The
SINGLE
EYE

The
SINGLE EYE

A Novel

by

Catrin Lewis

(THE ARCHITECTS: BOOK ONE)

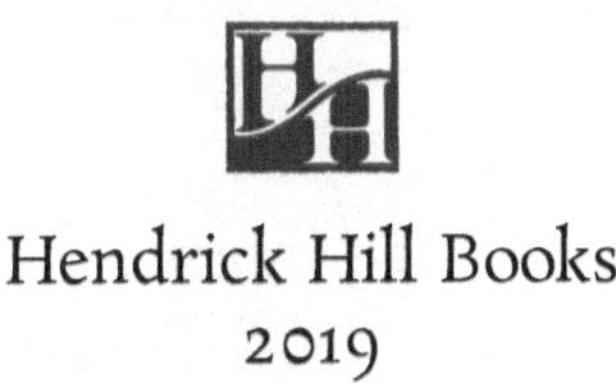

Hendrick Hill Books
2019

To my mother,
who has believed in me, regardless,
and
to the glory of God

TABLE OF CONTENTS

ACKNOWLEDGEMENTS

THIS NOVEL has been a long time in the making, three and a half decades long, in fact. Over that time the project has gathered to itself a large crowd of people to whom I owe thanks. With the awareness that this list cannot possibly be complete, my sincere gratitude goes out:

To Jane Austen, to Dame Mary Stewart, and especially to Dorothy L. Sayers for being my literary mentors and exemplars, though they passed from this life too soon for me to tell them so. If there is the faintest echo of them in this work, I count myself blessed.

To Valerie J. Meyers, who, back in the 1980s, gave me the incentive finally to take one of the story ideas that had been rattling around in my head and produce the novella that was the seed of this work. And to Joanne Herda, for inviting me to a novel-writing class in 2009, which got me going again.

To my colleagues at www.writingforums.org, for answering my questions, not only about my writing, but about book production and book marketing as well. Thank you for making me aware of contemporary developments in the writer's craft, and most of all for taking the time to critique the excerpts I posted in the forum Workshop. I may not have always taken your advice, but what you said encouraged me to rethink my prose and, I hope, make it better.

To the Pennwriters organization, its members, and the speakers and workshop leaders it provides at its annual conferences.

To the writers of the many excellent writing blogs and vlogs available on the Internet. In particular, thanks go to Kristine Kathryn Rusch for her business series at https://kriswrites.com, for helping me make the decision to publish independently. If I fail to do the business side of this thing right, it will be no fault of hers.

To retired Master Patrol Officer Bill LeBlanc for advising me on police equipment and procedure. Any undue creativity in that department must be laid at my door alone.

To my beta readers Mike Smith, Christopher Enoch, Jaina Moore, Corinne Brixton, and R. J. Conte. You asked the necessary hard questions about my plot and characters and pointed out my typographical errors and editing ghosts. I also thank you who began to beta read for me but withdrew because the story's genre or style did not meet your taste or expectations. The reasons you gave for not continuing made me look harder at my work and proved useful in revision.

To my friends Brenda Onufryk and Betsy Gidley. You have borne patiently with my constant chatter about my novel and its characters, allowed me to bounce ideas off you, and given me valuable feedback from the reader's point of view.

To the teachers and other experts of my acquaintance whose brains I have picked and whose reference books I have borrowed, especially during the formatting process.

To you, the many secondary school students who have been asking me for the past three years when the novel would come out so you could buy a copy. Even if you choose not to— this book is not Young Adult, after all— I've been warmed and encouraged by your interest.

And finally, I give all thanks, praise, and glory to the God and Father of my Lord Jesus Christ, acknowledging, as King David did long ago in connection with another offering of human creativity:

> All things come from You,
> and of Your own do we give You.
>
> – 1 Chronicles 29:14 (paraphrased).

TO THE READER

THIRTY-FIVE YEARS AGO, when this book started life as a novella called *Free Souls*, its setting and circumstances reflected everyday American life. But viewed from the perspective of the second decade of the 21st century, the milieu of 1981-82 can seem like something out of a fantasy novel, an alternative world.

Think of it. It was a time when architects got all their clients by personal reference and word of mouth, it being considered unethical— in fact it was professionally forbidden— to advertise. All drafting was done by hand and architectural drawings were reproduced by diazo whiteprint (oh! the stench of ammonia!), rather than being transmitted digitally as today. Computers were reserved for university think tanks and government agencies, and if you wanted to research a product or material there was no Internet; you phoned the manufacturer's representative or looked it up in a catalog you kept on your office shelf.

In the early '80s the cassette tape and the eight-track were in common use, but the compact disc and mp3s were unknown and true audiophiles stuck to the long-playing vinyl record. There were no mobile or cell phones, at least not for the general public, though the latest-model corded telephones had lost their rotary dials and gone to touch-tone buttons.

Back then, the 911 emergency system was unheard-of: you still had to dial "o" for the operator to summon an ambulance or the police. 1981 was before 9/11, too, and though we'd become aware of terrorists of various stripes even before the emergence of the Baader-Meinhof Gang and the massacre of the Israeli athletes at the Munich Olympics in 1972, we as Americans weren't sensitized to the effects terrorism could have within our borders. Good citizens like my protagonists had no reason automatically to report someone who might be stockpiling what we now call assault weapons, neither were we constantly being monitored by our government, such that law enforcement could readily detect arms trafficking of that kind.

And even more fantastic (in contrast to today's practices and assumptions), the early 1980s was a time when most people in America still got married before they moved in with each other. That said, the tide of sexual revolution that began in the 1960s was rising. Those who chose to take a stand for chastity, as my female protagonist does, did so against the general trend of the culture even if such a decision might have been less remarkable then than now.

Sex isn't the only area of life where my characters' habits and mindsets are at odds with the spirit of this present age. Christian and nonchristian alike, they still believe in objective values and objective reality, and some readers may find that to be the most fantastic— that is, the most incredible— thing of all.

But I hope not. I hope you, the reader, will suspend your Third Millennium disbelief and come along on what I intend should be an enjoyable, but not a "fantastic," ride.

And as you do, I beg you to allow me *some* bending of reality. I've endowed a world-renowned art gallery with fictitious paintings attributed to actual artists who never painted such images in their lives. I've fudged the American release date of a notable French film. Though I've done my best to be accurate with sunset times and the phases of the moon, I've arranged the weather to suit my own devices. And as for the real-life American university to which I've attributed a mid-1960s affirmative action admissions program, it's up to them to view that as good or bad. My male protagonist's opinion on the matter is his alone and should not be construed as being shared by me or by anyone else.

ON THE SPELLING

THE ORTHOGRAPHY in this novel purposely follows the old rule of preserving the short vowel by doubling the final consonant when writing the inflected forms. Examples: "remodel/ remodelling" and "focus/focussed." The point of view characters would have learned this form in elementary school and would still be using it at the time of the story, even though the one-consonant method was increasingly spreading from journalism into other types of written media.

"The light of the body is the eye:
if therefore thine eye be single,
thy whole body shall be full of light."

—Jesus Christ (Matthew 6:22, KJV)

The
SINGLE
EYE

For thou art my hope, O Lord GOD:
thou art my trust from my youth.

–Psalm 71:5

Train up a child in the way he should go:
and when he is old,
he will not depart from it.

–Proverbs 22:6

SATURDAY, 11 AUGUST 1962

THE KNOCKING CAME LOW on the door to his den. Dr. Roderick Beichten looked up from the chemical equation he was balancing. "Yes?"

The door opened slightly and the smiling face of a small girl peeked in. "Daddy, are you busy? Can I tell you something?"

"Sure, Honey Sandwich," he said. "Come on in."

His daughter Sandy slipped into the room, her lime green seersucker shorts and crop top a little oversized on her thin frame, the ribbon on one of her light brown pigtails as usual coming undone, and her eyes bright with enthusiasm.

"Daddy," she said, her feet planted wide and her back straight as if she were getting ready to sing with the Primary Choir up on the chancel steps of the Fourth Presbyterian Church, "Mark wants to be a doctor and Larry says he's going to be an airline pilot. Daddy, I've decided what I want to be when I grow up."

Roderick laid down his pencil and smiled at his youngest child. "So what do you want to be, sweetie?"

"I want to be an architect."

"An architect? I thought you wanted to be an artist."

"No . . . not anymore. Not an artist-artist anyway."

"Or an opera singer like Beverly Sills?"

"No, Daddy. An architect."

He suppressed his amusement. Every few weeks it was something new. Teacher. Archaeologist. UN translator. But never before had she come to him in his den on a Saturday afternoon to make an announcement about it.

"You know how we have a rendering in the church lobby to show what the new Sunday school addition will look like?" she said.

A "rendering," eh? Well, she had the terminology right. "Yes?"

"That's what I mean. An architect made that. It's going to be so beautiful! I want to be an architect and do drawings like that."

"Architects have to do more than draw pretty pictures of buildings," he said, his tone probing.

"I *know* that," she replied, and he nearly laughed at her impatience with his grownup stupidity. "They draw *plans*. And *elevations*. So they'll know how to build it and it won't fall down."

"I see. But why this all of a sudden?"

"Daddy, it *isn't* all of a sudden! I've been thinking *hard* about it!" She looked up at him, her face pleading.

And maybe it wasn't sudden. She'd always been precise and creative about the way she arranged her bedroom. For years she'd preferred playing with blocks over cuddling dolls. And didn't her drawings of houses always have their chimneys sticking straight up and their doors and windows in all the right places?

"I guess not. I'm proud to hear what you want to be."

She let out her breath. "That's good! Because somebody told me girls can't be architects. I'll tell them my daddy says they're wrong."

"Who said you couldn't?"

"Bobby Fyfield in my Sunday School class. His daddy made the plans for the new Sunday school rooms. I said I wanted to talk to him about being an architect and Bobby said I can't 'cause I'm a girl."

"Certainly you can talk to Mr. Fyfield! I'll call him on Monday and we'll make an appointment to go to his office together."

"I can't talk to him tomorrow at church?"

"Do you think that would be a good idea? He works hard all week. We need to give him a chance to rest on Sunday. You'll have to work very hard when you become an architect, too."

"I will!" she said. "I drew us a new house already. Want to see it?"

"Of course I do. And don't worry about what Bobby or anyone else says. You study hard and keep drawing, and I know you'll do as well as any boy out there. Maybe better." He winked. "Now go get those house drawings of yours."

She flew out of the den as fast as her sneakers could take her. Musing, Roderick looked through the open window. Out in the backyard, his teen-aged sons were playing catch in the summer sunshine. She was so much younger than they, but his nine-year-old Sandy was determined to keep up with them and be original about it, too.

From a window upstairs his daughter sounded a call of triumph. "Daddy says I can be an architect. Told you so!"

"Good for you!" said Mark. Larry, cocky as ever, pulled a hideously funny face and yelled, "Aw, you're still a baby! You'll chicken out." He gave his fingers an extra waggle, just for effect.

"Plzzzzzttt!" was the reaction from above. Roderick gave a hearty laugh.

A minute later, a girlish voice in the hallway drew his attention back into the room. "Daddy, look!"

Sandy came hurrying through the door, a half-unrolled scroll held out in her two hands, nearly tripping over a chair in her eagerness to lay it on his desk. "See, there's the living room, and there's the kitchen, and there's my room, and a new playroom and—"

"Hold on, hold on! Let me see." She'd used the white side of a sheet of wrapping paper and the drawing on its glossy surface was blotched with pencil smears and erasures. Nevertheless, he pushed up his glasses and examined it as carefully as he would a chemical analysis submitted to him by a promising junior at his research lab.

"Alexandra," he said, assuming a dignified tone he knew would please her, "these plans are excellent. May I have this drawing? I'd like to frame it and hang it on my wall, right over there." He pointed to the bare space over his bookcase.

Her mouth twisted up a little. "Daddy, can you wait? I still have to put the dimensions on. The measurements," she added helpfully.

"I see. All right, after that. But don't forget."

"I won't!" She hesitated, hands clasped, making fans with her fingers the way she did when something was bothering her.

"What is it?"

"Mommy says when I grow up I'm going to meet some boy and get married."

"Well, so you might. What's wrong with that?"

"Will I have to stop being an architect?"

"Oh, no! Your mother never meant to give you that idea." And if Karen did, bless her, she'd get over it. "You can do both, if you like."

Sandy's little forehead wrinkled in thought. "I think I would like to do both, someday. I mean, I like babies and all. But no boys, for years and years! I'm going to be an architect first!"

"You do that!" he said, laughing. "Shall we go to the store and get some real architect's supplies so you can start today?"

She considered. "No, let's go on Monday. I told Carole Peabody I'd meet her in the park to play. If that's all right with you? Mommy says I can."

"If your mother says you may, it's all right with me. Just be home before supper."

"I will!" And like a flash she was gone.

"Sandy!" called Karen's voice from the kitchen. "Don't let the screen door—"

Bang!

"—slam."

He laughed again. Monday morning he'd call Reg Fyfield. And before that day was out, he'd take his little girl to buy her first real set of architect's tools, even if he had to cancel ten meetings to do it.

*   *   *

"CAROLE," SAID SANDY, "what do you want to be when you grow up?"

The two girls sat on the curb of the fountain in the park, dabbling their bare feet in the cool water.

"I don't know. Sometimes I want to be an astronaut, but that's only boys. What do you want to be?"

"An architect. That's mostly boys, too, but my daddy says I can. He just told me."

Carole gaped at her. "You can do that? Wow."

"Well, not yet. I have to work hard and study. Daddy says so." She'd known Daddy would understand. He always did.

"Wow," Carole said again. "Someday I'll marry a boy with lots of money and you can design me a house!"

"Maybe I will, maybe I won't!" she said, tossing her pigtails. She clambered out and grabbed her shoes. "Race you to the top of the hill, last one up is a rotten egg!" And before her friend could splash her way out of the fountain, she'd left her behind and was flying like the wind down the path and up the hill.

In the end, Carole won the race. They'd been friends forever, since kindergarten at least, and Carole had always been bigger and stronger, with curly blonde hair that would have made her jealous if Carole hadn't been so nice.

The two girls flung themselves giggling onto the grassy slope. Pretty soon Sandy leapt to her feet and began to spin around.

"I can see everything from here, everything, everything!" she sang to a little tune she'd just made up.

"Even Africa?" said Carole. "Even China?"

"Well, maybe not quite China," Sandy said, shading her eyes. "But Africa for sure. And Brazil. Where the cannibals live."

"I know," exclaimed Carole, "let's play missionary!"

"Oh, good!" she said, turning dizzy-headed towards her friend. "I get first dibs on being the brave missionary!"

"You always get to be the missionary first. I thought of the game before you."

"Yeah, but whoever thinks of it doesn't get to go first. That's the rules."

"Oh, all right," said Carole, making a face. "But I don't want to be cannibals. Something else."

"What else, what else, what else?" sang Sandy to the same little tune. "I know! You can be the Nazis!"

"Why the Nazis?"

Carole was being *so* blockheaded today. "*Because.* The Nazis are always coming and killing people for being good. Don't you remember what your daddy and my daddy had to do in the war? Now, I'll be standing here telling people about Jesus—"

"Who's the people?"

"They are. Down there." She pointed at a group of little kids on the playground at the foot of the hill. "Okay, ready?"

Pretending to hold a large Bible, she said (loud but not too loud, since this was only pretend), "'Hey, people! Jesus died on the cross and God loves you and you can go to heaven!'"

Carole made her hand into a gun and waved it at her. 'You stop telling people about Jesus,'" she said in a voice that wouldn't have scared a kitten, "'or I'll kill you.'"

"Meaner!" Sandy hissed. "Sound meaner!"

"'If you don't stop telling people about Jesus,'" Carole bellowed, "'I'm going to run you through with my bayonet and put you on the barbecue!!!'"

Sandy stared at her. "Wow! That's scary! 'But'— she raised her eyes skyward, like she'd seen the saints do in pictures at the Civic Museum— "'you can't scare me. I'll *die* before I'll stop telling people about Jesus!'"

"Now I get to kill you," said Carole in her normal voice.

"Wait. I'm not done." She struck a dramatic pose, her hand over her heart. "'Jesus has always been good to me for eighty years and I'll never,

ever, *ever* betray Him!' That's St. Polycarp, in that book we had about martyrs," she explained, in case her friend had forgotten.

"You're not eighty," Carole objected. "You just turned nine last month."

"Who cares?" She put on the holiest expression she could. "'You need to believe in Jesus, too, Mr. Nazi, or you'll never go to heaven!'"

"'Ha-ha! Die, Christian missionary dog, die!'" Carole pretended to cut off her head, and Sandy fell to the grass kicking and flopping and waving her arms.

"Hey, die already. Your head's cut off," her friend pointed out.

"Yeah, but what about the chickens? I've seen them on my grandpa's farm. They run all around with no heads before they stop. *Schmock! schmock!*" She sprang up and tore crazily around the top of the hill before finally giving up the ghost at Carole's feet.

Then they switched and Carole got to be the missionary and Sandy was the Red Chinese who executed her, only Carole remembered to say "I forgive you" before she died so they had to play again so Sandy could say it, too.

After awhile, tired of the game, they lay on the grass looking up at the clouds.

"Carole," said Sandy, "maybe you could be a missionary when you grow up."

"I don't think so . . . Sandy, do people still have to die for Jesus?"

"No, that was just in the old days. Not even missionaries have to do it anymore. Not much, anyhow."

"Well, I'm glad," said Carole. "If I didn't have to die, it would be nice to do something for God. But girls can't be ministers."

"Mrs. Trumbell told us in choir we can do any kind of work for God. The main thing is keeping our eyes on Him. Like in that hymn."

"Which one?"

Sandy began to sing:

> "'Be Thou my Vision, O Lord of my heart,
> Naught be all else to me, save that Thou art!'

"Dr. Wallace said so, too, in the big church. Weren't you paying attention?"

"No, I guess I wasn't," Carole admitted.

"Well, it's true." They were both silent a moment, then Sandy spoke up again. "That's what I'm going to be. An architect for God. And nobody's going to stop me. They'll have to shoot me first!"

DIVISION A

WEDNESDAY, 19 AUGUST –

MONDAY, 9 NOVEMBER 1981

"But if thine eye be evil,
thy whole body shall be full of darkness.
If therefore the light in thee is darkness,
how great is that darkness!"

–St. Matthew 6:23

CHAPTER A.1

S HE WAS GLAD Eric was out when the stranger came.

The man wasn't there, then he was: a middle-aged, crewcut, gray-suited figure poised like an omen just inside the office door. He said nothing, only looked at her.

Sandy Beichten resisted the urge to flinch. "Good afternoon," she said, getting up from her drafting table. "What can I— um, won't you come . . . ?" She faltered, the greeting withering under his icy gaze.

He remained on the threshold, taking silent possession of the one-room studio like a conquistador planting his flag on the shores of a miserable little princedom.

What is he waiting for, a fanfare from the New York Philharmonic?

Sandy, that was rude. She stepped forward with what she hoped was a welcoming smile. "May I help you, sir?"

"Eric Baumann isn't here?" It was an accusation, not an inquiry.

"No, sir, he's out right now." Nor, to her frustration, had he been in all day. But that was no business of the man in the doorway.

"When *will* he be in?"

Incomprehensible. The visitor had dropped in unannounced. What, did he expect Eric to be clairvoyant and foresee his coming?

"I can't really say, sir. He has appointments . . . "

No answer. His pale glance raked over and rejected everything in the room, herself included, as if he owned the right of rejection. His eyes, there was something not quite right about his eyes . . . Behind their blank blueness some alien entity seemed to control his body like a machine, pulling levers and throwing switches for a purpose she couldn't conceive.

"If thine eye be evil…"

Sandy, stop it. She had no call to apply Jesus' words about the evil eye to someone she'd barely met. He was just an ordinary older guy, nothing to object to at all. *Except for those eyes.* She made her voice warm. "If you'll give me your name and number"— why did it feel she was crossing a line to ask?— "Mr. Baumann can arrange to see you another time."

"I'll be back," he announced curtly. Then he was gone, as if he'd conjured himself away.

"Bizarre," she whispered. A superstitious urge nearly drove her to peek out the door to confirm he'd been real. Who was he? He couldn't have been a product representative: he'd carried neither briefcase nor samples. She seriously doubted he was a personal friend of Eric's—

O Domine. What if he was a potential client?

She fervently hoped not. He was a first class jerk.

She went back to her drawing board, but for a minute her pencil didn't move. If that guy was a client, he should have appreciated what Eric had done with this space. Sure, it was small. But the ceiling was high, the double-hung windows were tall, and everything was painted a crisp, bright white. It was beautifully fitted out, with two drafting stations and a conference table, all custom-built by Eric and a couple of his friends.

The only thing missing this sunny summer afternoon— besides an air conditioner that actually worked— was Eric himself. She'd been working out these details for the Weisman laundry room tilework since Monday, and while it was going well enough, it would go even better if he was here to say so.

Never mind. Being left alone was sometimes a good thing. Like when it gave her the chance to head off characters like Mr. Demon Eyes.

Sometimes I think Eric would sell his soul if it'd make his architectural dreams come true.

On the thought she froze, despite the heat the AC could not overcome. *Jesus help us, what if it's true?*

Didn't he cheerfully put up with way too much from their clients? Arbitrary program changes. Demands that he redesign features that were already built and in place, because a client got a brainstorm. Joking insults about his looks from men who were toads compared to him. He never seemed to mind, as long as they would let him push the boundaries of innovation and realize his vision of what their house or office or whatever it was should be. Oh, yes, if she couldn't get Eric to see things her way, he'd definitely take on Demon Eyes— who'd pull all that and worse.

Stop it. Now. Probably the visitor was just one of those benighted souls who didn't think women should be architects. He'd made it clear he despised her. But that didn't excuse her being a jerk right back.

Pushing the thought of the strange-eyed man aside, she sharpened her pencil lead and proceeded to heavy up the lines she'd traced in earlier.

A few minutes later, " . . . soprano Regine Crispin," came the announcer's voice over the office radio, "singing Marguerite's aria '*D'amour l'ardente flamme*' from *La Damnation de Faust* by Hector Berlioz."

She sat bolt upright, her ears pricked. "I love this song!" She sprang to the shelf and turned up the volume, grateful, not for the first time, that theirs was the only occupied office on the wing. Sometimes, working in a ninety-year-old building with few modern amenities had its advantages. For awhile she stood there listening, then began to sing along with the French.

> *. . . His mouth with smiles of sweetness,*
> *the spell cast by his eye,*
> *his voice in its enchantment . . .*

If that's how she felt about him, shouldn't she get back to the work he'd given her to do? She turned down the radio and returned to her table.

> *. . . the caress of his hand—*
> *Alas! and his kiss*
> *of amorous, burning fire . . .*

That was never going to happen. She slid her parallel bar down and drew a bold dark cut line against its edge, as if the force of it could render her feelings similarly straightforward and settled.

It was no use, not while the aria still played.

> *. . . that I might see the day*
> *when I breathe out my soul*
> *in the kiss of his love!*

The last bars faded away and she shut the radio off.

Draw. Just draw. She flowed into the rhythm of it: bar, triangle, and pencil cooperating smoothly, almost organically, under her hands. " . . . I *stand at my window"*— she sang snatches of the aria to herself— *"to haste his return…"*

Eric, where are you? It was after 3:00. He'd said something last night about needing to get together with DeeDee and Sol Weisman and one of the subcontractors, but shouldn't he have gotten his beautiful self in by now?

Good grief, that last line was cockeyed. Her parallel bar must be loose. She fished in her drawer for a screwdriver then turned to tighten the screw that should have been holding the right hand wire taut against the surface of her table. As she did, she heard a step in the hall and her glance went to the open door.

The man passing through it was tall, nearly filling the frame. He wore his brown-black hair medium-short and wavy, in the style one would see on a bust of a young Caesar, and his judiciously-cut beard set off a strong chin and a humorous mouth. In his long rugged right hand he carried a tube of drawings like a scepter. The effect was so different from the one produced by the strange visitor that she could have gasped.

She did nothing of the kind. She spoke, and her tone was steady, controlled, even cool. "Hi, Eric," she said. "How was the meeting?"

CHAPTER A.2

"Eric?" Sandy raised her voice to be heard over the radio and the window AC's rattle. "Eric, take a look."

He inspected the sketch she'd been working on all morning. "Not too shabby! I'd say it's a good thing the chandelier the Weismans wanted isn't available anymore."

"And a good thing you convinced them we could design one that's even better-looking and fits their needs more."

He grinned a little sheepishly. "Well, yesterday when the electrical contractor pulled out his so-called alternative . . . You know the Lighting Innovations line?"

"Yes, but I try not to," she said wryly.

"Yeah. That awful. I headed him off by appealing to their art collector side. Didn't they want an original piece no one else had?"

"Perfect! Too bad we can't charge—"

"—If we could only—"

They laughed, and he began again. "I wish I could bill the clients what our design product is worth. But as it is . . . "

" . . . they all know each other and if you raised rates on one but not on the others, the one with the price hike would want to know why. And at the moment it wouldn't be . . . "

"That's right, it wouldn't be prudent to raise fees all around. I hate it, I really do. I wish I could pay you what you're worth. My gosh, I threw this light fixture problem at you practically at quitting time yesterday and here you're showing me something that will definitely fly."

She grinned with pleasure. "I don't mind. The way things are, we can put in the time to come up with what's right, not just what's good enough. Long as they're willing to pay the hourly rate . . . "

"... And a lot of them are. It's nice to be trusted," he said. "Anyway, your design is perfect. Heavy up the lines with black marker and slam some Prismacolor on it, and I'll take it around to the Weismans tomorrow."

For awhile they worked in relative silence. Then Eric's drafting chair creaked as he swivelled around. "Sandy," he said, "I've been thinking."

"Yes?"

"We really need to expand our client base. The Weismans, the Ryersons, the Eisenbaums, they're great, they're loyal, they appreciate our work, but..."

"But they're not a bottomless well. Right?"

"Exactly. And the economy's not out of the woods yet, whatever President Reagan plans to do. So if you hear of anything, let me know."

For the first time since the previous afternoon Sandy recalled the strange man who'd shown up and left so abruptly. Reluctantly she said, "Eric, I . . . I apologize, we got so wrapped up in what came out of your meeting yesterday that I forgot to say. A guy stopped in maybe an hour before you got back. I'm not sure if he wanted to hire us, but maybe he does."

Excitement lit up his face. "Who was he? You got his name?"

"No, he—" How could she put it without sounding prejudiced? "He wouldn't give it. He made it clear he only wanted to talk to you. He was a little, um, *strange*."

"Strange like how?"

"A little brusque, a little—" How *should* she describe it?

Eric shrugged dismissively. "So did he say when he'd be back?"

"No, he didn't. Just that he would be. Listen, maybe he was just a salesman. Maybe we shouldn't get our hopes up about him. I'll keep my ear to the ground for new clients, I promise."

"You do that. You carry your business cards with you?"

"Of course I do," she said, picking one up and admiring the way her name was teamed with that of Eric Baumann, Architect.

"Good. Flood all of Wapatomekie with them. Whether or not the guy from yesterday shows up again, we really need new work."

"WHOOPS!" Sandy stomped her foot down on the piece of tracing paper that had blown off the throw-off shelf in the cool breeze from the open window. "Got it!"

Eric set the air conditioner down near the door. "That's it for this season." He slid the heavy window closed and locked its sash. "That better?" he asked.

"Yes, thanks." She sat back down at his table, where they were working out some changes to the Weismans' new kitchen. "I should have brought a sweater . . . Funny, now that it's cooler outside the AC suddenly works. But what if it gets hot again? It's only the second week in September."

"Never mind. That thing hasn't functioned worth a nickel for months." He resumed his seat to her left, picked up his sketching pencil, and held it poised over a marked-up whiteprint of the kitchen floor plan. "All right. DeeDee's concerned about the circulation, now that we've worked in the latest changes. So . . ."

Pointing with her own pencil, Sandy said, "If we move the doorway *here,* it'll improve the flow . . . "

" . . . from the dining room? Yes, but she was also talking about more storage at that location. We have to fit that in."

"True. But I still think we should move the door."

"I agree. Here's what I'm thinking . . . " He took a roll of canary-yellow tracing paper and spread a piece over the drawing. His pencil began to move.

Deliberately, she focussed on the ideas taking shape under his hand, willing herself to follow every part of the solution he proposed and keep her reactions calm and cool. On the surface of the table lay the scheme to be rationally improved. Under the table, for her at least, surged fire and electricity racing through a world with no rationality at all.

His leg was close to hers, so near she could feel its warmth.

His sketching brought him closer. Their thighs touched. A thrill like a thousand tiny needles rippled through her.

Ah! Eric, you have no idea what you're doing to me.

What if he did know? Surely he wouldn't take advantage like—

A wave of horror crashed over her, so intense it made her say something absurd about the idea he'd just proposed. He peered at her quizzically, and continued to draw.

No. *Eric* wouldn't take advantage. Too many days, evenings, weekends alone together, and he'd never made a single pass.

Why not? Sure, she should be grateful, but— Was she repulsive to him? If he discovered how she felt, might he let her go out of a horror of his own?

How silly! She wasn't repulsive and she knew it. She needed to lose weight in her hips and thighs and she wished she'd been blessed with more upstairs. Even so, her figure was decent. Her long hair was a boring brown and its natural wave often had a mind of its own, but it was nothing she couldn't tame with a quick session with the hot rollers. No, her looks wouldn't repel him. More likely he'd explain patiently that he had a girlfriend already. Though how he found time to see the woman, she couldn't imagine. And he'd proceed to treat Sandy in a formal but big-brotherly way.

She didn't want a big brother. She had two of them already. From Eric she wanted— oh, what she could never get, what she should never *want* to get. And because she would never get it, she was making do with what she silently revelled in now: The pressure of his shoulder as he leaned towards her side of the drawing. The sensation of solid muscle and strong bone through his chino slacks as his leg accidentally pressed into hers. A life-giving pulse of pleasure from the sheer closeness of him, concentrated and intensified as she controlled her reaction to it.

He'd rolled up the sleeves of his windowpane check Oxford shirt to keep them from smearing the sketch, and the dark hairs lay along his bare forearm like prostrate worshippers.

"Looks good," she commented. "And if we use pull-out trays to get maximum use of the space . . . "

"Hey, that's right," he said, as if nothing mattered to him but spatial efficiency and achieving the best work triangle. As, she reflected, nothing probably did.

He'd made room for her between his chair and the deep throw-off shelf that ran from her table to his under the broad, high windows of the little room. He couldn't help it: as he drew he pressed in on her, but she didn't feel crowded, she felt sheltered and safe.

And I hate feeling trapped, ever since, ever since . . . No need to think about that now. Not when he was so close to her and his least inadvertent touch was a secret blessing.

"I can see where you're going with that," she said. "And maybe if we did *this* . . ." She took up her own pencil and altered his sketch.

Eric, do you realize where your foot just went? No, don't move it! . . . Oh, well . . .

"Right!" he said. Oblivious. Blessedly oblivious. "But don't forget we can do *this*, too."

He reached over with his pencil and as he did, his turned-up cuff caught, just for a moment, on the front of her blouse. In spite of herself she turned her face to his, her lips parted.

She never met his eyes. Past him, she recognized the wordless figure standing just inside the door. Struck mute, she alerted Eric to his presence by a gesture alone.

ERIC SIZED UP the visitor. Nondescript features, around middle height, maybe forty-three or forty-four years old, dressed in a dark business suit of admirable cut. The man's shrewd light blue eyes assessed him in return. Eric didn't mind. If this was a potential client, it was no one he couldn't handle.

"What can I do for you?" he greeted him. "Careful of the AC. I just, uh . . ."

The newcomer disregarded his outstretched hand, sidestepped the air conditioner, and without waiting to be asked sat down at the conference table near the door. "My name is Nick Hardt," he stated crisply. His diction was cultivated, without accent. A man of education. And taste? "You were told I had come?"

"Yes . . . my assistant mentioned it. I'm happy to see you."

"I'm going to lay my cards on the table," Hardt said. "I don't like people."

Eric stopped where he was, his head cocked.

"And I'm an egoist. I plan to build myself an empire."

"Good!" he replied as he sat down. "That's what we architects like to hear. We'll help you build it, if we can."

"I'm serious. I heard about you years ago but waited until you had your own office to come to you. Before I say anything further, what are your terms?"

He told him.

"All right. I have amassed some land in a remote, unspoiled area. On it I intend to build a large resort and conference center. Underground, most of it. 'Earth-sheltered'— isn't that the term you architects use? Totally private, utterly exclusive. Do you understand?"

"Certainly."

"I've chosen you to design it for me, but you don't need to know anything more about it just now. I have other consultations to make. I'll get back to you." He stood up. "And remember this, Baumann: you're to tell no one I was here, or about this project."

"I'll have to let my assistant in on anything concerning it."

Hardt looked around the room. "Who?"

"Miss Beichten." It was almost funny how people kept mistaking Sandy for a receptionist. "She's a licensed architect and she works with me on all my projects. She'll be working on yours."

"I see . . . !" It sounded oddly as if Hardt was implying something. Eric chose to ignore it; in any event, the man's face immediately went grim. "Well, listen to me, both of you: I don't care who it is. If you're married, you don't tell your spouse. You don't tell your father, mother, brother, or even your psychiatrist. No one is to know I was here, or what I came for. Do you understand?"

Eric met Sandy's eye, then nodded. "How may I get hold of you?"

"My number's unlisted. It's staying that way. If I want you to see me, I'll come see you."

⊞✐

"WOW. THAT'LL BE one interesting client," Eric said as he gingerly closed the door.

"Maybe *too* interesting," Sandy replied darkly, hoping he'd catch her meaning.

"Did you hear that part about not liking people?"

"I sure did. Made me wonder what he thought we were."

He rejoined her at his table. "Where's my pencil? . . . oh, thanks." He resumed drawing. "I guess he doesn't have to like us," he said, not looking at her, "only our work."

Your work, you mean. I doubt he has much interest in mine. His shoulder was touching hers, but he could have been a thousand miles away. "Yes," she said, "but what was all that about not telling anyone? What's he got to hide?"

For a few moments he said nothing, wholly engrossed, it appeared, in trying out sizes for DeeDee's custom kitchen island. Then, "You've never had a client demand a non-disclosure agreement?"

"No," she said, embarrassed. "At Phipps & Musgrave I wasn't that involved . . . I mean . . . "

He snorted. Obviously, his low opinion of the architects she used to work for had just gotten worse.

"It's not surprising he wants one," he said. "He probably hasn't got all the land use permissions worked out. Or maybe the deal hasn't gone through yet, whatever he says, and he doesn't want some other buyer getting there first." He ripped off another piece of tracing paper and continued to sketch.

"Yes, but why be such a jerk about it? 'Don't tell your shrink.' Good grief."

Laying down his pencil, Eric looked her full in the face. "He can be the biggest jerk in the world, as long as he pays our bills. This could be our big break. I'm tired of nothing but little renovation jobs."

"There's this project here for the Weismans," she reminded him. "That's all our design."

"Yeah, but it's still pretty small and we're almost done with it. Except for DeeDee's constant changes, that is." He grinned. "This could be a real chance to do something important architecturally. We don't have to *like* him. If this job goes through, we could . . . "

For the first time since she'd met him she wished he would shut up. Even as they worked, his speculations about the new client raced on, their mad dash cut short only by the phone. "Baumann here," he answered it. He waved towards the last of the sketches and said under his breath, "Use those."

She took them back to her table and plunged herself into the fourth redo of the Weisman kitchen as into a cleansing stream. Compared to the thought of working for the man who'd inflicted his presence upon them this afternoon, this project seemed almost holy.

CHAPTER A.3

"M IND IF I LET YOU OFF at Forty-fourth Street?" Eric drew up to the curb. "I've got to be at the McCulloughs' by 6:00."

"No, not at all," Sandy said. "What time do you think you'll be in in the morning?"

"Around 10:30 or so. See you tomorrow!"

She gazed after his late-'60s brown Ford Galaxie as it drove off down busy Meyers Trafficway. How funny— the rear bumper was about to lose hold. Again. How incongruous that a beautiful man like Eric should drive such a heap!

He would never, she was convinced, be one of the pretty boys on the cover of *GQ*, with their bland, regular features. He was more like the Gothic cathedrals she'd seen on her one trip to Europe. Not Greek god handsome— she'd had enough of that— but eclectic, intriguing, and fascinating altogether.

Her neighborhood was like him. The tall, healthy shade trees lining Forty-fourth Street were beginning to turn, the late afternoon sun illuminating the red and gold leaves against their background of green. The same light picked out the carvings in the ornamented window and cornice mouldings on the old stone and brick buildings, making them stand out like gems cut for everyone to enjoy. Whole stretches of the mellow brown brick sidewalk remained, and before the blocks of apartment buildings began in earnest she would pass a row of small, bustling stores: a grocery, a stationer's, a cleaner's, and, best of all, a little variety store— a curiosity shop, almost— with a window full of antique jewelry and hilariously useless toys.

In front of this shop, she paused. Amid the cloisonné brooches and old-fashioned pearl rings sat a little metal dog that when wound up leapt about, wagged its tail, and yelped in a high-pitched, mechanical tone. She had joked to Eric that it was just what he needed, since his landlord didn't allow real dogs in his building.

What did the McCulloughs want? They'd finished the restoration of their historic Arts and Crafts house months ago; surely nothing had gone wrong. No, how could it? They had Eric Baumann for an architect!

And she had him for an employer. Hadn't Frank Lloyd Wright's associates called him the Master? Well, Eric was hers.

So why not buy the Master a mechanical dog? The bell on the shop door jingled decisively as she pulled it open and went in. Yes, just what the man needed. It'd keep out the riffraff, like . . .

Like Nick Hardt. Why did the thought of him grind her bones? It'd been a whole week with no sign of him reappearing. Maybe Mr. Egotist had taken his dreams of empire somewhere else.

But Eric said they needed this job to keep the doors open. It was true, they didn't have much work in the pipeline. The interior drawings for the Weisman house would keep them busy into the fall, the job being so highly-customized, but the general contractor wouldn't wait forever. The other projects they had going were minor and seemed to cost them nearly as much money as they brought in. Nevertheless, she would be very happy if Mr. Hardt found himself another architect.

THE PHONE RANG for the third time. Eric, absorbed in his work, made no move to answer it.

"Eric Baumann's office," Sandy greeted the caller. "Oh, hello, Leah," she said, congratulating herself on how pleasant and relaxed her manner was. "Yes, he's here. . . . Eric, it's for you. Leah."

"Hi, Leah! . . . What?" he said, his voice bright and enthusiastic. "Yeah, that was great the other night, wasn't it?"

Sandy stopped drawing, her grip tense on her mechanical pencil. What was great? It better have been a movie or something.

She forced herself to relax. It was wrong for her to feel jealous. Wrong, and stupid. Leah Matthews was Eric's girlfriend. She had been for years. If anyone should resent another woman's demands on his attention, it was Miss Matthews. Funny, then, how Sandy felt her rights infringed upon whenever Leah would call. It was illogical, she wouldn't afflict Eric with it, but no way would she deny her own feelings.

Those feelings would behave themselves better, she was sure, if he hadn't broken up with Leah at least three times since Sandy had come to work for him a little over a year ago. It raised such hopeless hopes. Not that he ever mentioned his love life in the office; heavens, no. He'd "tell" her in other ways. Like, "If Leah calls, I'm busy"— and his hurt tone made it no surprise when they would get back together again.

They'd made up and then some after their big breakup early last spring, all lovey-dovey again right before the big deadline for the Eisenbaum office remodel. He'd shocked Sandy to the core when he'd handed the construction documents over to her so he could devote all his efforts to designing Leah's new cookware shop. Then he'd taken off another two weeks in July managing the shop's construction. Sandy was pretty sure he hadn't charged his girlfriend a cent for all that work, either.

After the store's grand opening August first, though . . . Something was definitely wrong then. It was irrelevant by now, for from the sound of his voice Eric and his girlfriend were thick as ever.

"Next Friday night? I really can't," he said regretfully. "I have a deadline like you wouldn't believe . . . I'm sorry, babe, it can't be helped . . . "

Charity was a lost cause. Monday they were submitting the Eisenbaum project for an award competition sponsored by *Design Mode* magazine and he would be devoting his weekend to completing the new presentation drawings required for it— instead of to Leah Matthews. And yesterday he'd asked Sandy if she'd be willing to come up to the office on Saturday and again on Sunday afternoon to help crank them out. As if her willingness could be in question!

"No, the weekend after doesn't look good, either," he said into the receiver. "I'm sorry, it's my stinking work schedule, it's so jammed . . . "

You'd think Leah wouldn't have time, either. But oh, yeah. She closed her store at 6:00.

" . . . I'll keep you posted, all right? . . . Yes. Uh-huh. Sure. . . . Well, babe, you go without me and tell me about it later. I'm sure you'll enjoy it. I'm sorry I can't go myself."

I'm not! thought Sandy with unholy glee.

It was unchristian of her to feel such satisfaction. Nevertheless, when Eric went down to the snack bar she permitted herself a nice greasy wallow in it. *I'd better watch out,* she thought luxuriously, *I'm liable to be punished for this!*

A shadow towards the doorway startled her. Eric returning with their pop? Of course not— it was Nick Hardt. And this time he'd stopped not just inside the entrance, but, exuding a defiant pride of ownership, had settled himself into one of their conference chairs.

She suppressed the urge to swear aloud. "Good afternoon, Mr. Hardt."

"Where's Baumann?" he snapped.

"He's stepped out for a moment, sir."

"He's got to learn not to waste my time. If I didn't think he was the only architect for this job, I'd—"

"I'll fetch him for you, if you like, sir." Without waiting for a reply she darted into the hallway.

She met Eric by the elevator. "Guess who's here?"

"Santa Claus?"

"No. Mephistopheles."

"Who?"

"Mephistopheles. I mean, Nick Hardt. I mean— good grief, he's like the devil in *The Damnation of Faust*: pops in, pops out, looks so contemptuous, and acts like he owns everything!"

"What an imagination! I suppose he'd like to speak with me? You *are* being polite to him?"

"Of course!"

"Good, because we need this job. Understand?"

"Yes, sir."

A transformed Nick Hardt awaited them back in the office, and Sandy could barely conceal her astonishment. She'd left a demanding tycoon sitting scowling and impatient; now a sweet-tempered uncle-type stood there relaxed, beaming at them angelically.

At them? No, at Eric.

"Sorry to keep you waiting, Mr. Hardt," Eric said.

"Not at all, not at all!" he replied, waving his hand genially. "You're a busy man with many demands on your time."

Like he hadn't noticed the cans of pop Eric had brought in, Sandy thought sourly.

"Before we start," Hardt said, "I want to apologize for my behavior last time."

Eric murmured that it was nothing.

"No, please," he continued. "I'd just come from a difficult meeting with a competitor, and . . . Well, I'm sure you understand. I'm a great admirer of your work and I was afraid we might have gotten off on the wrong foot. Please pardon me."

"It's no problem at all. Sandy," Eric said to her, "bring the memo pads and a roll of canary paper, okay?"

Hardt gave her a questioning look as she took her place at Eric's right hand. She smiled back at him sweetly.

He cleared his throat. "I've brought you," he said, pointedly addressing Eric alone, "my requirements for the building you're going to design for me."

HIS NEW CLIENT faced him across the table, unzipping a smooth leather portfolio. Change him out of that expensively-tailored suit, and the guy could have been a poster boy for Average. But one or two discreet inquiries had informed Eric that "average" was the last word to describe Nick Hardt's business acumen and brains.

"First of all," Hardt said, "I hope you don't mind signing a non-disclosure agreement on this project. *Both* of you."

"Of course not," Eric assured him. "It's common." He ran his eye over the document: the terms, conditions, and penalties were nothing unusual. He signed and pushed it over to Sandy.

"Couldn't I have more time to look at it? What if I—?"

"There's nothing wrong with it," he told her firmly. "Sign."

"If you say so," she muttered, and scrawled her signature below his.

"Thank you," said Hardt, beaming. He put his copy of the NDA away in his portfolio, then extracted a sheet of paper covered with typewriting.

But in mid-motion, he stopped. "I'm sorry," he said. "I shouldn't waste your time with this. A first class designer like yourself— You don't want to bother with a project that no one can see." He began to put the paper away. "I'm sorry. I'll go."

Eric's heart went leaden with fear. "No, it's all right! I don't need— We'll come up with a great solution together, and if that means no visible façade, that's fine with me."

"Oh, I'm so glad." Hardt's relief was palpable. "I knew you were a big proponent of energy-conscious design, so I figured you'd understand why I want it earth-sheltered . . . The site is rather exposed, and the winds—"

"You'll save a lot on heating and cooling bills. Besides, it'll be my pleasure to restore the landscape to its original state. When we get finished, no one will know the building is there."

"That's what I was thinking. Well, if you're sure . . ."

Eric glanced over the page Hardt handed him. It was a list of rooms and square footages, way too defined for this stage of the project. But that was typical for new clients.

He handed it to Sandy, then looked up. Hardt's eye was on her. Leaning across the table, he whispered, "Baumann, couldn't we keep this between us?" Eric shook his head. "No, I remember, you said that girl's in on everything. If you say it's all right," he said, raising his voice warmly, "it's all right with me. Miss . . . Miss . . . "

"Beichten," Eric reminded him.

"Miss Beichten, pardon me."

"Of course," Sandy said in a calm, low voice. She scanned the sheet front and back, then put her finger on one item to draw it to his attention. A shooting range. Another good reason to put the complex underground— no disturbing the neighbors, if any. He shrugged and took the paper back.

"Now," said Hardt, "I told you, didn't I, that my resort will be private and exclusive? But not in the way you might think. Baumann, the common man gets a raw deal in America these days, don't you agree? He needs a break, if it's only some time in the country with kindred spirits. I'll be setting up— let's call it a scholarship fund— so deserving men can get the recreation they need."

"And deserving women?" inquired Sandy.

Sandy, please. The question was reasonable enough, but did she really need to bring it up now?

Hardt didn't seem to mind. "Oh, most likely. Of course. Here's where the exclusivity comes in. I'll be reviewing the applications myself. I want to make sure the memberships go to the most deserving. And even those who can afford to pay, I'll be the one who decides who joins."

A little idealistic as a business model, Eric thought drily. Though if he could design the place to make it really attractive . . . "This is a nonprofit, then?"

"Well, no, not exactly . . . " Hardt demurred. His tone brightened. "But here's the best part. I won't be offering physical recreation only, but also refreshment for the mind. Lectures designed to help— to help men solve their deepest problems and become proud of being an American again. There's a real need for that these days, don't you agree?"

"Yes, I noticed you want an exhibition space and a large assembly room."

Too large, really, like most of the other square footages and dimensions Hardt had given him. Head down, he covered his mouth to disguise a chuckle. New clients were all the same, and the rich ones were the worst. They were always coming in with everything cut and dried, as if they only needed him to draw it up. They wouldn't do it to their physician or lawyer, would they? *"Doc, I've got this twinge in my chest; schedule me for open-heart surgery tomorrow."* So why did they think it worked that way with an architect? Never mind. Helping clients understand the process was part of the job.

"Oh, yes!" Hardt responded. "That room will be the heart of my— my resort. Even since I was a boy I've had the firm belief that things weren't the way they should be in these United States. This country needs a place where . . . "

Eric listened as his new client expounded on his vision for the complex. It seemed to involve bringing each member to realize his full place and potential as an American citizen, so none of them would let anyone take those rights away. The man's talk amused him. Eric loved his country well enough, but to find someone of Hardt's status wearing his patriotism on his sleeve, that was interesting, and again made him hide a smile.

"All my guests will leave there transformed," Hardt was saying. "It's so important that we restore the pride in America that was undermined in the 1960s, I'm sure you'll agree."

"Oh, certainly." It was frustrating. All these were good old motherhood-and-apple-pie objectives, wonderful to keep in mind during the design process. But did the guy really have to go on and on about them? It was time they got down to practicalities. Like, how flat or hilly was the site? What about access? How high was the water table? Maybe Hardt had gotten a geologist in to look at the conditions already. If Eric could get a word in edgewise he should ask.

The client talked on.

He seems to think things went wrong in America around 1964... Don't know about that, but he's got a lot of faith in Architecture to improve people's lives. That's good. So do I.

He visualized how the typical member would enter the reception lodge, ride down the main elevator, and step into a space that was truly inspirational. "Inspirational" was obviously what Hardt wanted . . .

Eric seemed to be standing in that grand reception hall himself. A little man with the face of a mole approached him and asked if he wanted to check his swim fins. He said no, he'd need them for the lecture later, and—

Oh, damn! I nearly fell asleep. That was what he got for staying up till

3:00 A.M. last night working in his home studio. He damped down the urge to ask Hardt to wind it up. To his right, Sandy made notes and little sketches on her memo pad. She didn't interrupt the man either.

Suddenly, Eric became aware of dead silence. Oh, no. This time had he actually drifted off and had the client seen it?

"Baumann," Hardt said, "Tell me something."

"Uh, yes?"

"What is your feeling on private citizens owning automatic weapons?"

From Sandy erupted a suppressed "*What?*"

"I— I suppose I'm fine with it. It depends."

"For recreation, and self-defense, perhaps?" the client probed.

"Well, in that case, certainly."

"Good." He smiled. "Some men of your profession run like scared rabbits when automatic weapons are mentioned. You're not that type."

"Oh, no, no. I'm not." Eric paused. "Does this have something to do with the shooting range I saw on the program?"

"It does. This is another unique facet of my plan. I intend for every man at my resort— every guest, I mean— to learn how to handle an automatic weapon."

At his side Sandy stirred, and on her pad she drew and circled a question mark.

"I'll have ordinary firearms available, and semi-automatics as well, but I think the big guns will be a real attraction. Don't you?"

"Yes, I can see that. We'll be sure to design your range to accommodate them."

"But, Eric," Sandy muttered.

"What's wrong?" he whispered back.

"You're not seriously—?"

"Not now." If Hardt could afford to collect guns like that, he must have really deep pockets. Not someone he wanted to offend. He spoke up. "Sandy, bring me *Architectural Graphic Standards*, would you? . . . Thanks."

He found the page detailing minimum requirements for shooting ranges and, spreading out a sheet of tracing paper, began to sketch.

"You must have gotten used to the M16 when you were in Vietnam," Hardt commented. "How did you like it?" Before Eric could answer, he said, "It's an elegant weapon. Light weight. Accurate at a great distance."

He grunted his agreement and kept drawing. There was something he needed to work out.

"The older ones had a tendency to jam, but they fixed that. It may surprise you—" Hardt gave a laugh— "but I like the Kalashnikov. A little heavy, but simple and rugged. Wonderful at close quarters."

Eric looked up. "I've been comparing what *Graphic Standards* recommends to the square footage you gave me. Even allowing for the more powerful weapons, you could get over thirty shooting lanes in. Are you sure there will be that much demand at a time?"

"I don't see why not. Do you?"

It did no good to contradict a client flat out. Let it rest for now. "You'll need secure storage for these guns, for the automatics in particular. About how many will you need to fit in?"

He hesitated. "The AKs and M16s? Several. Enough for my purposes."

"Five or ten of each?"

"You could say that. Maybe a few more."

How many was a few? Never mind, he'd stay flexible. "All right. You've called for nine hundred square feet for storage. How much of that will be for the weapons?"

"Oh, I was thinking most of it."

Really? A serious gun collector would know that wasn't necessary. Maybe this whole project was a pipe dream. A good joke on himself, if he put in a lot of time and the man turned out to be a debt-ridden pretender.

Eric stemmed his doubt. Everything he'd managed to find out told him Hardt had the cash to back up his talk. "I'm sure we can be way more efficient than that."

"Oh, of course. That's what I'm hiring you for! But, speaking of storage . . . " Hardt's tone grew even more friendly. "Baumann, I understand you're an expert in custom-fitted cabinetry."

"Yes, sir, I like to think so."

"Baumann, in this gun room I'm going to give you an opportunity to do custom design beyond your wildest dreams." He licked his lips. "You're going to design me racks, and shelves, and cabinets, and safes. All fitted up just the way I want them, all secured by fingerprint access only, all climate-controlled. What do you think of *that*?"

"Sounds fascinating. You want secret compartments? We love designing secret compartments. But I think we can get it a lot smaller."

"If you say so. Why the concern about the size?"

"Mr. Hardt," Sandy spoke up, "how many guests will you be accommodating? At capacity, I mean?"

"I was thinking about . . . oh, a couple th— maybe five hundred. For the bigger conferences."

A good question. Eric glanced over Hardt's figures again. "I hate to repeat myself, but I really think you need to trim this down. It's not that I object to designing a large complex, but if it's going to be underground, we need to keep it as economical as we can. Once you start digging— or blasting— you never know what you'll run into."

"Is that what you're worried about?" Hardt said, laughing. "You're used to cheapskate clients who make you redesign around hidden conditions and there goes your fee!"

Actually, no. His existing clients were good at paying for whatever came up.

Or they would be, a little voice responded, if he'd bill them for all the time he put in.

"I won't Jew you down like they do." Eric kept himself from scowling. Surprising, the terms educated people still used, but he wasn't jeopardizing this job by correcting the client on his language. "Any unforeseen circumstances, I'll pay. Don't worry about that."

"No, I'm not worrying. And they don't— um, now that I've seen the whole program, here's how we could organize these functions for you." He tore off another sheet of tracing paper and began to diagram how the spaces could fit together.

"That's good," Hardt said. "Yes, that'll work!"

The phone rang. "Sandy, get that, will you?" He went on drawing.

SHE KEPT LESS than half an ear for the fabric company representative who wanted to come show them their new line. It was plain that Hardt wasn't budging from the size and scope he'd outlined on the program he brought in, and equally plain that Eric wasn't hearing it.

"What do you think?" he asked, turning the sketch around so Hardt could see it. "Does that reflect what you had in mind?"

"Oh, yes," Hardt replied, and his voice was like warm tropical waters . . . with a shark lurking in the coral. "Baumann, I was right about you. We think alike. This is where it all begins, and you're the man to make it happen. Are we a team?"

"Certainly."

"Good," he said, his tone so innocent that Sandy doubted her senses, "because this will be bigger than you can imagine. Everything you've dreamed of since you were a boy— you work with me, and I'll see you have it all."

Have it all? How could any human being promise that? What could this complete stranger possibly know about Eric's boyhood dreams? Something here stunk and stunk bad. She focussed on the back of Eric's head and willed her thoughts into it: *Change your mind, please! Don't listen to him. Don't gain the whole world and lose your soul!*

Hardt raised his glance. The pale eyes burned into hers a look of hatred so stinging she nearly recoiled in pain. When she dared to look again, the man's face was serene and his attention was for Eric alone.

"No, Terry," she said to the rep on the phone, "Nothing's wrong. You were saying about a new line of tweeds?"

"Thank you, Mr. Hardt, I certainly appreciate—"

He waved off Eric's gratitude. "I'm convinced you can do this job; you're probably the only one I'd see doing it. I'll show you the site next week— assuming you're free?"

"Where is it? So I can plan—"

"Don't worry about transportation. I'll send a car for you. Just you, by the way. For now. You understand."

"Just you" for now and always, I'll bet.

Eric cleared his throat. "There is one thing—"

Finally!

"There," Hardt interrupted, ripping off a check and tossing it on the table. "For your retainer. Don't worry, I have enough for this. You'll get more when the job gets underway."

"No, Mr. Hardt. There's only one engineering firm in Wapatomekie I'd trust to associate with us on a project like this, and I need to make sure they're free to take it on. I know my limitations, and we'll need their help. We'd hate to get started and then disappoint you."

"Oh, is that what's bothering you? I have just the men for the job lined up. Have you heard of Plancher & McClelland?"

"Are they local? I'm not familiar with their work."

Me, neither. "Um, yes, Terry," she said into the receiver. "Jewel-toned velvets. We might be interested in that."

"Well, not exactly. But you'll like them. And Baumann," he said, those eyes still locked on him, "you needn't talk of disappointing me. I will not be disappointed.

"I have arrangements to make; once they're done I'll bring you a contract and have you sign." He slid his papers into his portfolio and rose from his chair. "And again, not a word of this leaves this room. You understand."

"Certainly," Eric agreed.

"Fine." With a nod, he silently slipped out the door.

"Good, Terry, we'll see you next week." Sandy hung up the phone. "How much is it for?" she asked, going to Eric's side.

"Ten thousand dollars."

"Ten thousand!" She stared at the check lying baldly on the table.

"He can afford it. I've made some calls. Did you know his money's behind the Broadmoor Industrial Park?"

"Really?" she said, trying to keep her voice casual. "I've never heard of him. I thought I knew the names of all the big Wapatomekie developers."

"He's not from around here. I'm told he always works through an agent."

"So why—?"

"Why what?"

"Nothing." She wouldn't step two inches towards implying that Eric's design product wasn't worth any client's personal time.

"He's involved in a lot of local land development, behind the scenes," Eric said. "It all makes money for him. He may be a little grandiose but he's not just a dreamer."

"Grandiose? You mean how big he wanted everything? It'd hold five times what he's saying, if the program stays how it is."

"Don't worry, we'll talk him down. I'm sure his agent will be more reasonable. We won't have to deal with him much after this."

"I don't want to deal with him at all."

"You won't have to. Leave that to me."

"You didn't hear what I said. I meant I don't think either of us should have anything to do with him, or this project, either."

He gaped at her, astonished. "Sandy, what's wrong? Is it because it's underground?"

"No, I get that part."

"Is it the shooting range? That's not the only recreational facility it'll have. And there's the lecture room. Look, Sandy, I value your input, but I can't lose this chance because you feel insulted."

"Who said I feel insulted?" The anger in her own voice appalled her. "It's not about me," she said more calmly. "It's more— my gosh, Eric, the guns he's talking about are illegal!"

He stared back, then broke into a grin.

"Aren't . . . they?"

"Actually, no. If you're not a felon or a minor, you can buy all the automatic weapons you can afford. Once you pay the taxes and fill out all the paperwork, that is. I don't know what you're worried about. He's only going to have a few of them. Or weren't you listening?"

"It's you who weren't listening," she retorted, more sharply than she intended.

"Meaning what?"

"You kept trying to convince him to make the project smaller, but everything he said back told me he has no intention of budging a single square foot. Especially for that gun room."

"I didn't hear that!"

"Of course you didn't. You were too busy drawing. Eric, he wants all that space, and he's going to fill it up, too. And for what?"

"For a resort and conference center. Seriously," he went on, "we could make a big name for ourselves on this project. Remember what he said about building an empire? 'Here's where it all begins.' I'd say this is only the first in a chain of resorts like this. We do well, we may be set to design them all."

She couldn't hold back a squeak of alarm.

He ignored her. "I'm excited about it. Wow. People will come there from all over the region. I know you don't like the guy," he said, giving her the appealing, little-boy look he sometimes turned on female clients when he was talking them into doing things his way, "but can't you get over your distaste for the sake of doing some really great design?"

Blast it, don't patronize me! "It's not distaste!" she sputtered. "It's— well, I've done all I can not to push my religion on you or the clients and still be the best Christian I can in this job. But I can't be tactful or discreet about this. He's got something nasty— something immoral— in mind, and we shouldn't be involved in it!"

"'Immoral,' huh?" The cynicism in his laugh twisted her heart. "Like he's planning some massive prostitution ring."

"That's not the only kind of immoral— Good grief, why won't he tell us where the site is? Why use some engineering firm nobody's ever heard of? What if we end up helping him, I don't know, carry out some kind of plot? We'd be involved, and where would we be then?"

"Don't be ridiculous!"

"Don't you be so blind!"

"Me, blind?" shouted Eric. He stepped back and in a quiet, maddening voice inquired, "Haven't you heard of something called the Second Amendment?" He sounded so reasonable she could scream. "I thought you conservative Christians made that part of your creed."

How could he be so unfair? Her love for him made the cut hurt all the more. With great effort she forced down her rising fury and modulated her tone to match his. "Some of us put God first. And the Second Amendment has nothing to do with it. Nine hundred square feet for guns and ammunition? At a private resort? I mean . . . "

It was too much. Her ability to be cerebral fell to pieces. "Please, Eric, you know there's something wrong with this from start to finish! You really believed all that rot about patriotism and the common man? Really?"

"Humph," he said, his eyes refusing to meet hers.

"Please," she begged, "I don't know what it is, but he intends something, something terrible, and how you of all people could think of helping him, I can't—!"

Turning his back, he gathered his meeting notes. "Sandy, be reasonable," he said coldly. "I don't think you realize how little work we have left. You like your job, don't you? We need this project to keep the office open." He wheeled and stared her in the face, his jaw set. "And I for one will enjoy doing it."

"I am being reasonable!" she said, her voice rising. "You can fire me or throw me out or whatever, but as a Christian I can't and won't do this job and I don't want you doing it, either!"

She clapped her hand to her mouth. *O Domine.* Now he'd remember everything he had against Christianity. Throw in her face how his Lutheran missionary father had abandoned the family to minister on some Indian reservation in North Dakota. Remind her of the poverty he, his mom, and his little brother struggled through in Bismarck and how the local church left them on their own. And wind it all up with a lecture on the uselessness of faith in Christ.

. . . What was she thinking? Eric wouldn't do that, he never had.

What he did do was worse.

He said nothing at all. The advance check, so brazenly lying there, mocked her from the table's surface. He put out a hand to pick it up, but, abruptly pulling back, stalked over to his drawing board and with ostentatious busyness returned to work.

Silence slammed its icy barrier between them. The frigid stillness imprisoned her in the room for one hour, two hours . . . so oppressive that she wished to flee, but so ominous that she dared not go even to the restroom, lest she return to find he'd locked the door past appeal against her.

She prayed frantically, her thoughts refusing to cohere. Maybe she was wrong. There was no one thing she could put her finger on, not if those guns could be owned legally. But taken all together . . . *O Domine, don't let him— Make him— Please, God, oh, in Jesus' name, please . . . !*

It was late in the day when Eric rose. She sucked in her breath and sat up straighter to steel herself against the inevitable.

Here it comes. I've had it. I'll be a martyr for the faith. But the melodrama of it all struck her so hard she let out a giggle.

"What's so funny?" he inquired, and she was amazed to see he was smiling, too.

"Oh, me. Wallowing in self-pity."

"You've got no monopoly on that, I'm afraid. I want to apologize and say you're right: we can't do that job for Nick Hardt. Questions of Christian morality aside— I'm an agnostic, remember— I don't think it's legitimate."

"You mean it's illegal?"

"I doubt he's conspiring to take over the world, if that's what you're afraid of. But a complex that big, out in the middle of nowhere . . . and that silly idea about vetting all the guests himself . . . There's no way it would work financially."

Is that how he saw it? Why should she be surprised?

"He might get in trouble with the civil rights laws, too," she said.

"What? No, that's for public accommodations. He said this would be private."

"Oh, that's right. But those automatic weapons . . . ?"

"Those? They're terribly hard to get. You can't import them and you can't ship them across state lines. How's he going to come up with more than a handful for his little shooting gallery after spending all that money on construction? That bothered me, too. If he's that unrealistic . . . The place'll go belly up in a year and everyone will call it 'Baumann's Money Pit.' No, thank you."

"You're not mad at me, then?"

"For bringing me to my senses? Certainly not." He smiled. "It's late. Are you ready to—"

"Wait a minute. Could we— I mean, Mr. Hardt should be in his office by now; couldn't you— we— call him now and, well, save him the trip back?"

"Well— all right. His number should be on the check." He stepped over to the conference table, not touching the draft where it lay. "Oh, no, it's not. Just the company name and a post office box here in town."

"It's not?" She joined him at the table and looked at the check. "'White Way Ventures,'" she read off the name. "Sounds like Broadway plays."

"More likely some road or creek on the property." Eric shrugged. "I'll write tomorrow and let him know I've changed my mind."

"You think he'll try somebody else?"

"I doubt any sane architect will touch it." He took her hand and shook it, and the pressure of his fingers around hers was firm and reassuring. "Sandy, I don't know what I'd do without you. Forget what I said before. Not taking this job will *not* kill us."

How dear he was to her, how very dear!

Too soon, he released her hand. "Now let's get out of here."

"Okay, but I almost forgot. Here's something I got for you yesterday." She reached under her table and handed him the sack containing the mechanical dog.

He pulled out the box and opened it. "It's wonderful! Where did you get it?"

"At that little store on the corner of Adams and Forty-fourth."

"Oh, I know it; they have fascinating stuff, don't they? Gadgets and jewelry all mixed up together . . . "

"I really like the pearl rings," she threw in. "So much more subtle than the usual diamond." He looked puzzled, and she hurriedly said, "And old watches, too. So classic."

"Well, this'll make a great 'watch' dog," he said. "Look, you wind him up in just the same way!"

They laughed as the tiny contraption hopped and yelped with mechanized ferocity across the conference table.

"Look at those ears and tail spin!" he said. "What shall we name it?"

"Up to you. He's your dog!"

"Oh, come on."

"How about . . . no . . . oh, wasn't it Le Corbusier who called a house a 'machine for living'? Well, this is a 'machine for dogging.' Let's call him Corb!"

"Well," said Eric, smiling, "I don't know if that's quite an appropriate memorial, but yes, the point is well-taken. His name is Corb."

Sandy looked up at him as he watched the toy, his face again clear and serene. He would do what he promised. The ice was melted; she had him back.

CHAPTER A.4

NICK HARDT REAPPEARED the very next day. Sandy prayed intently as he swung himself into "his" conference chair— and was confronted with the ten thousand dollar check lying exactly as he had tossed it down the afternoon before.

His eyes narrowed. "What's this?"

Thank God, Eric didn't waver. "Mr. Hardt, we can't do your job for you. I've got the letter written to say so."

"You're telling me you're incapable?"

"It's just not prudent for us at this time. Don't get me wrong, you can build whatever you want. But if I were you . . . " He made a conciliatory gesture. "I'd rethink it, myself."

Hardt sprang to his feet. "Don't be a damned imbecile! You were eager enough yesterday. What's gotten into you? Unless . . . " His eyes turned on her, pinning her down. "Is it that bitch you use for an assistant?" Sandy sucked in her breath. "Damn you, Baumann, if she's in the way, get rid of her. If you don't have the guts, I'll get rid of her for you. Be a man! I will have this job done, and you're going to do it."

Eric repeated quietly, "I'm sorry, Mr. Hardt. We will not do this job. That is final."

"You have the sense of this doorknob! Listen to me. Refuse me, and you'll never have another client here in Wapatomekie or anywhere else!" The words pierced in like some unalterable truth. "I can arrange it. You work for me, or I'll ruin you. I'll ruin you!"

"Mr. Hardt, we will not do this job. Kindly take your check and go."

His face stripped of yesterday's genial mask, rage darting from his uncanny eyes, Nick Hardt crumpled the check between his fingers. This time, they heard him go, stalking furiously off down the hall and out to the elevators.

"Well, at least he *is* human," she whispered.

Eric closed the door as against a dreaded pestilence and sat down in his chair, hard, his head in his hands. "O god, O god!"

Finally looking up, he said, "I'm sorry I didn't say anything to him about that name he called you. He actually offered to help me fire you!" He shook his head in wonder. "I'm sorry. I had to keep on the subject. You're a brave girl."

"You're a brave man. It's all right. You did wonderfully."

"Not as much as you. You saw it from the beginning, didn't you? You were right. I don't think I could ever work for that man, even if what he wanted *was* feasible." He shuddered. "Better the firm should fail than survive on someone like that."

"Eric," she ventured, "what about what he said about, you know, the clients . . . ?"

"I don't know. It could be all bluster; people say things like that all the time. We'll just have to wait and see."

"'Jump off that bridge when we get to it'?"

"Exactly!" His laugh made fair approach to merriment. "Hey, listen, we've been through a hell of a lot this afternoon. Why don't we go get us a hamburger and drive over to my place and listen to some Bach? I could use cleaning out my soul."

"'*Magnificat anima mea Dominum*'," she replied, softly. "My soul doth magnify the Lord!"

"*The Magnificat?* Yes, we could listen to that if you like."

He had not understood her, but standing there, her heart overflowing with love for him, she knew exactly what she had meant.

HOW DID Nick Hardt know Eric was in the Army? And apparently did a tour in Vietnam?

The thought struck her that night as she turned off her bedside lamp. He'd never mentioned it to her.

One of those guy things, most likely. Eric probably hadn't thought she'd care.

CHAPTER A.5

"**T**RICK OR TREAT!" Eric greeted her as he came into the office one morning early in October. He was wearing a black-toned wool sweater and charcoal flannel slacks and looked a little dashing and dangerous.

"You're in luck, you ghoul. Here's doughnuts." Sandy pushed the box his way.

"Great!" he said, taking one and biting into it. "Any messages?"

"Mrs. Ryerson called. I can't swear to it, but she sounded worried."

"Wonder what about. I'll call her and see."

He pushed the phone buttons with firm, even strokes of his long artist's hands. "Hi, Annette," he said to the maid, "is Mrs. Ryerson in? Tell her Eric Baumann is returning her call."

His voice was like a cello played by Pablo Casals . . . She could let the sound of it flow over her all day. How unfair it was to him that he could never say the same about hers! And, she lamented to herself, she was such a shrimp, she didn't give him much to look at. Tall, stunning girls with legs that went up to infinity, that was Eric's type. Girls like Leah Matthews. She suppressed a mock-melancholy sigh.

"Hello, Sheila? Eric. What is it? Sandy said you sounded worried."

The client's anxious excitement burst shrilly out of the phone.

"My side of what?" said Eric, and she spun her chair around. Whatever Mrs. Ryerson said in response, it made his eyes meet hers in blank horror. "No! What happened? When? Why didn't—?"

What was going on? The blare of Mrs. Ryerson's voice was audible enough, but she couldn't make out the words.

"Hey, wait a minute," said Eric. "When did she say this happened?"

Sandy clutched her drawing pencil tight and forced herself to be patient.

Another long pause while Mrs. Ryerson spoke.

"Sheila, hold on! Nobody's dead. I don't know where that woman got her information, but she's wrong. I was there just yesterday and the roof is in one piece. The shingles are on, the insulation is in. Even if it had collapsed last week, there's no way they could've repaired all that by now. It's not—" He was cut off by another noisy expostulation from Sheila.

Something had collapsed at the Weisman site? Someone was dead? Why hadn't Sandy heard?

"Sheila, please. We'd be in the middle of an investigation. We aren't. Everything's all right." He was calmer now. "Listen, if you're worried about it, the contractor's Bill Worthington. He built your remodel, you know what a good craftsman he is. Call him up and tell him to take you through. You'll see nothing has come down, I promise."

Of course nothing was wrong. Sandy allowed herself to relax. But where had all this come from?

Eric listened again. Then, "I understand. Of course. Call Bill if anything's still worrying you." Another pause. "I'd appreciate that, Sheila. Thank you. Goodbye."

He grabbed his head in both hands and shook it in frustration. "I don't have time for this!" She watched him sympathetically. "I guess I should have expected it, but oh, damn, why now?"

"Something happened, or I guess, didn't?" she ventured.

"Oh, Sheila was at some party last night and some woman she barely knows told her the ridge beam at the Weisman job came down last week and killed one of the workmen."

"That's stupid. You don't design like that, Bill doesn't build like that, and besides, we would have heard."

"That's just the thing. How could she have believed it for a New York minute?"

"Do you think Nick Hardt's behind it?"

"Who else?" He shook his head. "But dammit, if that's the best he can do, I'm not going to worry about it. Sheila said she'd speak up for us and that should be the end of that."

A nice thought, but . . . "Eric," she said hesitantly, "I was in the deli yesterday noon getting lunch, and I ran into another architect, a girl I knew at college."

"And?"

"And immediately she saw me, she came rushing up and yelled— so embarrassing, I thought the whole counter could hear— 'Oh, I hear your office is getting sued for cheating a client!' It didn't surprise me; we never got along in school and I think she's still jealous. I asked her what on God's green earth she was talking about, and she said she'd just heard we'd been caught cutting corners on somebody's project. No specifics, of course, and she couldn't for the life of her say where she'd heard this report, it was just sort of floating around her office."

"What did you say?"

"I pulled the Aggrieved Artist act. I said trash like that didn't deserve a reply and if the people in her office spent more time discussing the history and theory of architecture instead of passing on stupid gossip they'd profit greatly by it."

"Whoo! A little harsh, weren't you!"

"Yeah, maybe. But I *could've* told her maybe then they'd stop turning out those misbegotten Post-Modernist abortions they're so fond of."

"I congratulate you on your kindness and restraint," he said, bowing in mock gravity.

"I didn't mention it because I thought it was just Mona being Mona. But—"

"Maybe it was. I refuse to give Hardt more credit than he deserves."

"Me neither. I'll—"

"Knock-knock!" a cheery female voice sounded behind her. A comfort-ably-plump young woman in a chic pale-blue woollen suit trundled a large sample case into the room. Rosie Crenshaw, the StudioFabrik representa-tive. "I'm not too early, am I?"

"Oh, no," said Eric. "Sandy and I were just talking."

"I wondered," said Rosie, wheeling the case into position by the conference table. "You two looked like you were in the middle of a conspiracy."

"Nothing like that," Sandy assured her. "What do you have for us? Terry from FabTex was here last week," she said slyly, "and showed us their winter line."

"Oh, FabTex!" Rosie scoffed. "You'll want to throw all their samples out once you see what *we* have."

Sandy and Eric admired the upholstery and wall fabrics in silk, wool, and fine cotton that Rosie produced for their inspection. When she had made note of all the lines they wanted larger samples of, she latched the case and said, "You know, I almost called to find out if our appointment was still on."

"Why?" he asked, his voice a little too casual.

"I was having drinks the other night with Paula, the David Stockhouse Textiles rep, and she had the strangest thing to say about your office. I wouldn't even mention it if I hadn't heard something like it before."

"What was it?" Sandy admired how he managed to sound curious, nothing more.

"She'd heard on good authority that your firm was going belly-up and you were about to declare bankruptcy."

"Oh, Rosie!" Sandy exclaimed. "And you believed it?"

"Bankruptcy happens; it's nothing to be ashamed of." She shrugged matter-of-factly. "I didn't want to embarrass you by showing you product you couldn't sell."

"But you decided it wasn't true," said Eric.

"Oh, yeah. Paula had no idea who the source was. The other place I heard it, that guy will say anything for a good story. And nobody else I talked to'd heard anything like it."

"You asked people if we were going bankrupt?" Sandy asked, appalled.

"God bless America, no! I've got more finesse than that."

"So why say anything to us?" said Eric.

"Well . . . I like you guys. You're friends. And you may be small, but you're one of my best customers. The bankruptcy rumor is trash, obviously, but there's other stuff going around. Eric, if you can stop it, you should."

"Tell me what you've heard. I'd better know it all."

THEIR REJECTED CLIENT, Eric concluded grimly when she had finished, was a man who kept his promises— or his threats. No point in letting the fabric rep know her news bothered him, even if she was dating one of his closest friends. "Well," he said, cheerfully enough, "it's not good, but nothing we can't handle."

"You see why I wanted to tell you," said Rosie, as he helped her on with her coat.

"Certainly. I'm glad you did. I'll deal with it."

"Of course. See you in the spring." He was grateful for the good-natured emphasis in her voice. At least she had some confidence that he and his firm would still be there then.

At the door she paused. "Want me to say hi to Mike for you?"

"Sure." It'd been months since he'd seen him, August, at least. Never mind, he and Mike Laurence had been on the same project team at Richardson & Greene where he used to work. They both knew how hectic architectural practice could be. "Tell him to behave himself."

She snorted, and left. He closed the door behind her and looked at Sandy, shaking his head in disbelief. "Clever, isn't he? All that, and not a mention of anyone named Hardt."

"If that's the kind of thing it is," she said, her worry undisguised, "how can we stop it?"

"I think . . . well, considering that our clients are bound to speak up for us, and we can only do what we can do . . . the same way I shut up the fools who thought I was an idiot to go out on my own a year and a half ago: trust in our reputation and let our work speak for itself."

"SANDY, DIDN'T SHAKESPEARE say something about reputation, how useless it is?"

She looked up from her board, and he couldn't help noticing that her eyes seemed tired and a little sad. "Someplace in *Henry IV*? But I don't think it was reputation, it was honor."

"Same thing. Ours doesn't seem to be doing us much good."

"I don't think—" She shook her head, gave him a thin smile, and turned back to her work.

Bitterly he stared at his own drawing, almost too disgusted to go on with it. He'd found out these past few weeks how fragile reputation was, and the influence of longtime clients was almost as insecure. Every day it was something new: Worried calls from people whose projects he'd managed when he'd been an associate with Richardson & Greene. People he'd thought of as friends avoiding him at the last AIA meeting. Shocking tidbits "I heard about you" dumped on him— with far less tact than Rosie Crenshaw had shown— by acquaintances on the street. Sandy told him she was getting the same. A mounting tide of false reports was beating mercilessly against the good name of his firm and against them both as professionals.

None of his current clients had withdrawn their agreements, but no more work was coming in. Oh, the business was out there, but now, men he'd thought of as prime leads wouldn't talk to him at all. Without new prospects, once the Weisman house was finished he'd have to close the doors. He'd dreamed of having his own architecture firm since he was a small boy in North Dakota, and to have his vision undermined like this was gall to his soul.

And somehow Hardt managed to keep his name out of it. Even the middlemen his would-be client had worked with previously had neither seen nor heard from him since the end of September. Eric asked his friends to keep their ears open for anything that could connect Hardt to the smear campaign, and they all came up blank. He had no proof Hardt was doing anything to damage him at all.

None, that was, until the afternoon he got a call from a fellow-architect.

"Sandy," he said grimly when he got off the phone, "that was Miles Pinter."

"Yes, he's got a firm specializing in strip malls, that kind of thing." She rolled her eyes.

"Right. Miles was a year or two ahead of me in architecture school and we've been friends ever since. Can't imagine why: his work can be really generic. Which makes it all the stranger that . . . "

"That what?"

"That anybody should come to him wanting a distinctive office design, drop-dead reception space, impressive executive suite, the whole package."

"Well," said Sandy, her brow wrinkling in puzzlement, "if that's the case, he'd better learn how to do distinctive design. Or recommend someone who already does."

"He tried to. He recommended us. And the client said, yeah, originally he had intended to talk to us about it. But he knew a guy who knew a guy named Hardt who said we banked his retainer then refused to do any work. So now there's no way he'd trust us with anything at all."

"Oh, no!"

"Oh, yes. He's tired of screwing us from behind the scenes; he wants the glory. I'll give him glory, all right. Where's that phone gotten to? I'm calling my lawyer."

A few minutes later, he hung up, deflated.

"What did he say?" Sandy asked.

"Chuck told me yes, I have cause for civil action. Miles, if he's willing, can testify and that'll help prove that we've suffered material harm."

"So what's the problem?"

"Where to serve the papers."

"Oh my gosh, that's right. What about the check? No, I remember, it only had a post office box on it."

"I'm having Chuck look into this White Way outfit. It should be on file with the state. Meanwhile I'll keep asking my contacts where to find the SOB. But there's no point starting legal action if I can't run him down."

THE NEXT DAY brought him no further light.

"Eric, it's Chuck Stiegel on the line," Sandy said, handing him the receiver.

"Good. Maybe he's discovered something." He gave her an encouraging wink. "Baumann here. What do you have for me?"

"Sorry, it's no-go," the attorney said. "I called Merchants Federal to get a line on that account, and they told me it was closed four weeks ago. We can't get any more information about the account holder without going through a lot of government paperwork. You want me to follow up on it?"

Eric considered. Expenses were tight. "You think that'll get us the information we need?"

"Doubt it. I checked with the state, and there's no record of a corporation or even a sole proprietorship called White Way Ventures. It's possible it's registered in another state, but in my opinion it's a dummy entity. No reason to hope that any contact information isn't bogus as well."

"I see." *Damn.*

"You find out anything?" asked Stiegel.

"No. The engineers he mentioned aren't on file with the state licensing board, and they aren't registered with any surrounding states, either— I checked the day after he was here. All my sources on Hardt tell me they've had no word of him in weeks. And he's not in the phone book, though I'm sure you checked that already."

"The name could be an alias."

"Could be."

"Anything else I can do for you at the moment?"

"No, I'm afraid not. Thanks for trying, Chuck." He felt like an emptied-out bag of cement powder. "Send me a bill for the time you put in."

"Will do. Let me know if anything comes up. Although . . . here's something else you could try."

"What?"

"Ever think of hiring a private investigator?"

"Really?" Eric said. "You mean like *Magnum, P.I.*? I doubt I could afford the red Ferrari."

"I'm serious. I've got a guy I recommend, very reputable. He'd have sources I don't and his fee would be a hell of a lot cheaper than mine."

Maybe the idea wasn't far-fetched after all. "All right," said Eric, "who is it?"

"His name's Gino Lupelli," said Chuck. "Here's his number . . . " Eric read it back, and Stiegel said, "You really need to go after this bastard. Sorry I can't do anything more myself, but it's been like tracking a ghost or a demon trying to run him down."

To his dismay, Eric had to agree.

CHAPTER A.6

LUPELLI THE PRIVATE DETECTIVE couldn't locate Nick Hardt either. Two things only did he provide in return for the three days Eric could afford: first, not only had Hardt not been seen around town since the third week in September, he had also liquidated all his local holdings before the end of that month. And second, he apparently owned the controlling interest in an industrial gold mine up in the Dakotas. But which Dakota and what mine and where, nobody could say.

"You want me to go up there and poke around some more, boss?"

"How long would you need?"

"Week, maybe two." Mr. Lupelli would be happy to undertake it— for his regular fee, plus travel expenses.

The amount quoted was more than Eric paid himself in a month.

"No, I don't think so. Not now, anyway." And he and Sandy were back to weathering the gale on their own.

"WHAT THE *HELL?*"

The expletive startled Sandy out of her concentration. Eric stood at the conference table reading the enclosure from the plain, unmarked envelope a private messenger had dropped off at their office while he was out. "Is this his idea of a Halloween prank?"

"What is it?" she asked, coming over.

"That SOB Hardt expects me to put a double-width classified ad in the *News-Herald* on Friday the sixth, with the words 'I'll Deal' in 50-point type with my name under it. Then he'll let bygones be bygones and we can get on with the project."

"Is he crazy?"

"Probably. He says we're destined to work together and it's pointless for me to dodge my fate." He laughed contemptuously. "Clever, how he kept that from sounding like a physical threat. Even so . . . Do you mind fetching me a nine-by-eleven envelope?"

She brought it to him, and carefully, holding the letter and its cover by the edges, he slipped them inside.

"For Chuck Stiegel?" she asked.

"Yes. Just in case."

She sighed and resolved to work all the harder on the custom cornice moulding she was designing for the Weisman dining room. Eric, too, once he'd applied the address sticker, stamped the envelope, and put it aside, pulled up his chair and doubled down on his tasks. Ironic, considering that once this house was finished they might be left with nothing to do and no one willing to hire them to do it.

Let it be so. In the meantime they'd keep up their standards as their mutual act of defiance. She picked up a french curve and redrew one of the lines. There. That was better still.

THE EVENING of November sixth was cool without being cold, and Eric made a point of relishing the walk from his apartment to the Wapatomekie Civic Museum, a few blocks away. No advertisement from him had appeared in the day's newspaper, and if Hardt had expected to see one he was a fool.

Screw Nick Hardt. The man was trying to grind him into poverty. Well, he'd been poor before, growing up in that gray, dingy third floor walk-up in Bismarck, North Dakota. Going into architecture had been his way of escaping that ugliness— no, more than that, to transcend it— and whatever Hardt threatened, architecture would raise him from the dust again.

And he wasn't in the dust yet. He still had his membership in the museum's Fine Arts Guild, he was headed for a private reception to mark the opening of an exhibition of Old Master paintings from the National Gallery in London, and he intended to enjoy it to the hilt.

Sandy, it occurred to him, would have enjoyed the preview too. Maybe he should have asked her along as his guest.

But why think of her? You didn't take your female employee out unless it was business. He should have asked Leah. But she was up to her neck at her new store. Besides, Leah didn't like Old Masters.

Just as well to go by himself. Maybe he could slip away from the cocktails and chatter and see the paintings alone and in peace. It'd be a mob scene once the exhibition opened to the public tomorrow and no telling what he'd hear being said about himself. Tonight he was safe: his fellow Guild members would be too polite to mention the rumors.

But Sandy… she'd certainly been good company that evening they'd listened to Bach. (Come to think of it, Leah didn't like Bach, either.) Funny how she seemed to think just like he did whenever they listened to music. Well, not exactly like him, but when she came up with something new, it just revealed to him what he'd felt all along. And wasn't it remarkable how her serious Christianity made him better appreciate Bach's or Mendelssohn's intentions in the sacred works? He'd had enough of religion as a boy, but on her it sat very well.

And it wasn't just music. In the office, too . . . damn, he was lucky to have her. Good thing he'd taken the time at American Institute of Architects chapter meetings to discover her stance on practice and design. And when he'd followed his gut and hired her away from those imposters Phipps & Musgrave, he'd done the right thing there, too. Most employees would have resigned the moment Hardt made good on his threats, but she was as dedicated to architecture as he was himself. And steady? She had hardly let the rumor campaign affect her production at all. At least he'd had that to rely on these past few weeks. A lot of employees would have—

"Eric!" a female voice trumpeted as he entered the museum's reception hall. His meditations scattered like birds at a shot. "I wondered if you were going to show your face!" exclaimed Sheila Ryerson, descending on him with a glint of satisfied accomplishment in her eye. "Let's get you some wine and some of these nice sandwiches, and then I have something to tell you!"

"What?" he said drily. "Somebody's hundred-year-old foundation caved in and it's all my fault?"

"No, you silly boy! As for that, I got together with a group of my friends who are also your clients, and we compared notes. We'd all heard the most *disastrous* stories about each others' houses, and as you may expect, not a word of them was true. Somebody is spreading *vile* gossip about you and we resolved not to let them get away with it."

"That's very good of you all."

"You don't know who it could be?" Sheila inquired narrowly.

"Jacob didn't tell you? A guy named Hardt. Nobody in your circle."

"That's a relief! Now what was I going to say? Oh, yes! You know that family room we'd just had redecorated when you started working for us and we wouldn't let you touch?"

"Yes, what about it?"

"Well, Jacob and I enjoy your part of the house so much, we feel so comfortable in it, we absolutely *hate* going into that room. The kids have parties in there occasionally, but even they complain that it's gloomy. We've actually moved the TV to the spare bedroom!"

The Ryerson family room— Eric winced at the mere mental picture of it. It was the sole blaring sour note in the finely-tuned symphony of his redesign. Monstrous and dark with its over-stained panelling, it flaunted black fiberboard beams traversing the oppressively-low dropped ceiling, a ponderous brick fireplace, and a lurid orange shag carpet that could have been the progeny of an English sheepdog outraged by a Las Vegas stage set. He wondered why it'd taken them so long to be repelled by it.

"So," Sheila went on, "I've talked to Jacob, and especially after all this awful gossip, and knowing how painful that room is to you— no, don't deny it— we decided you deserved a chance to bring it up to the level of the rest of the house."

He veiled his excitement. "Sheila, I'd be happy to make whatever improvements you like in your family room."

"Improvements, shimprovements! Rip the whole thing out! It's useless the way it is."

"What's useless?" inquired Jacob Ryerson, strolling up beside his wife. A short man in his early fifties with a frizzled ring of gray-black hair combed over a thinning pate, he trained on Eric a sly, appraising look that gave him the uncomfortable feeling he was onto something about him.

"Our family room," she explained.

"Oy, you can say that again." Ryerson lit up a cigarette. "Say, Eric, hear anything lately from our old friend Hardt?"

"With 'friends' like that—" began Sheila.

"Too bad about all those rumors flying about you," her husband cut in over her. The ash flew from his cigarette's end and settled on the breast of his expensive gray pinstriped suit. "Though I wouldn't be all that sorry if one of them is true, if I were you."

Oh-oh. What do they say I've done now? "Which one?" he said lightly, hoping to mask his apprehension.

"Why," Jacob said, brushing off the ash with studied deliberation, "didn't I hear that secretary of yours got you in the sack and now she's pregnant?"

"That's ridiculous. I don't have a secretary."

"Well then, Whatsername, your cute assistant, Miss Bei—"

"What the *hell* are you saying?" It surged up before he could consider. "*You* may think that's funny, but Alexandra Beichten is a Christian. She'd die before she'd do anything like that and it's disgusting you'd even think of it!"

A thrown bomb could not have transfixed them in a more appalling glare. Had he just set Sandy's Christian morality over against how Jacob Ryerson might behave as a Jew? Eric stood paralyzed, aghast at what he'd implied.

A voice was speaking, a woman's, saying sensible, commonplace things: "Well, Eric," it said, "When would you like to come over and discuss the family room with us?"

"Oh, yes— Sheila, this next week, I'm— Jacob, I'm terribly sorry, that was offensive of me."

"No," replied the older man heartily, "the offense was mine. I had no business talking about that girl like that. Come to think of it, I hear she's too much of a prude to—" His wife's eyes narrowed, and he faltered. "Well, Eric, let's call it even. Agreed?"

"Agreed."

"And Sheila's right. Come have dinner and tell us what to do with that room. It's, um, wasted space as it is." Fumbling a little, he took a drag on his cigarette. "And um, yes, I have something for you as well. Just have to run down Delkirk . . . Oh, there he is, over at the buffet. Come on, I'll introduce you."

Curious, Eric accompanied them to a long table spread with finger sandwiches and hors-d'oeuvres. Jacob tapped the shoulder of a stout, balding man with reddish-gray whiskers and a bright, cheerful face.

"Oh, hello, Jacob, Sheila!" The stout man gestured to his plate. "I don't know how the Guild did it, they got us genuine black caviar. They'll be raising our dues after this. Tried it yet?"

"Sturgeon roe?" said Jacob. "Sorry, no can do. 'Tain't kosher."

"You don't know what you're missing. Nothing's better." He took a bite out of the canapé. His eyes went to Eric. "You'll try some? You are—?"

"Sure," Eric said.

"Sam," said Jacob, "this is Eric Baumann, the architect. Eric, this is Sam Delkirk, my partner at FirstCon Packaging." They shook hands, and Jacob said, "Sam, you do the honors, all right?"

"Glad to." Between bites of caviar on toast, he said, "We've run FirstCon out of a rented facility the last seven years. Now that we've acquired a smaller concern and opened some new markets, it's high time we moved into a plant of our own."

"You have a building in mind?" Eric said.

"No," said Jacob with great satisfaction. "That's where you come in. We have the land. The building we want you to design and build."

Their first large-scale project! He could do it; he'd managed other such jobs at Richardson & Greene. It couldn't have come at a better time.

"Certainly, I'd be happy to design—"

"It won't be more than mid-sized, as corrugated box making plants go," said Mr. Delkirk, "but our offices will be attached, so it should be worth your—"

"Something to keep you busy," Jacob cut in, "when you get bored dealing with that schmuck Hardt."

"—worth your while. I've seen your work, Baumann, and it's as good as any I've come across in New York or Boston. Maybe better."

"Thanks. It'll be an honor—"

"It's settled, then," said Sheila with cheerful finality. "Eric, you and Sam come over for dinner Tuesday night and we'll discuss the great new inroads we're going to make in local architecture!"

They all laughed and Sam Delkirk proposed a toast. Eric's head whirled— and it had nothing whatever to do with the Chardonnay.

✥

WALKING HOME, Eric turned up his coat collar against the nip in the wind and laughed.

Take that, Hardt, you bastard.

He'd always done right by his clients and now his clients were finally doing right by him. He'd nearly blown it, though, getting on Jacob for saying that about Sandy. Charged in with lance levelled like Sir Somebody-or-Other.

Like Don Quixote, more like it.

But that'd been the right thing, too. He owed it to her, after saying nothing to Hardt when he called her that foul name back in September.

. . . Hang on a second. Was someone hiding in the entryway of that vacant storefront up ahead? As he drew even with the shadowy recess, he spotted within it the figure of a man in a nondescript overcoat, shrinking back as if he didn't want to be seen. Instinctively Eric's muscles tensed.

Baumann, relax. He's just trying to keep out of the wind.

Nevertheless, he quickened his pace. A little past the doorway, he heard footsteps approaching from behind. He told himself not to be ridiculous, but fear like an icy hand clutched at his chest, impelling him to walk faster. He reached the corner. The lights and the traffic were against him. The footsteps kept coming.

Dammit, he was not letting Hardt mess with his head. Deliberately, he turned and grinned at the stranger . . . who glanced at him curiously and stopped at the bus stop a few feet short of the intersection. As Eric's signal turned green, a city bus full of lights and people lumbered up to the curb and took the man away.

Chuckling at himself for feeling so relieved, Eric shrugged and crossed the street.

What had he been thinking about before? Oh, yes, Sandy. He wouldn't tell her what Jacob had said about him and her. The very idea of them carrying like that would be as unthinkable to her as it had been to him. But maybe he should phone her right away with the good news about FirstCon. She'd be thrilled to hear it.

No, it can wait till Monday.

Call her anyway, his gut said. *She'll be relieved as you are.*

He ignored his gut. She was doing just fine through all this. A couple more days wouldn't matter.

Besides, he had plans to make for the office. He began to whistle the "Esurientes" from the Bach *Magnificat*.

> *He filleth the hungry with good things,*
> *And the rich he hath sent empty away.*

When he got home he'd call Leah. A guy he knew could get him good cheap seats for the touring company production of *Woman of the Year*, and tomorrow night he'd drag her away from that store of hers and they'd go. Sandy could wait.

CHAPTER A.7

ON SUNDAY AFTERNOON, Eric returned to the exhibition. Somehow the thought of the crowds no longer bothered him. Today he would actually look at the paintings and enjoy some people-watching as well. *Thanks, Sheila, Jacob, Sam. Just in time.*

In the seventeenth century Dutch gallery he came across a pretty girl he couldn't help noticing. Wearing a broad-brimmed felt hat over her long brown hair, a plum velvet jacket, and a soft dark blue sprigged wool skirt, she stood with her back to him contemplating a Rembrandt. The outfit was unfamiliar, but something about her stance told him she might be someone he knew.

With amused surprise it dawned on him. "Hi, Sandy."

The full skirt swirled gracefully about her calves as she turned at his greeting. That was a nice blouse she had on, ivory with a narrow ruff of lace about her throat, and the wine-colored hat gave her brown eyes a luminosity he'd never noticed before.

"Enjoying the Old Masters?" he asked her gravely.

"Yes, immensely. I feel rather guilty about it. I feel I should like the Moderns better."

"You look like an Old Master yourself."

She laughed awkwardly and glanced down at her attire. "Oh!" she said. "You mean the spattered smock, the paint in the hair and under the finger-nails, the general odor of the garret?"

"No," he persisted, "like one of their paintings."

"Oh, like that?" She pointed toward a genre study of a madwoman begging in an Amsterdam street.

"I swear, you're impossible!" His unrepressed laughter caused several other exhibit-goers to turn their heads in shocked admonishment. "You know. You look very nice."

She flashed him an indecipherable smile, sketched the semblance of a curtsy, then turned back towards the painting she'd been examining when he walked in.

Strange. He'd meant nothing by the compliment. It was like commending a fellow-architect on a well-designed building. She'd put together an ensemble that suited her. He'd said so. Why had she found it so difficult to accept?

It was none of his business. Nevertheless, he continued to watch her, suddenly curious. What would she say when he told her what he had in mind for the office?

That was no mystery. She'd be thrilled.

"YOU LOOK very nice," he'd finally said.

Such a statement was prosaic enough to be borne, so Sandy had accepted it with equally prosaic grace. She was now trying to immerse herself in the study of Rembrandt's portrait of his mistress Hendrickje Stoffels, but every cell in her body was a separate antenna picking up the frequency of Eric's continued presence behind her. There had been poetry in what he said, and she dared not credit that from him. It might engender a hope too fragile to endure.

He never paid her personal compliments. Why suddenly today? She faced him boldly. "Has something happened since Friday afternoon that I shouldn't know about?"

"Absolutely not! I mean, yes, you should know about it."

Eagerly she heard the news. Lucrative new commissions after all they'd been through— yes, that would put him in an expansive mood. She nearly danced for pleasure herself.

"I won't know all the details till Tuesday night," he said, "and probably not then. But I'd say for sure they're ours."

"And Mrs. Ryerson and Mrs. Eisenbaum and everyone got together and agreed to close down the rumor mill?"

"Seems that way. And if what Sheila told me later is any indication, they're all so angry they might give us work just to show Hardt he can't get away with it."

"I love it! He's definitely been 'hoist with his own petard.' That's Shakespeare," she added.

"*Hamlet*," Eric confirmed. "Hardt's blown himself up with his own landmine, all right."

She dropped her tone confidentially. "I have news, too. Reg Fyfield belongs to my church, and this morning after service I spoke with him. Sorry, I should have done it before."

He made no comment, so she went on. "I said I knew he couldn't send out any edicts or decrees, but since he's our AIA chapter president, could he circulate the report— the truth, I mean— among the local firms that, well, that we're good upstanding professionals 'in whom no iniquity is found' and so on, and ask our colleagues to treat us the way they'd like to be treated. He agreed to do it, and it may work. He's got enough influence."

Eric was silent a moment. "He'll just drop a word here and there? No soapbox lectures on the evils of gossip?"

"Goodness, no! He'll do it discreetly, don't worry. He's not AIA president for nothing. Besides, he's a Christian gentleman."

"Hmm."

"Something else. There's a couple of jobs that've just come into his office they don't have the time to take on. He said you should call and see if you'd be interested."

"You think the clients'll want to work with us under the circumstances?"

"Reg said he'd put in an extra-good word for us."

"Okay, I'll call him. I'm glad you acted on your impulse. If things work out, our reputations and the business both should be saved."

"I hope so."

"Well, enough of this. Have you been through the exhibit?"

"Not all of it."

"Did you see the Raeburn in the English room? Come on, I'll show it to you."

She followed sedately, and indeed, the portrait was very beautiful. He accompanied her through the rest of the galleries, he elucidating the finer artistic points of the paintings, she illuminating him on the religious or mythological backgrounds of many of their subjects. After a while they came to the Spanish room, where Eric was drawn away by a remarkable Velasquez. Sandy, in her turn, stood fascinated before a large canvas by El Greco.

Its subject was a young Spanish saint, a soldier by his dress, with that peculiar attenuation of the bone structure so characteristic of the artist's work. The young man stood on a high, moonlit, weather-shrouded hill, the instruments of his martyrdom in his hand and on his face an expression of eternal joy mingled with an awareness of the futilities of the world.

It took her breath away: as a work of art, certainly; but also because, had he been born a sixteenth century Spaniard while yet remaining himself, she could have sworn the young soldier-saint was Eric Baumann. It was all there: the dark-bearded face, the long hands, even the attitude of the body— the only thing Eric lacked was the look of spiritual assurance. In that moment, if someone told her that he'd been transported to the late 1500s and sat for the artist, or that El Greco had time-travelled to the twentieth century that he might paint him, she would have accepted it without question or doubt.

A hand was laid gently on her shoulder. She turned and in a kind of delicious shock recognized the seeming original of the painting. "I'm not the only one who looks like an Old Master . . . " she murmured with soft recklessness.

If he heard, he gave no sign. "Sorry, I couldn't get your attention. You like this El Greco?"

"Yes, I do. Very much."

"Maybe I should give it to you for Christmas." He sounded oddly serious.

"Uh, well," she said, purposely quelling him, "I doubt the accountant would let you take it off the taxes." It was no secret that he deducted the cost of Christmas gifts to her and the engineers they worked with. "I mean, the fee on the FirstCon job won't be *that* big, will it?" She laughed nervously.

"No, I guess not." He frowned and looked away.

Around them the carefree murmur of art lovers flowed mercilessly on. She realized she was playing with her fingers. She made herself stop, but filling the speechless void was beyond anything she could do.

"Um, tell me," she managed to say after a few excruciating seconds, "what did you think of the Velasquez?"

The awkward mood dissolved. "Oh, yes," he said, "come and see it!"

With enthusiasm he pointed out its salient features, but after her appreciative responses died away, a silence, now warm and comfortable, closed around them. They did the rest of the exhibition with hardly a word, marking each other's reactions only by the curving of a mouth, the widening of an eye, the gesture of a hand.

He did not touch her again, yet her skin retained the electric charge of his long hand upon her shoulder. Increasingly distracted from the masterworks, she resolved to come again, alone. Today her rebellious energies demanded leave to flow out to the man at her side, and it was fear and pride, as much as prudence, that with difficulty kept them dammed in.

ERIC EXAMINED the painting before them. It was Italian; its subject, three elegantly-dressed ladies surrounding a gentleman plainly-clad. Well no, he corrected his first impression, only two ladies, as they understood the term in the 1700s: the third woman appeared to be a serving maid. But even she was beautifully attired. He glanced down at his own employee. She really did look especially nice today. She always did him credit with the outfits she wore to the office, but this one did credit to her. She'd taken off the broad-brimmed hat and held it loosely in her hand, exposing her warm-brown hair. Did it always fall in those waves, or had she done something different with it today?

She's got a life outside working hours.

And he couldn't shake the newly-born urge to wonder what it was like. He knew comparably little about her. Even talking in his car in front of her building those nights he gave her a lift home, they always kept to ideas. Oh, he'd picked up things about her from the way she spoke about the buildings she loved and the music she enjoyed. But here was this human person he spent hours with every week, and there were whole levels of her personality he couldn't conceive.

Keep out of her business. You're here to look at paintings.

Like this one of Moses and the burning bush. He knew the story well enough; his mother had drummed it into his head when he was a kid, between dragging him to church and forcing him to memorize Luther's *Small Catechism.* "*I will now turn aside and see this great sight . . .*"

Apparently, amazing things showed up in all kinds of unexpected places. Take Sandy here. Just an ordinary girl— again, as on Friday night, his gut told him he wasn't being wholly fair— an *ordinary* girl, and suddenly she speaks up all passionate about their not working for Nick Hardt . . . On fire, yet not burned . . . Like some kind of angel, or the voice of God, guiding him to what he should do.

He shuddered. Angels and God were no part of his universe. But he'd listened to her in September, and even with all the trouble after, he was grateful he had.

Go ahead. Tell her the plans for the office. Tonight. Why not?

When they were through, he asked quietly, "How were you planning to get home?"

"I thought I'd get the bus, as usual."

"On a Sunday evening? Don't be ridiculous. You'll be standing there in the cold for an hour. Come on, get your things. I'll drive you home."

"Yes, sir," she replied in a tone that was an almost perfect counterfeit of her normal workday voice. He started at the slight difference, then pushed it out of his mind.

CHAPTER A.8

RIDING THROUGH THE GRAY LATE SUNDAY AFTERNOON, neither of them said a word. Eric at the wheel seemed deep in thought, and an amazed silence had laid its hand on Sandy and rendered her mute.

Somehow this afternoon had been different. Never before had she felt herself so enveloped in his presence, never before had the air they breathed been so charged with excitement and peace. All of it, everything he'd said and done, spoke of far more than liberation from financial worry. It sang of— but no, it couldn't mean that. What's more, her conscience reminded her, it mustn't mean that.

After a few blocks, he spoke up. "You know, if we have these new jobs I'll have to hire some new people in the office."

She flinched, as if the point of a knife were prodding between her ribs.

O Domine! That was why he'd been so attentive this afternoon. All these months they'd enjoyed an exclusive bond between them; now it would have to break. Today's kindness had been his way of bidding it farewell.

You idiot! she savaged herself. He'd never thought of the two of them as exclusive and bound. Not now, not ever.

"Interesting," she said, making her tone light and humorous. "You didn't talk about staffing up when Nick Hardt wanted to undermine half the state." She couldn't exclude a note of irritation, and she didn't care.

"You didn't give me the chance to think about it, remember?" he said cheerfully. "Maybe in my gut I knew he was crazy, too. But this is different. We need help or we'll run ourselves ragged. We put in too much time in the office as it is."

"Too much time in the office"? He was there less than half of most days as it was. And now he was going to make her share him with strangers?

"We have a few months before the FirstCon project starts," he went on. "I'll interview a few people and submit them to your judgement. If you find anything wrong with them, they're not hired, okay?"

"Hey, you're the boss," she said, shocked at how ungracious she sounded. "You know better than I do what you want in an employee."

"Sandy, you know I respect your opinion! What's wrong?"

Everything. Especially me. "I'm sorry. I'm tired, I guess. Long day."

"Long weekend," he agreed. "But you're right, I do know what I want in employees, and one of those things is that they be agreeable to you. I also know what I want in an associate."

"Oh," she said as if nothing affected her less, "you have an old college friend or something who's coming back to join the firm?"

"No," he said, glancing over curiously. "I thought you'd just assume. You don't think you can handle a promotion?"

A promotion? Like a flash of revelation she saw it all: The two of them on different schedules, most likely working on different projects. Touching base only by appointment, and then not for very long. All very businesslike, efficient— and desolating.

"What— *me?*" It came out as if she thought he'd lost his mind.

"Well, yes!" He looked at her and grinned. "With a raise and all the rest of it. The room next to ours is empty; I'll see if I can rent it. We can put the catalogs and the help back there."

"What a marvellously dehumanizing way of speaking of them! 'The catalogs and the help'!" Safer to joke about peripheral issues. It kept her mind off the widening void in her soul.

"Well, you know me!" he answered. "A regular Simon Legree. Anyway, you and I will stay up front for the time being." For what *that* was worth, she reflected bitterly. "Nothing's official until I speak to the Ryersons and Delkirk Tuesday night, but I'd say it's a sure thing."

"I'll have to think about it . . . " she said, as much to herself as to him.

"I've always wanted to do something like this, once enough work came in," Eric went on with that same maddening enthusiasm. "This FirstCon project, once it gets into the building phase, should give you the opportunity to get out of the office and get some solid experience in construction management."

Oh, yes. Out of the office. In a car of her own, of course, and with a higher salary she couldn't plead poverty not to buy one— and there she'd be, out by herself on construction sites, then returning to the office late in the day to find it empty; well, empty except for some new kids, whoever *they'd* turn out to be. No more rides home with him, no more long conversations outside her building. Not occasionally, but day after day. "I guess so," she replied dully.

"You don't seem too happy about it," he said in surprise. "I thought you'd like more autonomy. From that portfolio you showed me in our interview, I'd say you've got plenty of ideas under that hat you're dying to try. There will be new projects, I'm sure, that you'll be able to handle on your own. I can't see you playing second fiddle forever."

He was right. Why, *why* was she resisting this so hard? "Sure I'm excited; it's just that, well, I'm—" She tried again. "I mean, have you really thought about it? What if I'm not ready?"

"Of course you're ready!" His amazement struck her like an open hand. "You don't think I'm a good judge of your work?"

"Yes, but it's not just the work and me doing it, it's also—" She stopped still. It was also what? It wasn't like he would ever fall in love with her, no matter how much time they spent alone together. And if by ten special miracles he did, she could never marry him. On his best days he thought Christianity was a quaint historical artifact good for understanding old works of art and nothing more. On his worst . . .

He didn't believe in marriage, either. Without actually bringing up the topic, he'd made his antipathy towards it more than clear. So why should she let her stupid, useless feelings get in the way?

"I don't understand," he said with some irritation. "Are you telling me you don't have the stomach for it? I thought you were stronger than that. The way you stood up to me about Nick Hardt, I liked that. I admired your courage. And you're getting cold feet about this?"

He'd admired something about her. He *had*, past tense. If she wanted to guarantee he'd never love her, she'd just accomplished it.

"No, Eric, you don't understand. It's just— do you really think this is the best time to discuss this? Can't you give it a couple of days at least?"

"What is there to think about? Do you want the promotion, or don't you?"

He must've seen the pain on her face, for he went on more mildly. "I want to help you out, to forward your career. But this is about the firm and the work we're doing. I need somebody with standing to deal with major clients and contractors. That should be you. Whether you take the position or not, I have to have somebody in it."

Face reality, a sensible inner voice told her. *There's nothing between you, nothing that matters. The work is all you have together. Give up your stupid hopes and say yes.*

"I thought we were in agreement on these things," he said. "But if we aren't, we aren't. I'll get somebody else, maybe that old college friend you mentioned—" He glanced over and his smile was grim— "and hire him in over you, if that's what you want. I have to do what's best for the office."

"That's not it. I just—" Tongue-tied, she fell silent.

Outside the car windows, the November dusk was settling in gloomy and damp, exactly fitting her mood. Angry tears forced their way out from behind her eyelids; she wiped them furtively, turning her body away from him. No reason she shouldn't look out the passenger side window. Wonderful view out the side window. Dark closed stores, bare scraggly street trees, blowing litter. Beautiful.

She made herself sit up and look forward, to pretend everything was all right. She owed herself at least that.

The Galaxie drew up to a stoplight. She could see Eric out of the corner of her eye, his hands squarely at ten and two on the steering wheel. For a few long silent seconds he stared straight ahead out the front window. Then he relaxed and turned towards her. "Don't worry," he said. "I won't force you into anything. Whatever you want to do, wherever you want to go, I'll support you."

"You don't understand. Of course I want the office to be successful, even if— even if— I mean, I don't want—" She gave up and started over. "I'm sorry. I don't know what came over me."

After what seemed like an eternity, he spoke. "No, I should apologize. This business with Nick Hardt must be putting a lot of stress on you. It's been rough on me, too. But I'm used to being cussed at. I guess it's been worse for you."

She seized on the idea. "Maybe that's it. Maybe I thought I was handling it better than I was."

Silence again. She had to say something more. "I'll get through it. We both will. Hopefully he'll give up now. And I'm not— I'm not saying absolutely no, really I'm not. I just think we should give it some time. Please?"

He was watching the stoplight, waiting for the change. "I won't make you do anything you're not comfortable with," he said. "Forget I brought it up."

"No, I don't mean—"

"Get some rest," he said. His tone was detached, noncommittal. "We'll talk in the morning."

The light turned green, and the car moved on.

CHAPTER A.9

SANDY CLIMBED THE STAIRS to her apartment, hardly noticing where she was. She flung herself in the door, yanked off her hat, and crammed it on its hook. Her coat and scarf kept slipping through her fingers as she tried to hang them in the closet, but she didn't care. Something panicky and tight had laid claim to the pit of her stomach and would not let her look back on the afternoon with any degree of contentment or rest.

She kicked her shoes across the room and drew herself up on the sofa, her arms clasped around her legs as if the hardness of her knees against her skull could ground her and restore her to sanity and sense.

Hypocrite, hypocrite, *hypocrite!* She didn't care one dime about Architecture, did she? Twenty-eight years old, and she was behaving like a lovesick teenybopper. *"Don't change anything, Eric,"* she imagined herself saying in an eye-batting, breathless baby-voice. *"Don't grow the firm. Keep me in exactly the position I'm in now; let it be just you and me designing side by side, forever and ever, amen!"*

Whatever had possessed her to answer him the way she had? Was Eric's presence some kind of drug she couldn't live without? He was about to give her exactly what she needed to get ahead and to serve God in her profession, but she was no better than a junkie. She would willingly trample on it all if it catered to her pointless cravings. And they were all the more pointless because if she didn't focus and do what was best for the office, eventually she would be pushed out and wouldn't have him to get high on at all.

Sighing, she heaved herself off the sofa and retrieved her shoes from under the armchair. *Could* she separate her work from how she felt about him? She couldn't dispose of the question as easily as she could hang up the plum blazer and the blue challis skirt. By the time she emerged from her bedroom in a pair of old jeans and a turtleneck, she was deep in it still.

The sandwich she put together in the kitchen was about as appealing as cardboard. She sat down at the breakfast room table and forced herself to swallow it anyway.

Outside the window, a light snow was falling, the scattered flakes blowing listlessly in the glow of the street lamp lurid through the naked branches of the sycamore tree growing by the curb. She shivered a little as the wind's cold breath penetrated between the pane and the wooden sash. The landlord needed to caulk that. Or she could do it herself and send him the bill.

Sandy, focus. Was the change Eric was proposing that radical? Even if they would be more independent of each other in the office, wouldn't they still be friends?

Friends? Were they really, truly, even that? Sure, they communicated well over their projects. But even those few occasions they'd listened to music at his place in River Hill, what did it amount to but casual encounters— she gave a grim laugh at how risque that sounded— over art and music? So spur-of-the-moment and intellectual that even his girlfriend Leah didn't mind. And those long after-hours discussions about their work and architecture in general were just an extension of their work in the office. Strictly business, and it was foolish of her to think otherwise.

She took her supper plate to the sink and rinsed it, watching the crumbs spiral inexorably down the drain.

No, she thought, setting the dish down on the counter a little too hard. *I refuse to believe that. I have to be more to him! He puts the needle on the record, the music begins, and it feels … it feels like … it wraps us up together … unites us as one …*

Stop it! How could she let herself think like that? Chastened, she returned to the living room and stared out at the weakly falling snow.

All right, then. Suppose she *was* useful to him merely as a fellow-intellect. She could still take joy in the pleasure the works of art gave him, especially the ones she knew better than he did.

Or formerly, she could. Now, she wouldn't even have that. He wouldn't make time to see her outside the office whether he had a girlfriend in the picture or not. And once she had her own car, how likely was it that she could have him up to listen to music here? All right, it was just that one time, last spring. He'd asked to use her bathroom, and she'd been so excited that the classical station would be playing Berlioz' *La Damnation de Faust* for their evening concert she'd boldly urged him to stay. He'd enjoyed it so much he'd bought his own recording of the piece the following weekend.

All that was past. A new dynamic was coming and the sooner she got used to the idea, the better off she'd be.

Focus, Sandy. Keep the single eye— on your career. You did the right thing with Nick Hardt, you can do this, too.

Resolutely squaring her shoulders, she went to the telephone. Nearly 7:00 p.m. by her watch. Even if he'd stopped for something to eat, by now he should be home. She rehearsed what she would say: "Eric, I've thought it over, and I'll be happy to be your associate." Very professional and mature. No apologies— that would only remind him of how she had failed him earlier.

She picked up the receiver. She dialed his number.

Busy.

Sandy stared at the telephone as if it were a car she'd seen driving sideways. Busy? When she'd resolved to do the right thing and followed through? How could Eric's phone possibly be busy?

She turned on the radio. Something by Schubert. She adored Schubert, even though it was her cheating ex-fiancé Werner who had introduced her to his work. But tonight, his music only increased her restlessness. She shut it off.

Eric would be off the phone by now. She tried calling again.

Still busy.

Maybe he did have a back-up candidate in mind, and he'd given up on her. Maybe it was worse. Maybe he was talking to Leah, telling her how that silly little Sandy Beichten had gone all wishy-washy on him when he'd tried to give her a promotion.

Immediately she repented. He might think all that about her, but he'd never speak it to anyone else.

She picked up the latest issue of *Architectural Record*. The perfectly-composed photographs of white buildings shot against impossibly blue skies nearly made her scream.

I can't stand it anymore. She hurried to the phone and dialed Eric's apartment again.

Baaah-beep! Baaah-beep! The busy signal mocked her like a demon of hell.

God help me!

Maybe he was just asking a friend what he should do. Maybe she should do the same, call someone and hash it out with her.

But who? Someone from church? She hadn't made it to a meeting of the Presbyterian Young Professionals group in ages.

Perhaps her best friend Carole Peabody. Carole Fenton now, married with her own job as a lawyer and a husband and little boy out in the suburbs. But she and Carole hadn't spoken since they'd seen each other at their Blakewell Public Academy ten year reunion in July, despite Sandy's firm promise to stay in touch. Carole could have had tried to call her ten times since then, but when was she ever there to answer the phone? So how would it look if she called just to dump on her now?

Maybe her mother. No, Mom couldn't possibly understand. She'd looked forward to Sandy's marrying a good Christian man and providing her with grandchildren ages ago. Now Mom was beginning to worry that her only daughter would never find a husband. Last year when Sandy had called down to Florida to tell her she was joining Eric's firm, Mom had wanted to know all about her "new young man." Only with difficulty had she convinced her that Eric Baumann was merely her new boss. Her own errant desires were hard enough to curb without tempting her mother to indulge them too.

Besides, she was perfectly capable of seeing the truth on her own. It was foolish to jeopardize her God-given vocation to save a relationship that didn't exist and couldn't go anywhere if it did. Foolish and cowardly. When had she lost her focus? How could her eye have strayed so far off her goal?

She plopped down on the sofa and once more drew her knees up under her chin. She had started her career so dedicated . . . That August night the summer after her high school graduation, just before they'd all gone off to college, she'd had a slumber party at her house. They'd been down in the rec room, herself and Carole and Pat Trehorne and Brenda Streicher and a few other girls from their Blakewell Classical Honors program. They'd spoken long and earnestly about their roles as women planning to enter traditionally-male fields. They'd discussed sex and temptation and not letting shallow, self-gratifying affairs divert them from their God-given vocations. They'd talked about marriage and its sanctity and about waiting for Him to send them a good Christian man. In the end, they'd taken a Bible oath to devote themselves, their careers, and their lives to focus and purity.

They had vowed to serve Jesus as Knights of the Single Eye.

CHAPTER A.10

THE SNOW HAD GIVEN UP, and the wind had swept the street clean. She felt cold: the building thermostat must have adjusted the heat downward for the night. What time was it, anyway? She looked at the clock on the end table.

"Good grief, it's nearly 2:00 a.m."

She remained on the sofa, her head in her hands.

Lord, I should have been faithful, shouldn't I? We all promised. "Be Thou my vision, O Lord of my heart; Naught be all else to me, save that Thou art." My idea, to take that for our anthem. But my eye didn't stay single.

She'd adhered to the pledge when it came to architecture. But with men, she hadn't waited. No use boasting that she'd never had full-blown sex with any of them— any physical purity she had left was by the grace of God and the skin of her teeth. And not one of the relationships she'd grabbed for herself had ended well.

Not that she'd been a victim— not really. Whatever those men did, she'd committed her own sins right back. That meant she could repent and do better.

So, what about Eric? Was he just one more example of her setting her sights on the wrong thing? Maybe she shouldn't accept the promotion after all. Tomorrow morning, maybe she should present herself before him and announce that she was quitting him and his firm forever!

She laughed. Forget it. When it came to keeping her mind and eye on her architectural vocation, with Eric was exactly where she needed to be.

All right. Since their relationship could never go anywhere . . . and if loving him made her act like she did this evening . . . should she— should she just stop loving him? Relate to him only as an employee and otherwise just not care?

Impossible.

What then?

By the time she had brushed her teeth, the solution was as obvious as the dark circles rimming her eyes in the mirror.

Don't love him less. Love him more.

Starting tomorrow— no, right now, tonight— she would pull back from loving him as a woman loves a man. She'd stop focussing on the romantic feelings he gave her and objectively seek his good. Be like the sister he never had. She would love him as Christ loved her.

Meanwhile, she thought as she vigorously scrubbed her face, she'd keep the single eye on her vocation and pursue it to the glory of God, not for her own pleasure. When she saw Eric in the office in a few hours she'd have a civilized, friendly, *adult* conversation with him and say she'd be happy to take the position of associate architect in his office. And if God wanted her to be loved as she desired, He'd bring that long-awaited good Christian man into her life.

Singing, she slipped into her nightgown.

> *Riches I heed not, nor man's empty praise;*
> *Thou mine inheritance, now and always.*
> *Thou and Thou only, first in my heart:*
> *High King of heaven, my treasure Thou art.*

The clock radio by the bed said half past two. Four and a half hours of sleep if she was lucky. Eric rarely got in before 10:30 but she would take no chances. She'd catch an earlier bus and be there by 8:30 just in case.

After praying for them both, she reached over and shut off the lamp.

SHE WAS standing in an unlighted church, at the chancel steps. Fourth Presbyterian? It didn't feel like it. She was wearing a long white dress. It seemed odd that she should be and she tried to figure out why.

But was it really a church? No, no walls. Someplace flat and open and cold. And dark, dusky dark. Up north, it seemed. North Dakota?

She was getting married. She knew that now. To whom? Someone was standing at her side. Werner? She looked up. No, it was Eric! Joy pierced through her like a jagged knife. He was dressed like the soldier-saint in the El Greco painting . . . but not glorified. No— bloody, wounded. Dying! His pleading eyes met hers; he tried to speak; he swayed, falling. She caught him in her arms, they were both falling; the minister standing there ready to marry them, why *was* he just standing there?

"Help me, please!" she screamed.

It was no pastor. The pale, inhuman eyes glistening in the darkness belonged to Nick Hardt.

The scene changed. It was full daylight. She seemed to be lying in bed in her own room, her tensed body subsiding into relief. She'd just escaped something terrible; what was it?

Broad daylight gleaming through the window on a November morning . . .

"Oh my gosh, look at the time!"

She'd forgotten to set the alarm. And even with skipping breakfast and catching a bus within a minute of arriving breathless at the stop, she didn't get into the office till after 10:00.

It was all right. It was still morning. Eric had said he'd be in before noon.

Then she saw the note lying open under her parallel bar.

> Unexpected meeting with Bill W & HVAC sub. Out rest
> of day. I'll call Reg Fyfield about those jobs later. Try to
> finish range hood details ASAP.
>
> E.

She'd missed him. She'd missed him, he was gone till tomorrow or who knew when, and in his place the fears and tensions of yesterday came flooding back. It was all still up in the air between them. Or maybe for him it was settled— against her.

No! I don't believe it! Yesterday couldn't speak the last word between them. He had to have left her something more.

She turned the piece of scratch paper over. There was nothing on the reverse. As she put it down, she noticed under her bar another piece of letter paper, folded, with her name on it. She undid the tape and read it. Then, dropping into her chair, she put her hands to her face and wept.

CHAPTER A.11

THE FAMILIAR AROMA of hamburger grease and coffee greeted Eric on the other side of the stainless steel door of the Dine Time Diner. He gave a nod and a grunt to acknowledge some familiar faces from the usual Sunday night crowd and slipped into a booth at the far end. There he sat in confusion, his chin on his hand.

What the hell had just happened with Sandy? That wasn't at all what he'd had in mind.

Somebody back in the dishroom was a jazz fan; he could hear the radio clearly over the rush of water and the crashing of the dish machine. He made himself concentrate on the music, willing it to distract him from the scene in the car.

It was no use.

He'd tried to do the right thing. There on Friday he'd been marvelling over how much the two of them thought alike. Even when they differed temporarily over a point of design or— or— on something like what to do about Nick Hardt . . . even then, it only went to show how thoroughly they were in tune. And now, tonight? They'd been totally at odds— over her taking a promotion! How could she disagree with him on that?

Deft hands placed a menu and a mug of steaming black coffee on the table in front of him. He looked up, signalled with his eye for more time, and the waitress moved away.

Sandy was licensed, she had six years of experience, including four years with a top firm in Boston and nearly a year and a half with him. How could she possibly think she wasn't ready to be an associate? Had the wrong girl gotten into the car with him at the Civic Museum?

The radio in the dishroom began to play a blues number.

> *Since my baby left me,*
> *Hear me cryin' all alone . . .*

He sat up. Good lord, "The Lone Woman Blues." When was the last time he'd heard that?

> *I don't get no lovin',*
> *I just hang my head and moan.*

It was all too easy to remember the first. It had been a Saturday night in the apartment in Bismarck. He was eleven, Paul was three, and they and Momma were sitting at the kitchen table listening to some old wire recordings Eric had found in her closet when she'd asked him to fetch something. Poppa wasn't there, of course; he was at some synod meeting in Minot or somewhere and wasn't expected back till Sunday afternoon. That was, if he didn't go straight back to the reservation. They'd been listening for a good hour or two when Eric happened to put on a recording of this song.

> *Hopped that midnight freight train,*
> *Said he'd ride it down the line . . .*

It was his mother singing with a USO band during the war. She'd joined it Stateside while his father was in Europe serving as a chaplain to the troops. Eric had been transfixed. Sure, he was used to hearing her sing hymns at their Lutheran church. But this song and his mother's voice singing it had spoken to him of worlds unexplored, of feelings he'd never known existed, of loss and hope and yearning all tied up together with something else he couldn't define.

Not then, anyway.

> *Come on home and love me,*
> *Rock your baby all night long . . .*

That was when Poppa had decided to walk through the door for the first time in weeks. The song sent him into a rage and he'd practically called Momma a bitch and a whore for playing it in front of Eric and little Paul. Poppa had shoved the player and all the spools to the floor and stomped them into ruin, every one.

He'd done his best to defend Momma. He'd been her Little Man, the real man of the family, ever since he was four and Poppa had abandoned them for the Indians on the reservation. Screaming that Jesus would send him to hell for saying such awful things about Momma, he'd charged at him with all his strength. Unmoved, Poppa had stood there and knocked him across the room. After that, he'd forced him to feed the machine and all the tangled wires to the incinerator in the apartment house basement. "There, boy," his father had said. "Let *that* teach you about hell!"

"EARTH TO ERIC!" said a female voice.

"Huh, what?" he said, looking up to see the waitress. "Oh, hi, Lisa. What did you say?"

"I *said*," she retorted, "aren't you too old to be playing with blocks?"

"Oh!" he said, regarding the wall he was absentmindedly building out of jelly packets. He hurriedly returned them to the rack.

"What'll it be tonight?" She rattled off the specials.

"Right," he said, only half listening. "Give me a second."

He tried to study the glossy laminated menu, but his thoughts wouldn't cohere. "I'll have . . . oh, gosh, I don't know. Bring me the special, the— hell, the one you mentioned first."

She repeated something he didn't catch. The mood he was in, it didn't matter. "Comin' right up," she said, and left him alone.

. . . That was one of the worst things about religion. It stomped on people's dreams. He'd found out the next day that Momma had always wanted to be a professional singer and Poppa had been just fine with it— until he'd decided to buy off God and become a pastor. Eric's first sister, Ruth Adelaide, had died suddenly as a baby and Momma told him that Poppa had gone to seminary out of sheer guilt.

Funny how that guilt didn't do their family any good when his second sister, Gretchen Louise— Lou-Lou— got pneumonia when Eric was just five and she was six. That was after Poppa had let his God convince him it wasn't enough for him to pastor two churches in Wisconsin, he had to move them all to North Dakota then head off to the reservation on his own. Convenient how God never convinced him to come home to Bismarck when his little daughter was dying. He didn't even send Momma any money for the doctor.

One of the wire recordings Poppa destroyed that night was of Lou-Lou singing "Mary Had a Little Lamb." Poppa hadn't listened when he'd begged him to save it. He'd just called him names and gone on with his rampage.

Poppa wasn't like that with the little Sioux children. The one time Eric and Momma and Paul had visited the reservation, it was sickening how the ragged red kids clung to Poppa and danced around him and looked up at him with those big black adoring eyes like he was the Great White Father. And the grownup Indians weren't much better.

Poppa had eaten it up, of course. Though if Eric could have idolized him that way, the stinking hypocrite wouldn't have cared.

God, he still missed Lou-Lou. He would have helped her be whatever she wanted, just like he wanted to help Sandy. But Sandy wouldn't—

"Here's your rolls," said the waitress, setting down a basket covered with a red and white napkin. "Nice and hot, just like ya like 'em." She turned to go and nearly collided with a dirty-blond young man in a faded Wapatomekie Warriors baseball jersey.

"Hey, sorry, Lisa."

"Hey, Mike, no problem," she said easily. "Just don't do it when I'm carrying hot liquids, okay?"

The young man greeted Eric. "Hey, pariah."

"Hey yourself, Laurence," he said moodily. "What's the latest at Richardson & Greene?" He waved toward the opposite bench in a take-it-or-leave-it fashion. "Have a seat."

"Oh, we're doing great. I'm heading up a cool project for a new branch library over in Springvale. But you. You sure it's safe being seen with you, Baumann?" said Mike Laurence, grinning. He slid into the booth. "The stories going around, you'd think you'd been poisoning the water at all your job sites."

"Very funny," Eric said. "Got any new ones?"

"What are you doing in this ptomaine joint, anyway?" his friend went on relentlessly. "With all the money they say you've been taking under the table, you should be able to afford haute cuisine."

"All right, Laurence. Can it. If you only came over to be a pain in the ass, you can leave."

"Okay, okay! I didn't say I believed all that, did I? What's up with the rumors, anyway?"

"Disgruntled would-be client. Delusions of grandeur. Plenty of money but more trouble than he'd be worth. I turned him down."

"Bastard meter going haywire, huh? So now he's proving what a bastard he is by undermining your business?"

"Something like that."

"Hey, your office isn't really in danger, is it? You may not know it, but you're an inspiration to the rest of us peons. If you can do it, maybe so can we someday. It'd be crap on wheels if something like this put you under."

That made Eric smile. "No, I've got loyal clients. And more work coming in. I might even be hiring."

"So what's with the antisocial act? Haven't seen you in weeks and you sit there like all the world can go to hell, your friends included. Be like that and Rosie and I won't invite you to our wedding."

Out of his mouth it erupted before he could think: "Why do you want to do that?"

"Do what? Invite you?"

"No, tie that poor girl down by marrying her."

"Huh. Rosie Crenshaw is not a 'poor girl.' And getting married was her idea, not mine." He picked up the menu and began looking it over.

"Probably just giving in to social pressure. You two have been dating long enough, her family was probably on her to make an honest man out of you."

"Oh, I don't know. She's pretty independent."

"That's just the problem. She is. And one day she's going to wake up and say, 'Oh crap, I could have gone on with my career and now I'm stuck being Mrs. Mike Laurence.'"

"She'll still be repping StudioFabrik once we're married," Mike said coolly. "She'll just hyphenate her name on her business cards."

"Yeah, but what if she wants to do something different? What if she wants to go away to school and there she is, stuck in Wapatomekie because hubby Mike likes his job and doesn't want to go anywhere?"

"We'll deal with that when it comes up," he said, shrugging.

Eric shook his head. "Well, good luck," he said cynically. "That's what my—" *mother thought when she got married.*

"So we should save the stamp and the fancy engraved invitation?" Mike teased him. "It's not until the sixteenth of January, you can still change your mind."

Before Eric could reply, the waitress brought his meal, slapping the plate smartly down in front of him. She turned to Mike and pulled out her order pad. Mike shrugged optimistically. Eric said, "Laurence is a colossal turkey, Lisa, but he'll be joining me." He looked at his food. "What the hell is this? Slop on a shingle!"

"You said you wanted the Veterans' Week Special," she replied primly, hands on hips. Mike laughed.

"Oh, crap, I guess I did," he said. Yikes. Creamed chipped beef on toast and pork and beans with a side of fruit cocktail. Probably left over from World War II.

"Want me to change it?"

"No, it's food. Long as it shuts my stomach up."

"Right you are." She took Mike's order, brought him a cup of coffee, and departed.

"So what's eating you?" Mike asked. "Besides the idea of me and Rosie getting married, that is?"

Eric hesitated. No, better to say something than to have his mind going around like a hamster on a wheel.

"I told you I had more work coming in, right?"

"Yep. Little remodelling jobs?"

"That, but also something big. Found out about it Friday night. Can't say too much about it till the paperwork's signed, but the budget could run to two or three million dollars."

"Whew!" Mike whistled, impressed.

"So over the weekend I'm thinking about this, and I realize there's no way the office can deal with a job of that size the way it's organized now. I've got other work as well, and I need two of us with the authority to meet with clients and make decisions and all the rest of it."

"Sounds like it."

"So I decided I'd promote Sandy to Associate and hire a couple other people."

Mike took a drink of his coffee and nodded.

"I was going to talk to her about it tomorrow, but I ran into her at the Civic Museum this afternoon." He swallowed a forkful of the chipped beef. He'd had worse.

"What's going on over there?"

"You don't belong to the Fine Arts Guild? You should join, you'd get the notices. Spectacular exhibition of Old Masters from the National Gallery in London. Take Rosie to see it; she'll appreciate it even if you won't, you Philistine."

"I'm more a Roy Lichtenstein fan," Mike said, shrugging, "but it wouldn't kill me. Oh, thanks, Lisa," he said as the waitress put down his Reuben sandwich and withdrew. He took a bite. "Mmmm, not bad. So you saw Sandy over at the Museum. What then?"

"I told her about the new project. Then I'm giving her a lift home, and I tell her what I had in mind, that I was promoting her to Associate."

"I bet she jumped on that."

For a few long seconds, Eric said nothing. He gestured that he needed time to chew; what he really wanted was time to think. How to put this without embarrassing either himself or his employee?

"Laurence, you know how when we interviewed at Richardson & Greene and they asked us where we saw ourselves in five years?"

Mike's brow wrinkled. "Yeah?"

"Well, when I interviewed Sandy last year I guess I forgot to ask her that question." He dragged his fork back and forth in the pork and beans, making a grid pattern where the plate showed through. "I just assumed . . . Or maybe I wasn't thinking about the future at all."

"You've lost me. So tonight you promoted her to Associate. What's the problem?"

"She turned me down."

"She did *what?*" sputtered Mike, sauerkraut hanging down his chin.

"Well, no, not exactly. She put me off and told me she'd have to think about it."

"What's wrong with that?" Mike said, wiping his face. "Hey, Lisa, can I get some more napkins?" he asked as she refilled their coffee cups. "Thanks."

"It wasn't what she said, it's how she said it. Not like herself at all. Nervous and angry at the same time. She refused to look me in the eye."

"Well, if you were driving . . . "

"You know what I mean. Came out with talk about was I really sure and her not being ready. Dammit, Laurence," he said in frustration, "for awhile there I thought she was going to cry!"

"You're right. That doesn't sound like the Sandy Beichten I know."

"I didn't think you knew her at all."

"Sure I do. Sandy and I go way back." Mike chomped down on his sandwich. "Architecture school, State U at Mount Athens. We both had Ruben first year, then Avery when we were juniors. You could have known her back then, too, if you'd ever emerged from Studio. Though I guess juniors didn't hang out much with freshmen."

"No," said Eric, looking past his head to the faded travel poster on the wall. The radio in the dishroom was playing something complicated by John Coltrane. He listened for a few bars, trying to decide. Should he ask?

For the sake of the office, he had to know. "What was she like in school? I mean, did she ever say what her ambitions were, how far she wanted to go in the profession?"

"Intense," said Mike. "Crusading. Evangelical."

"In *religion?*" he nearly yelped.

"Hell, no. In *architecture.*" Mike pronounced the word "ahhhh-ki-teck-shah," drawing out the first syllable in a way the most snobbish of society matrons could not have bettered.

"Well, good for her," Eric said. "I'm the same myself."

"Yeah, but she drove us all crazy. Always going on about *Mister* Wright and *Mister* van der Rohe and *Mister* Gropius. Like she thought the rest of us weren't being respectful enough." He took another huge bite of corned beef and sauerkraut.

"But anything about her career goals, like being a partner in a top firm?"

Mike must not have heard over the noise of the dish machine because his next words were, "She loosened up, though, when she started dating Marv Jansovic second year."

"Marv Jansovic!" Eric exclaimed in spite of himself. "Medium height, stringy hair, loud talker? I know who he is." The memory, long-forgotten, came back of a party, in April of 1980, wasn't it? at Leah's place. This guy Marvin had somehow gotten invited and brought along a new girl—Sandy— and left her standing on her own. Eric had approached her with a survey he was taking about the new public library on Commerce Avenue and once they discovered they were in the same field they'd ended up talking about architecture for the next hour. The Jansovic character had disappeared and Sandy had never mentioned him nor seemed to miss him at all. And here Mike was telling him they'd actually dated? No. It went against his whole image of her.

"Yeah, him. Amazing, what that guy could hold. He could out-drink anybody in one bar, then go to two more and do the same. Impressive." He shook his head.

"I doubt he can still— Who she goes out with isn't my business," Eric said hurriedly.

"Like *this* for over a year." Mike persisted, holding up his first two fingers firmly intertwined. "Her and him, would you believe it?" He laughed hilariously.

You find that funny? I should wipe that smirk off your face, that'd *be funny.*

But no. This conversation was about the office. "Never mind that," he said. "It's not what I need to know."

"No, but listen. She was really into him. Must've been, everybody knew she did half his work for him. She must've been a mess when he dropped out before the end of junior year. Not that I saw it myself," he allowed generously, taking a slurp of coffee and wiping his mouth. "We were in different studios by then."

"Oh."

"He's still around," Mike said. "Works for ChillWell Systems, pushes heating and cooling equipment."

"Remind me," Eric said dryly, "never to use ChillWell as a subcontractor."

"Why?" Mike grinned. "You taking this personally? You're not jealous, are you?"

Eric fixed him with what he hoped was his most repressive glare. But Mike was not to be quelled. "Hey, didn't I hear something about you two, that you and she—"

Something inside urged him to charge to her defense just as he had on Friday night. But wouldn't that imply there was something to what his friend was saying? He cut him off with a chuckle. "No, it's just I'd rather use subcontractors I can trust. Any company that would hire Jansovic as its field rep . . . "

"Oh, I dunno. Maybe he's dried out by now."

"I doubt it," said Eric. "I picked him up at a party a couple years ago—"

Mike's eyebrows catapulted up into his hairline and he spit coffee onto the front of his sweatshirt. "Wha—?"

"—off the floor of Leah's closet," he went on, smoothly. "He was using her best boots for a pillow. Hauled him home dead drunk and I doubt he's doing any better since." He said nothing about Sandy's involvement in the matter, nor that once they'd literally dropped Marvin off at his place it'd been quite natural for them to continue their talk about architecture for a few minutes outside her building.

"Oh. Well. That's funny! Never would have pegged old Marv for a man with a shoe fetish. Cars were more his thing. He had this orange '70 Firebird he got from a wrecker, rebuilt it from the chassis up. You ever see it? That was one zoomy ride! For looks and speed both."

The idea of the guy driving Sandy around in an over-powered machine while several points over the legal limit was deeply offensive. If she'd been one of his sisters— if either of them had lived— he would have said something about it.

"Yeah, I saw it. And heard it." It had made a damn lot of noise under the Studio window. "But," he said firmly, "that doesn't answer my question. She never said what her career goals were?"

"Not that I remember. You know how it was, only goal we had in school was getting the projects in and actually getting some sleep!" He took another gulp of coffee. "I'll say this for her, she always cranked out what the profs liked, even when she was dating Marv. Some people have it easy."

Easy? Do you have any idea how hard Sandy works?

It dawned on him that if anyone was jealous, it was Mike. Had he hoped he'd bring him into the new office as his right-hand man? They'd worked together a lot at Richardson & Greene; it was possible.

"All right, sounds like you don't—"

"She won the Senior Design Award our fourth year, if that helps," Mike interrupted. "Can't remember what the project was, though."

"Yes, it was on her résumé," he said dryly. He wasn't hearing anything he didn't already know— or anything new he wanted to hear. "Well, thanks," he said, closing the subject. "I can work it out on my own."

"You sure?"

"I'm sure. So tell me some more about this Springvale library project."

To Eric's relief, Mike was perfectly happy to forget about Sandy, and talk shop instead. From his account, his current project at Richardson & Greene would be a handsome addition to the local streetscape. It was when Eric reverted to the new projects coming into his own office that Mike said, "Wait a minute. This big new job you're talking about, it's just verbal? You don't have anything in writing yet?"

"Yeah, why?"

"You think maybe you're getting ahead of things, planning to expand the office right away?" He leaned back in the booth and howled. "Good grief, Baumann, you amaze me. According to you, you've got some creep trying to drive you out of business, your reputation is mud, but you're going to hire new people and make Sandy an associate. Are you *crazy?*"

Eric sat there, stunned. So that was it. She'd been more sensible than he was. He was ashamed to admit it out loud, but his friend said it for him. "Sandy probably thought you were crazy too, and was pissed off because you weren't listening. Boy, I don't envy you." Mike laughed again. "You're going to have to go in there tomorrow and tell her you take it all back."

Take it all back? No. Ryerson and Delkirk were men of their word. After Tuesday night everything would be fine. But Mike was onto one thing: he needed to take it a little slower. He hadn't even calculated what kind of promotion package he could offer. She'd been right not to commit herself. He'd tell her so first thing tomorrow.

"Mike, if I know anything about Sandy it's that she's a levelheaded girl. She's proved it the past few weeks. She'll understand. Since you've known her all this time, you know that's true."

"Levelheaded? Yeah, once she got off the Crusader Rabbit high horse. Though there was this one time . . . "

"That's okay, Laurence, you don't have to—"

"End of freshman year," Mike went on regardless. "Like overnight she got weird. Touchy. Started throwing off these sarcastic one-liners about herself and other people. Odd, because like you said, she's religious. I sat next to her in Ruben's and I came in for it a time or two. She ever let you have it? No? Believe me, she could let it fly."

"But she got over it."

"Yeah. Start of sophomore year, she was fine." Mike sounded almost disappointed.

"Whatever it was, I doubt it's relevant now."

Maybe he should call her tonight. No, he needed to sit down and do the numbers first.

You could still apologize, his conscience prodded him. *You dumped her out at the curb and didn't spend two minutes talking about the exhibition or anything else. Not your usual at all. Now she thinks you're a jerk as well as a fool.*

He doubted that. But calling her would be a good idea anyway. He'd do it, soon as he got home.

"We'll work it out," he said. "You'll see. Now, whose chances do you like for the NFL playoffs?"

CHAPTER A.12

IT WAS TWENTY TO SEVEN by the Art Deco clock on the mantelpiece when Eric let himself into his apartment. Good. He'd make that quick phone call to Sandy, then do some thinking on the new salary and benefits he could offer her. Something similar to what he'd had as an associate at Richardson & Greene, though not so lucrative— he couldn't afford it, yet. After that he could bury himself in his studio and play with some ideas that had come to him from the National Gallery exhibition.

But he'd hardly put away his coat when the phone rang.

"Hello? Baumann here."

"Eric? Hey, how're you doing!"

It was Paul. Unusual for him to phone on a Sunday evening, or any time, for that matter. Something about Momma? But he sounded upbeat, so the news couldn't be bad.

"Fine. Great to hear from you. What's up?"

"I've got news!" His brother's voice burst with enthusiasm. "How'd you like to have a sister?"

"You mean a live one? It's a little late for that," Eric said dryly. The image of his elderly father, estranged from the family and living who knew where, and that of his mother, merely existing with Alzheimer's in a nursing home across town from Paul's place in Boise, rose to his mind's eye.

"All right, turkey, I'll spell it out. 'Sister-in-law.' Sophie and I are getting married."

"Oh." His good mood deflated. In a leaden tone he said, "So you're doing it, too." He sat down heavily on the sofa.

There was dead silence on the line. Then Paul said in a quelled, hurt voice, "You're supposed to congratulate me."

"Why? And give Sophie my condolences? You know how I feel about marriage. Seems you'd be warned off doing it to her, from what Momma went through when we were kids. I'm surprised you'd think of it."

"And I'm surprised my only brother doesn't think I can do better."

"Can you? Our parents set us a hell of an example. Poppa did, at least."

"You're right," Paul said calmly. "But not everyone's marriage is like theirs. His missionary work, being gone so much, that had to put a strain on things."

"You think so?" said Eric, his voice laden with irony. "And when Poppa was home he'd talk about nothing but his precious Indians or fight with Momma about how she was running the household. And she just put up with it. Why didn't she divorce him?"

"It was against her religion."

"That's another thing I have no use for." He picked up the phone on its long cord and began to pace back and forth across the living room. "Her religion made her hang in there and be miserable and we were miserable, too. That's what comes of tying yourself down like that."

"Yeah, I guess you had it harder. You could remember back when Poppa had a church and things were more settled. And then he had to go and get the missionary bug. With me it was all I knew, so I got used to it."

Eric stopped still. Really? He'd always assumed Paul resented their father's absence as much as he did. Could he actually have been happy with the way things were in Bismarck, or at least content?

"Besides, I had my big brother. I had you. In a lot of ways you *were* my poppa. Did you know that?"

Oh, god. Something soft, convoluted, and insistent was forcing its way from his gut, threatening to make his mouth and eyes do something he couldn't allow. He sat down in Grandma Schmidt's Morris rocker, his head in his hand.

"Paul, I—"

"So I hoped you'd be my best man." It was almost a question. "But I guess there's no point asking?"

"Paul, I'm sorry. Right now, I don't know. Let me think about it, will you?"

"Let me think about it." Where have we heard that before, this evening?

Shut up. I'll call her as soon as I get off the phone with Paul..

The convoluted thing had lodged itself behind his cheekbones, hard and pushy and making him want to cry out. "Besides," he said, forcing it back, "what's the rush? Why not—" he took a breath— "just move in to-gether?" He focussed his gaze on the framed black and white image of an architectural detail that hung over his sofa. It calmed him and he went on more easily. "More and more people are doing it these days, no one has a problem with it. No one who matters. You can be together without getting the preachers and the lawyers involved. Before *or* after."

"Because Sophie and I aren't planning to just live together," he said patiently, like a kindergarten teacher going over the ABCs with a slow learner. "We want to be *married*. Committed for life. Full weight."

"But *why?*" Eric couldn't explain, even to himself, why the thought of Paul's binding himself to a wife made him want to pull out his beard. He began to pace again. What business was it of his? Paul was twenty-six and Sophie was, too. They were both grownups; they could do as they pleased.

But as Paul's brother, he couldn't like it. "Listen, brat, you're only thinking of yourself. Did Momma ever tell you what she gave up, marrying Poppa? It took her a few years to realize it, and then it was too late."

"What did she give up? She had us, didn't she? She knew Poppa was a clergyman when she married him. You go into these things with your eyes open and deal with it like adults."

"No, she didn't, Paul. She didn't." It was vitally important he should set his brother straight. "He wasn't in the church when they got married. He was a civil engineer. He didn't became a pastor until after our sister Ruth Adelaide died. Didn't Momma ever tell you about that?"

"First I've heard of it," said his brother. "Why didn't she tell me?"

She had shared this with him alone? The discovery gratified him strangely. "I don't know. But it's true. Poppa treated her like she was his appendage. He didn't ask her to come along when he changed professions, he just expected her to. With no regard for what she cared for or what she wanted. Did you ever hear her sing, I mean, really *sing?*"

"Lots of times," said Paul. "Remember how she'd cut loose with those descants in church? Wow."

Eric remembered. Hearing his mother soaring on the last verse of "A Mighty Fortress Is Our God" had given him his first and only idea of hea-ven. "No," he replied a little roughly. "I mean real music. That's what she wanted to sing. She wanted— she was going to get an agent and be a recording artist."

"Momma? Really?"

"Hell, yes, really. But Poppa shut her down and said no because it didn't fit his image of a pastor's wife."

"You and I are the new generation," Paul said complacently. "We're used to women having careers."

"You think that's all it takes? I don't want to rain on your parade, but are you really thinking this through? It's not just Momma and Poppa, marriages are going bad all over." He felt the tightness welling up again. "You think you can do a better job at it, I can't stop you. But you'd be making a terrible mistake."

His brother was silent.

"Paul, I'm sorry, I . . . You know me, I'm not the type to . . . Well, you know. Oh hell, man, I just don't want you to be hurt. Or Sophie, either. She sounds like such a nice girl, why put her through it?"

Slowly, Paul replied. "I know, Eric. I know. It's okay. You just have to understand that living without Sophie would hurt even more. And she feels the same about me. We can't do it. We just can't.

"Listen, can you get out here for Christmas? You can meet her and see what a great girl she is."

"No, I can't leave, there's too much—"

"Seriously? You haven't hired anybody yet? There's nobody you'd trust to hold the fort for a few days?"

"No, I— No, yes, there is. She's very reliable."

"She?"

"Great employee, that's all." And a good friend, but he didn't want Paul to get the wrong idea.

"Oh. No, I was just assuming all architects were men. Chauvinist of me, sorry."

Damn. Now he *had* given Paul the wrong idea.

"Unless you and Leah had plans already?"

"Leah?"

"Yeah, Leah. Your girlfriend. Or is she still your girlfriend? Is that what this is all about? You two fight or something?"

"No, nothing like that. We've just haven't had much time to get together lately."

His eye went to a photograph of the pair of them at the ski lodge at

Crested Butte two or three years ago. They'd been nearly inseparable then. But recently . . . Last night was the first time they'd gone out in four or five weeks. Funny, he didn't feel that guilty about it. Why should he, after the crack she made at the store opening in August? She'd been talking to a prominent local restauranteur, a guy he would love to work for. She'd said, *"If I'd had the money, I would've hired a real architect and it'd look even better."* Then she'd grinned at Eric over her drink as if it were a great joke between them. She had to know it would hurt.

But that was months ago. He'd enjoyed himself at the play last night, hadn't he?

Yeah, *Woman of the Year* was good. Raquel Welch in the lead was good.

"She's busy with her new cookware shop, and I'm up to my neck at the office. But everything's fine."

"I was wondering. You don't seem your usual happy self. Something wrong?"

Should he say something about Nick Hardt and the smear campaign? No, it might be over. He wouldn't trouble Paul with it.

"Come on, big brother," Paul urged. "You can't carry the weight of the family all the time. Spit it out. Let me give you some advice and you can reject it, too." He laughed, and Eric laughed with him.

"No, nothing in particular. I mean, just growing pains." He sat back down on the sofa. "I just got a big new seven-figure project in the office. I'm going to have to staff up and it's hitting me that being a boss won't be as easy as I'd thought."

"Thought you said you had an employee already."

"Yes, but that's different."

Different how? an inner voice inquired.

"Different how?" his brother inadvertently echoed.

"I don't know— I guess we're just a good team. You ever feel you wanted an extra pair of hands to get something done? It's like that with her. We've only disagreed a couple of times, and that was when I was wrong and she was right!" He laughed, a little uncomfortably.

"I'd be careful if I were you," Paul said.

"What? Hey, don't read this the wrong way. She's a nice girl— Christian, if that means anything— but it's strictly business."

"That's not what I was getting at. It's what you said earlier, about how

Poppa used Momma as an appendage. You just said it yourself— that working with this girl is like having a spare set of arms. She may not mind it now, she may be as dedicated to the work as you are—"

"She is," Eric interrupted.

"—but someday you're going to send out a signal and she's not going to jump. What will you do then?"

"I said I'm willing to admit when she's right!"

"Sounds to me like you're already treating one employee like an extension of yourself. Loosen up now, or you'll expect all your employees to be that way. And they may not be as patient as she is."

Was that part of it, too? His own voice from just a few hours earlier sounded in his inward ear: "My new associate, that's you," he'd said to her. "I just *assumed* you'd know . . . "

Shaken, he stared at the painting over the fireplace, an abstract he'd done himself in a class at Mount Athens, as if it could assure him that his behavior in the car this afternoon was a fluke and Paul knew nothing about the subject at all. "Where'd you get all this wisdom?" he joked.

"Observation. Experience. The brass in the accounting firm I work for just had to let an upper-level manager go. He expected his subordinates to read his mind and got mad when they didn't. Jeopardized a couple of important accounts. We're having to scramble to keep things covered, but the atmosphere is a lot better."

Did he expect Sandy to read his mind? Seemed much of the time she did. But Paul was right— he couldn't expect that from everyone who worked for him. Even with her, he shouldn't have expected it tonight.

"You never were like Poppa," his brother went on, "yelling and throwing things when people don't do what you want. But you can be pushy in your own way. If you'll take your little brother's advice, get your head on straight before you hire anybody else. Okay?"

"Okay, and when *Paul Baumann's Hiring Tips for Young Entrepreneurs* comes out, I'll buy the first copy."

"I mean it."

"So do I. Really, you've been a big help. Luckily the new work won't start until February, so I've got time to think things through."

Starting with his relations with Sandy. Crap. The last thing he wanted was to be like his father.

"Sounds like you've already found somebody as sold out to architecture as you are," Paul said. "Treat her well, you hear? And I'll see you at Christmas."

"Sure thing. Tell Sophie she's making a big mistake," he said cheerfully, "but give her my best."

He hung up the phone and stood there for a moment, thinking. Should he call Sandy and smooth things over between them right away? Or should he have the pay and benefits package in hand first, in case she asked?

He'd call now.

His hand was on the receiver when the phone rang again.

"Hi, Paul," he said. "Did you need—? Oh! Mrs. Eisenbaum. How are you?"

Gerrie Eisenbaum was fine. It was the custom-upholstered couch he'd ordered for her living room that wasn't in the best condition.

"I know it's not your fault that Kai Lung scratched it," she apologized, "but it really needs to be repaired, and could you come over tomorrow night and look at it, please?"

He suppressed a sigh. Why didn't she just call the upholsterer? The Eisenbaums should put him on a retainer, the way she constantly assumed he'd solve these problems for her. But this kind of service kept the clients coming back, so what could he do?

He took the phone over to the Morris rocker and steeled himself for a long session. Once Mrs. Eisenbaum got going she seldom came up for air.

"And you'll stay for dinner, won't you?" she said almost two hours later. Eric jumped. Crap, he'd fallen asleep. "Levvie and I haven't seen you since forever."

Lev Eisenbaum was a man worth talking with. After repeating himself several times, Eric finally convinced her he would join them for the meal and got himself free.

He was in the kitchen brewing a cup of coffee when he remembered he still needed to call Sandy. But it was late, after 10:00. She wouldn't want him bothering her at that hour. Never mind, he'd get into the office bright and early for a change and make it right with her in the morning.

CHAPTER A.13

"SANDY, YOU HERE?" Eric called as he strode down the corridor towards their office.

The door was still locked. No matter, it was only 8:30 and she usually got there at 9:00. She'd be in soon. In the meantime he busied himself returning a few phone calls. He was reaching for the receiver again when the telephone rang.

"Eric Baumann, Architect. Eric Baumann speaking."

"Eric? Bill Worthington. Glad you're in early. Something's come up with the Weisman job."

Oh, damn. Sabotage. Had Hardt finally resorted to sabotage?

"What is it?" he said with a little too much urgency.

"Oh, nothing earth-shaking. Just another change DeeDee Weisman wants. But it'll affect the ductwork for the heating and cooling, so we need to meet on it this morning, right away."

"Right away," Eric repeated, feeling deflated as an old balloon. There went all his noble resolutions. For the thousandth time, it seemed, Sandy would have to wait. Unless she got an earlier bus?

"Yes. I've got the HVAC subcontractor here, but he needs to leave by 10:30 to get to another job. Sooner you get out here, the better."

"Uh, Bill, there's a little thing I need to take care of here at the office first." He calculated. Twenty minutes to get there ordinarily; twenty-five or thirty with traffic. "I'll meet you by 9:15. 9:30 at the latest. Anything I should bring? Okay. See you there. Bye."

Fifteen till nine. He couldn't take the chance and wait for her to arrive; there wouldn't be time for them to talk about the office changes anyway.

He'd better write a note. A quick one, letting her know why he wasn't in and what she needed to concentrate on.

That part was easy. When would he be back? He ran over his commitments for the day. Crap. Once this meeting with Bill was finished, he doubted he'd be in till tomorrow. Better be honest and say so.

He finished the note and slid it face up under Sandy's parallel bar.

Ten till.

He regarded it critically. It wasn't enough. He'd said they'd discuss the matter of her promotion in the morning and now they couldn't. There wasn't room on the scrap of paper he'd grabbed before, so he tore a piece of letter paper in two and started a second message.

> Sorry I couldn't stay to talk to you about

No, that sounded too personal.

> Sorry I had to leave before

Not that, either. He started over on another half sheet.

> Looks like it's happened again. Hoped to catch you
> early but Bill insisted we meet right away. Nothing un-
> usual, just DeeDee W. changing her mind again.

He took a breath. She'd understand that. They'd laughed together over that kind of thing before.

> About what we talked about yesterday. Maybe it was
> premature

That implied it'd been premature for him to ask. Start over again? No, draft it out and recopy it when he had it done.

> About what we talked about yesterday. ~~Maybe it was~~
> ~~premature~~ I don't blame you if you thought it should
> wait till after I meet with Jacob and Sam tomorrow
> night. So let's revisit

Was that the word he wanted? No, not exactly.

> let's ~~revisit~~ wait and make things final on Wednesday.
> Keep lunchtime open and we'll

Crap. Her lunch hour was her own time; he had no right to dictate what she did with it. But over lunch would be the best time to discuss the plans for the office. They needed to get away from their drafting tables and the phone and the random visitors. Besides, everything went better with food.

> ~~Keep lunchtime open and we'll~~ If you don't have other plans

Hell! again. What business was that of his? That implied that whatever they were, she should give them up to be at his beck and call. Try again.

> ~~If you don't have other plans~~ If you're available I'd like to take you out to lunch and

That sounded too social. This was business.

You're right, it is business. Why are you sweating so hard over this? If she doesn't like how you put it, that's her problem.

No. It was important. He had to get it right.

> ~~plans If you're available I'd like to take you out to lunch and~~ We can have lunch somewhere and work out our strategy for the next few months.

There. That sounded good and collaborative.

> I can't help feeling optimistic about this new project, so I'm resubmitting to you the offer of a promotion to the position of Associate. I'm putting together a package I hope will please

Not "please"; that wasn't quite the right word . . .

> hope ~~will please~~ you will find favorable to your interests, though of course it will be open to your input and negotiation.

Rather formal, but that might be best under the circumstances. And knowing Sandy, she'd get a kick out of it.

This time he took a full sheet of office stationery and recopied it. His handwriting was the best he could make it, considering he had to rush.

> Looks like it's happened again. Hoped to catch you
> early but Bill insisted we meet right away. Nothing
> unusual, just DeeDee W. changing her mind again.
>
> About what we talked about yesterday. I don't blame you
> if you thought it should wait till after I meet with Jacob
> and Sam tomorrow night. So let's wait and make
> things final on Wednesday. We can have lunch
> somewhere and work out our strategy for the next few
> months.
>
> I can't help feeling optimistic about this new project, so
> I'm resubmitting to you the offer of a promotion to the
> position of Associate. I'm putting together a package I
> hope you will find favorable to your interests, though of
> course it will be open to your input and negotiation.
>
> Yours, Eric B.

He had folded the note and even pulled off a piece of tape to seal it (why did he think he had to seal it?), when it occurred to him he'd forgotten the most important message of all. He flattened it out on her table once more and without pausing to think he wrote,

> P.S.: I'm sorry I acted like a jerk in the car last night. If
> you ever catch me doing anything like that again, tell me
> and I'll stop. I apologize for not being here this morning
> when you get in to tell you that. I'll be here tomorrow and
> we'll talk about it, if you want— I promise.   EEB

He picked up the paper again to seal it, but again laid it down.

> P.P.S.: I hope you're all right. The office couldn't get
> along without you.   E.

Fifteen after. "Bill will have my head!" He refolded the note, taped it shut, scribbled her name on it, and slid it under her parallel bar. Snatching up his portfolio, he ran out of the office. And if Bill was ticked because he was late, so be it.

DIVISION B

WEDNESDAY, 11 NOVEMBER 1981
– MONDAY, 1 FEBRUARY 1982

There be three things which are too wonderful for me,
yea, four which I know not:
The way of an eagle in the air;
the way of a serpent upon a rock;
the way of a ship in the midst of the sea;
and the way of a man with a maid.

—Proverbs 30:18-19

L E BISTROT SOUFFLOT SUITED ERIC so much he could have designed it himself. The decor was elegant yet clean-lined and airy, while the food was excellent in its simplicity. And it didn't hurt that Chef André Gautier was a personal friend of his and Leah's.

"But yes, the firm, it is growing? You are ready for the big new things?" Chef André had said Monday when Eric called for reservations. "We must celebrate. When you order, I will bring you the ideal wine out of my private stock. *Non*, you will not pay. The wine is on me."

Now his friend the chef had retired to the kitchen, and Eric poured out a glass for Sandy and one for himself.

"'We're good to go," he said. "We settled the business on FirstCon last night after dinner."

"Oh, what great news!" She beamed with pleasure, and he was glad he'd left his last morning appointment a little early to make sure to meet her in time. So much depended on having her on his team. "I take it they still want us to start the beginning of February?" she asked.

Purposely he hesitated. "Yes . . . that's the same . . . though we may do some preliminary site work prior to that. But . . . "

"But what?" Her eyes flew to his, suddenly wary.

"There is one change to what we discussed yesterday. It's about your Associate's package."

Her face clouded. For a moment she looked down at her bread plate. Then straightening her shoulders, she said, "That's all right. If we can't afford it, we can't afford it."

He really shouldn't tease her like this. But he was in so deep already, he may as well play it out. He continued, putting on his most sympathetic frown. "Yes. Jacob and Sam thought— they both thought—" He struggled to keep his composure. "They both thought I'm asking way too little for the design product we put out, and they told me— no, they ordered me— to set your rate at a dollar more per hour."

She stared at him in blank disbelief. He couldn't help but laugh. "Oh, Sandy, I'm sorry, but if you could see your face!"

"What? You mean—? Is that instead of what we discussed yesterday?"

"No," and he laughed again, "it's on top of it!"

"Oh. Oh! Wow. Are you sure?" She relaxed then again drew herself erect. The pride in the gesture pleased him. "That was so nice of them! Whose idea was it," she said eagerly, "Mr. Ryerson's or Mr. Delkirk's?"

He wasn't about to give either man more credit than he deserved. "Actually, I don't think Jacob understood the contribution you make to this firm until I explained it to him. Fortunately, he's a fast learner."

"I shall endeavor to reinforce the lesson," she said with mock formality.

"I doubt you'll have any trouble doing that."

There was a pause. "Eric," she said, looking at him over her wine, "what about you? Did you teach him how many hours you've been putting in and not billing?"

He smiled. "Maybe. I'd say that was taken care of, too."

The waiter approached and set their plates before them. "Thank you, René," Eric said.

"Are you sure?" Sandy asked. "I mean—"

"Shh. Chef André slaved over this coq au vin all morning. No more talking. Let's eat."

⁜

"THAT WAS a great lecture at the AIA meeting last night," Eric commented one afternoon a week later. He'd been writing Weisman specifications since lunch and it was a good time for a break. "We were lucky to get Richard Meier to come speak to us."

"I wasn't too familiar with his work before this," Sandy said. "I like it a lot."

"I'm glad Hartford Seminary took a chance on him for their new main building—"

"—Especially since he'd mainly done residences before?" she completed his thought, smiling impishly. "Kind of reminded me of a certain architect I know."

"Well, yeah . . . You know, I might consider that porcelain enamel cladding for FirstCon. I admire that clean white look."

"I saw you talking with him after."

"Why didn't you come over and join us? He was really interested in what I was telling him about the Weisman house."

She made a face. "I wanted to. But . . . you know that woman Mona Silvestri, the one I heard the first Hardt rumor from?"

"Yes?"

"She was there, and she practically corners me and says, 'Too bad Baumann turned out to be such a disappointment.' Before I could say anything, she goes, 'I hear Phipps & Musgrave is looking for junior space planners. They *might* take you back on.'"

"Seems she didn't get the memo."

"Guess not. She grabbed some guy I don't know by the arm and says, 'Hey, come listen to this about Eric Baumann's office,' and just then there's Reg Fyfield at her elbow. I said, 'Good evening, Reg,' and Mona shut up and went away. By that time Mr. Meier was talking to someone else and I decided not to interrupt."

"I'm sure the program committee will bring him in again." He went back to his spec writing.

But Sandy said, "Eric?"

"Yes?" he said over his shoulder.

"It hasn't ended yet, has it?"

"What hasn't?"

"Nick Hardt's smear campaign. The filthy rumors. Yes, we've got work coming in again, but people like Mona are still talking. Saying horrible things."

He turned around. She was nervously playing with a 45-degree triangle, turning it over and over, pressing the points into her fingertips. "I wouldn't let that bother you," he reassured her. "You said yourself that this Mona has been a rival of yours since architecture school. Everything I've heard the past couple of weeks has been personal. It's just the turkeys taking advantage."

She was silent a moment, then said, "You mean it's not as orchestrated as it was before. It's more petty now, not the kind of thing that could undermine the firm."

"Exactly. We can stop worrying."

She puffed out her breath. "Well, if you say so . . . It's just— Eric, did Hardt push back after you didn't put that ad in the *News-Herald* on the sixth? Have you heard from him at all?"

"Not a word."

"That's the trouble. It's not like him. And I'm grateful for what the Ryersons and all are doing for us, but do they really have that much influence? He's put a lot of effort into trying to ruin us. Did it really take only our clients banding together to make him give up and go away?"

"Who cares why it happened? Let's relax and enjoy it."

She put the triangle down and looked away, out the window. "I keep waiting for the other shoe to drop," she said. "Like he's out there planning the second stage and this is only the calm before the storm."

He laughed. "It's not much of a calm, is it? That's what makes me think this is over. Face it, we've won. He swore that we'd never work again in this city and here we are with substantial new projects and more to come. He was wrong, and we proved it. We, and our loyal clients. Now let's forget about Nick Hardt and focus on doing architecture, okay?"

"You know, you're right. We're getting along very well without his project, and— well, yes." She gave him a thumbs-up and went back to her drafting.

A few minutes later, the phone rang. "Baumann here," he answered it.

"That was Vicky McCullough," he said to Sandy after he hung up. "She and Jameson want to show their support, so they've asked me to supper tomorrow evening."

"Good for them!"

"Actually, it's more the Charles Rennie Mackintosh bedroom set we ordered for their third floor guest room."

"Oh, is it—?"

"It's finally in from Scotland."

"That's wonderful! I wish I could see it sometime. That furniture is just what they needed in that beautiful old house."

"I'll make sure you do. Right now, it's still in the box. Vicky's asked me to inspect it and make sure it's set up right."

"Meaning you and Jameson get to do the unpacking and put it together while Vicky tells you where it all should go? Have fun." She gave him a cheeky grin.

He laughed. "I'll make sure he doesn't strain himself. It'd be easier with Jim there to help, but he's got a night class at the community college. He's studying architectural drafting, if you'll believe that. Looks like my adventures haven't scared him off."

"Hmm," Sandy said. "Will he get his Bachelor of Architecture eventually? Why doesn't he just go up to Mount Athens and do the thing properly?"

"Not sure. I gathered there was a girlfriend in the picture."

"Mistake." The word came out hard-edged and grim.

"What? I'm sure I heard Vicky right."

"No. Mistake to let that get in the way of your vocation."

There was that disturbing hardness again. Quickly, he reverted to the original subject. "Elaine won't be there, either. I gather she has something going on at the high school. But I'm sure Megan will be right there in the thick of it." He rolled his eyes.

"She's in third grade by now, isn't she?" Sandy asked, her voice again warm and cheerful.

"Yeah. Cute kid. I guess she'll tell Uncle Eric just how it's done."

"I'm sure she will. Well, have a nice time."

"If the Mackintosh furniture looks the way it should, I certainly will."

CHAPTER B.2

IT NEVER FAILED. Halfway out his apartment door and running late on a Tuesday morning, and the phone had to yank him back.

For a moment, Eric was tempted to let it go. No, better not. It might be a client.

It was— the one he had an appointment to meet.

"Hi, DeeDee. Don't worry, I'm on my way."

"Oh, Eric!" said Mrs. Weisman. "I'm so glad I caught you! Sol and I got together with the Kornblums last night, and she has the most *adorable* warming drawer in her new kitchen! So I was thinking, as long as you're bringing the finish samples for the cabinets, could you bring me something on three or four brands? I could really use one."

Oh gosh, another change. Was this job never going to be done? Never mind, if the Weismans were willing to pay them to redraw it, they'd do it— as long as it didn't compromise the basic design.

"Sure, DeeDee, that'd be a nice feature. I'll run by the office and get you some catalog cuts. It'll be more like 10:30 before I can get to your place. Is that all right?"

"Of course. See you then."

Downtown, he was in luck. There was an open parking space out front with just enough time left on the meter. He'd run upstairs, do a quick rummage through the kitchen appliance binders, make copies of the likely models, and still have a minute or two to spare. He dashed inside and took the elevator to the seventh floor.

As he made the turn to his corridor, he heard music drifting from the far end.

> *...De sa main, de sa main la caresse—*
>> *hélas! et son baiser...*

"*...hand the caress... Alas, kiss*"? he attempted to translate. The piece playing was operatic. A soprano aria, French, and vaguely familiar.

> *...d'une amoureuse flamme*
>> *consument mes beaux jours!...*

"*...amorous flame consumes my beautiful days...*"? He couldn't quite—something sounded odd about it. Before he'd taken another step, Eric realized what it was: the woman's voice was unaccompanied.

> *...Ah! la paix de mon âme*
>> *a donc fui pour toujours...*

..."*The peace of my soul,*" something, "*gone forever*"?

Some kind of on-air experiment? A live contest, maybe. Although the pitch was true and the tone was full and sweet, his ear told him the singer was not a professional.

> *...a donc fui pour toujours!*

Still, the soprano, whoever she was, was very good. She cared about the song and sang it with true feeling.

As he approached, the voice, which had ached with passion in the phrases he'd heard before, now sounded rushed, even desperate.

> *Je suis à ma fenêtre,*
>> *ou dehors, tout le jour...*

Frustrating. He was hearing the French but he couldn't quite work out what it meant. "*I'm at my window...*" something, something "*...all day long...*"

Never mind the translation. The announcer would identify the song and the singer, and he could look it up later. Right now, he needed to go through appliance catalogs.

> *...C'est pour le voir paraître,*
>> *ou hâter son retour.*

But just outside the office he stopped short. Through the half-open door he had a clear view of Sandy's table, and it was not the radio that was playing: the singer was Sandy herself.

Oh, gosh. Like Momma.

Though when his mother sang classical, it was something light, *The Daughter of the Regiment,* maybe; nothing like this. Only in that wire recording of "Lone Woman Blues" had he ever heard Momma singing anything so heartfelt.

He had time. Let her sing. He drew back a little and remained in the hall, listening.

Her voice accelerated, grew staccato, breathless, her intensity mounting.

> *Mon cœur bat, mon cœur bat, et se presse*
> *dès qu'il le sent venir …*

"… *my heart beats …*" and to his surprise he found his own heart beating faster, too.

Damn, she's good. Almost as good as Momma.

Her voice was doing something inexplicable in him, and playing critic stopped the sensation cold. But faster and faster came the song,

> *… au gré de ma tendresse*
> *puis-je le …*

till the tension was nearly unbearable . . . then once again the tempo slowed and the wistful, yearning note returned.

> *… retenir!*

"My tenderness, I can't hold it back"? No. Quiet. Listen.

Her hands, which he could still see, laid down triangle and pencil and all her being seemed poured into the poetry she sang.

> *O caresses de flamme!*
> *que je voudrais un jour*
> *voir s'exhaler mon âme*
> *dans ses baisers d'amour!*

He took a deep, silent breath. Not a professional singer, not professional at all, but her artless sincerity was drawing the soul, *l'âme*, right out of his breast.

His good sense saved him. *The meter's running out. You'll be late for your meeting.* He glanced at his watch. Good grief, nearly ten o'clock.

It's almost done. Just one more line. One more.

> *Voir s'exhaler mon âme …*

No. He had work to do. And so did she. He pushed the door wide open, and walked in.

> *… dans ses baisers—*

Around she spun in her revolving chair as if snared by a whip. Her face flamed red then drained white, and for a moment he thought she would faint. Her lips parted, but no words came out.

"Hey," he said heartily, "you never told me you could sing!"

"I— I— I'm sorry, I didn't think you— I mean, I—" She faltered and went silent.

"That's all right," he said, suddenly feeling embarrassed and clumsy himself. "You're good. I mean, you sing good. I mean, 'well.'"

She contemplated her hands in her lap for a moment, then drew herself up straight. "The Weisman kitchen cabinetry details, they're— they're almost done." But still her voice quavered, and she avoided meeting his eye.

"Actually, no, they're not."

"What?"

That sounded more like the Sandy he knew.

"Another change, I'm afraid. DeeDee wants a warming drawer. It's the latest thing, I gather. Guess I should have thought of it myself."

"Do you want me to look them up for you?"

"No, I have something in mind. I'm due over there at half past. Leave off finishing the island; that's probably where we'll fit it in."

"Okay." She turned back to her drawing, but a strange tension shimmered in the air between them. He forced himself to ignore it and focus on warming drawers. His hands fumbled a little with the pages; the heat of her embarrassment seemed to have affected him, too.

"Good . . . I think I have what I want." He held up the catalog pages he'd selected.

"Do you want me to go down and—?"

"No, I'll run the copies for DeeDee myself. No point in you running down to the sub-basement and back up again." He flashed her his best indulgent boss smile, as much for his sake as for hers. "Put the binders away for me, all right? I mean, don't put them away, I'll have to put the pages back in when I get back, I mean, I should be back around 2:30 . . ."

"Oh. Okay."

He picked up his portfolio and escaped for the elevator.

THAT AFTERNOON everything seemed back to normal, and the only music in the office came from the radio. As usual, they spent a few minutes talking in his car before she got out at her apartment building, and all constraint between them— if there had actually been constraint before— had disappeared.

But between her place in Summerside and his in River Hill Eric recalled the name of the aria he had caught her singing that morning. It was Marguerite's from Berlioz' *La Damnation de Faust,* "D'Amour l'ardente flamme"— "The Burning Flame of Love."

He parked his car in the lot at the rear of his building and hurried to the back door, nearly cannoning into a man wearing some kind of brown uniform. "Excuse me," he said, abruptly pushing by him. He dashed up the stairs to his apartment, dumped his coat on the sofa, and went straight to the record shelf. Finding the *Faust* album and sitting down, he pulled out the liner notes with the French lyrics and the translations in English and German.

> *I stand at my window*
> *Or outside, all the day,*
> *To glimpse his appearing,*
> *Or haste his return.*

"*To haste his return*"? A flush of heat went through him. Oh, no. No. It wasn't possible. Not safe, sane, levelheaded Sandy Beichten.

Besides, the part before,

> *The caress of his hand,*
> *Alas! and his kiss . . .*

. . . nothing had ever happened, there was nothing to make him think that she— that he was— Never had he touched her like that. Not once.

But if he did, would she—?

Just for a moment he let his imagination off its rein. He saw his hand reaching out and putting aside the lock of shining brown hair that often fell over her face as she bent over their design, then tilting that face to his and—

Inconceivable. What would become of his work? And dammit, wasn't Leah the only one he should be thinking of in that way?

But something compelled him to go on reading. He skipped up to the previous lines.

His voice in its enchantment
(He knows it sets me ablaze) . . .

He groaned. There'd been that time, last summer, when he'd been giving Sandy some instruction or other. She'd looked at him intently, seemingly taking in every word. But she kept coming back to him later, needing to be reminded of the simplest part of what he'd said. Could the sound of his voice really do that to her? But he hadn't known. Never!

It couldn't be. She just hadn't slept enough the night before. Or it had been the July heat.

He read the lyrics to the aria from start to finish; they only stirred up his unrest.

O! caresses of flame!
That I might see the day
When I breathe out my soul
In the kiss of his love.

Once more he could hear the passion as she sang the French. He began to pace the room.

She meant it. For somebody, not him. For whom? For Marvin Jansovic?

His stomach turned. Marv Jansovic? He refused to believe it. It had to be somebody from that church of hers, some man whose name she'd kept private from him, even through the days and late evenings and long weekends they worked together.

His legs felt inexplicably weak and it was hard to breathe. She hardly had time to be with anyone but him. Would it be so bad if they . . . ? That was, if he and Leah ever . . . ?

Yes, more than bad. He had to think of his career. He had to put a stop to it.

How? Hell, he was just flattering himself. She *was* an attractive girl; he'd finally figured that out a couple Sundays ago at the museum. What was he going to do, put up a sign saying "NO SINGING ON THE JOB"?

It's not the singing. It's the— I mean, if she really feels like that— crap!

He sat down hard on the sofa, the liner notes in his hand.

But what was he stressing over? There was nothing he needed to do about it right now. He should fix himself something to eat, then get into his studio and work on some ideas for the Ryerson family room. Or he could call Leah and see if she wanted to go out.

He did neither. He put the disk on the turntable and submitted to the aria, following every word. Then, starting at the beginning, he played Berlioz' dramatic legend all the way through to the end. When the last note had faded away he felt better; the music was its own distraction.

But the problem remained.

Thursday was Thanksgiving. He'd given her the Friday off. Tomorrow was Wednesday; he could give her the afternoon off with pay, too. He'd have four whole days to think what he should do— if he had to do anything at all. No, three, since he was going over to Leah's for the holiday. Good old Leah.

Three days, that should be enough time to think of something.

D'amour l'ardente flamme
consument mes beaux jours …

O lord, it had better be.

CHAPTER B.3

"SOUNDS LIKE YOU HANDLED IT WELL," said Sandy's friend Carole as they relaxed together after Thanksgiving dinner. With Carole's husband and five-year-old son down in the recreation room watching the football game, the women had the living room to themselves.

Oh, Carole. You wouldn't say that if you knew the stupid, stupid *thing I did on Tuesday.* How could she sing Eric love songs in the office when he might come in at any minute . . . and she'd sworn she wouldn't feel that way about him anymore?

"Yes," she said aloud, "being an associate will be different, and I think I've got my head around what that'll mean. When I think how I nearly lost the opportunity, letting myself get too attached to him . . . "

"I hear you," Carole said, stroking the calico cat that lay purring on her lap. "The last thing you want to do is mess up your vocation getting emotionally involved with the man you're working for."

I'm emotionally involved already. And trying hard not to be. But it wasn't Carole's fault if she was working in the dark where Sandy's heart was concerned. *Maybe if I'd pick up the phone and call her every so often we'd be on the same page.* "Some people," she began, and she peered at her friend intently, "some *Christian* people would say I should quit and take myself out of the way of temptation entirely."

"Oh, I don't know. Temptation's everywhere. It's how you handle it."

"Exactly. And I always said I was going to do architecture to the glory of God and working for Eric's the best chance I have at doing that around here. If you saw his work, you'd know what I mean. The man is brilliant, and that's not just me talking. Though maybe that means I should get out of Wapatomekie and go work someplace bigger. But I tried that already," she defended herself. "Four years in Boston, and, well . . ."

"True. The grass isn't always greener on the East Coast. Or the West Coast, either. I know. And I am familiar with your boss's work. A friend of mine has an office Eric did while he was still at his old firm, and David wouldn't change a thing."

"Where is it?" Sandy couldn't help asking.

"Not quite out here in the 'burbs, and not all the way into town. I think it's on Meyers, near Josepha Park."

"I know the location," Sandy said. "And that reminds me. Thank you for sending George all the way into town to pick me up. It was pretty cheeky of me to call Monday night and invite myself to Thanksgiving dinner."

"No, not at all! I'd been wondering how you were, and besides, we love having guests. It's just that with our law practices and Robbie to keep track of, we rarely have the time."

"I'd say you were using your time well. You both seem really happy." Sandy paused. "But did it ever seem *you'd* gone wrong with your profession?"

Carole thought for a moment, sipped her tea, and said, "Yes. And it's funny, I told you I'd been thinking of you; well, I was also thinking of that pledge some of us Classical Honors girls took the summer after our senior year."

"'The Knights of the Single Eye,'" Sandy said, automatically.

"That. All that about purity and focus and all the rest of it."

"You sound a little cynical. You haven't changed your thinking on—?"

"Oh, no, I think the standards were good. Still are. But wasn't it a little presumptuous of us to pledge ourselves like that?"

"What?" If anyone was still going to be carrying the banner high ten years later, it was Carole Peabody Fenton.

"I mean," Carole went on, "our baptismal vows and the promises we made when we joined the church should have been good enough, don't you think? Did we really need to set ourselves up as something extra special?"

"I guess it came with the Blakewell Classical Honors territory."

"I guess so. I don't know how the ordinary kids put up with us. All the Latin and Shakespeare and the whole knights-and-ladies chivalry act."

"Me neither," Sandy agreed, laughing.

"Anyway, I didn't have any problem with the bodily purity side of it. Stanford was quite a shock for a Midwestern girl like me, and when I found out that George was from Wapatomekie, too, I latched onto him like a sucking leech."

Sandy doubted it. "I think it was probably him latching onto you."

"Well, a lot of both. I'm still surprised our parents let us get married the summer after our sophomore year." She smiled apologetically. "But they did and I'm glad of it. No, where I had trouble keeping the pledge was on the professional side."

"How? You did really well in law school. Came out with honors and everything."

"I did," said Carole, picking up a pristine crystal ashtray and carefully setting it down again on the mahogany end table. "I'd even get on George because I thought he wasn't hungry enough for legal knowledge. Then I interned at a corporate law firm. I enjoyed that, too. Too much."

Sandy stared at her, perplexed.

"Don't get me wrong, corporations need good legal counsel. But I was learning to fight for the corporate clients to the harm of everyday people. I stopped caring if our client's cause was just or fair, I simply wanted to win. And God help me, I justified it by saying I was pursuing excellence for the sake of Jesus Christ. Talk about taking the Lord's name in vain!"

"So what happened?"

"I suggested a way to spin some evidence to make a certain plaintiff's case look weaker than it was, and the jury bought it. When I looked in the faces of that poor man and his family and saw how crushed they were, it hit me what I'd become. The company owed him compensation; by rights they should have paid every last penny of his medical bills with damages on top. And I'd helped rob him." She put her hand to her head, then looked up, pain in her face.

"Don't get me wrong," she said again, "you can be a Christian and a corporate lawyer. But not me. That's when I approached my advisor and begged him to get me a new internship with a firm doing consumer law. He did, and I've been at it ever since. And with George's tax law business, we're each serving God in the way He's called us to, and He's blessed us beyond anything we could deserve.

"But what about you?" she asked Sandy. "Seems like you've upheld the good old vow pretty well."

Sandy gave a self-deprecating snort. "Never believe it. I started messing up as soon as I started architecture school." One confession deserved another, and she told her a little about Jeff. Not what happened that night down in the student store. Back then she was ashamed to tell and swore she never would. Now she'd forgiven what he did; why dredge it up?

Her own error in dedicating her freshman year to a mere man like Jeff instead of to Christ, that she could admit. "Ridiculous how I let myself make an idol of him, just because he was the best designer in the school and had auburn curls and a perfect Grecian profile."

"And a fabulous bod?"

"Apollo in the flesh!" She grew serious. "My grandmother Fleming used to say, 'Handsome is as handsome does.' I guess that made him rather ugly."

"You always seemed the most dedicated of any of us when it came to your work," mused Carole. "I'm just sorry you've never found a good Christian man as well."

"I thought I had, once," said Sandy. "My senior year in college. A guy from West Germany, named Werner."

"Wait a minute. I think you wrote me something about him. In the fall of '74, but nothing after that."

"I'm sorry . . . But yes. We were even engaged. For about a half an hour."

"Really!"

"Until I found out that not everything that calls itself Christianity really is, and what people believe matters to who they are."

Carole laughed ironically. "Ain't that the truth."

"Funny, though. He loved me more than I did him. He was studying violin and composition and we'd listen to classical music for hours on end. We'd be lying together in this humongous beanbag chair—"

"Stuffed with real beans?"

"Of course! And oh, how they *smelled!* But other than that, it was nice. And I liked having him talk German philosophy to me, Schleiermacher and Hegel and all. And the way Eastern mysticism tied in with Christianity."

"But it doesn't."

"I know that. Maybe that's why I didn't write you much about him. It wasn't the gospel like we got at Fourth Pres. But I let myself think it was. Made me feel really advanced and wise, you know?"

Carole smiled. "That's not surprising, if you were in love."

"But I wasn't in love with him, not then. And I wouldn't sleep with him just for fun. But that spring he gave his Master's recital. And that night something changed. I'd be lying if I said it wasn't more wonderful than anything I could have imagined . . . "

She tried to suppress the more intimate details of what happened that May evening. Carole wasn't fooled. "You slept with him?"

"All but," she admitted. "The way I thought about it then, if the guy said he loved you and asked you to marry him, it was all right."

Sometimes I still think that way . . . Forgive me, Lord. Vows first, "before God and all the neighbors."

"I won't lie," she said, staring at her fingers. "I *wanted* him to take me. He knew I was a virgin. He was so slow and considerate and artistic about it he nearly drove me nuts. I thought I was going to blow sky-high! And then . . . just before . . . he blurted out that making love to me was like making love to all the women in the world. I tried to get him to take it back and he said no, Love with a capital-L was too big to confine to one woman and I should be glad to know he was thinking of me when he did it with 'the others.' *Blast!* . . . Sorry, it still makes me mad."

"He was sleeping around?" Carole asked sympathetically.

"Yes. And intended to keep doing it after we were married."

"So you dumped him."

Sandy gave a doubtful laugh. "I could have killed him." *Literally.* "Afterwards, when I calmed down, I thought my heart would break. I wanted to take him back so badly . . . " She sighed. "Thank God we didn't go through with it. The sex, I mean. I would have been so tied to him I never could have left him. We would have made each other miserable." She took a sip of her tea. It had gone cold.

A pause. "It must have hurt for a long time," Carole said. "What, Posey? You want down? There you go." The cat jumped off her lap, scratched at the closed door to the kitchen, then headed off downstairs.

"It still does, sometimes, especially when I see his name in the paper."

"Wait a minute. You're talking about *the* Werner Edelstein? The violinist?"

Sandy couldn't suppress a flush of pride. "Yes, though he's not quite international caliber yet."

"You're nuts. He's extraordinary! We heard him play with the Wapato-mekie Symphony a year or two ago. You didn't go?"

Sandy shook her head.

"Oh, I am so sorry. It must have been terrible for you. Back then, I mean."

"Yes, but better to find out what he meant by Universal Love when we were only engaged. That's why I have to keep my head on straight about Eric. If it didn't work out with Werner, who at least claimed to believe in Jesus Christ as Lord, what can I expect out of a lapsed Lutheran missionary's kid who rejects God altogether?"

"I hear you. I don't know what I did to deserve George. He's a better Christian than I am."

Sandy nodded. "After that I swore I'd only date Evangelicals. And I did. Did I tell you I attended a big nondenominational church when I lived in Boston? I had all the dates I wanted. But . . . "

"No one ever worked out?"

"Worse than that. Carole, it was awful! All they wanted to talk about was the Red Sox and male authority. I had one guy tell me he'd be making all the decisions in our relationship because he was the man."

"You were going steady with him?"

"Heavens, no. That was when we were planning our first date."

"Wow!"

"And then, get this: I got laid off, and the guy I was dating at the time, he said— he said—"

"Okay, spit it out."

"He said Jesus told him my being out of a job was a sign I should move in with him! That's when I beat it out of there and came back to Wapatomekie."

"And you haven't dated anybody since?"

"Not really. But maybe God wants me to devote the rest of my life to my work and give up on marriage . . . and love . . . and all the rest of it."

"Don't be too sure," Carole said slowly. "Maybe you just need to meet the right guy. Would you mind being fixed up? There's a really sweet single man at my church. He likes art and music too and I think you'd like him a lot."

Carole, no. I don't want—

Why should she refuse? Because he wasn't Eric Baumann?

"Sure. Give him my number." She took a deep breath. "And as for Eric, I need to focus on loving him the way Jesus does. Even if he becomes a Christian— and I pray he does—"

"Amen," said Carole.

"—it'll be for him and for God, not for me. Maybe some nice girl will thank me some day."

"Maybe so!" Her friend glanced out the window at the early evening darkness, then at the clock on the mantelpiece. "I wonder if that football game is over. Shall we call the boys upstairs for pie?"

THE FENTON KITCHEN, though not small, seemed crowded. Maybe it was all the pans and dishes sitting out from Thanksgiving dinner. Maybe it was little Robbie Fenton riding his plastic three-wheeler around and around under the grownups' feet. Maybe it was the cat who had stolen in, keenly curious about the turkey carcass and the whipped cream that stood ready in the stainless steel bowl. Maybe it was the bad layout Sandy had inwardly criticized from the moment she'd first walked in. But there hardly seemed room for anything.

They managed regardless. Carole had cut the pies (two kinds, pumpkin and apple) and Sandy stood at the counter near the doorway, a filled dessert plate in each hand, ready to take them out to the dining room.

"Carole, honey," said George, "you want me to build a fire in the fireplace?"

Sandy watched his eyes as he entered the kitchen, and it was with joy for her friend that she saw his look was for his wife alone. She stood back to let him pass.

An unearthly yowl surged up from the floor. Carole's husband staggered into Sandy, his hands seizing her by the waist and arm, his weight pinning her tightly against the counter's edge.

Fear washed crimson through her body, blinding her eyes, enraging her mind. Frantic, she hurled the pie plate at his head. Dish and dessert sailed past his ear and crashed broken to the floor. For a horrified moment their eyes locked, then he released his grip and stepped back.

"I'm sorry! I'm sorry!" she blurted. Trembling, she set the other dish down on the counter. "Carole, your plate, I'm so sorry!" That was it. Make them think she was apologizing for the damage, not for her meaningless rage. She stooped to pick up the pieces.

"No, my fault," George said quickly. "I should have been watching for the cat. Robbie," he addressed the transfixed, wide-eyed boy, "take that tricycle out of here and go sit down in the dining room. No, find Posey first and make sure she's okay. I think I stepped on her tail. Sandy, I'm sorry. I guess I gave you a scare."

"That's— that's all right," she answered, still shaken. "I'm so sorry!" she pleaded, stooping for a porcelain shard under the refrigerator.

"Sandy, stop," said Carole. "I'll pick that up. I'm always telling George the circulation in this kitchen stinks. Maybe one of these days we'll have you guys redo it for us."

"Are you sure?" asked Sandy, meaning the mess on the floor. "I'll pay for the plate."

"Don't be silly. I can get a new one at Monkey Ward's. Now go sit down and relax. George and I will be out with dessert in a minute."

She acquiesced, and as she left the room she heard Carole whisper to her husband: "Stress."

"SANDY, CAROLE TELLS ME you've been going through an adventure at your office."

It was an hour later, and she and George sat in the living room chatting while Carole put Robbie to bed. Sandy looked at him, a little startled.

"Something about a sinister client?" he asked.

"Would-be client," she clarified, and sketched out the Nick Hardt saga for him. She said nothing about the project itself; a non-disclosure was a non-disclosure, signed reluctantly or not. "We're still hearing stuff, but less and less, and it's nothing new. And the work is coming in again. Did Carole tell you I'm being made an associate as of the first of the year? Eric's waiting till then for tax purposes."

"Very wise. If I was his tax advisor I'd tell him the same."

"The big commission won't start till February, but these new little jobs should keep us off the streets in the meantime."

George cleared his throat and looked pleased with himself. "Well, if you need anything else to tide you over . . . "

"Oh, sure! You have something in mind?"

"Do you do planning studies?"

"We haven't done any yet together," she said frankly, "but we both have experience at that from our former firms."

"Well, good. I have a friend, he's the head of the planning commission for Fort Randolph City, and they've budgeted the funds for a study and master plan to revitalize their downtown shopping area."

"Sounds like fun."

"You'll have to submit a proposal to the city council, of course, but I can put you in touch with him and get you qualified for the bidders' list."

"What's his name?"

"Theophilus Duggins. He's a great guy; I met him through the first law firm I worked for after I passed the Bar."

"'Theophilus'! Sounds like his parents were Christians. Is he?"

"Yes. Deacon in the A.M.E. church up there. I'll give you his contact info." George noted it down on the back of one of his business cards. "Be sure to say I sent you."

"George, did you tell Sandy about Phil?" asked Carole as she came back into the room.

"Yes, just did."

"Good. Robbie's asleep, so let's pour the wine and have a toast."

George obliged, and said, "What shall we toast to?"

"To pure focus!" said Carole, laughing.

"And to focussed purity!" Sandy returned.

"In Jesus' strength, not our own," Carole amended.

"Absolutely. Of course!"

George shook his head. "I have no idea what you ladies are talking about, but here goes: To focus and purity, in the strength of Christ!"

"Amen!"

"And amen!"

CHAPTER B.4

B Y THE MONDAY AFTER THANKSGIVING, Eric knew what he had to do to restore order in the office.

Stay businesslike. Make sure Sandy understands you're her boss, not her . . .

His mind refused to complete the thought.

He was able to put his resolution into practice shortly after he got in. She told him about a lead she'd picked up over the weekend for a master planning study for Fort Randolph City, and a brief "Follow up on it," was all the response he made her.

She did, the same day. "Mr. Duggins was in a meeting," she reported, "but his secretary said he'd be happy to speak with me about the study in the new year. I'm to call back in January and make an appointment to see him."

"Good," he said. "By then you'll be drawing your new salary, and you can buy a car." He observed her closely to see how she'd take it. As he did, he couldn't help noticing how her teal-blue sweater brought out the green flecks in her brown eyes.

"That'll work out well," she agreed.

He persisted. He'd picked up how much she enjoyed their conversations sitting in his car evenings after work. Maybe she enjoyed them too much. "Without a car you wouldn't be able to take on jobs like that."

"Of course not. I'd thought of that myself."

He felt oddly deflated. This was too easy. But maybe for her, "after the new year" still seemed a long way off. Suddenly he wished it were a very long way off, himself. If she was going to be this sane and sensible, why rush the change?

All that week he managed to be in the office at the right time to give her a ride home. They had a lot to discuss about the new projects and no time to do it during work hours. It was the same the week after. It made sense. Besides, he concluded, he'd been mistaken. That aria was just a song she liked and could throw herself into. Still, in unguarded moments, he wondered what he would do if he returned unexpectedly to the office some day and caught her singing to herself again. Once or twice he thought he had, but it was only the radio.

Good thing. The Weismans had decided they wanted to be moved into their new house by the start of Passover the coming year. That was early April, so the drawings had to be finished by mid-December, no more changes, no more delays. Eric had the Ryerson family room to deal with, and there was a new project for a retail space for a man named Millerson, one of the jobs that had come in from Reg Fyfield. On top of that he had to see about hiring more staff. There was no time for drama in the office, and Eric thanked his stars that Sandy wasn't giving him any.

"Let's get these ads written before the phone rings and interrupts us," he said one afternoon towards the end of the first week in December.

"Right!"

She sat opposite him, a legal pad in her lap, her pen in hand. He liked the way she held it. It was a fountain pen, and he liked that, too. He even liked the little smudge of ink it left on the first knuckle of her middle finger.

"So, what kind of people *are* we looking for?" Her confident voice shook him out of his reverie.

"A good nuts-and-bolts man— or woman," Eric said judiciously. "Unless *you* want to write the specs."

"No thanks!"

"And someone to help you with the slave-labor drafting. You'll be supervising that one. Then we'll see what a heartless creature you are!"

"Oh," Sandy said cheerfully, "I'm as bad as you are, if not worse!"

Two hours later he looked over the finished copy. "That'll do it," he said.

THE ADVERTISEMENT went to the Wapatomekie *News-Herald* and into the Opportunities file at the local American Institute of Architects office. By the middle of the next week, the résumés started to trickle in.

"Any possibilities?" Sandy asked him one day after lunch, looking over his shoulder as he perused one of the latest.

The nearness of her pleased him. He looked up. "I think so. Not as many as I would have expected, so far."

She considered. "Maybe Nick Hardt did us a favor. Only the people who really know us and really want to work for you are applying."

"That could be it." He smiled. "Trouble is, a lot of them want to design, and they can probably do it, too!"

"That could get awkward," she agreed.

"I'd hate to be an overbearing creep like Ayn Rand's Howard Roark, but I need to set some kind of steady design course before hiring anybody else to concentrate mainly on that end of things. Other than you, of course."

"I think you're right . . . The firm's not even two years old, and if you don't establish a design standard now we'll just be blowing in the wind and won't be known— or hired— for anything."

"Exactly!" He picked up a short stack of résumés and handed them to her. "Getting the Weismans' done is first priority, but when you have a minute, look these over. These are the people I think we should interview."

"No problem." She took them back to her table and he returned to the detail he was working out. After a time the soft whirr of her parallel bar ceased and he could hear the rustle of letter paper.

He was deep in a sketch when she cried out, "Oh, no!"

He jumped. "What is it?"

"Nothing."

A few minutes later, Sandy stood at his side. "Eric," she said, "most of these look like good candidates. I'm looking forward to having them in for interviews. I *will* be interviewing them with you, won't I?"

"Of course."

"But there's one . . . "

She held out the résumé by its corner, as if she were loath to have it touch her.

"Yes?"

Wordlessly, she handed it to him.

"'Jeffrey A. Chesters,'" he read out the name of the applicant. "What's wrong with him?"

"I don't think he'd be a good fit."

"That's funny, he's one of my top candidates. He's got over nine years' experience with Architects' Group International. Didn't you read the letter of recommendation?"

"Yes," she said, looking very unhappy.

"From one of the partners at AGI's New York office. He says Chesters is one of the best specs men he's ever known, and has a real talent for custom design."

Oddly, that seemed to encourage her. "Yes, that's just the problem. I'm not sure how or why he got into writing specifications, but design is his real strength. But it's not the same as yours. You two would never agree."

"Funny, that's not how he presents himself. But you sound like you know him. Do you?"

"You don't?" She sounded shocked.

"No, should I?"

"Check out his architecture school."

He flipped to the Education section. "'Bachelor of Environmental Design, School of Architecture, State University at Mount Athens, Class of 1972; Bachelor of Architecture, 1973.'" He thought for a moment. "Yes, the name is vaguely familiar. Wasn't he . . . wasn't he . . . ?"

"He was a year ahead of you and three ahead of me. Senior Design Award, 1972. Now do you remember?"

"A little." He shrugged. "I kept my head down in Studio and didn't get much involved with anybody else."

"Yes, I've wondered why I never knew you there. Anyway, if I know anything about Jeff Chesters, it's that if AGI had him doing specs, it was because he— I mean—" She grimaced. "Anyway, we shouldn't take the risk."

"Risk?" Eric questioned. "Well, just to be fair, let's have him in and let him explain."

Still she stood there. She took a breath and seemed to make up her mind about something.

"Eric," she said with more conviction, "I could keep arguing against Jeff Chesters because I think he'd compete with you in design. But it wouldn't be the whole truth. After all, I think I design pretty well, and you and I— I mean, together we—"

"Yes, we do. Go on."

"It has to do with design, but it's different. It's his personality. No," she corrected herself, "his character."

"His character?"

"Yes." She went on, more resolutely now. "Jeff Chesters has a rotten, lousy character. He's arrogant. He's not trustworthy or reliable. Believe me. Our reputation is on the fragile side now; if he was working here it would only get worse."

"You've been in touch with him since school?"

"No." And she uttered a quiet "Thank God!" under her breath.

"Don't you Christians think people can change?"

"Yes, but . . . let's not stake our futures on it. It's not like he's the only applicant for the job."

He looked at her, then at Jeffrey Chesters' résumé, then back at her again. He'd told her the new hires had to be pleasing to her. Hadn't he meant it?

"All right," he said finally, "into the circular file it goes." And tearing it in pieces to show his good faith, he dropped the résumé into the wastebasket.

"Thank you," she said simply, and got back to work.

There was a story there. No time to wonder about it now.

CHAPTER B.5

AND SHE'D THOUGHT job seekers had it hard.

"Goodbye, we'll let you know," said Eric as yet another interviewee left the office. He looked at her, his eyebrows raised.

"No, I don't think so," Sandy said. "Maybe the next one?"

It was only Wednesday morning and this was the fourth candidate they'd interviewed this week; they'd seen three the week before. But so far they hadn't found one person, let alone two, who met all the requirements of their ads.

An hour or two before lunch, Eric called her over to work out a problem in the Ryerson concept drawing. She made herself avoid that sweet seductive spot between his right side and the throw-off shelf, but even sitting to his left Sandy could see the business-sized envelopes piled up under the window, untouched since the day before.

"Looks like there's a few résumés you haven't had the chance to open yet," she commented once the Ryerson issue was solved. "You mind if I look them over and vet them for you? I think I'm about finished with the Weismans' dressing room details."

"Sure, would you?" He handed her the stack.

Back at her table, she skimmed each one, carefully rereading those with promise.

"Eric," she said, approaching his table a few minutes later. "Here's one I'd say we should interview for sure."

"What's the name?"

"Homer Tahatan. If half what he says is true, he's a specifications whiz."

"Sounds like a Sue," he said dismissively.

"A what?" The Johnny Cash song "A Boy Named Sue" began to play in her head.

"A Sioux Indian," he said.

Bizarre. That sounded almost prejudiced. And if anyone didn't have a prejudiced bone in his body, it was Eric Baumann. "But what does that have to do—?"

"Let me see that," he interrupted. He looked the résumé over. "Yes, just what I thought," he said. "Remember what you said about Jeff Chesters? Not the character part, the design part. Something in his résumé tells me this Tahatan guy would rather design. I may be wrong, but unless we get desperate, let's not push it."

He'd used her own argument against her. Annoying. "Hmm. I say bring him in and see what he says. Besides, look, he's from North Dakota, like you. His degree's from North Dakota State in Fargo."

The moment the words were out of her mouth she knew she'd said something very wrong.

"I'm from Wisconsin," he said, his expression set and cold.

"I'm sorry. I forgot." *O Domine!* If only she could reach out and comfort the virtually-fatherless little boy he used to be! Impossible, but he'd taken her word for it on Jeff; she'd do the same with Homer Tahatan. "Okay. Whatever you say." She shrugged and returned to her seat.

But Jeff. He wasn't a local boy; he'd come to the university at Mount Athens from out of state. Was he living in Wapatomekie already, or was he thinking of moving here from New York? She'd gotten Eric to throw his résumé in the trash last week and now she'd never know where he was writing from. She envisioned running into him at AIA meetings and shuddered. Forgiveness was an excellent thing, but it didn't mean she wanted to be in the same room with the man she'd had to forgive.

Please, Jesus. Let him leave New York, if he wants, but please grant he moves anywhere else but here!

✎

LATE THAT AFTERNOON, hearing Eric push back from his table and heave a mighty stretch, Sandy swivelled her chair around and said, "I was wondering, why didn't you attend NDSU? How'd you end up down here?"

"You're sure you want to know? It's a long story."

Usually she would say, "The longer, the better," but she needed to make some final decisions on the Weisman dressing room hardware before quitting time. "Give me the *Reader's Digest Condensed Version*."

"Well, I originally had a scholarship to Yale."

"Wow, did you? What happened?"

"Uncle Sam. Well, poverty, actually. I decided to put off the scholarship for a year so I could work and build up my cash reserves. It never occurred to me that I'd lose my student deferment."

"You got drafted that soon?"

"The September after I graduated from high school. I did my tour in Vietnam and when it looked like I was getting out of country in one piece, I reapplied to Yale. But they wouldn't renew my funding. In fact, I got the distinct idea that they didn't want anyone like me."

Sandy hung her head for a moment. "I'm sorry."

"It wasn't your fault."

"No, I used to feel the same way. All the names people stick on Vietnam vets. I used them, too. Maybe it's a good thing we never met during architecture school. I might have insulted you beyond forgiveness!"

"I doubt that." He smiled. "Anyway, I had to go somewhere so I applied to North Dakota State. Even with the GI Bill, I needed that in-state tuition. They wrote back and said my application for '67–'68 didn't get to them in time. Maybe it didn't. I hadn't shipped home yet; things happen."

"Did you come down here after that?"

"No, I went back to Bismarck, moved back into the family apartment. Reapplied to NDSU for the following year. This time they said— well, never mind what they said."

"They turned you down?" she said, aghast. "That far ahead?"

"They did. Nothing personal. Some bureaucratic snafu."

"Well, they were fools," she said hotly.

"I totally agree," he said, and she laughed with him. "So I started looking around for Midwestern architecture schools that were both good and affordable, and decided on the one down here. I moved to Wapatomekie, worked a year to establish residency, got accepted at Mount Athens, and there I was."

"And there you were. That explains why you were only two years ahead of me. I was wondering. Thanks."

"For what?"

"For letting me . . . I mean . . . " She changed the subject. "Have you checked today's mail? Any new candidates?

"Oh, yeah. I've been so busy I forgot." He dug the stack from under some discarded sketch paper. "Okay . . . bill . . . bill . . . yeah, this looks like a résumé . . . gallery opening notice . . . hmm, what's this? Somebody sending money?"

She came closer as he opened the cheap envelope. As he read its contents, his face grew grim.

"Eric, what is it?"

"I'm not sure you should see this. No, you shouldn't."

But she already had. It was one of those collages of letters cut out of magazines and newspapers and stuck on a sheet of child's tablet paper to form a message.

You KIke loVer You1l PAY

4 What you DId   get rEadY

tO DIE   Your wARNed

"Eric!" she gasped. "That's awful!"

"I doubt he was trying for a Pulitzer."

"You know what I mean!" The sickening memory flooded in of her dream the month before, with him lying bloody and dying in her arms. "You've got to call the police!"

"And have them do what? There's no return address, no signature even. Probably just some crackpot trying to get my goat."

"Really? Eric, please, I don't want you to— for anything to— to—" Quickly she said, "Nick Hardt. Isn't it from him?" She bit her lip and looked out the window.

"I'm not so sure."

Astonished, she searched his face. "You're serious?"

"Yes. Has he ever sent us anything without letting us know it's from him?"

"No, but the only thing he's sent us was—"

"Besides," he interrupted, "he's a businessman. It's one thing for him to try to do us down professionally. But is someone like that going to make threats he can be arrested for? He has too much to lose."

"You said he'd sold out all his holdings here."

"That doesn't mean he never wants to do business anywhere again. How's a murder conviction going to help him? Unless you're suggesting he's in the Mafia?"

She kept silent. Against her will, tears began forcing their way out of the corners of her eyes.

"Hey!" he said. "Nothing's going to happen. And if anything does, we have evidence— this letter."

"You'll at least send it to Chuck for safekeeping?"

"Good idea. Too late this afternoon; I'll take care of it tomorrow." He replaced the paper in its flimsy envelope and put it in his portfolio.

"But you won't call the police."

"What good would that do? Hey, look. I'll see what Chuck says. Let's get back to work. Nothing's going to happen."

You don't own him. You have no right to tell him what to do. "You have to be the most stubborn— well, okay," she gave in. "Do whatever you think is best. But so help me, if you get hurt, I'll— I'll shoot you myself!

CHAPTER B.6

NOTHING DID HAPPEN. Not over the weekend, not on the Monday, nor on the Tuesday. By then, Sandy's nerves were so taut she could almost have brained him herself for how lightly he was taking it.

"Eric," she ventured to say that afternoon, "is everything all right?"

"Of course," he said, not looking up from his board. "Why shouldn't it be?"

"Because . . . well, that note."

"Oh, that! I forgot to tell you. I think I know who's behind it, and he's harmless, really."

"You do?"

"Yes. I ran into Mike Laurence on Saturday and he thinks it might be this guy at Urban Atelier."

Urban Atelier? Their little firm was a mere crouton on UA's lobster salad. "Good grief, why?"

"A year or two ago the *News-Herald* asked me to write a guest review on the new Commerce Avenue library. I'm afraid I didn't pull any punches about its failings."

"The library on Commerce? Wasn't that what you were running that survey on at . . . ?" She faltered, afraid she might blush recalling the night they first met. It had been so wonderful, the way they'd talked in his car for hours after leaving Marvin snoring on his couch.

If she did go red, he didn't notice. "That's right. What a great memory you have. Mike reminded me that after that, the library board stopped using Urban Atelier and brought all their work to Richardson & Greene. He's managing one of their projects now."

"But what about the bad grammar and spelling?" she asked. "And the ethnic slur?"

"Probably trying to throw me off. The guy at UA wrote a pretty fierce letter to the editor at the time, practically accusing me of libel and a few other nasty things. I was surprised the paper printed it."

"Okay," she said, "but somebody like that could still do a lot of damage, if he's bearing a grudge after all this time."

"No, if he'd meant me physical harm he would have broken my neck for me before this. Likely he figures I'm nervous after the smear campaign, so now's a good time to mess with my head. Everyone else is doing it, why shouldn't he?"

She considered. "Well, all right . . . I won't ask who it is, but I'll take your word he's harmless . . . You'll take care anyway?"

He shrugged. "Of course I will."

"I know, but—"

Just then, a building materials representative appeared at the door and the subject was dropped.

ANYBODY WHO TALKED about things winding down for the holidays, decided Sandy, must be nuts. It was less than an hour to quitting time the Friday before Christmas and here she was, hip deep, banging out the alternatives Mr. Millerson wanted to see Monday afternoon for his store. If the client couldn't relax, neither could she.

"Sandy?"

"Uh!"

"Sorry to startle you," Eric said. "I was just wondering. Were you planning to hit the Grant Street galleries for the Third Friday openings? I could give you a lift over."

"I can't. I have things to do tonight."

"Oh, come on. The Weisman plans are finally done, you should go out and celebrate."

You? Not *"we"*?

She couldn't, anyway. She'd finally made arrangements to go out with Carole's church friend Bradley Wellborn, and he was taking her to a play. Why was she reluctant to tell Eric? If he'd been any of the guys at Phipps & Musgrave, it would have been just another piece of news.

Treat him like one of the guys at Phipps & Musgrave. For both your sakes.

"No, actually," she said, "I have a date tonight."

His eyes narrowed. "You do?" He sounded astonished, and she didn't like it. Did he think no one would want to go out with her?

No, it wasn't astonishment. He was disappointed. Blast. Couldn't Bradley have asked her out for tomorrow? With any luck she and Eric could have gone through all the galleries together and maybe had supper, too. All strictly platonic, but fun.

"Well, okay," he said. "But tell him if he tries anything your big brother will come and beat him up."

"Huh?" she said. "My brothers don't live here anymore."

"No," he said a little awkwardly, "I meant me."

"Oh! . . . Um, thanks . . . I think. Um, what about you? You're going gallery-hopping, are you?"

"No. No, I don't think so." She could have sworn he'd intended just the opposite the minute before. "I need to get home and accomplish something on the Ryerson family room."

She took that at face value. "I haven't seen anything on it the last few days. Anything developing?"

"I think so . . . something's coming, but I'm keeping it at home. Maybe I'm afraid if I bring it down here I'll lose the idea. I've been putting a lot of hours into it."

"You're not staying up too late, are you?" Did that sound maternal? Whatever she was to him, she didn't want to come off as motherly.

"Me? Stay up too late? Nonsense! I've been in bed by 6:00 a.m. every night this week!"

"Idiot! When do I get to see these marvels?"

"By Monday. I'm going to bury myself in my studio this weekend and emerge with . . . " He groped for the word.

"'The tablets of the Law'?" she suggested.

"Yes, exactly!" His look immediately changed to one of discomfort: he must have realized the line was from the Bible. "Well, um, you'll be ready to do some drawing on that by Tuesday? You've got something to show Millerson?"

"Yes, almost. I think I can get the color on the third alternative by the time I leave tonight."

He was silent for a moment. "Get that done, then I'll take you home. And I meant it: Make sure that guy, whoever he is, treats you well."

HIS WORDS struck her with irony on Saturday morning as she came downstairs to get her mail. Bradley Wellborn, far from treating her badly, had been the nicest of Christian gentlemen. Too nice, in fact.

Though had it been truly gentlemanlike in him to take her to what turned out to be his nephew's junior high Christmas play? That might have been charming, had it not been a cobbled-together hash of out-of-context Bible verses and re-worded pop songs, complete with the girl playing the Virgin Mary singing "You Light Up My Life" with Jesus' name thrown in. The show had left her with the impression that the director thought Christ was born to make everyone into nice people. What was worse, Brad hadn't been happy with anything short of wild enthusiasm for the script and for his nephew's performance. But the poor kid, who played the Second Wise Man, couldn't carry a tune in an oil tanker. Avoid being a hypocrite or preserve her date's feelings— she couldn't do both. She'd erred on the side of charity and said everything he expected her to. But it was galling to be forced into it.

Afterwards he'd treated her to a late supper at a cheap chain restaurant, where he'd lavished praise on the food (bland and congealed), the service (careless and slow), and the decor (plastic and dingy). He was so nice it made her feel like a shrew.

All the way back to her apartment Bradley had talked on and on about the comparative merits of various computer languages— "You're into technology too, right?" he'd kept saying— while she sat in the passenger seat trying not to yawn. He hadn't gotten her home till way after midnight, and she didn't care if she never went out with a real nice guy again.

Down in the tiny entrance lobby she found Mrs. Lopez, who lived below her on the ground floor, locking up her mailbox. Glancing this way and that as if they were being watched, the elderly woman said in a low, excited voice, "Did you see him?"

"Him, who?" Sandy asked.

"That *man!*"

"What man?" Only half paying attention, she opened her box and extracted her mail.

The woman grabbed her sleeve and pulled her close. "The man I saw outside last night!"

She suppressed a sigh. Mrs. Lopez was up to her spying tricks again. More than once Sandy had caught her peeking out between the slats of her blinds, watching her and Eric sitting out front in his car. They must really spoil her fun, never doing anything but talk.

"I'm sorry, no, I didn't see anyone," she said politely. "I wasn't home. I hope he wasn't right outside your window?"

"No," Mrs. Lopez replied in a conspiratorial whisper. "He was hiding in those pointy bushes in front of the apartment building across the street. He was watching me!"

Like meets like. "Are you sure? It's pretty dark over there. Sometimes those Alberta spruces look like somebody's there."

"No, it was a man!" the woman insisted. "I saw his face. He was standing in there, from ten o'clock on, watching."

Probably nothing but a fast food bag caught in the branches. Sandy glanced through the glass outer door, across the street to the evergreens clumped together in the opposite building's shallow front yard. Nothing there now.

"How long did you see him?" she asked. No harm in letting her neighbor feel important, if that's what she needed.

"A long time! Nearly an hour and a half!"

"Really!"

"Until that man from the building down the street came along with that big vicious dog."

She meant that ridiculously friendly Great Dane.

"It went for him!" Mrs. Lopez said, her little eyes glittering.

"Him who?"

"The man in the bushes! He ran out the side of them and into the driveway. I saw him then; you know how the building next door over there has that light. He was wearing brown coveralls and carrying a doctor's bag. He ran down the driveway to the back of the building. I didn't see him again," she said, shaking her head with apparent regret, "but the dog jumped on him and his bag came open and something fell out!"

Maybe she did see someone. "Mrs. Lopez, did you call—"

"I went across first thing this morning and picked it up."

"Picked what up? How do you know it's what he dropped?"

"It *was*," Mrs. Lopez insisted. "Here it is." She dug in the pocket of her housecoat and drew out a red rag.

Even without being a car owner Sandy recognized it as the kind auto mechanics used, and though fairly unspotted it gave off a faint whiff of some petroleum substance, gasoline or kerosene, she wasn't sure which. If the watcher wore brown coveralls like a mechanic, it'd make sense to assume the rag was his . . . But why would a mechanic be lurking in the landscaping across the street with a doctor's bag?

"Mrs. Lopez, listen. You need to turn this over to the police. You know that young woman with the little boy who moved into an apartment over there last month? I heard her husband's an abuser and she's trying to keep out of his way. He's probably tracked them down."

"*No.*" She was adamant. "He was looking over here, watching *me.*"

Sandy suppressed a sigh. "Well, in that case," she said, humoring her, "you definitely need to talk to the police."

"I could never do that! That would be raising a fuss!"

"Please? We don't want people like that hanging around. Do you want me to call for you?"

"I suppose you *could*," she said, as if it were Sandy who was making too big a deal of things.

No use standing on pride. "All right. I'll ask them to let you know when they're coming over." Though why she needed to, she couldn't conceive. Her neighbor would spot them through the blinds first.

"If you really think it's necessary," Mrs. Lopez said impatiently, and unlocked the inner door and went upstairs.

Sandy stood in the vestibule a little while longer, contemplating the building across the street.

That poor young woman. And her poor little boy.

For some reason, it made her think of Eric as a child. She ran upstairs and made the call.

LATER THAT MORNING, Sandy was retrieving a book off her living room window sill when she saw two policemen in the yard across the street, stooping near the shrubbery.

Eventually, one of them picked up an object that glinted in the winter sunshine. Though the branches of the sycamore obscured her view, she could tell it was too small to be a weapon, not even a pocketknife.

The policemen didn't seem to find anything else, and after a few minutes, they got in their squad car and drove away.

Lord, I know You're sovereign and all, and You've got everything under control. But if I hadn't had to go out with Brad last night I would have been home and called the police myself. Even if I had gone gallery-hopping. That guy would be in jail now and that poor woman would be safe.

She sent up a prayer for the fugitive wife and child. God willing, the man in brown would not be seen on their street again.

CHAPTER B.7

RIC LEANED BACK ON HIS STOOL and cast a critical eye on the sketch he'd just made. True to what he'd told Sandy that afternoon, after supper he'd sequestered himself in his back room studio and for the past hour he'd kept himself hard at work on the Ryerson family room. But the design wasn't emerging as smoothly as he would have liked.

Not like Athena from the head of Zeus. Not quite full-grown.

His eye wandered to the battered couch on the other side of the room. Sometimes when he was stuck a short nap would allow his thoughts to clear. Not this evening. If he kept pushing . . . Besides, the sofa was piled with clean laundry he needed to fold and put away.

Now that he'd noticed them, though, the clothes were a distraction. He pulled the quilt over the offending piles; that would suffice until he was finished drawing.

As long as he was up, he tugged a volume on Finnish woodworking out of the crammed bookcase that stood against the back wall of the room and examined the photographs. Working in the new built-ins with the existing fireplace location, that would be the key . . . Fairly easy, if only the west windows weren't in the way.

Maybe Jacob and Sheila would let him move them?

He sat down and sketched a little more. Whatever happened with the windows on this project, he'd be putting in the same energy-efficient units he'd specified for the rest of the Ryerson remodel. Better than the leaky sashes he had here. All shut tight and his studio was still freezing.

He pulled his kerosene space heater into the middle of the room and plugged it in. At least the old thing had an electric ignition. He could be grateful for that.

As the element danced with flame it sent out air currents that lifted the edges of the discarded sheets of yellow tracing paper that littered the floor. Eric glanced from them to the threatening note he'd tacked to his bulletin board, almost lost amid the layers of sketches that festooned it. He'd never gotten around to sending it to Chuck. Stripped of its menace, it gave him an odd sense of pride— see what he was prepared to face for his art! But now common sense took over. *If I don't watch it, nobody'll have to do me in, I'll fry myself.* He cleared off his rolling supply cart and put the heater on top of it, first laying a large ceramic tile sample underneath to protect the surface. Better.

Hardly was he back to his table when the phone out in the living room rang. He hoped it was nobody who wanted to talk.

It wasn't. The minute he picked up the receiver and said "Baumann here," the line clicked dead. Wrong number.

Taking a bottle of pop from the refrigerator in the kitchen, he pried off the cap and returned to his studio. He worked steadily for another hour or more. His ideas began to coalesce. Sheet after sheet of yellow paper was covered with sketches, then tossed to the floor as the design progressed.

Now he was too warm. Blast that heater, the thermostat knob was broken. He'd have to open a window or suffer in an impromptu sauna. Not the one on the wall next to his drafting table: it faced north, right into the wind. Nevertheless he raised it and leaned out, drawing in deep breaths of clean cold air. Above the buildings a blank gray sky blocked out the stars. The windows of the second floor apartment opposite were lit by a holiday party, the novelty song about Grandma and the reindeer penetrating through the panes.

He closed the sash and locked it. No partying for him tonight: he had to come up with something to show the Ryersons on Monday. Sheila had broadly hinted that she was counting on it for a Hanukkah present.

The west window would do better for ventilation. It gave onto the fire escape, but that landed in the parking lot where people came and went all the time, and his was a safe neighborhood. Besides, the steps ended at his floor and it wasn't as if anyone could catch the ladder from the ground. As he lowered the upper sash a few inches, a clanging from the living room made him jump.

1.   *Damn phone!*

Again, he ran out to answer it. "Hello? Eric Baumann here."

Once more, silence and a click. Couldn't people get their numbers right?

A tingle of unease stole over him. He shook it off: there was nothing behind that pasted-up note; something would have happened by now. The only thing he had to worry about tonight was coming up with a good plan.

So, where was he? Right, working out the best viewing angle for the built-in TV. And if it went *there*, it would fit in nicely with the games cupboard over here, and yes, the stereo could fit in there, and he could throw up a bulkhead for the new ductwork here, and . . . Faster and faster he drew, his excitement mounting. This is what he loved about design, this was what he lived for, there was nothing better in life—

"What the *hell?*"

Someone was knocking on his door. He flew into the living room, his heart pounding.

The knocking ceased. Slowly, the knob began to turn . . . Then, the unmistakable scratching of a key.

It was his killer. He had a crazy vision of grabbing the fireplace poker and bringing it down on the head of whomever was about to enter his door. Then he relaxed and laughed out loud. Only one person other than himself and the landlord had a key to his apartment and no compunction about walking right in whether he was there or not.

"Hello, Leah," he said as a tall, beautiful woman with curly black hair and mischief in her eyes stepped into the room.

"So you are here," Leah said, coming up and giving him a peck on the lips. "Why didn't you answer the door?"

"I'm sorry, babe, I was designing. I guess I got into it pretty deep."

"Huh," she said. "I was sure you'd drowned yourself in the bathtub. Be just like you to make me call the coroner to pick you up."

"No, nothing like that . . . Hey," he said, "come see what I'm getting. It's for the Ryersons."

"Oh, shit, do I have to?"

"Torture time, huh?" He laughed. "Come on, babe, tell me what you think."

"Oh, all right," Leah said, rolling her eyes.

As she stepped through the studio doorway, she gave a shriek and clapped her hands to her mouth. Then laughing and butting her head against his shoulder, she said, "Shit, Eric! For a second there, I thought there *was* a dead body!"

"Huh?" He looked around in confusion. "Where?"

"There, on your sofa!" She pointed.

"Oh, no, my dear," he said, twirling his mustache in his best imitation of Snidely Whiplash, "that's Something So Much Worse! Nyah, hah, hah!"

"*What?*"

"Clean clothes from last week's wash!"

"Oh! Well, I won't volunteer to fold them."

"I wouldn't expect you to. But come look at what I've been working on."

"There's no time. I've come to kidnap you."

"Oh, so it was *you* who—" He stopped himself. Leah didn't need to know. "Who what?"

"Never mind. Kidnap me? What's the ransom?"

"There's a new French film showing over at the Grant Street Cinema and I won't let you go until you come watch it with me."

"Oh, Leah, look," he protested, "I've got *work* to do!"

"You always have work to do. Never time for me— or for yourself. Come on, it'll do you good. Besides, it's the one I told you about, *Le Pont du Nord.* Pascale Ogier's in it," she cajoled, smiling flirtatiously. "You always like *her.*"

"Hey, you're right. I hear it's got some great views of Paris, too. For that," he joked, "I'll even go out with you!"

"I should be enough without the film," she replied tartly.

"Very true, very true. Can we get there for the 9:35 showing? Give me a second, I have a couple of things to shut off in here . . . "

"I'll use your john," she said, "and meet you at the door."

"Well, kidnapper, let's go," he said a few minutes later as they clattered down the stairs. "And don't keep me out past my bedtime!"

"I'M GLAD I convinced you to come," said Leah, glancing over from the driver's seat. "I haven't seen you since Thanksgiving."

"Sorry," he apologized. "I've been busy."

"I was beginning to think you'd forgotten what I looked like."

Forgotten ... "Babe, hang on, go back."

"What?"

"Go back. I don't think I turned off the lamp over my drafting table."

"Oh, shit, Eric! You and your energy-consciousness! That's only, what, a 75-watt bulb?"

"100."

"Not that much anyway. You turned off the rest of the lights, I know that. Now relax. We've got just enough time to make it to the film."

CHAPTER B.8

"**Y**OU'RE KIDDING!" Sandy exclaimed Monday morning.

"Kidding about what?" Eric rummaged through the piles on the throw-off shelf. Where was that roll of tracing paper, anyway? "That I don't have the Ryerson scheme or that I had a fire?"

"Eric Edward Baumann, you think I give a flying turd for those damned drawings when you could have been *killed?*" She stood there trembling in a cute royal blue dress with a black blazer over it, her fists balled at her sides. "You think I'm made of dammit *stone?*"

He couldn't help it, her reaction gratified him. He tried to look stern. "Such language! And you a nice Christian girl."

"And you didn't even call and tell me!"

"I didn't want to worry you."

"You didn't want to *worry* me?" She was staring at him as if he were raving mad.

"Okay, I admit it. I was sure you'd think it had something to do with that anonymous note I got a couple weeks ago." He found the roll under some drawings, ripped off a length of paper, and taped it to his board.

"And it *doesn't?*"

"Not according to the battalion chief. It was my own damn fault. I knew that space heater had been recalled, but I was too busy to make the landlord replace it and too cheap to get a new one myself. The firemen found it tipped over on the floor."

"And how did that happen?" she asked suspiciously.

"Another problem with it. It wobbles a little. I thought I had it safely up on my cart, but I guess not."

"One of those plastic ones with all the drawers? Oh, Eric, for you of all people to go out and leave it there! It probably melted straight through!"

"Well, I thought I'd turned it off. At least, I'm pretty sure I did. I might have left the light over the table on. I thought of it when we were almost to Grant Street, you'd think I'd remember the heater. But I guess I was so into the design, my head wasn't on straight." He shrugged.

"I guess not! Eric, how— how can you be so blasted *calm* about it?" She looked around helplessly, then faced him, distress filling her brown eyes. "Your apartment— your work— and you could've been— I'm sorry— oh, Eric, I'm finished with the Millerson presentation; please, give me something to do! I don't want to think about it. I just— God help me, if Leah Matthews ever justified her existence, it was Friday night. If anyth—" She threw her hands over her mouth, her eyes wide with embarrassment.

Odd. Why would Sandy say that about Leah?

She picked up a pencil off her board, then let it fall. Bracing herself against the table's edge, she said in a voice that was more disciplined, "Well, I thank God you weren't there. Your stuff was insured?"

"Um, no."

"It *wasn't?*"

"Something else I didn't get around to."

The horror in her face appalled him. "Look," he protested, "it could have been worse. Guy across the hall's an ex-Marine. He heard the heater explode, grabbed the fire extinguisher, and was in there with the door kicked open before it spread very far. Couple other neighbors grabbed the other extinguishers and, well . . . I guess I should be grateful the fire station's only two blocks away, but . . . " He made a face. "The books will be the worst of it. Two big cabinets full, and all crammed in so tight they hardly burned at all."

"But if they weren't burnt—?"

"Water damage. The guy downstairs is out of his apartment for a while, too. It came through his ceiling."

"You mean—?"

"Well, they had to make sure the fire was totally out, didn't they?"

That made her laugh if nothing else did.

"The landlord's insurance will take care of repairing the structure and getting the smoke stink out of the walls and so on. It was his heater. Dealing with the furniture and the rest of the contents will be up to me."

"Oh, gosh, I'm sorry. Can you at least deduct new reference books as a business expense?"

"That's an idea, I'll ask the accountant."

"Well, if there's anything I can do . . . I mean," she said hurriedly, "I can loan you some books in the meantime, if you need them. But you can't stay there for a while, can you? Until the landlord does the repairs?"

"No, I'm going over to Mike Laurence's tonight after work. If I can't talk him out of getting married"— that made her frown— "at least I can make sure he does the thing right. But only till Thursday when I go out to Idaho for Christmas."

"Oh. But after . . . ?"

The truth was, he didn't know. Could he ask the McCulloughs if he could stay in their Mackintosh guest room? But maybe his landlord would have his place refurbished by then.

And Sandy didn't ask and he wouldn't tell her where he'd spent the past three nights. He'd been at Leah's, and early on the Saturday morning after the excitement was over they'd slept together, for the first time in weeks. The physical release had been there, but nothing more. They'd gone through the motions again Saturday night, but they'd both turned over and gone to sleep unsatisfied; the glad heart-passion he'd once found in her was gone, and mere mechanical coupling wasn't enough. No need to ask Leah how it had been for her: she had been bored. Maybe they would make love again in a week or a month or next spring when the situation was different, but, by mutual unspoken consent, last night he'd slept on her couch.

He put a good, sharp point on his pencil lead and began to draw. For several minutes only the radio broke the silence.

Then, "Eric," Sandy said, "are you sure your fire had nothing to do with that note? Or . . . Nick Hardt?"

"If it'll make you happy, I told the battalion chief about the note— it was destroyed, so I couldn't show it to them— and I asked was there any evidence of a firebomb. He said there was a broken bottle—"

"And?" she gasped.

"—and the pieces appeared to have some kerosene residue on them. But it was near the heater. Probably the one I had at my table, and it got blown off. And all the windows were closed."

"Oh," she said, not looking convinced.

"Hey, don't worry," he said. "I'm a big boy. It was just stuff, I can replace it. The important thing's up here." He tapped his forehead. "Come on, pull your chair over. I want to show you what I was getting Friday night."

He drew back his own chair to leave the space open at his right hand. She seemed to approach reluctantly; even so, she fitted into it like . . . like he hoped the Ryerson family room would fit together once he'd recaptured his design.

As he knew he would.

CHAPTER B.9

OUTSIDE THE OFFICE WINDOW, fat flakes drifted down from clouds heavy with more to come. Had there been a white Christmas in Wapato-mekie since he moved here a few years ago? Eric doubted it.

"Good thing we already planned to close up at noon," he commented to Sandy, who was busy with a drawing at her table.

"Really?" she said humorously, her back still to him. "I can just see you, happily snowed in here doing nothing but work."

"Not this time, I'm afraid. Almost finished?"

"Yes . . . in a minute."

He glanced over her shoulder at the perspective she was inking up. "That'll do for now. Sheila isn't expecting to see it till I get back after Christmas."

"You sure?"

"I'm sure. I'm hungry, anyway. Aren't you?"

"Yes." She looked up and smiled. "Funny to think that next year there'll be more people at the Christmas Eve lunch, not just . . . I mean, God willing and the work keeps coming in."

"Which, if I have anything to do with it, it will," he said. "Now, before I forget, here's your year-end bonus check."

She thanked him warmly and put it into her purse.

"Don't thank me; you earned it. But about your Christmas present . . . " He shook his head with regret.

"No, don't worry about it! With your fire I don't expect you to— There's no way you could . . . But anyway, here's yours." She reached into her tote bag and pulled out a tiny box wrapped in parchment paper and a wisp of red ribbon. "I hope you like it."

Inside were a pair of sterling silver Wiener Werkstätte-inspired cuff-links. "For really important client meetings," she explained.

"Thank you. They're beautiful." He smiled. There'd been that time when one of his went missing and he'd had to secure his French cuff with a bent paperclip. "I won't lose these."

"I'm glad you like them. And don't worry about anything for me. I understand, really."

He pretended to look solemn. Her generous attitude dovetailed perfectly with what he was about to do. "Well, I have a thing or two to take care of before we go eat; you probably need to visit the ladies' or something?"

"Oh! Yes, that would be a good idea."

"Take your time. The reservation isn't until 12:30."

She left the room, and Eric dove into the dark corner under his table and pulled out a large flat package wrapped in brown kraft paper. He laid it under her drafting table, stood back to gauge the effect, then pushed it in farther still. When she returned he was busily straightening papers at his end of the throw-off ledge.

"I'm ready," she announced. "Just let me get my coat."

He was ushering her out the door when with studied casualness he glanced back and said, "Wait a minute. You forgot something."

She checked her belongings. "Got my purse . . . We're coming back to the office after, aren't we?"

"Yes, but you left something there, under your table. You might forget later."

"No, I didn't. I—"

"No, there, by your wastebasket. Go see what it is."

"Eric, it isn't mine . . . Oh, all right."

She was getting dust on her long burgundy coat as she stooped down and reached for the package. Was it really fair to do it this way?

Too late now.

"This isn't mine," she said, laying it flat on the conference table.

"It might be. Open it."

Carefully lifting the tape on one end, she slid out the contents. He watched her face as she took it in: a framed reproduction poster of the El Greco painting of the martyred saint he had seen her admire at the exhibition in November.

"See, I said I would get it for you for Christmas."

She wasn't listening. She was again standing as she had that Sunday afternoon, her hands clasped before her, and again her rapt countenance moved him and made him afraid.

For a fleeting moment the expression lasted, then she frowned, just a little, and it was gone.

He coughed, and looked out the window. Yes, they were definitely getting a hard snow. "If you don't like the frame or the color of the mat, tell me. I can have it changed."

"Oh, no, it's perfect! Thank you!" She again looked and sounded like her everyday, professional self. He was relieved.

"Well, I hope you like it. I was in luck; that is, you were: it was still at the framer's last Friday."

"Oh, yes!" She seemed to think a little. "I believe I know just the place for it."

He helped her slide it back into the wrapper.

"But Eric," she said, "you are so sneaky! You really had me thinking that . . . well . . ."

"No," he corrected, "that's what you assumed."

"You're right, I did. But you let me! So, are there any more surprises this afternoon?"

"No— unless you mind trying Chinese instead of French for Christmas Eve lunch. I thought we'd go to the Dragon Palace for a change."

"THE STRANGE THING was, we kept the doors locked and he didn't have a key." Sitting across from Sandy in the red and gold ambiance of the Dragon Palace Restaurant, he was telling her of the time when he was seventeen and discovered his brother Paul was sneaking out of the apartment at night to go skylarking with a young friend. Up to now, the memory had been a grim one, fraught with fear for the nine-year-old and resentment at his father for not being there to deal with it himself. But today he could recall it with affection, even amusement.

"What did your mother say? She must've wanted to tan his hide," she said. "This tea-smoked duck is wonderful, by the way. Have you had some?" She pushed the dish towards him.

"Yes, it's good, isn't it?" He watched as she separated the tender slices into bite-sized pieces. How well she used her chopsticks! Where had she learned? "No, I didn't tell Momma. She had enough on her plate without a worry like that. He always came home. I just couldn't figure out *how*."

"And?" She put down her chopsticks, waiting for him to go on.

"He and Stevie got *too* adventurous. One night they decided to go skiing."

"In Bismarck, North Dakota? I thought that was pretty flat."

"Cross-country. He borrowed Stevie's brother's skis and they fit him so badly, he kept falling over. So the next morning my mother goes to the icebox and it's dripping wet all down the front. She says, 'The ice box is leaking!' So I looked, and hey, what's this? There's Paul's sopping wet coat all bunched up on top of it and the hatch in the wall is standing open!"

"Oh, one of those little doors over the refrigerator they used to deliver groceries through? My apartment has one."

"Yes. It was all up then. Paul had to confess and Momma gave him a paddling. Nothing severe— she never did ... You want any more of the gingered oysters?"

"I'll split them with you," she said. "So did Paul really think no one was going to notice the wet coat?"

"Don't think he thought that far." He laughed. "Guess I was sitting down on him a little hard if he thought he had to sneak out to get any freedom."

"You're not like that now."

"No? And neither is he. Paul the accountant— he's more responsible than I am!"

She responded with a story about the first time she tried to ski. "I'm surprised my rear wasn't one big bruise, I fell down so many times. And that was on the bunny slope! I'm still a beginner, I'm afraid."

"You need to get out on the slopes more," he advised. "I'm sure you'd do great if you did."

She looked at him with friendly skepticism. "Slopes? Around Wapato-mekie? We have some nice hills, but ... "

"Well, someday we—" What was he saying? He'd never go skiing with Sandy Beichten. Still, he couldn't help imagining how she'd look flying down a mountainside. Like a brown-haired sprite.

She hadn't heard him. She was saying, " ... working for you, anyway."

"What'd you say?" he said, startled.

"I said, I have too much work to do to go skiing anyway. But I'm not complaining!" She beamed, and gestured towards the remains of their lunch. "Eric, this was a wonderful idea. Thanks!"

"Did you get enough to eat?"

"Plenty and to spare."

"You take the leftovers. I'm flying out to Boise this afternoon."

That should have been the cue for them to gather their things and leave. But he had no inclination to go. He sat back and began telling her what he and Paul planned to do over Christmas. How satisfying that she was content to linger, too.

"You like take-out boxes?" asked the waiter, stopping by their table.

"Sure, thanks," they said in unison. Amused, he met her eye.

"Here, finish the pepper beef," she said, pushing the dish towards him. "There's not enough to take home."

"Thanks."

He was laying his chopsticks on his plate when, laughing, she said, "Eric, you have sauce on your beard."

"Where, here?" He made an attempt to wipe it away. "Did I get it?"

"No, up higher. There." She pointed.

"Here?"

"No." Taking her napkin and leaning across the table, she cleaned away the errant sauce. As she withdrew her hand, her fingers, just for an instant, stroked the skin of his cheek.

Her touch was fire blazing through him. He couldn't move, or think, or speak. "*L'ardente flamme . . .*"

"Sorry, napkin," he blurted, and bent over to pretend to pick his up. When he sat up again, she was cheerfully talking to the waiter.

Had she touched him on purpose? No. *Even so, shut it down. Now.*

"We've really been too long," he said bluntly. "I don't want to miss my plane, and I'm sure you've got better things to do."

She looked startled. "Oh, yes. Of course. Uh . . . you'll be back in the office Tuesday morning, right?"

He nodded stiffly.

"Okay, I've got plenty to do till then. I'll call you long distance if anything comes up."

"I doubt anything will." Suddenly, it was imperative that he see or hear nothing of her the next four or five days. "When I get back, I'll make sure you know how to negotiate for a car." Her expression remained neutral. "I can go with you to the dealership." If she took that to mean he wanted to make sure she bought one, that was fine with him.

She inclined her head in acquiescence. "That might be helpful."

There was an awkward pause.

"Are you going to open your fortune cookie?" he said at last.

"No," she said, pushing back her chair and picking up her purse, "I'll have it later."

He put his own in his pocket.

He drove her home. They spoke little, and when they did, it was him giving her instructions for while he was gone. Too many, she didn't need them, but something was compelling him to— to do what? Keep her in her place? She took it well, better than he deserved.

By the time he turned the corner onto her street he was ashamed of himself. "Sandy, I— Have a merry Christmas, okay?"

"Sure," she said, her tone committing her to nothing. "You, too."

He pulled up to the curb. Without looking at him, she gathered her things.

"Let me help you with that poster."

She hesitated, then said, "Okay."

They entered the vestibule.

"Can you manage everything by yourself?"

"Of course. I always do. Have a good flight." It was a mere formality. Juggling the framed poster, the bag with the remnants of their lunch, her tote bag, and her purse, she pushed open the inner door and disappeared up the stairs.

ON THE LEG between Portland and Boise, Eric's stomach began to growl. There was no food service and he remembered the fortune cookie he'd dropped into his jacket pocket hours before. He pulled out the fortune, popped the cookie into his mouth, then read the slip of paper:

The wise man recognizes the diamond in the sand

CHAPTER B.10

Late Christmas Day, and the setting sun was painting an ever-changing fresco of color and light on the west face of the Boise Mountains.

From the parking lot of his mother's nursing home, Eric drank in the effect. Such a watercolor palette of scarlets and purples and golds: the sight could wash a man's troubled mind clear so he could think— or fill it so full of beauty he didn't have to think at all.

A week after his fire, and he was having misgivings about the battalion chief's on-scene verdict.

Not that he doubted the man's professionalism. It was more that the night it happened he'd only had time to take a quick glance at his burned-out studio before a fireman shooed him away. It was a black, wet, reeking hole, more stomach-turning than he would let on to, even to Leah. "Total loss in here," the chief said. "What a stink!" said Mr. Price, his landlord, who had arrived at the scene. "My other tenants aren't going to put up with it. Now, if you'll let me clear it out soon as possible . . ." Eric had agreed. But who would have thought that Price would show some diligence for a change? By the time Eric arrived back late the next morning, there was a dump chute rigged up to the north window and most of the studio's charred and soaked contents were in the rented bin below. But what if he could have dried some of the books out? More than that, what if he could have found some clue, some piece of evidence to satisfy him totally that he indeed had left that heater on and the fire didn't stem from anything else?

Stop tormenting yourself. Think of something happy.

Like the good time he had with Sandy yesterday at lunch.

No. Not that. The alpenglow on the mountains— that was beautiful, and safe. That alone deserved his attention just now.

A few steps away, his brother Paul was saying a slow goodbye to his fiancée. "Thanks for coming to visit Momma with us, darling. I know you're anxious to see your family."

"I wanted to come, sweetest," Sophie Lang replied, kissing him again. "In a few months she'll be my mother too, even if she can't really get to know me."

A nice girl, Sophie. Too bad his brother wanted to ruin her life for her.

"I think she recognizes you," Paul said in that rapturous tone Eric had never heard him use till today. "She brightens up when she sees you, I've noticed that before."

"Oh, have you? I'm glad!"

"Anyone would be happy to see *you*."

The engaged couple nuzzled and kissed. Eric turned away. His mother had not recognized him. She hadn't treated him like a stranger. It had been much worse. She'd mistaken him for Poppa.

"Norrie!" she'd cried out as he entered the room. "Where have you been?" And she'd stretched out her arms to welcome him.

He couldn't not give her a hug, but as he'd tentatively put his arms around her he'd said, "No, Momma, it's Eric. Your son."

She had ignored the correction. "Norrie!" she'd said again, and as he'd tried to kiss her cheek, her lips had made for his mouth. They'd met the corner of his mustache as he and his mother collided in an awkward, embarrassing clinch; embarrassing to him only, for she'd remained unconscious of her mistake.

"Norrie, when did you grow that beard? I don't like it." She'd gotten increasingly upset until Sophie had come forward and distracted her.

The "Reverend" *Norbert E. Baumann, some husband* he *was,* Eric thought now. That Momma could remember his father with love made him sick. Just as well the old man had gone off somewhere years ago and they hadn't heard from him since.

Eric eased his heart again with the view of the mountains.

> I lift up mine eyes to the hills;
> from whence cometh my help?

Where had *that* emerged from? Some psalm or other. He should have expected it, after visiting Momma.

Still, the hills were a help. He watched till the rose and vermilion faded to mauve then went dark as the last of the sun's rays disappeared. He turned around. Skimming the trees, an old moon hung in the western sky, the mere paring of a fingernail just visible in the growing dark.

"Eric," Paul said.

"What?"

"Say goodbye to Sophie. She has to get over to her aunt's."

"Oh, sorry. I was . . . Sophie, I'm glad to finally meet you. Paul didn't tell me half the good things about you he should have."

"And not half the bad?" she teased.

"Well, since half of zero is zero . . ."

"Good gracious, Paul, you didn't tell me your brother was such a ladies' man."

"He isn't," Paul said, playfully punching him in the ribs. "He's a clod of the first order."

"Don't listen to him, Sophie. He's always been a brat. You're coming skiing with us tomorrow?"

"I'll be over bright and early."

Eric stood with his hands in his coat pockets while his brother gave his fiancée one last kiss good night. After she drove away, Paul turned to him with a wide grin and said, "Well, what do you think?"

"It's what I said before, brat. You don't deserve that girl."

"I know!" Paul said. "That's why I love her! Come on, let's go home."

PAUL RETURNED to the living room, pulling the tab off a can of beer. "Are you all right?" he asked him.

"All right about what?" Eric had been sprawled at his ease on the sofa with his own can of Coors, but the question made him sit up straight.

"Your fire."

"Oh, that." Not what happened in their mother's room. He relaxed.

"Yeah, that. How can you be so casual about it?"

"These things happen." And if it was more than happenstance, his little brother didn't need to know.

Paul shook his head and looked entirely too skeptical. "Don't you think there's something basically creepy about a fire? The damage it does . . ." He gestured around his living room, at the second-hand furniture and the lopsided plastic Christmas tree that had been even more pathetic before Eric and Sophie had rearranged the ornaments on it a few hours before.

"My house isn't much, and I don't go in for art like you do, but if I lost it all in a fire, I'd be devastated."

"I didn't lose everything," Eric corrected him. "I'll need to spend a good chunk of change getting the smoke smell out, but the things in the living room and my bedroom should be okay."

"Including Grandma Schmidt's rocker?"

"Including that. Nothing I can't cope with."

"You sure? Something's eating you. Why not tell me what it is?"

He hesitated. Hadn't it always been his job to shield Paul from trouble? "Well, all right. They told me it was accidental. But my gut tells me they could be wrong."

"You mean arson? What makes you think so?"

"Long story."

Paul motioned with his beer for him to continue.

"It's like this. This past September a guy I didn't know showed up in my office. I can't legally say anything about the project he wanted me to design, the NDA is still in effect. What I can tell you is . . ."

" . . . SO THAT'S THE PROBLEM," he concluded. "I need to find out where our Mr. Hardt is in case anything like this comes up again. But I don't know his address from a hole in the ground."

For a moment his brother looked as if he'd been struck silly. Then he shook his head like a dog coming in out of the rain and said, "Sorry, I was thinking. Didn't your detective say your boy has a literal hole in the ground?"

"What?"

"That gold mine in the Dakotas. Why not track him down there? His people there could tell you where he hangs out. He has to have someone to run that operation for him, doesn't he?"

"Great idea— if I knew what mine and where."

Paul grinned. "That's where I come in. Our firm handles the accounting for several big mining firms. Idaho, Montana, the Dakotas. One of our clients might know something. You want me to ask around?"

Did he? At the office, at least, things were going well. If he had Hardt's address, he'd have to follow up. It'd cost time and money. It might stir up trouble. On the other hand, if anything else bad happened . . . "Sure, go ahead. I don't have the money to use the information right away, but yeah. It'd be good to pin him down, just in case."

"Okay. Other than that, anything I can do?"

"Got a couple thousand you can loan me?"

Paul shook his head and half-grinned.

"Yeah, I figured," Eric said, smiling ruefully. "I've got the cost of cleanup and a boatload of books and equipment to replace. That fire couldn't have come at a worse time."

"Any savings?"

"Yes— for expanding the office; I'm taking two more rooms as of the first of the year, and they'll need to be furnished. And some padding for the new salaries to tide us over until I can start billing out the work. But now . . . Damn, it'll be tight."

"Credit cards?"

"No. I asked my accountant about opening a business line of credit, and he recommended I wait."

"I agree with him. You need to be on a more solid footing. So no personal credit card, either."

"No."

"It would have come in handy." He shrugged. "Well, you'll get by without it. You're good at making do."

"I'll be eating a lot of beans," said Eric. "No, check that. I don't want to drive away the clients and the new employees."

Paul hooted. "What about the one you've got?"

"Oh, she puts up with me regardless." Eric grinned and took a pull of his beer. "I really will be getting by with a little help from my friends, as the song goes . . . When I go home Monday night, I'll be staying with the McCulloughs till the landlord finishes redoing the apartment. He says by mid-month, so it shouldn't be long. And he isn't charging me rent till I'm back in. So I'll manage."

Paul raised his can in salute. "More power to you. I'll let you know as soon as I find anything out."

"Thanks. No hurry— I've got to concentrate on that manufacturing plant once the new year begins."

"Put your head down and focus?"

Eric laughed. "Yeah. Something like that."

CHAPTER B.11

THEY HAD EXCELLENT SKIING the next day, and thanks to the guest discount that came with Paul's resort membership, Eric could enjoy the fresh powder with a good conscience. Now, sitting with him and Sophie in the lodge's atrium lounge, he was treating himself to an overpriced but very satisfying drink.

He settled his happily-fatigued body deeper into the big leather-upholstered chair and contemplated the high, lacquered-wood cathedral ceiling. This lounge was a good space, protective and uplifting at the same time. The mountain view outside the two-storey, south-facing window wall was so perfect it seemed to have emerged from some artist's imagination, and the architect had made sure to specify semi-sheer drapes to filter out the sun when it got too hot. Electronically controlled, he noted with approval.

He took a sip of his whiskey and brandy-laced hot coffee. "So, when are you and Paul getting married?" he asked Sophie, feeling indulgent.

"Not till next Christmas. Or early in '83. We're not sure."

"So he's being slippery?" He darted his brother a significant half-smile.

"Oh, no!" Sophie defended him. "We're working around my family's schedules. And the weather, I'm afraid."

"Yes," said Paul, answering Eric's look with one that clearly warned him not to reopen the marriage debate, "there are more Langs than Baumanns to consider. Which is why *you*, old man, need to toe the line and do your part to build the family back up. What does Leah say?"

"Right now," he said cheerfully, "she'd say I should keep out of her hair and let her run her business."

"Oh, yes, the cookware shop!" said Sophie. "Tell me more about it."

They discussed Leah's new store for a while, and Eric made a mental note to be a good sport and buy them something there for a wedding present.

"It sounds like she's a lot like you, Eric," Sophie commented. "Very dedicated."

"She is. Which is why I don't think . . . No, you'll just have to put up with me as the bachelor uncle."

Paul seemed about to protest, but Sophie broke in, musing. "Yes . . . two dedicated people won't necessarily work out, if they're dedicated to different things.

"Eric," she went on, "I admire you. Don't worry, Paul knows what I mean. He loves accounting, but it's not the same, is it? Architecture is something a person can really get into. More than a job, really. Almost something spiritual. It's like you don't need anyone else. I'm glad Paul is just an ordinary boring accountant." She leaned over and gave her ordinary boring accountant fiancé a kiss.

So he, Eric, was some kind of secular monk? He thought of Leah and smiled inwardly. Not hardly.

But their last time together . . . His attitude sobered. He didn't seem to need her the way he used to. Maybe Sophie was onto something. Maybe his work *was* enough.

Then, without prelude or invitation, he seemed again to feel Sandy's fingers soft on his face only two days before. He trembled a little at the memory, then shook his head.

"You disagree?" asked Paul.

"Not at all. Sophie, you're probably right. Now, how about those conditions on Bullnose Run? I thought they were a little rough, but maybe that was just me being out of practice."

He directed the conversation safely back to the day's skiing. Fates willing, he wouldn't be confronted with his work *versus* his personal relationships again during this visit.

❖

"I'VE BEEN THINKING about something," said his brother that evening.

They were in Paul's kitchen, putting together turkey sandwiches for supper. "Thinking is good," Eric said, not paying attention. He was rooting through the cabinets. "Where's the hot sauce, anyway?"

"Right there." Paul pointed to an appalling object sitting on the counter. It looked like a melted version of the Eiffel Tower with a spout protruding from the top. "We got it in Paris."

Eric didn't believe it. The French could never come up with anything so vile.

"About what Sophie said, about how dedicated you are to architecture."

"Hmm." The subject wasn't worth pursuing.

They took their food to the living room and settled down in front of the TV. There was nothing on worth watching. Eric could have put up with that: watching television at all was a rare indulgence, and indulge himself he would.

But Paul turned the set off. "Really," he said. "I've been thinking about it. You are."

"I am what?"

"Dedicated to architecture. Lock, stock, and barrel."

"So?" He went on eating his sandwich.

"It's been on my mind the past few weeks, since you tried to convince me not to marry Sophie."

"Really?"

"Really. You were being the enlightened feminist guy and laying down this line about marriage not being fair to women and cramping their style and all. But it has more to do with Poppa than you think. And Momma as well."

"Well, of course it does. Didn't I remind you of how Poppa treated her? Hell, he wouldn't even have her and us with him on the reservation."

"That was Momma's idea," Paul said flatly.

"What?" Eric stopped chewing in mid-bite. "You're kidding me!"

"I'm not," Paul said. "When I was twelve, after you got drafted and went to 'Nam, I heard him asking her if she'd be willing to go. She smiled real big and said she would, once the weather got warmer. Then he came home in the spring and she said maybe they should wait till I finished junior high. And then it was 'Wait till Paul graduates from high school.' He was unhappy about it every time, but she said she wanted to come and one day she would."

"Poppa? You're telling me he actually cared?"

"He sounded like he did. But Momma, after he went back to the mission, she'd tell me he was crazy to ask her, the reservation was dirty and smelly and she wasn't living there and she wished he'd stop asking her to."

"I don't believe it." He smiled confidently as he said it, but he put his plate down on the coffee table and wandered over to the window.

"It's true," Paul said. "She said she had no calling to be a missionary's wife and she wasn't about to work herself to death among savages for no pay."

"She had something there," Eric commented. "The no pay part, I mean." He parted the drapes and looked out into the darkness. On the other side of town sat their mother, confined to that nursing home, and never could she tell him if this was true.

"Yes, but don't you see?" insisted Paul. "It isn't all marriage, it was *their* marriage."

Eric turned to face him. "Even if you're remembering something real"— his brother stirred a little, as if to object— "and let's say you are, you can't defend what else the institution of marriage let him get away with."

"Like what?"

"Like . . . " Like when Lou-Lou died? But perhaps his mother bore as much responsibility for that as his father did? She could have done more to get his sister the care she needed; was it pride that kept her from asking? Or resentment at his father, kind of a "See what you made me do?" Would Momma have been willing to let her daughter die to express it?

The idea made him physically sick and he shut it out. No, never while Momma was unable to answer such a charge would he entertain it.

"Like . . . Like suppressing her singing career," he answered instead.

Paul shrugged. "She might have been that good, she might not. If she'd tried it he might have pushed her too hard and exploited her talent and that would have been bad, too. Their marriage was what they made of it. Don't write off a good thing because of one bad example."

"If you say so," said Eric, not conceding the point. "You want another beer as long as I'm up?"

"Sure."

He pulled a couple from the refrigerator, handed a can to his brother, and sat back down. "I'm not— I mean, I'm willing to believe you and Sophie are a good team. Maybe you'll be better off together. But I still don't think marriage is a good idea."

"For everybody or for you?"

"In principle."

"Are you sure? Sophie said it: you're dedicated to your career. Maybe you *are* being smart just to focus on that and not tie up a woman in it. But I think it's something else hanging you up. I think you're scared."

"What?"

"Yes, scared." Paul leaned towards him in challenge, the same stubborn look on his face that sometimes made Eric want to punch him as a teenager.

He glared back. "You're nuts. I'm not afraid of anything."

"Sure you are. You're afraid you'll find out you're just like Poppa."

"What?" he growled. "Just like *Poppa?*"

"No, no," Paul placated him. "I don't mean in everything. I mean you're afraid that if you got married you'd be just like him, the way he sacrificed everything to his work."

"It's not the same at all! With architecture I've got something real, worth sacrificing for! Poppa's religion was nothing but fantasy!" He snorted in disdain. "He should have left those people alone. We all would have been better off."

"Maybe so. But didn't Poppa believe as much in Christianity as you do in architecture?"

"He *said* he did." Eric shrugged. "He was willing to sacrifice us to it, at any rate."

"So I'm thinking you're afraid you might be the same way with architecture, and if you got married you might sacrifice your wife and kids to it like Poppa did us."

Eric refused to answer. He picked up the *TV Guide,* leafed through it, and put it down again. He took up the newspaper. Special Christmas edition from yesterday, with a two-page photo spread on local Nativity pageants.

Paul's eyes didn't let him go. "Or maybe," he said, his tone daring, *"maybe* you think a wife and kids would cramp *your* style."

"Damn you, brat! What business is that of yours?"

He's right, you know, said that interfering inner voice. *That's what you like about Leah. She doesn't want to get all that involved, either.*

"So maybe you *should* swear off marriage," Paul said, not rising to the insult. "But it'd be the same if you were just living with a girl, wouldn't it?"

"Or we could just date and have our own places. Like with Leah."

"So how's that working out, again? Women are funny. They expect things— like us being there for them."

Yeah, Leah expected that from him— usually just when he was coming up with the perfect design solution. True, that one time may have saved his life, but in general . . .

"Maybe." Eric stood and rubbed the back of his neck. "Not saying you're right, but suppose. I'm kind of stuck, aren't I?"

He was not cut out for the celibate life. He could deal with it for a while, if he was really involved in a project. But not forever. What was the alternative? A long string of one-night stands? Nauseating.

"Not necessarily," Paul said. "Maybe you're going after the wrong kind of girl."

"Wrong kind—? Hold on there, brat. There's nothing wrong with Leah Matthews."

"I don't mean 'wrong' like that. I mean, maybe you need a woman who's as much into architecture as you are. And if things are cooling off with Leah . . . "

He began to protest, then stopped. "Cooling off," maybe that was the right way to put it. Lately, Leah and he . . . No, before that. Things had started to go flat when he'd opened the office a year and a half ago. Time and again she'd be talking as if his work in architecture was just a job. If he'd been content to remain an employee at Richardson & Greene, the flame might be there still. And lately when he did want her, she was never around.

"Leah and I go way back," he retorted nevertheless. "We'll work something out."

"Maybe you will," said Paul. "But if you can't, maybe next time you should look for a girl in your own field. You still know women from your old employer, don't you? Ask one of them out sometime. Or find a nice girl at one of your architects' meetings."

"Guess I could," he said, keeping his tone noncommittal. But at his brother's words his imagination ran over the female architects he knew from R & G, past the ones he encountered at AIA events, and came to rest on the petite brown-haired woman who labored back to back with him in his own office.

No. Don't ruin a good thing.

"Maybe," he said. "We'll see."

CHAPTER B.12

FUNNY *HOW THINGS TURNED OUT*, Sandy reflected the Tuesday after New Year's. She'd dreaded having to drive a car of her own to work, and so far it wasn't half bad. Enjoyable, in fact.

True, it was only her second day, but it was nice not to have to stand shivering in the cold at the bus stop. With his home studio still out of commission, Eric was doing all his drawing in the office. And it wasn't as if he could give her a ride anyway. He often had to leave early to meet with clients or stayed downtown deep into the evening to get more drawing done.

He'd been back from Idaho for a week, and she still had no idea what had been eating him towards the end of their Christmas Eve lunch. Something to do with the office that he didn't want to burden her with? Delayed reaction to his apartment fire? Whatever it was, he'd returned in a good, if thoughtful, mood. Last Wednesday he'd initiated her into the mysteries of used-car buying (she'd already made a study of the *Kelley Blue Book* over Christmas), and the next day, the afternoon of New Year's Eve, they'd gone to the lot together to do the deed. Good timing: the dealer was eager to get all the vehicles he could off the lot before the end of the year, and she was now the owner of a very affordable, decent 1979 Honda Civic. Just how decent she knew because she'd taken it to Eric's mechanic on Saturday to be checked out. He'd made the dealer put a line in the sales agreement saying she could bring it back if it turned out to be a lemon.

Eric rotated his chair her way. He said, "Sandy?"

"Yes?"

"You're enjoying having your car?"

Funny, he was thinking about it, too. She smiled. "Yes, actually, I am."

"Good, because I need you to pick up some meetings for me this week."

"What's up?"

"I have to go out of town again. Tonight."

Her heart took a sudden plunge.

Sandy, don't. "Okay, let me know when and where. Where the meetings are, I mean." She hesitated. "Where *are* you off to?"

"To Pierre, South Dakota, and then to Deadwood."

"In the dead of winter? How come?"

"My brother called last night. He's found out about the mine Nick Hardt owns up there. The White Star, it's called."

Oh, blast, Nick Hardt again. She'd been so hoping he was out of their lives for good. "You're not going to— I mean— "

Eric laughed. "I'm not going to challenge him to atom bombs at twenty paces, if that's what you're imagining. He's probably not even up there. But Paul has put up the money for the plane ticket and I agree with him— even if I can't talk to him— Hardt, that is— I need to pin him down somehow. I just need to find out where we stand with all this. You understand."

She did. "Okay, don't worry, I'll take care of things here. Isn't that what associates do? When will you be back?"

"Friday afternoon. I can't be away any longer." He put some papers into his portfolio. "Let's do this," he said, latching it with a determined click. "My plane's due back in Wapatomekie at 2:45. You take the bus in, Friday morning. I'll try to get into the office by 4:30; we'll grab supper at the Dine Time and I'll let you know what I find out."

No, she couldn't possibly mistake a burger at the Dine Time Diner for a hot date— as if a hot date was what she should want with him anyway. "All right. Now who do I need to wrestle into submission these next few days?"

"Two subcontractors, a consulting engineer, and a granite supplier. Bring your calendar over here and we'll get it all down."

As she made note of the appointments, a piece of her brain wondered if Eric's trip north would prove to be nothing but a wild goose chase. But he was right: They needed to know where they stood.

LEAVING ASIDE the fact that Eric was out of the office, her Friday was going quite well. The design development drawings for the Ryerson family room were coming together, and that morning she'd had a successful meeting with the electrical sub on the Weisman house.

Around 3:50 the phone rang.

"Sandy? It's Eric."

"Hi, where are you?" It was too quiet to be the airport.

"At home. I mean, the McCulloughs'." His voice was tired, even subdued. "Listen, I've got a message here that DeeDee wants me to come see her about some urgent matter this afternoon."

Why hadn't Mrs. Weisman called her about whatever it was?

"She should have called you," he said, and her heart did a flip. "She expects me at the job site at 4:15 so I guess I'd better move. I'll try to get downtown by 5:20 at the latest. You don't mind, do you?"

"No, of course not. I have plenty to do."

"All right." There was silence on the line and for a moment she thought he had hung up. Then he said, "I can't go into this now, but I think you should know."

Her heart caught in her throat. "What is it?"

"I talked to his partner at the mine yesterday evening, and we don't have to worry about Nick Hardt anymore. He's dead."

SHE DID have plenty to do. She thanked God she had plenty to do. Her mood was swinging from relief, to guilt at feeling relieved, to sadness that the man had most likely died in his sins, and back to a perverse joy that he was getting what he deserved— which made her feel guilty all over again.

It had been some kind of car accident, sometime in November. That's all Eric had had time to tell her; he'd fill in the details this evening.

> *High King of heaven, my victory won,*
> *May I reach heaven's joys, O bright heaven's Son!*

Nick Hardt wouldn't have that to look forward to. She wouldn't have it either, she reminded herself soberly, were it not for God's own grace. She doubled down on the detail for the Ryersons' pull-out TV.

Awhile later, she stretched and looked out the window. The gray afternoon light was fading. In less than thirty minutes Eric would be there and she would learn just how Hardt had met his end.

On the sill Corb the mechanical dog lay half hidden by tracing paper.

"Oh, Corb, have we been neglecting you? Here."

She wound up the toy and let it gambol and bark its way through the debris on the throw-off shelf. "Not exactly in time with the radio …" But it did her heart good to watch it go. "That's all for now. I have a drawing to finish up."

But 5:20 came and Eric didn't appear. She hadn't really expected him to be on time. 5:30 passed with no sign of him. She shrugged and smiled to herself. DeeDee had likely thought of ten more things she needed to discuss. But he would be in at any minute. He wouldn't want to wait to give her all the news.

A few minutes later, she looked at the clock and frowned. Fifteen till six and blast him, he still hadn't shown his face. But why should she feel angry? It wasn't like he was making her stay past her ordinary working hours. The supper meeting she was looking forward to was only about their professional lives. What was her gripe?

Maybe just that she'd finished the task she was working on and now she had to gear herself up to shift to something else, with no idea how much time she could devote to it . That would frustrate anybody.

Why couldn't Eric tell DeeDee he had another appointment and just go?

The linoleum floor around her table was sprinkled with eraser crumbs and the janitor didn't come in on Friday nights. Sweeping it would give her something brainless to do.

It took extra work to get all the debris out of the broken spot in a tile a little behind her chair. They really ought to get that repaired, with new people coming.

Still, good enough for now.

She stashed the broom and dustpan back behind the tall file cabinet and sighed. No Eric still.

You know how he is. You may as well go home.

Her tote bag was packed up; the radio was off. The phone rang.

"Eric, hello!" She couldn't keep the joy and relief out of her voice. "Where are you?"

"At the Weismans'. Their old house, not the job site. Sandy, I'm afraid I can't make it this evening."

But you promised!

"I'm really tired," he went on, "and Sol's asked me to stay for supper. I'll fill you in on South Dakota on Monday, all right?"

No, it's not all right. Why do I always come second? But that was foolish. He paid her salary, didn't he? He was the ideal boss, wasn't he? He could arrange his schedule any way he wanted. If she was really loving him as her neighbor, this was her chance to prove it. "Sure, don't worry about it. Anything I can do for you before I leave?"

"Actually, um, there is." At least he had the decency to sound embarrassed. "Could you call down to the management office and see if they'll hold the print room open so you can run off two more sets of the Weisman working drawings?"

"I can do that. What's up?"

"Oh"— She could hear the eye-roll in his voice— "just before we left the site, DeeDee mentioned they're throwing a party Sunday evening, some kind of premature housewarming or sneak peek or something. She thought they'd take the guests through the construction, but Bill put his foot down. So she's making do with two more sets of their house plans. Bound, of course."

"Of course. Did you tell her she'd better invite you?"

He dropped his voice. "She did. I'm trying to get out of it."

"Oh. Well."

"They should invite you, too," he said, moodily. "I'm really sorry about this. I've cancelled out on you and now I'm telling you you have to stay later. You want to get out of there."

"It's all right," she reassured him, delighted that she'd gotten her head on straight and could say that sincerely. "Anything to keep the clients happy. It's part of the job."

"You're sure? You won't be stranded downtown?"

"Of course not. I can get the bus at 6:40 if I'm done and there's two more after that."

"Oh. Okay. I'll swing by tomorrow and pick up the sets. Roll them up and leave them in a tube on my table."

"Two tubes, more like it." She laughed.

"Yeah, probably. Thanks. I'm sorry to— I really appreciate it."

She glanced at the clock. Seven minutes to 6:00. "I'd better hang up so I can call downstairs. See you Monday. Bye!"

Yes, the management office would trust her with the print room key. Just drop it through their letter slot before she went home.

She sang as she pulled the tracings from the drawer. Funny, she was remembering a fifth verse of the hymn, one she'd learned only when she and her mother had visited Scotland the summer after her college graduation.

> *Be Thou my breastplate, my sword for the fight,*
> *Be Thou my whole armor and Thou my true might,*
> *Be Thou my soul's shelter and Thou my high tower,*
> *Raise Thou me heavenward, great Power of my power.*

The construction documents were exquisitely drawn, if she did say so herself. Only a time or two had Bill Worthington spotted an error in them, and he had an eagle's eye for a mistake.

She penciled the date— *8 Jan. 1982*— onto the twenty-four sheets. That was more than some firms devoted to whole office buildings. It had been worth it: the house stood an excellent chance of winning them a design award in next summer's AIA competition. And after that? Fame, publicity, more clients . . . ?

By the time she ran all the tracings through the diazo machine in the sub-basement and brought everything back upstairs, it was nearly 6:30. No way she was going to make that 6:40 bus. She laid the ammonia-suffused whiteprints on the throw-off shelf and slid the tracings over to the side, ready to be put back into the drawer. But now there was no hurry.

"Well, Corb, you're going to be keeping me company awhile longer." She gave the toy a good winding and watched it gyrate a few seconds till it came to a rest against her compass case. "All run down? I can't make that excuse. I still have work to do."

On the other hand, the call of nature was suddenly insistent. She was thirsty as well. Taking her water glass, she headed out to the restroom.

CHAPTER B.13

There was always something a little eerie about the seventh floor of their building after hours on a Friday night, especially if Eric wasn't there with her. Tonight, as usual, everyone else on the floor had gone home an hour ago, but the atmosphere felt vigilant, even taut. If she believed in ghosts, she thought as she returned from the ladies' room, she'd say she was being watched.

The office door. Didn't I pull it shut when I went to the john?

It was just slightly open now, and she had the impression someone was inside, though with the Venetian blinds on its window closed she couldn't see.

Don't be silly. No one's there.

Wait. There *was* someone inside, making a noise. Eric? she thought, her hope rising absurdly. Taking great care (and mocking herself for taking it), she eased open the door.

A broad-bodied man in a grimy nylon ski jacket stooped with his back to her, rummaging through their file cabinet, half its contents already on the floor.

"What?" she cried out in spite of herself. "Who are you?"

Startled, he turned towards her. It was a stranger, his face burnt and creased by the sun, with yellow, crooked teeth. He looked stupid and slow; with any luck she could make it to the stairs before he was halfway down the hall. She stepped backwards into the corridor and turned to flee. But with surprising quickness he darted through the door and seized her by the wrist, sending her water glass shattering to the terrazzo. She gasped as he yanked her inside, kicked the door closed, and extinguished the overhead lights.

"Oh, this is a peach," he exulted in a voice like stickleburrs drowned in honey. "It sure is a peach!"

"What? No!"

"I got help now. You're goin' to help me, sweetheart, yes, you are."

Don't get sick, Sandy. Don't get sick.

He pulled her to him like a partner in a vicious dance. He smelled of flatulence and cheap cigarettes, and the odor reminded her of a fart joke she'd heard in second grade.

Oh, heavens, she was thinking of that now?

"Heh— help you?"

He gave her arm a twist.

It wasn't happening. Not again.

Jeff. Don't think of Jeff. Think of Larry and Mark; think of annoying teenaged brothers wrestling with their little sister. She could break their holds; she could break his. Just a quick, hard twirl of the wrist, out, around, and out again, and—

"Oh no, you don't!" the man snarled. Swinging her around, he flung her into her chair. It skidded back till it hit the edge of the throw-off shelf with a bang; if he hadn't followed and grabbed her arm again she would have tumbled to the floor. "I pegged you for a real cooperative little girl, sweetheart, but it looks like I'll have to learn you to mind your manners!" He struck her a blow across the face, sending a spearing pain through her neck as it snapped to the side.

I won't cry. I won't. I won't give him that. O Jesus, help me!

He yanked her drafting lamp over so it glared down on them like a spotlight. In a daze of disbelief, she watched him draw a large, folded knife and a length of cord from his jacket pocket. It was such a filthy pocket in such a filthy coat; somehow that made it worse. She tried to stand. He punched her in the gut, forcing her back into the chair. Bent over in pain, trying to catch her breath, she could put up no resistance as he doubled her left arm behind her back and tied it to the upright metal bar that supported the backrest of the chair. Once he'd wound the long end of the cord tightly around her body and made the knot secure, he hooked Eric's chair with his foot and sat down in it, his knees touching hers. He tightened his hold on her right arm, flicked the knife open, and held it up close to her face.

"Now," he said, "we can talk. Tell me what I wanta know and you go free, okay, sweetheart? All you gotta do is tell me where Cole Rutherford's setting up his operation. How many men you building for? How far along has he gotten?"

This wasn't real. It was a play. A play, like the ones she used to act in in high school.

"C— C— Cole Rutherford? I don't know any Cole Rutherford!"

"Don't give me that shit!" He struck her again, and the metal of a ring he wore grazed her cheek. "You know, all right!"

Don't panic. Don't panic. Say all your lines right, it'll be okay. Think of something. Stall him. Anything!

"You— you want to kn— know about one of our clients?"

"That's right, sweetheart. A real important client. Thinks he's too important for Al McNair. I'll learn him he can't shut me out. No sirree. I'll find out what he's up to, 'cause you're going to tell me!"

She fought down the wild panic rising within her. "You don't mean Nick Hardt? He's dead!"

He drew back. For a long moment he gaped at her. Then the fist with the knife in it slammed into her cheekbone, the blade barely missing her eye. "Don't try me, bitch," he snarled. "Don't you distract me with no Mick Harts!"

"Please believe me, we don't have any client named Cole Rutherford!"

"You little liar!" He squeezed her wrist till she cried out in pain. "I got me a reliable source that says you do!"

"You— Mr. McNair—" Some ridiculous idea had entered her mind that if she showed him respect, they could settle this like civilized human beings. "You can check our files. We don't!"

"Oh, I was doin' that. But I'd rather find out *this way!*" Wrenching her to him violently, he pressed the blade to her throat.

God help her, she was going to die, a martyr to a stupid mistake. A stupid, damnfoolish mistake, and she couldn't do a thing about it.

Or could she? Pinned against a counter's edge ten years ago, she'd found herself a knife. Her tormenter had one; there had to be a knife for her, too. Only a craft knife, only a one-inch X-Acto blade. But razor sharp. It'd been enough the last time. She could make it be enough again. She could distract him and get it. Where was it? Where *was* it! Yes, there it lay, open, ready . . . O heavens! open, ready, and out of reach on Eric's parallel bar!

A scream was powering up from her gut like magma from a volcano; the scream that couldn't come that night Jeff had violated her body in the basement of the architecture building; the scream she must not let emerge now. No one would hear her. For all she knew, she and McNair were alone in the building. If she screamed, she would die.

Her tormenter glanced around. "Nice cozy little office ya'll got here." His insinuating drawl infested the room with unseen cockroaches. "All the way down this nice, empty hallway. You and Baumann probably have a real nice time in here. A real *nice* time." From between the creased lids his hard little eyes leered at her and she saw in them Jeff Chesters' lascivious gaze, so ugly in its false beauty.

She wouldn't look at him. She wouldn't let him look at her. She bent her head down, trying to hide it in her shoulder. But the man jerked her back by the hair and forced her to meet his eyes.

"A real nice time," he repeated. His blade pressed against the skin of her throat. "Me and you don't wanta miss out on the fun, do we?" He winked grotesquely. "Pity you're so puny. I like me a gal with more meat on her. But that won't stop us, will it, sweetheart? All cats are gray in the dark . . . "

His reeky breath hot against her cheek, he reached under her skirt and began to stroke her thigh. "You like that, don't you?"

On reflex her right hand, now free, reached out to grab that violating arm, to yank it away from her. But before she could grasp him, he brought the butt of the knife down hard on her wrist bone, paralyzing her with the pain.

"Don't you touch me, sweetheart!" He gave a cruel chuckle. "You'll do that later, the way *I* like. Now keep still!"

Her arm hanging throbbing and useless at her side, the knife again at her gullet, she bit her lip to hold back the fatal scream. *Be Thou my breastplate, be Thou my breastplate!* Oh, that she could go berserk, flail out at him, at Jeff in the past, at her own helplessness! Even now she could kick and bite and bathe the room and everything in it in her blood and his— and everything in her was focussed on not letting that happen. If she let herself go, she would bleed and she alone.

"You like that!" he repeated, his left hand kneading the flesh of her leg as he pressed the knife's edge to her windpipe. "Right?"

"No. I don't know!" Her voice came out high, strangled, ludicrous, an object of shame. She tried to conceive of Eric's being there, of his strength making everything sane and sensible once more, but he was distant and unreal, like a song whose words she could never recall.

Her assailant gave her thigh another squeeze and withdrew his hand. "Well, that's just a taste, sweetheart. We want to leave the best for last, don't we?" He grabbed her right wrist again, so she winced with the pain.

"Now fess up about Cole Rutherford!"

Detach, Sandy, detach. Breathe. Breathe!

Was she the girl in pain, sitting there half tied up with her breath coming "huh-uh-uh-uh, huh-uh-uh-uh"? The one who wasn't crying only because she was petrified of what would happen if she did? Was she the terrified woman again trapped in a little room with a man who meant only evil, who wouldn't stop till he'd worked his evil on her?

It had nothing to do with her. So many other things were so much more important and her matter-of-fact brain registered them all. The graphite smudge on her right shirt sleeve. The hairy mole on her assailant's forehead. The racket the steam radiator was making under the windows. The acrid scent of the whiteprints behind her. The slat high on the door's Venetian blinds that was tilted cockeyed. The floor where the corner of the linoleum tile had broken out.

I really should patch that.

She considered that she might pray, but all the prayers had been said long ago and it was the time for answers, whether she liked them or not.

The man was speaking, his voice more stickleburrs than honey. "Fuck you, don't toy with me! You know about Cole Rutherford and you're goin' to tell me, now!"

"I— I— I—"

"You're going to take some convincing, huh?" He looked over her right shoulder at the Weisman tracings lying behind her on the throw-off shelf. He moved around to where he could reach them. "These are real purty drawings," he singsonged, turning up one sheet after the other, "real purty. You do 'em?"

Cursing herself for it, she nodded her head yes.

He let the tracings fall back to the counter and grasped her right wrist more tightly than before. "You do 'em with this hand?"

She opened her eyes wide at the implication.

"Well, I figure you won't be much use to Baumann or anybody else if you can't do them purty drawings. No right hand and you're on the trash heap— or dead." His lips contorted in a sickening grin.

Sweet Jesus, no. Evil like that couldn't exist.

But against all reason, it did. He unbuttoned her shirt cuff and the fact he didn't just rip it open magnified the horror. He rolled it up, exposing the winter-white flesh just above the palm, and held the knife there, barely touching it.

"Now tell me about Cole Rutherford." He pressed the edge harder against her wrist. *"Tell me about Cole Rutherford!"*

She stared at him, speechless.

"All right, bitch, all right." And slowly, calmly, methodically, he drew the razor-sharp blade across the blue-veined skin of her right wrist, shallowly, almost delicately. A red thread followed in its wake, widening to a ribbon as the blood oozed forth from the wound.

That's going to hurt like all get-out later.

Blood was dripping on her skirt. And on the floor. She'd have to clean it up before Eric saw it. That tile certainly did need to be fixed . . .

"See, bitch, I mean it!" he said, slapping her again. "It'll be deeper next time, I guarantee it!" Once more he dug his fingers into her hair and turned her face to his. A hellish light dawned in his eyes. "Oh, I know how to make you talk. I know now."

A sick sharp ache bit at the cut, but it was nothing to the pain that tore through her shoulder as he wrenched her right arm back so her hand and wrist hung over the throw-off ledge. The blood, her blood, was overflowing, dripping, running down, staining everything under it with red.

"Thou shalt not bleed on the drawings."

That had been a joke in architecture school, but now—

"Oh dear God, the tracings!" she exclaimed, reflexively jerking her arm in towards him. As she and the chair whirled sideways, her left elbow hit her compass case.

"BARK-BARK-BARK! YIP-YIP! ARF-ARF-ARF-ARF! BARK-BARK-BARK-YIP-YIP-YIP!"

McNair jumped back. Eyes screwed shut, Sandy sensed rather than saw some object swinging through the air. She flailed up with her bloody right hand to protect herself. Something gave a hollow *clunk!* then a *crack!* and a heavy weight thudded to the floor.

She opened her eyes. Eric was kneeling next to her assailant, whose body lay sprawled on the linoleum that so badly needed repair.

CHAPTER B.14

"ᴇRIC. ERIC, STOP."

His fist seemed to have a will of its own. He drew it back to punch the intruder again.

"No. It's enough. He's out cold."

Sandy's voice, nearly drowned out by the pulse that thudded madly in his ears, finally penetrated his rage. He hesitated, shook his head like a surfacing diver, then let one last blow connect with the man's temple. Raising him by the lapels, he glared into the slack face, then let its owner lapse to the floor.

"Out cold? I guess so."

He reached under his table to retrieve the stranger's knife.

"No, don't touch it," Sandy cautioned, her voice impossibly calm. "It's evidence."

"My god," he said, wrapping the switchblade in a sheet of tracing paper and getting to his feet, "are you all right?"

Bizarrely, she remained sitting in her chair.

"Eric, please. Let me loose."

"My god," he said again as he used his X-Acto knife to cut the cords, "I didn't know . . . I'm sorry . . . I saw the broken glass and the water in the hallway, I knew something was wrong but something told me not to come right in. There was that open place in the blinds, he blocked my view but I could tell he had a knife to your throat, I should have come in sooner, but if he heard me I was afraid he would—" He couldn't think it, let alone say it. "Then he bent your arm back and you moved and Corb began to bark and he got clear of you and I— I hit him across the head with this tube of drawings." He picked it up off the floor so she could see. "I think it's dent-ed," he added lamely.

He took a deep shaky breath. At his feet, the intruder gave a snort, his mouth lax, and again was still.

That could have been Sandy lying there.

"What *did* he do to you?" he asked.

"Nothing," she said briskly. She stood out of the light of the drafting lamp, holding both hands behind her back. "Nothing. I'm going to call the cops. And an ambulance. They'd better haul him away before he throws up and messes up the linoleum any worse."

Without hesitation she stepped over her assailant and picked up the phone, turning her back as she made the call. Something wasn't right about the way she was hitting the buttons; she was holding the receiver between her shoulder and ear and dialing with her left hand. But nothing was right this evening.

"Yes, Operator? Could you send the police and an ambulance to 102 North Fifth Street? Room 724. Yes, an assault. No, he's here. The ambulance is for him. Unconscious, flat on his back. Concussion, probably. Yes, Opera-tor. That's fine, we'll do that. Thank you."

She hung up and turned around, her arms oddly crossed over her body, as if she were hugging herself. "The cops will be here in a few minutes, so that's taken care of." Her voice was businesslike, flat. "And the operator says we need to turn him on his side to make sure his airway stays open."

"Oh. Right," Eric said, still dazed. He rolled the man over, the arms flopping loosely against the floor.

"Should we tie him up?" Sandy suggested. She nodded towards the cut pieces of rope lying on the floor around her chair.

"Oh, uh. Certainly." He made the knots as tight as he dared. How could she watch so dispassionately? His own nerves were sizzling like grease in a red-hot pan. "I guess that will do till the paramedics come."

"Yes, it should," she pronounced. "What brought you in tonight after all?" She could have been inquiring about the weather.

"Oh, I needed to look at the building code manual. I was—"

He looked at her harder. She was standing in the shadows near his table like a cardboard cutout of a woman. Except cardboard cutouts didn't bleed.

"Good god, Sandy!" he exclaimed, and turned on the ceiling lights. She was still holding her right arm across her front, but now her left hand pressed a wad of Kleenex to the wrist, a spreading stain seeping through them and dripping red to the floor. There was blood on her dark brown wool skirt, blood on her Fair Isle sweater vest, and blood from a scratch on her face as well. "*What* did he do to you?"

"Oh, nothing," she repeated, again concealing her right hand behind her back. The words came out hard, light, and artificial, like the simulated computer voice in a movie he once saw. "Just threatened to amputate my drafting hand and then slit the wrist to prove he meant it. After he nearly broke it, you know. It'll hurt like hell later," she said, and began to laugh. "Oh gosh, Eric, isn't this the biggest joke?" The burst of hilarity chilled him. "Some jerk practically tries to kill me and here I am, running around like it's business as usual. Isn't it the biggest joke in the world? Come on, Eric, laugh!"

He stared at her, appalled.

"It's funny, really!" she persisted. "Here I go, just like Corb, just like the damn mechanical dog! It's funny, Eric, funny, funny, *funny!*" She laughed hysterically, hiccupping, choking, as the fit seized her, held her, then finally drove her out of laughter and into sobs. She collapsed into her drafting chair then sprang out of it as if it burned, flinched from his, then subsided into one of the seats at the conference table. Burying her head in her arms, her blood dyeing the white painted surface crimson, she huddled there weeping.

His heart turned over in pity. He laid a comforting hand on her shoulder, but to his surprise she stiffened, jerked her body away, and continued to sob.

If I'd kept my promise, this wouldn't have happened.

"Dammit," he said gruffly, "let me see that wrist."

She raised her head. Still shaking, she held out her right hand.

He took it in his and reined in a red raging urge to take the right arm of the man on the floor and stomp it seven levels down into the building lobby. "Well, you've got some bruising but the cut's not too deep," he said, taking his cue from her. "You should see a doctor, though."

"No. I don't need a doctor."

"Sandy!"

She shook her head.

"You need something better than that Kleenex, at any rate. I think we have some cotton memo samples in here that're big enough . . . " He reached down a box. "Yes, here's one. And clean." She barely moved as he wrapped the folded fabric around her wrist and bound it firmly with drafting tape. The blood seeped through the cloth a little, then ceased. She sat there so frozen, so pale; only her eyes held a terrible mixture of agonized need and frantic rejection. It was his fault, and there was nothing he could do.

He turned away, only now seeing the clotting blood on the Weisman tracings. He reached for a Kleenex then let his hand fall helplessly.

No, let them alone. Evidence.

WHY, *WHY* had she told him she didn't want to see the doctor?

In the end, the detective who took charge of the scene had insisted she go, and now, sitting in a side room off the Emergency Department of St. Stephen's Hospital, she had only herself to thank for making Eric look like a negligent clod.

"That's a nasty cut you've got there, young lady," the emergency room physician observed in that overly-hearty manner doctors sometimes used. "You're lucky you didn't sever a tendon."

That I *didn't sever a tendon? Lovely. Just lovely.* But what did it matter? She was too drained and depressed to care.

With lowered voice the doctor addressed Eric, who had automatically accompanied her into the treatment room. " . . . Counselling is available . . . persuade her to talk to somebody . . . no repetition of the act . . . "

Eric's eyebrows went up, his expression passing from incomprehension to indignation.

That roused her.

O Domine. He thinks I did this myself. And that I'm Eric's wife. No, his girl-friend — no ring on my finger. The idea must make Eric sick.

"Eric," she interrupted, her voice falsely bright, "did the police say anything about how soon McNair would be charged?" The ambulance had taken her still-unconscious assailant to City Hospital. He'd be booked, the detective had said, when he came to.

He caught her drift immediately, thank heaven for that. "Yes," he replied in a tone that was just as staged, "probably tomorrow morning."

"Do you think they're finished photographing the office? Will they need a picture of my wrist for evidence at his trial?"

At least the doctor had the grace to look embarrassed. "Uh, no, my report should be enough. Busy night," he muttered. "I didn't catch . . . " He returned his attention to her wound. "You're lucky, it'll only take a couple-three stitches. We'll numb it up first, so, um . . ."

She nearly told him not to bother with the anesthetic. Any physical pain he caused her would be nothing compared to what she'd suffered this evening already, and it was only what she deserved. But Eric's stricken face convinced her to submit.

"We'll just dress it now," the doctor said as he completed the last of the sutures, "and medicate that cut on your face. I'll give you an ice pack for those contusions. You'll need a tetanus shot . . . don't worry, it won't hurt."

"I know," she said apathetically. She watched Eric as he looked over some public health pamphlet he'd found in the waiting room. What had been wrong with her back in the office? She'd held it together through the whole ordeal then dumped it all on him. He'd only wanted to help.

Correction: he did help. He saved my life.

The thought didn't make her happy. It only depressed her more. And she was thanking him by making some doctor think they were closer than they were.

Lord, why again? Is there some lesson I didn't learn ten years ago?

She had no leisure to think about it. The waiting detective sent in to say they were wanted at the station to give their statements, now.

⌈⫯⌉

YOU'D THINK these cops could ask a question once and get it over with. I'm exhausted, and it's a wonder Sandy's holding up at all.

He'd had a bad moment earlier. "Mr. Baumann," one of the officers had said, turning a too-knowing eye on him, "how many times did you strike the alleged perpetrator with your fist? Two times? Ten times? More?"

"I, uh—" He couldn't remember. He didn't know. And written on the blankness of his mind was just the one terrible possibility, that they might arrest him, too. "Maybe—" he tried to give an answer. "I think—"

"The bruising was extensive," the officer pressed him. "I wonder if—"

"That's all right, Officer," the lead detective cut in, flashing Eric what he hoped was a friendly smile. "Mr. Baumann, I'm sure you only hit him enough to neutralize the threat."

"Yes, sir. Only that."

That had been a relief, but it didn't make the long, tedious interview comfortable or easy. Nursing his sore right hand, he worked not to betray his irritation as they made Sandy repeat her story, the one cop interrupting to remind her that the suspect's guilt was only "alleged." He was Afro-American, and Eric wondered if he was going strictly by the book on the redneck prisoner because he felt he had something to prove. Whatever it was, it was chilling to witness Sandy's impossible calm as she answered, describing yet again what Al McNair had done to her. No wonder she'd reacted the way she had back in the office. Already there'd been a time when she'd asked to speak to a policewoman alone. What that implied, he didn't like to think.

And all for a case of mistaken identity. That was what disturbed him the most. The intruder was the lowest variety of white trash hick; it was impossible he could have any connection with any client of theirs.

Not even—?

No, not even the late Nick Hardt. According to Sandy, McNair had disavowed all knowledge of the man, and why would he do that, if it was information he wanted?

The names of Cole Rutherford and Al McNair were run through the police computer, but it brought them no closer to solving the mystery.

"Well," the detective reported, "our perp's not from around here, and he's got an outstanding warrant against him in Kentucky for illegal gun sales. Nothing on Rutherford; not here, at least. We'll follow it up. This guy McNair begins to talk, we'll get more of an idea who he really was after. We'll need you both to testify at his trial."

"When's that likely to be?" Sandy asked.

"He won't be in any shape for it for a while," the detective said, sounding almost jaunty, "and Kentucky'll probably want a crack at him first. If he doesn't plea out on your case and it goes to trial . . . I'd say, with the usual delays, next summer sometime. Fall, could be. Even so, check with us before either of you go out of town. You might be needed."

SHE GOT her ride home with Eric after all.

"Are you hungry?"

"No."

But also to insist she call her mother in Florida, something Sandy had resolved she would not do, and then to pray with her and for her, and for Eric, too; that was true uncomplicated friendship.

"Carole, I'm thinking there's something we still need to do . . . "

"What's that?"

"Pray for Al McNair. And this Cole Rutherford, whoever he is. They need it more than any of us."

It was while they were interceding for them that the phone rang. "Uh!" she groaned, her nerves still strained. She stilled herself and they let it go until the prayer was through.

"I'll get it," said Carole. "Hello?" She put her hand over the mouthpiece. "It's Eric. Do you feel like talking to him?"

Sandy went to the phone. "Hi," she said, a little shyly.

"Hi, how are you doing?"

"Better. My friend Carole's here." She flashed her a smile. "We've been praying."

"Oh. Well. I'm glad. I mean, glad she's there. I was calling to see how you were. And if you needed anything. Like *patisserie* from Le Bistro Soufflot."

"*Pain au chocolate?* I always need that. But it's snowing. Don't drive all the way over just for that."

"I'm not driving all the way over. I'm at the phone booth on Meyers. And I've got the goods. I'll be there in three minutes."

And before she could protest, he'd hung up.

"I have to change my sweater," she announced. "Eric's coming over." Carole opened her mouth, but before she could speak Sandy dashed to her bedroom and picked out one he liked for its color and design. After last night, it was the least she could do. Besides, she had her professional image to uphold.

The ache in her wrist and right shoulder made it hard to change quickly. Scarcely was she out of her bedroom when the door buzzer began to sound: Eric ringing the lobby bell to be let in.

She pressed the door release button. This was the first time he'd been up to her apartment since the night they'd listened to *La Damnation* together. Thank goodness Carole was here; it kept things from . . . it made things more . . . there was no time to sort it out; he was out in the hallway, knocking at her door.

The moment she saw him on the threshold she knew she'd made a mistake letting him come. Even in the snow-wet, beat-up tweed overcoat he wore on weekends he was so beautiful that only Carole's presence kept her from throwing her arms around him and burying her head in his chest.

Then he stepped inside and the spell broke. He was merely her boss, who also happened to be her friend.

"Instant fortitude," he said, offering her the box of pastries.

"Thanks, I need it. Come meet my friend Carole. We've known each other since grade school."

The two got acquainted as Sandy passed the pastries around. Choosing a *palmier* for herself, she sank back onto the sofa, grateful to be relieved from the burden of conversation.

"I'm glad you're here to take care of Sandy," Eric told Carole earnestly.

Should she resent that? But she was too full of wine and flaky pastry. Besides, self-sufficiency could be vastly overrated. Even now she could hardly bear to think about what happened last night, let alone of what could have happened had Eric not arrived.

Ten years after the last time. Escaped again. Thank God. I think I'm stronger now, but still—

Hush. Trust in God, not yourself.

"I got here around noon," Carole said, "and found out she hadn't eaten since yesterday's lunch. Fortunately, she keeps her kitchen pretty well stocked."

"Rough night?" he asked Sandy, a little tentatively.

"You might say that," she replied, taking a croissant and putting a little too much care into tearing off a morsel. She looked up at him. "You haven't— I still don't know exactly how you felt about your— fire— but last night I couldn't help feeling that *I* was the one who'd wielded the knife. I felt filthy. I felt I should be sitting on a dungheap in sackcloth and ashes!"

"No," Carole said, shaking her head and smiling, "how could it be your fault?"

Eric made no comment, just continued to listen.

"Music helped a little. All the requiem settings I own. Especially the *Lacrymosa* from the Berlioz. Over and over."

"From what she tells me," Carole said, "the neighbors got quite a concert."

Sandy stared at her lap, pretending to be occupied with the buttery flakes that had fallen there. "I'm sorry I acted like such an idiot last night, breaking down and all. Will you forgive me?"

At this, Carol shot out of her seat. "I'll be in the kitchen."

"Please, don't worry about it," Eric said.

"But I do. I was so rude to you, after you— you—"

He cut her off. "It was my fault. I should have told DeeDee I was already booked for supper. I made an appointment with you and I broke it. I'm sorry."

"Eric, don't. You were exhausted from your trip, and then they made you rush out to the site as soon as you got home."

"It was nothing she really needed me for," he said with disgust. "I could have left as soon as I took care of it, instead of tramping all over the new house gawking at how good it looked. If I'd come and picked you up like I promised, yesterday wouldn't have happened."

"Oh, Eric, you sound like me! Don't worry about it." How strange it was, even humorous, that she should be comforting him. "It can't be helped now."

She paused. "But please. Tell me what happened to Nick Hardt."

He looked at her curiously. "Are you sure you want to talk about that now?"

"Actually," she said, making a wry face, "I think it will help."

"All right. I got up there late Tuesday night. Spent the night in Pierre, then next day, I rented a car and drove out to the White Star Mine. You should see it— real throwback kind of place, up in the Black Hills, about thirty miles outside of Deadwood. Got there around noon; there were three or four cars in the lot, but nobody was around. Just one guy who looked like a miner; he ignored me and took the elevator down the shaft. I did a little exploring in the Black Hills, then came back later that afternoon. This time there was a secretary in the office. She wouldn't talk much. She said if I needed to know anything about Hardt I should make an appointment to see the managing partner, Mr. Simmons, and he and his calendar wouldn't be in till Thursday morning."

"So what did you do?"

"What could I? I drove back to Deadwood and called first thing the next day from the hotel."

"And? Was Simmons there?"

"He actually was. I told him I needed to speak with his partner, and he said he'd meet me about it that evening. Was Hardt there in South Dakota? I asked him. He told me to wait. He absolutely couldn't meet me till then. It made me mad."

Meaning, Sandy reflected, that Eric had let him know what he thought in the most deadly-polite way possible. It hadn't done any good, because Simmons had stuck fast to 8:30 that night, at a coffee shop in a town midway between Deadwood and the mine.

"When I finally had the guy face to face, he tells me, 'You want to get in touch with my partner Nick. I'm sorry, but he's no longer with us.' For a minute I thought Hardt had sold his holdings like he did down here. But then he said, 'He was killed in a car accident up here the first of November. He's gone.' I didn't believe him at first. Then he handed me this clipping."

Eric took a piece of newsprint out of his wallet and handed it to her.

"'Blizzard Claims Mine Owner in Crash,'" she read out the headline. "Where is this from?"

"Check the left hand margin."

Along it somebody, Simmons probably, had scrawled in ballpoint pen "*Black Hills Pioneer*, Nov. 4, 1981." She scanned the article quickly. Apparently there'd been an early-season snowstorm the past November first. Hardt had been driving from the mine back to Deadwood that evening and in the white-out conditions had hit something on the road: a deer or maybe an elk. Whatever it was, it had sent him into a skid and pitched car and driver down the mountainside, where the vehicle caught fire.

"It says here," Sandy said, "that the body was burned beyond recognition. How'd they know it was him?"

"Simmons said the reporter exaggerated. He identified Hardt himself. And no one else up there drove that model BMW."

"Oh." She went on reading. The last known permanent address for "Nicholas R. Hardt" was Frankfort, Kentucky, and for some reason they couldn't lay hands on his will. Anyone with information as to its location or to the identity of next of kin was to contact attorneys Logan, Rothfels and Brightwood of Pierre, South Dakota.

"Any chance to talk to these lawyers?" she asked.

"Yes, yesterday morning just before I caught the flight home. The only thing they could tell me was that the will had been located and the heir turned out to be some nephew down South. Hardt's share in the mine was transferred over a couple of weeks ago."

"Oh, well." She passed the clipping back. "So we've been safe since the beginning of November?"

"Looks like it," Eric said. "I'd wondered why he didn't react after I refused to put that ad in. Simmons said they cremated what was left of him and he scattered the ashes up there in the Black Hills."

For a moment, neither of them spoke. Then, "I suppose this means the authorities are right about your fire. Unless," she said cynically, "he put on a contract out on you in advance and hired a conscientious arsonist."

Eric shook his head. "No, I doubt that. Like I said, he's— he was— a businessman. Doing something like that, he'd have too much to lose."

There was an awkward silence, and against her will, she shuddered.

"What's wrong?"

"Nothing. No, actually, I was just thinking how much worse things could have been. With your fire and last night, both."

"I'm sorry." He seemed to study her for a moment, then said, "About Monday. Would you— would you rather avoid the place for a day or two? I could give you some time off."

"No . . . ?" she questioned. It hadn't occurred to her to dread returning to the office. Room 724 meant Eric, never Al McNair. That was one thing she wasn't going to let last night change. "Actually, I was thinking of driving in later this afternoon and cleaning up the mess I made. If the cops are finished, I mean."

"You could do that?"

"Yes. Why not? I mean . . . " Flexing her right wrist, she considered. "I guess I feel better if there's something I can do . . . Gosh, Eric, I hated feeling so helpless last night. I hated it!"

"And here I've gone and—"

"Gone and what?"

"I did it already."

"What?"

"I cleaned up the blood. This morning."

The mental image, suddenly, of Eric on his knees, scrubbing the blood— *her* blood— off the floor of their office . . . *O Domine!*

"I didn't want you to have to face it on Monday," he said simply. "I'm sorry if I interfered or took anything away from you."

"Oh, Eric!" She threw her hands up to her face and began to weep quietly. He regarded her from the armchair, his brow furrowed, his palm running anxiously over his beard, and again the urge nearly overtook her to run to his arms. She fought it down and dried her tears.

"Thank you," she said. "You didn't need to do that, but thank you."

From the kitchen came the sound of Carole noisily opening cupboards and the refrigerator, as if trying to cover the sound of their private talk.

He spoke. "There's something else I've arranged to do, and I hope you'll let me."

"What is it?"

"I'm taking on a new employee starting Monday morning."

"What?" She sat up, surprised. "Don't we have a few more interviews to do?"

"It's not one of them. I'm talking about Jim McCullough, Vicky and Jameson's boy. The architectural drafting student."

"We're taking on an intern? But I thought we—"

He glanced down at the rug and picked at something— she hoped it wasn't dried food— on the arm of the chair. "He played fullback in high school."

What did that have to do with architecture?

"I hope you don't think I'm being paternalistic," he said, raising his eyes to hers with a look of apology, "and he has no impression he's being hired as a bodyguard, but—"

"Surely last night was a fluke? McNair got you mixed up with somebody else. And we don't have to worry about Nick Hardt anymore."

"I know. But I'll still feel better knowing someone's with you when I can't be. For a while, anyway."

Oh. "I will, too," she said, almost hoping he wouldn't hear.

His face told her he had. But he only said, "I'm afraid he can only work part time— he has classes to attend. But you shouldn't be alone." He glanced out the window, where snow was falling softly, then cleared his throat. "I haven't asked about your cut. Is it feeling better?"

She was glad the wound was concealed under the cuff of her sweater and she didn't need to show it to him. The less he saw of it, the sooner they could both forget.

"Yes . . . About Jim," she said, "what exactly will he be doing?"

"No 'real' architecture, unfortunately for him. There's no board for him anyway, though I can bring in a portable if you want to throw him a bone on the Millerson design development. Mainly I want him to build the tables and throw-off ledge for the new people, and knock together some shelves for the catalogs and samples."

"Same as in our room, right?"

"Right."

Carole emerged from the kitchen with a plate of cheese and crackers and a clean wine glass. "Some Bordeaux?" she offered in a tone that expected Eric to say yes.

"No thanks. I have to get moving," he said. "I've got things I need to take care of."

"Sounds interesting," said Carole.

He looked a little sheepish. "Not really. Tonight's Mike's bachelor party—"

"Mike Laurence," Sandy put in. "I knew him in architecture school and he worked with Eric at Richardson & Greene. He's getting married next week to one of our fabric reps."

"Yeah," Eric went on. "Rosie doesn't trust the best man. She wants me to make sure Mike doesn't go overboard."

"'Overboard'?" asked Carole.

"Good luck," Sandy said. "I have to say, 'overboard' was just the word for Mike Laurence's parties. It's what they say about Woodstock: if you can remember it, you weren't there."

"Oh, I'll make sure he remembers." He paused. "I'll call you tomorrow evening after I get home from the Weismans'."

"You're going, then?"

"Only long enough to shake a few hands and drum up some business. I have to take them the drawings; why make two trips?"

She clapped her hand to her mouth. "Oh my gosh, the drawings! I forgot, they're still sitting on the counter! Carole," she said, turning to her friend, "that's what I'd just run off when I came back and . . . " She faltered and couldn't go on.

His eyes met hers. "No," he reassured her, "I've got them, in the car. All collated and bound." He paused. "Sandy . . . if you're not too sore, on Monday could you take the tracings you— that you put so much of yourself into, and . . . "

He looked a little embarrassed. But she laughed and said, "You could put it that way!"

His expression changed to one of relief. "And run them on mylar and doctor them up so they look like they did before? That is, if you really are determined to get back on the horse that threw you?"

"I am," she said. "Besides, that's not the horse that threw me. *He's* going to jail."

"Amen," said Carole.

"Well, I'd better run. You'll be all right? Anything more I can do?"

"No, just keep me busy come Monday. Thanks for the dose of fortitude. And for the pastries. Drive safely."

When the door closed behind him Carole said, "So that's the famous Eric Baumann."

"It is."

"You're sure he's not a Christian?"

"You heard what he did? This morning in the office?"

"You've got a small apartment. I couldn't help hearing."

"It boggles me, too. But no. He's not."

"Too bad."

"I know. Believe me, I know."

CHAPTER B.16

"I COULD ASK THE CONGREGATION to pray for you." The Rev. Dr. Malcolm Kennerdene regarded her across his desk. Outside the slightly-open door of the pastor's study, the church secretary, Mrs. Rogers, exclaimed over a dropped stitch in her knitting. It was supposed to be her day off and Sandy felt a little guilty making her come in in the evening, but Dr. Kennerdene had said not to worry. If he needed to meet with someone on short notice, Mrs. Rogers didn't mind.

Yesterday morning in church Sandy had requested prayer for "a private matter." The long sleeves of her jacket hid the welt on her wrist and if her fellow-members noticed the bruises and the cut on her face, they were too polite to mention it. But she could not conceal her trouble from her pastor when he inquired about it discreetly after the service.

"No thank you," she said now. "Things are just settling down after what we went through last fall, but if this got out, well . . . " She shrugged. "I doubt it'd be good for business."

"If your workplace is unsafe for yourself or for others," Dr. Kennerdene said gravely, "you have a duty to make it known."

"Oh, no, no!" she said, dismayed. "That issue last fall, the man involved is dead. And the guy I walked in on, he's in police custody. It was just a coincidence, anyway. Or no," she went on cheerfully, "maybe it was God sending me some adversity so I'd learn to trust Him more!"

The leather of his chair creaked as he leaned forward. Smiling a little doubtfully, he nodded. "All right. Though I'm sure the leaders of your Young Professionals group would maintain confidentiality if you told them."

"Of course. I could do that." Had she just fibbed to her pastor? The fact was, she didn't know if they could be trusted or not. She'd been trying to attend more activities with the PYPs; still, she couldn't name any one member she knew well enough to unburden her soul to. "But it's all right," she assured him. "You've really helped me. And my friend Carole— she used to go here— she's keeping tabs on me. And my boss, Er— Mr. Baumann— has been very understanding, too. I'm doing a lot better already. Thank you."

She *was* doing a lot better. A lot better than she did that terrible summer of '72, after her illusions about Jeff had been shattered. Back then, not even Carole had been trusted with her outrage and pain, and it had taken her months to say anything to Dr. Wallace, Dr. Kennerdene's beloved late predecessor. And when she had, it was only to ask him in a general way about forgiveness. She'd refused to tell him whom and why she needed to forgive.

Was she learning to rest in Jesus better? *Thank You, Lord.* They had too much going on in the office. She couldn't afford to fall apart now.

SHE COULD HEAR her phone ringing down the hall even before she reached the top of the stairway to her floor. Could it be Eric? No, Carole, more likely, calling to check up on her. She hurried down the corridor, quickly unlocked her door, and dashed into the breakfast room where the phone sat jangling.

"Hello?" she said cheerfully.

"Hello? Is that Sandy Beichten?" said a breezy male voice she couldn't place.

"Yes? Who is this speaking?"

"You don't remember me?" The voice bled disappointment. "This is Rick Johnson, from high school."

Rick Johnson? There'd been several boys named Rick at Blakewell. But Johnson? It was nobody in her Honors program, not that she recalled.

"Uh, yes, Rick? How are you?"

"Fine! How's the architecture business?"

"Um, fine." She still couldn't raise a picture of his face. "Rick, sorry, remind me what classes we had together. It's been awhile."

"English, don't you remember? Hey, that was fun times. That old King Lear, he was sure a stitch!"

King Lear? Funny? "You mean the Fool, don't you?"

"Oh, yeah, sure, the Fool."

Wait a minute. We did a lot of Shakespeare, but they never gave us King Lear.

"Rick, I'm sorry, what year did we have English together?"

"Come on, you know, when we were seniors. You remember."

Senior English had been all Classical Honors people. They'd definitely had no Rick Johnson that year.

"Um, thanks for calling, but I think you're mistaking me for someone else."

"No, Sandy Beichten." The voice suddenly ran iron-cold, chilling her to the core. "I am not mistaking you for anyone else. You always think you're right about everything, *Sandy Beichten*—"

It wasn't McNair, it couldn't be; this voice lacked the redneck accent McNair's had; it—

"—but this time you're wrong. Dead wrong."

THANK GOD for Jim McCullough and his advent in their office. His college-boy humor poked holes in Eric's dignity, frequently made Sandy blush, and seemed custom-designed to take her mind off her troubles.

Not that she saw much of the kid the first part of the week. Jim's first day, Eric (who by some miracle of scheduling had nothing to take him out of the office) had sent him to the lumberyard to purchase materials for the new drafting stations. When the plywood and paint— in Eric's favorite shade of white— were delivered on Tuesday she could hear the two of them through the open adjoining door, measuring, sawing, hammering. It would have been fun to help and discover more about the hands-on side of carpentry. Her father had never been one to build things in the basement and that side of her education had been sadly neglected. But she had more than enough to do on her drafting board and she judged it better to keep out of the way.

Getting out of the office helped her forget, too. On Wednesday she drove up to be interviewed by Theophilus Duggins, the Fort Randolph City planning director. Mr. Duggins turned out to be a clean-cut, slim, efficient but personable man in his mid-thirties who'd studied urban planning at the Illinois Institute of Technology and property law at Howard. She took to him right away: he was no mere government functionary, but a professional who cared deeply about good design and would do his best to get it for his city on the budget allowed. He was sure their firm would have no trouble being approved for the proposal list; he would put their request on the city council agenda for the meeting the first week in February.

In the midst of it all she and Eric managed to interview two or three more people, and by Thursday his mind was made up.

"Though," he said, "I wonder sometimes if I should bring anybody in, with what happened last week."

"That was a fluke, wasn't it?" They'd never be able to manage FirstCon without new blood.

Oops. Not quite the way to put it.

"Yes, I think so. And with Nick Hardt out of the way . . ."

"So it should be all right," she assured him.

What about the phone calls you've been getting?

Never mind them. I can handle it.

"So, who made the cut?" she asked.

"I want Neil Hughes for our specs man."

"Good choice," Sandy agreed. If what he'd said in the interview was any indication, Hughes had Marvin's ear for a tight specification, without the antagonism towards contractors and suppliers her former boyfriend had shown. He'd been president of the black architecture students' association at his school, so he had incentive and leadership potential, too. "Who else?"

"Ruth Parrish. Her drafting style will fit right in."

"She's expecting. I forget, how long will we have her?"

"At least six months. Long enough to produce the working set. She'll be answering to you first, so behave yourself!"

"Yes, sir, I shall remember my long months under your lash and be tender and merciful. Anyone else?" she asked.

"No, I don't think we're ready for that big a big time yet. I might lose my clawlike control!" They grinned at one another mischievously.

Ruth, they decided, would join them the eighth of February; Neil, closer to the end of that month. In the meantime, they'd lay some groundwork: tomorrow the two of them were going to meet Jacob Ryerson and Sam Delkirk on the FirstCon site.

"Bring the hundred foot tape," he said. "Unless it's too muddy with this thaw we should be able to measure off the setback lines and get an idea of exactly where the building can go."

"Aye-aye, Captain!"

Poor Jim. Tomorrow she and Eric would have all the fun.

CHAPTER B.17

IF IT WEREN'T FOR THE MUD, Eric would have said Nature had given them the perfect day for a January site visit. In the upper 50s, lightly-overcast with no chance of rain— it was the best anyone could ask for this time of year.

Life was good. Despite everything, it was.

This site at the top of a broad plateau, first of all. Plenty of level land to accommodate the program and provide for future expansion, and elevated enough that his new building would be visible from miles around.

And so gratifying to have such good clients. Jacob, for all his rough humor, had a good eye, and in combination with him Sam Delkirk was shaping up to be as knowledgeable and collaborative a patron as even Eric could wish.

Jacob sauntered along at his side as the four of them made their way up the rutted track, regaling him with something Sheila had said after their last meeting on the family room. Eric only half-listened; his attention was on Sandy as she walked a few paces ahead of them, in earnest conversation with Sam.

He chose well.

Not just in making her his first associate, but in asking her to come work for him in the first place.

Look at her. She's five-foot-one if she's lucky, but she comes off like she's six-foot-two.

How erect she carried herself, with her shoulders straight and her head held high. No one would guess that a week ago she was in danger of her life. Not just skill, but guts, too. Definitely an asset to the firm.

There's more to her than her role in the office, an inner voice reminded him.

True. He smiled to himself. She was like his sister Lou-Lou would have been, had she lived. Paul's Sophie was a fine girl too, but she was in Idaho. So much better to have Sandy as an "adopted" sister close by.

Jacob had switched to a slightly risqué tale involving some woman in his office. Eric made the necessary conversational noises and pursued his own thoughts.

There was music in her walk. What song was running through her head to give her that firm, easy rhythm? Something optimistic and sure, not the aria he'd come upon her singing in November. Ridiculous, how he'd tied himself in knots over that.

That was a handsome pair of boots she had on. Warm Cordovan leather that hugged her calves, but with a low heel, just the thing to allow her to negotiate this sorry excuse for a road. She was wearing a rust-colored cropped jacket he particularly liked, and below it her jeans fit her like the upholstery on a sleek designer chair.

His eyes lingered there, on the curve of her thighs, on the graceful swing of her hips as she ascended the hill, on the inverted heart-shape of her bottom . . . *Gut Form,* as the German designers put it . . . His gaze was like a hand, reaching out, touching, caressing . . . Her body was supple and warm to his imagination, and the warmth suffused his own body, setting every nerve gloriously on fire.

Wait. No. My sister? The good of the office . . .

She turned, and in her face was a glow that lit up the gray morning with the blaze of a dozen suns. "Oh, Eric!" she said. "Sam tells me they want us to design all four elevations to respond to the environment! Aren't you *glad?*"

Speech, movement, thought: all were beyond his doing. There was nothing but her smile, nothing he could do but whirl suspended in the bright orb of it. Staring, wondering, he at last stammered out, "Y– yes. Glad!"

To his left a harsh noise intruded, bringing him to himself.

It was Jacob Ryerson, laughing.

" . . . I'LL MAKE SURE Sandy sends you a memo on today's meeting, and I'll see that she has the preliminary site plan done by Tuesday. Do you want to come over on Wednesday and discuss it?"

"I can fit that in," said Sam.

"I'll check with my secretary, but I think that's doable," said Jacob.

"Great!" Eric said with enthusiasm. He turned to Sandy and made his voice hard. "You *do* have everything, don't you?" He didn't meet her eye or address her by name.

It'd been like that all day. They'd measured and documented the proposed building site, checking it against the survey Sam and Jacob provided. They'd shot out three or four rolls of film on existing conditions. It was no different from any other preliminary site visit they'd gone on, but today he'd cut her no slack. Reminded her to do things that were her second nature. Made unaccustomed demands as to promptness and accuracy. She had taken it in stride, completing each task in her usual quiet, efficient way. He felt like a jerk.

But he couldn't stop.

"Tape, clipboard . . . all but the camera," she said. "You have that." There was mystification in her voice, but more than that, concern.

"Here," he said brusquely, pulling it from around his neck and thrusting it at her. "Don't drop it."

A questioning flash in her eyes (which he'd still meant to avoid), then her face went blank. She took the camera in silence.

"Don't forget to run the film by the camera store this afternoon and ask for one-hour processing."

"Good grief, Eric, that's what we always—!" First sign of temper. She turned away, hitched the equipment bag more securely on her shoulder, and stalked down the hill ahead of them all.

Was he trying to convince Jacob Ryerson he hadn't seen him make a fool of himself this morning? Or himself, that he hadn't felt what he definitely had?

So? He liked women, and women liked him. She was easy on the eyes. What was the harm?

It'll screw up my work, that's what.

He stared with deliberate harshness at her retreating form, which was no longer erect. "Diminished" was the only word to describe her now. Even as he noted this, she tossed her head, drew herself to her full height, and strode on, as if she'd felt his critical gaze boring into her spine and wanted to defy what she couldn't understand.

At the bottom of the slope, their cars were parked on a sweep of mud and gravel just off the access road. Under the windshield wipers of all three he discerned something white flapping in the chilly breeze. She must have seen it too, for she accelerated her pace and, arriving at his Ford, pulled the paper out and began to read.

He watched her, with curiosity now. Her eyes went wide and, as he drew nearer, she clapped her hand to her mouth in horror.

"What is it?" he called anxiously. He closed the distance between them, and the wall he'd been building all day broke down.

She held out the paper, her hand trembling, then glanced up the slope to Jacob and Sam, within a few yards of joining them.

He did his best to take it in. The graphics and layout were hideous; that he noticed first of all. But the words printed didn't deserve good graphics. "WHAT'S WRONG WITH AMERICA?" screamed the headline. "Jungle Savages Overrunning Our Cities!" "Degenerate Colored Race Pollution!" "Stop the Nigger Menace NOW!" And, over and over: "Jews at the Bottom of it!" "Hebrew Fiends Strangling White America!" "Destroy the Kikes and Niggers!" "Kill all Niggers and Jews!"

"Don't let Jacob see!" Sandy pleaded.

It was too late. "See what?" Ryerson said casually. He angled himself to get a view of the flyer in Eric's hand. "What is this dreck!"

He snatched the sheet away, then yanked the other copies out from under the wipers on his and Sam's cars.

"What is it, Jacob?" asked Sam.

"Never mind." Pinching the flyers together by one corner, he pulled out his lighter and set them on fire. "I'll send these right where they belong."

"Wait, Jacob," Eric tried to stop him, "I wanted to see—"

But the white letter paper rapidly turned to black ash that Ryerson ground underfoot. "There. I'll try to forget it's polluting my property."

No chance, now, of his verifying what he thought he'd seen, there at the bottom of the repellant screed:

**THE WHITE WAY
IS THE RIGHT WAY**

CHAPTER B.18

IT WAS TOO MUCH. He'd hardly spoken to her in the car on the way back from the FirstCon site. She had hoped— prayed— he would apologize for his behavior, or at least explain it, but he'd sat behind the steering wheel like a stone image and given her nothing. Even if it was the shock of seeing that flyer, he could have shared it with her.

She told him she had a lot to do at home and left the office right after bringing back the developed site photos. Entering her apartment, she let her purse and tote bag drop like rocks to the floor. Her feet begged to be released from the confines of the brown boots, but her mind refused to tell her hands to do anything about it.

All the distance she'd come since the attack, erased. All the strength she'd mustered the past seven days, gone. Her shoulder hurt, her wrist hurt, her heart hurt. She sat on the sofa and stared.

Riiiinnnngggggg!!!

"*No!*" She flew into the breakfast room and yanked the phone cord out of the wall. For a moment she stood there, paralyzed. The picture rose in her mind of a half-gallon of ice cream in the freezer, a spoon in the drawer, and a long-neglected TV in her bedroom. Why not? Why the heck not?

No. She had too much pride to waste a whole evening on *The Dukes of Hazzard* and *Dallas*. She marched into the bedroom, deliberately ignoring the television sitting on the bookcase opposite the end of the bed. From her closet she dragged a portable drafting board, a small toolbox, and a roll of sketches. Blast it, Eric wasn't the only one who could drown his sorrows in work. It'd been ages since she'd touched the plans for her dream house, she'd been too busy expending her energies for him.

Back in the breakfast room, she set up her board. Two hours later, she congratulated herself. She was getting into the project again, the ideas were coming back to her, and best of all, this was a design that would never, ever, have anything to do with Eric Edward Baumann.

MONDAY MORNING, he was in before her. She gathered he was reviewing the photographs they'd taken at the site on Friday, but she wouldn't bother herself to look.

"Hey, Sandy," he said in his usual friendly tones, "you got some really great shots."

"Good," she said without expression, and focussed on her own work.

"I, uh, saw an interesting film on Grant Street over the weekend . . . "

"That's nice," she barely responded.

Keep your distance. You've got enough to cope with without letting him break your heart. No more sharing personal stuff. Just keep it to the office, you hear?

Her resolve held until Thursday.

"Hey, Sandy," he said when he came in that afternoon, "I tried to call you last night and it said your number was out of service. What's going on?"

For a moment an irrational hope lifted her heart— and immediately let it crash to the floor. He must have called her about work. That's all she should want him to call her about.

"I've gotten an unlisted number," she said with deliberate coolness. "Sorry, I should have given it to you." She wrote it on a slip of paper and handed it over. There. He had the information he needed, subject closed.

"But why?" he asked, mystified.

She hesitated.

Don't overdo it. If you're too reserved, it'll raise questions.

In the next room Jim McCullough was muttering under his breath as he applied edge banding to the new plywood drafting tables. She lowered her voice. "Because . . . for a while I've been, um, I *was* getting rude telephone calls."

He looked puzzled. "Prank calls, like 'Is your refrigerator running, you better go catch it'?"

"No. You really think I would change my number for *that?*"

He winced.

"I'm sorry," she said. "It's just that it was so creepy, and I didn't want to bother you with it."

"Why would you think that?"

Last Friday, maybe?

"You can tell me," he offered. "If you want. You didn't recognize the voice?"

"No. Actually, it was several voices. All men, but different. That's what was so awful about it, like being ganged up on. It'd be someone supposedly calling for a charity, or a wrong number, or even claiming to be an old friend of mine. Then when I'd relax and think it was okay, they'd launch into the worst . . ."

"Nothing violent, I hope? That's the last thing you need."

"Well, most of it was pretty general, just things like 'You won't get away with it' and 'If you don't quit you'll be sorry.' It got so they were coming in maybe four or five times a night, all different voices."

"Sandy! How long has this been going on? You should have told me."

"Since . . . since Monday before last." "Rick Johnson" had been only the first, and the insinuating voices had made it clear that what she was supposed to quit was her employment with Eric Baumann, Architect.

"Well, I hope you told them to go ream themselves."

"I couldn't do that! That wouldn't be Christian!"

He laughed. "I suppose not. Was any of it about the office?"

He had her.

"Um, well . . ."

"Tell me the truth."

"In a way, yes." There had been one call, particularly terrible, when before she could slam the receiver down a quick soft voice had whispered that some less than pleasant things would happen to Eric if she didn't leave him. "The office was mentioned. And you."

"I gather it wasn't complimentary . . ."

"Outright threats."

"To the office? Anything about damage to the premises?"

"No, it was all personal."

"I can take care of myself. As long as it doesn't keep me from practicing architecture."

"It might," she said wryly, "put you in practice for the Vienna Boys Choir."

"*What?*"

"I told you it was rude."

"Somebody's getting obscene phone calls?" said Jim from the connecting doorway, grinning.

"That's none of your business," Eric warned.

"Might be fun, if you could keep 'em going long enough."

"Jim!" they said together.

"Jim, get back to work." Eric glared at him, and the boy disappeared into the next room.

"By last Saturday— no, Friday— I couldn't stand even to answer the phone," Sandy said. "So I got my number changed. It was final yesterday morning."

He shook his head. "I'm so sorry . . ."

"Nothing you could do about it. Don't share the number around, if you don't mind. But you tried to call last night? What about?"

"I was hoping to pull you off FirstCon first thing this morning so you could check into prices and lead times for ebony and rosewood veneers."

"Sounds interesting. What for?"

"For these." He opened a folder labelled "McCullough Table" and spread the sketches out on the throw-off ledge.

"These are lovely! This is for their library?"

"Yes, I've been staying there since the end of December and it's about time I upheld my end of the bargain."

"Any sign of daylight with your apartment?"

"No, I've given up. I don't think my landlord's ever going to get it repaired. Not for me, anyway. In fact, he's been hinting that I should pay for the damage, since I supposedly left the heater on. I could swear I turned it off . . . It was his defective heater, not mine."

Sandy grunted her agreement. "So what will you do?"

"I've found a new apartment. Guess that's something I forgot to tell *you*. It's on Bryce Avenue, still in River Hill, but a little closer to the office. No fireplace, though." He shook his head in regret. "But I can't get the key till Monday the first. I'll take a day or two to paint it, then I should be out of Vicky and Jameson's hair."

"I can still call the hardwood suppliers this afternoon."

"No, let's get them some drawings first. So take this one . . . " He selected a sketch and laid it on her table. " . . . this one . . . " He removed another drawing from the pile. " . . . and this one . . . " He followed it with a third. " . . . and draw them up to scale. Work your usual magic with the presentation . . . I want some alternatives to show them by next Monday."

He pulled his coat off the stand. "I've got a meeting with Sheila Ryerson. Shouldn't take long; I'll be back by 4:30 or so."

She smiled skeptically.

"I mean it. If I stay over there longer she'll blow my eardrums out."

He leaned into the adjoining room. "Jim, you're almost done with that trim? After that I want you to get the catalogs and samples onto the shelves in the resource room. Sandy will tell you where they go."

"Sarright!"

"That's enough, Baba Looey. Sandy, I'll see you both this afternoon. Keep him busy, okay?"

IN THE END, it worked better for Jim to hand her the catalogs while she shelved them. She hadn't been getting any drawing done, not with all the questions he'd been asking.

"Jim, there's a biggish box of granite samples under the conference table. Could you go get it? It needs to go about there." She pointed to a spot on the shelf.

"No problemo!" He disappeared into the main office.

She got off the step stool and assessed the progress they'd made on the new resource room so far. Through the intervening doorways she could hear the scrape of the heavy box as Jim hauled it out from where it had been stashed. Then, the tread of footsteps approaching the main door, and a clatter that told her Jim had set the box down again.

"May I help you?" the boy's voice inquired.

"Yes, maybe you can," a man's responded. "Is Eric Baumann here?"

"No, sir, he isn't."

"Well, it's *really* important I get ahold of him. I've tried his home number but no one answers. You wouldn't by any chance know where he's staying, would you?"

Sandy didn't like the way the man sounded. Whiny, insinuating. Anybody who needed to know that Eric was at the McCulloughs' knew already, and since her attack they'd agreed it was just as well the information went no further.

"Why, sure!" responded Jim avidly. "He's at—"

"Jim! Come in here right now! I need you!"

Thank heaven he was a kid who listened. He appeared in the doorway.

"Jim, I just remembered," she said loudly, so the visitor would hear. "I need you to look up double-glazed aluminum windows right away. Eric needs the information right away."

"Really?"

She shook her head no. "Right away," she repeated, hoping her words carried to the front room. "Jim," she said for his ears only, "I don't know what Eric's told you, but he really doesn't want people bothering him at your house."

"But why?"

"Shhh. Keep your voice down. He just doesn't. Now you keep working in here, and I'll take care of this guy."

In the main office she confronted the visitor, the lurid red cut on her wrist throbbing in fearful remembrance. She braced herself. "Yes, sir, you needed to see Mr. Baumann?"

He was no one she'd laid eyes on before. A little under average height, fidgety, wearing a gray-green conventional overcoat and dark hat; his only accouterment of note was a large emerald— or green glass— ring that scintillated on his right hand.

"He'll be back in an hour or so," she said. "I'm sure he'll see you if you come back then." She looked at him steadily.

"Are you *sure* I can't get ahold of him at home?" the man importuned, gesturing nervously. "It's *real* important, see?"

"I can make an appointment for you to see him during office hours."

"That won't work. This is private." He reached into an inside pocket. "See, I've got money." He riffled a sheaf of bills before her. "You could use some extra cash, couldn't you?" he said, shifting his weight from one foot to the other.

"Sir, I'm afraid I'm going to have to ask you to leave."

The man opened his mouth to speak but just then Jim appeared in the communicating doorway, filling it with his considerable bulk. The young former fullback glowered down as if the visitor were an undersized defenseman about to get run over on the football field. The man's eyes darted from Jim to Sandy and back to Jim; he opened his mouth, shut it again, and hurried out.

"Maybe you should've told him where the can is," young Mr. McCullough suggested. "He looked like he needed it."

CHAPTER B.19

W HAT A BEAUTIFUL COLD, CRISP EVENING it was, Eric rejoiced as he drove home. *Well, my temporary home.* On a night like this, you could probably see the stars, even in the city.

On the seat next to him was a box of *Mozartkugeln*, bought to celebrate the composer's birthday the next day. Sandy hadn't had any of the chocolate-covered hazelnut confection since she visited Vienna years ago, and for Jim it would be a new experience.

In the back lay his portfolio containing their presentation for the side table he was designing for the McCulloughs' library. He hoped they'd like the approach he was taking. It had been so good of them to let him stay in their Mackintosh bedroom, and Vicky's cooking deserved his utmost gratitude.

He parked the car on the street and ran up the steps from the sidewalk. In the yard was a half-finished snowman, two balls lying separate in the trampled snow. One of Megan's efforts, no doubt.

Elaine McCullough met him at the door. "Daddy wants to see you in the library right away."

"Certainly," he said, hanging up his coat in the entry hall closet. How he loved this space, with its rich dark oak woodwork, encaustic floor tile, and the stained-glass transom over the broad door! The whole house was the same. It had been a privilege to help the McCulloughs rescue it from the depredations of the former owner. How could anyone cut a lovely Arts and Crafts house like this up into cheap apartments? If that wasn't immoral, nothing was.

"Any idea what about?" he asked the teenager, idly.

"No," was her reply, and there was something about its brevity that admitted a trickle of doubt. Did Jameson think he was taking unfair advantage of their hospitality? He grabbed the portfolio and headed straight to the library, where his host sat behind his massive Neo-Gothic oak desk, arranging some papers. What a find that was! Who would have thought it was hiding in that secondhand shop in the Rhinelander District?

Jameson McCullough rose. "Eric, have a seat," he said, gesturing to one of the lounge chairs that sat in the library corner. There was a grimness to the offer that told Eric to keep silent and wait. "Scotch?"

"No, thanks," he replied. Whatever Jameson had to say, he'd receive it without filtering it through alcohol.

Jameson grunted and poured himself a glass. But instead of joining him, he went and stood by the door. "Before I begin, I want Megan to tell you something."

Megan? Why?

"Megan, honey, come here," he called.

When the child appeared, Jameson laid a reassuring hand on her shoulder. "Go ahead, honey," he said gently, "tell Mr. Eric your story."

She glanced at her father, then approached. "Mr. Eric, we didn't have much homework from school today and I was ahead so I got some cookies out of the pantry and—"

"Not that part, honey. The part after you went outside."

"Oh! I'm sorry, Daddy," said the third-grader. "Well, okay, anyway, I went out and I wanted to make this one snowman and I started making it and it was a lot of work but I got this one really big ball made for the bottom part. And a medium one for the middle part."

"Yes, I noticed that, coming in," Eric said. "Why didn't you finish it?"

The child's face darkened. "There was this one man . . ."

"A man?" He held his breath. Over Megan's head Jameson caught his eye and nodded.

"Yeah. Not in a car or anything, just walking."

"Tell Mr. Eric what he looked like."

"He wasn't very big and he had on a sort-of green coat and a hat and he was just ordinary, I guess."

"Think. What did he have on his hand?"

"Oh, yeah!" she said. "He wasn't wearing any gloves and it was so cold this afternoon I thought his hands must be cold and he had on this one big ring with a big green emerald on it. Gosh, it was big! Daddy, do you think it was real?"

"I have no idea, honey. Tell Mr. Eric what the man asked you."

"Well," she went on forthrightly, "he was real, *real* jumpy, like he had ants in his pants—" She giggled— "and he asked me if you were staying here with us."

Oh, crap. He frowned and began to worry his beard. The child hesitated. "It's all right, Megan," he said. "Tell me the rest."

"Well, I don't talk to strangers, like you told me, Daddy." She glanced back for his approval. "So I didn't say anything."

Eric waited.

"So he said he'd give me candy if I'd tell him if you were but I didn't like him so I wouldn't tell him *anything*. Then he said something bad would happen to me if I didn't tell the truth so I ran up on the porch and I threw a piece of ice at him but I missed."

In spite of it all, Eric had to laugh. "Oh, good job, Megan! You're smarter than your brother!"

Jameson's smile was grim. "I gathered that. Megan, thank you. See if your mother needs you in the kitchen."

He shut the door behind her, brought his drink to the chair opposite Eric, and sat down. "She told Vicky, of course, and then Jim when he got home from class. A man bearing the same description visited your office looking for you one day last week?"

"Yes, Jameson, I suppose it could be the same person."

"And the same *modus operandi*, I take it. Bribery, then threats." He took a drink of his Scotch, then set it down on the ugly table between them— the table his design would replace.

The creep didn't threaten Sandy, he wanted to say.

So why threaten an eight-year-old girl?

"I'm so sorry that happened. I have no idea why someone like that would want to see me," he said defensively. "I mean—"

"Eric," Jameson cut him off, "whatever course you're pursuing, I'm sure it's an honorable one. But I'm a businessman myself and I know that 'cut-throat' isn't always a figure of speech. I hate to do this, and it won't affect our business relations, but for the sake of my wife and children I'll have to ask you to find another place to stay."

"Oh, of course, I totally understand!" But when? Now? Where on earth could he go? "Are you sure?" he blurted out. "That guy had to be a one-off. I doubt he'll be back." Even as the words spilled out he was ashamed at how disingenuous they were.

"It doesn't seem one-off to me. Remarkably persistent fellow, wouldn't you say? And taking it with your fire—" Eric opened his mouth to object but Jameson put up his hand— "With your fire and the smear campaign that Hardt character waged against you last fall, your luck hasn't exactly been good lately. Especially if none of this is connected.

"Call me superstitious," Jameson went on, "but Jim will no longer be working in your office, as of now. If he were older, more mature . . . But as long as he's under my roof, I have to decide what's best for him."

It wasn't wrong for me to bring Jim in! The kid wanted a job, and I just want to do my work . . .

But he'd told Sandy he was hiring Jim as a bodyguard. Why, unless he feared something else would happen?

That was just to make her feel better. Not because I thought they'd declared open season on us.

" . . . difficult day at the office anyway. One of my employees brought in a flyer he'd picked up somewhere—"

Flyer?

"—full of racial slurs and calls for a white revolution of some sort, not the kind of thing you want around. Of course everyone had to come look at it." Jameson rolled his eyes and took another sip. "One of my Afro-American employees saw it. He objected strenuously, as you might expect, and then someone was fool enough to say that maybe whoever put out the flyer had a point, that the civil rights movement went way too far, too fast."

"Really? What happened then?"

"I nearly had a race war right there at the water cooler. I can't blame Varnell for being upset, but if there's to be a fight, they should take it out in the alley like gentlemen."

"Huh?"

"I'm joking, of course. I've had to put everyone involved under warning, which I hate to do since Varnell Gates is one of my best workers. Les Whittaker, on the other hand . . . his mouth has gotten him in trouble before. But that doesn't make it any less difficult for me."

"I may have seen that flyer," Eric admitted. "At the FirstCon site, when we were out there measuring. Somebody stuck them under our windshield wipers. Jacob Ryerson— you know him— burned them all, but it could be the same."

"Was this it?" Jameson pulled a folded-up piece of white letter paper out of his jacket pocket and handed it to Eric.

"Yes, that's the one." He shook his head. "Why do people persist in this kind of backward thinking?"

"Why, indeed? You have any idea who's behind it?"

Was Jameson insinuating that he did?

Well, did he? He glanced at the bottom of the paper. Yes, there it was:

THE WHITE WAY
IS THE RIGHT WAY

But it couldn't be the "White Way Ventures" printed on Hardt's advance check last September. That was just a business, if a fake one. And Nick Hardt was dead.

"No one I'm associated with, that's for sure."

"That goes without saying," Jameson said drily.

But what about that threatening note? It had an anti-Jewish slur.

Dammit, he wasn't going there. That note was only cheap talk from a pissed-off fellow architect. If the UA guy was an anti-Semite it didn't mean he'd set up a branch of the Ku Klux Klan. Or was Eric supposed to believe that Hardt had somehow resurrected himself and all this White Way propaganda was his? If he thought that, he might as well join the UFO hunters' club.

His host was holding his drink up to the light, swirling it around and staring into its golden depths as if about to make some prognostication. "We won't throw you out tonight," he said humorously. "Wouldn't look good to have the best architect in town sleeping in his car when it's down to fifteen degrees."

"Um, thanks. I appreciate that."

"But if you could find a new place by tomorrow night, that would be best. And no hard feelings, agreed?"

"Of course not."

Suck it up, Baumann. You've got friends who'll take you in. Just don't let it affect your work.

He grasped his portfolio like a life preserver.

"You have some drawings to show me?" inquired Jameson, gesturing towards it.

"Yes!" he said, relieved. "So you can get rid of this thing." He gave the table next to him a little shove.

"Save it till after supper. We'll all look at them then. Now let's see what Vicky's got us to eat."

CHAPTER B.20

"YOU'RE IN EARLY TODAY!" Sandy forgot to conceal her delight. "You even beat eager-beaver Jim to work. Or wait, does he have a class this morning? I forget."

"He won't be in at all today," Eric said morosely, hanging his coat on the rack. "Or ever. Paternal edict."

"What?"

"And I've been evicted. Same cause."

"*What?*"

"You heard me. Cast into the cold, cruel world. Seems the creep who was here the other day somehow tracked me down to the McCulloughs' and approached little Megan. She didn't tell, no, but even so, Jameson decided the black cat had better cross someone else's path from now on."

"'Black cat'?"

"I'm bad luck, didn't you realize?"

"There's no such thing as—" The look on his face told her not to pursue it. "Don't be so morbid. When did you say your new apartment would be ready?"

"I'm not being morbid, it's the truth." He thrust a decorated metal tin towards her. "Have a *Mozartkugel*. In fact, let's both have a *Mozartkugel*. It'll make me feel better. Happy birthday, Amadeus," he said ironically.

Unwrapping her candy, she slyly sang a few bars of the Mozart *Requiem*. "*Lacrimosa dies illa!*"

"You said it. I can't get in till the first," he answered her question. "Old tenant's still in there, remember?"

"There must be some place you can stay. How about Mike Laurence?"

"Uh, I doubt he and Rosie will want company so soon."

"Blast, you're right. I'm sure you'll think of something . . . do you want me to get back on the FirstCon programming, or did you get a chance to present the table design to the McCulloughs?"

"Yeah, get on with FirstCon, whatever," he said.

Behind her as she worked she could feel his fretfulness as acutely as if the trouble was her very own.

Wasn't it? If only she could invite him . . .

Don't be an idiot.

He made several phone calls asking around for places to stay, apparently without result. Shortly before noon he announced, "I'm going to get something for lunch. You want anything from the deli?"

"No, I brought mine."

Should she say something?

Don't be a coward.

"Eric, what's the problem? I'm sure there's a motel you can go to . . . "

"You don't understand. Right now I don't even have enough to pay myself this Friday. There was that trip up north and the two new rooms and your—"

And my new salary. Well, he'd shut his mouth in time. But she could still give her opinion.

"You're still not billing out all your hours?"

He gave her a crooked smile.

"You've got to stop doing that! . . . Anyway, I'll be praying something turns up."

"It can't hurt." He swung on his coat and headed out the door.

2:12 P.M. IT WAS painful to overhear all the calls he was making, striking out every time. Was he like her? Had he lost touch with his friends for the sake of the work?

"Eric," she spoke up, "what about the Allisons? They have a mother-in-law apartment over their garage, if I remember correctly."

"They also have a new baby. I don't need a reputation as a danger to innocent children."

"I do believe you're feeling sorry for yourself . . . I don't mean to sound cold, but could you stay here?"

"And sleep on the floor? Afraid not. It's against the rules. I could lose the lease."

"Oh."

She got back to work.

A LITTLE AFTER 2:30, she quietly rummaged in her purse for her checkbook. She ought to have enough to put him up at a decent motel the next few days.

Oh, blast. Of course she didn't. There'd been the down payment on the car. And the sales tax, insurance, and registration fees. Her balance would get her through to Friday and payday, but no further. There wasn't even enough to rent him a room in a flophouse— if they still had flophouses.

But wait. There was something else she could try.

Really? You can't afford that! Look out for yourself.

Look out for herself? Shameful. Now she *had* to follow through on her impulse. She untaped the drawing she had on her board, brought it over to him, and when it seemed he had relaxed a little looking at it, she said, "I've got an idea."

"Yes?"

Quickly, before she lost her nerve, she said, "I've got a decent amount in savings, in a certificate of deposit. I could cash it in and loan it—"

"*No,*" he said, holding up his palm like a stop sign. "I can't let you do that."

"It's okay—"

"I said, no. How many years do you have to run on that thing?"

"It's a five-year," she admitted. "I opened it last August."

"They'd hit you with a massive penalty. Sandy," he said, sounding more than a little frustrated, "I have enough on my shoulders without making you lose your money and feeling guilty about that, too."

"But—"

He held up his hand again and shook his head. Admitting defeat, she took the sketch and returned to her board.

2:51.

"Eric?" she asked.

"What?" he said over his shoulder, irritably.

"What's your theory on that guy who was here the other day?"

"Theory?"

"Yes. Like what did he want with you and all?"

Nothing for a few seconds, then, "I think he's connected with McNair. Stupid bastard— sorry, bad language, but . . ."

She waited. She could hear his parallel bar going, though its rhythm was broken and disjointed.

Finally he said, "You'd think he'd have gotten the point by now. Maybe he thinks cash will work where a knife didn't."

"Maybe. I was thinking the same thing."

She let a few more minutes go by. "Did Jameson call the police about him?"

"He didn't say he did."

"Do you think we should?"

"You can if you want," he said, shrugging. "Doubt it will do any good."

She dialed the precinct number and asked for the detective who'd handled her case with McNair. He was busy, said the desk sergeant. He'd have him call back later.

3:48.

Don't turn around. He doesn't need you staring at him.

She could tell he was getting very little done, on the phone or on his board. Had he called Leah? She didn't think so. No, he hadn't.

Why not?

None of her business.

An inner voice was saying, "Be noble. Suggest he call her." For more reasons than she could count, it was quickly suppressed.

4:23. HE WAS DOING something in the middle room. She went to the communicating door and saw him on his knees, sanding the supports of the new drafting tables. A job that should have been Jim's.

"I was thinking," she said. "I could call Carole and George. They could put you up. It's far enough out. That guy wouldn't look for you there."

"They have a little boy, don't they? Can't risk it."

He seemed to be over the self-pity; that was a relief. But this flat resignation was little improvement. He took up the sandpaper again, and she went back to her board.

4:57 P.M. HE WAS at his own table again, drawing— or pretending to. Had he had any luck? No, he would have told her.

There was nothing more she could do about it.

Or was there?

For a few minutes more she tried to work. Then, turning her chair around, she gave a little laugh. "Eric?"

"What?"

"Um, a wise man once said, 'If you see your brother or sister lacking clothes or food and you say, "Depart in peace, be warm and filled," and you do nothing for his physical needs, what good is it?'"

"That's Bible, isn't it?" he said over his shoulder.

"*Ach!* and I meant to be so subtle." Purposely, she remained on her side of the room. "Yes, from *James*. The point is, you're kind of like a brother to me, and I've got a sofa bed that's pretty new, and well, if you get desperate, I suppose you could come use it."

He couldn't possibly read that as a come on. Besides, her feelings were under control. His sleeve had brushed hers at his drafting table on Monday and it hadn't raised a flutter.

Because Jim had been there with them?

No. Not a flutter. She could exercise Christian hospitality and everything would be fine.

He looked up and gave her a thin smile. "Thank you," he said quietly. "I doubt it'll come to that, but I appreciate the offer."

5:11. THE PHONE rang and Eric nearly knocked it off the counter grabbing for it. "Oh," he said, and his disappointment was palpable. "It's for you."

It was her detective. Sure, he'd make a note about last week's visitor. But had the subject actually made any threats? No? Well, if he came back and did, be sure to let him know. She was about to ask him about a connection with McNair when he said there was something he had to attend to, wished her a nice day, and ended the call.

"He didn't seem to think it was important," she told Eric.

"Let's hope he's right."

5:50 P.M.

"Sandy, are you leaving any time soon?"

"No . . . I want to get this programming as far along as I can, and they'll be playing the last three Mozart symphonies in a row starting at 6:00. I want to listen to No. 39 all the way through, at least."

"Ah. Okay."

6:13.

"Sandy?"

"Yes, Eric?"

"Have you given your new number out to many people?"

"No, just to my mother, and Carole. And you."

He said nothing more and went back to his work.

6:21. THE BROADCAST recording of the Mozart 39th may have been the best rendition ever, or it could have been the worst. Either way, her ear missed it, and so did her heart.

Dear Father, what is he going to do?

6:37 P.M. SHE'D SAID she was staying for the 39th; the 39th was over. Would he think she was babysitting him if she didn't leave? Still, she had to know he was settled and safe.

Please, God, do something! Provide for him, now!

6:42 P.M. THE FIRST bars of Mozart's *Great Symphony No. 40* in g minor were sounding from the radio on the shelf. Eric swivelled around in his chair and said, "Sandy?"

"Yes?"

"If your offer's still open . . . I think I need to take you up on it."

CHAPTER B.21

HE ARRIVED AT HER APARTMENT later that evening. "I don't think I was followed," he said, dropping his bags just inside the door. "I parked over on Forty-sixth Street, just in case."

"Followed?" She hadn't thought of that.

"It'd be just my luck," he clarified.

Oh. "Have you eaten?"

"Oh, yeah. They fed me pretty well," he said fatalistically. "My last supper."

She couldn't resist. "Don't worry, my sofa bed's not that bad. It won't crucify you."

Besides, Someone's already been through that in your place.

He gave a nervous laugh, then his face went sober. "You're sure I'm not taking advantage of you?"

"Well, it depends on what you call 'taking advantage,'" she joked, and immediately repented of it. "I'm sorry, that was—"

"No, sorry, that was the wrong term," he said. "I mean . . . "

End this.

"But no," she said, "I'm always glad to help out a friend."

They lapsed into an awkward silence.

This is silly. This isn't us at all.

"Here," she said briskly. "You can put your bags in the closet, out of the way." Did that sound like his luggage was in her way? And him, too? "I mean, where we won't trip over them. Sorry my place is so small."

"That's all right." He pointed at the wall next to the entry door. "You've got the El Greco poster up."

"Yes. It looks good there, don't you think?"

She wasn't about to tell him that after his sudden coldness at the end of their Christmas lunch she had shoved his gift in the back of the closet and refused to look at it for weeks. By now she felt more settled about both gift and giver, and last Saturday she'd finally gotten around to hanging the poster. She could be reasonably detached about the image of the martyred saint now.

"Yes." He stood there, uncertainly. Why didn't he sit down?

You haven't invited him to.

"Have a seat," she said, trying her best to act casual. What was wrong with her? This had to stop or they'd drive each other bats. "Um, this hasn't been much of a Mozart's birthday celebration. I've . . . I've got a recording of the *Quintet for Clarinet and Strings* I think you'll like. Tashi, with Richard Stoltzman."

"That'd be nice. I've got the rest of the *Mozartkugeln* with me . . . " He dug out the box and offered her one.

"In a minute, as soon as I put the record on . . . . Thanks. Perfect." She bit into the bonbon, then made rather a fuss of getting them both napkins and coffee. "I'm sorry I don't have any—"

"Any what?"

"Nothing. Isn't his playing superb?"

Any wine, she'd been about to say, but that was a good thing. She'd come a long way since mid-November when she'd nearly destroyed her career over the silly idea of being in love with him. Even so, sharing a glass of wine with Eric Baumann tonight would be neither politic nor wise.

They both said all the right things about the quintet's performance, and about the pieces she put on the turntable after that. But something in the atmosphere kept their talk from being anything but superficial and constrained.

We're both loners. Neither of us is used to spending this time of evening with anyone else.

That couldn't be true. He had Leah, and there were those evenings she herself had spent at his place . . .

Shut up.

She looked at her watch. 10:15. She never went to bed this early.

I can't stand it any more.

"Well," she joked, rising, "I'm afraid tonight you'll have to go to bed at a civilized hour like a real human being."

"That's okay. The McCulloughs made me turn in when Megan did!"

What a relief he could kid her again. "Oh, horrors, and she staying up for the *Late Late Late Show*." She fetched a set of bedclothes from the linen cupboard in the hall. "Here's a pillow for you, and some sheets, and a blanket. All aesthetically-matched and fashion-coordinated."

"Gee, thanks!"

"I'll pull this thing out for you." She made a move towards the sofa.

"No, I'll get it. If you don't mind, that is. I'd like to sit up a while longer."

"Oh, sure, go ahead. I've got a book I'm rereading. You can play the stereo or whatever you want. I won't be going to sleep for a while yet."

"Okay. Well, pleasant dreams."

"Same to you."

In the bathroom, brushing her teeth, she wondered. Was she doing the right thing?

But the image of him sleeping bootleg on the office floor, or worse, freezing all night in his car, filled her with such horrified pity that her heart could only say that she was.

ERIC WATCHED her pad off to the bathroom. He heard the water running, then took in the silence as she settled in with her book behind the closed bedroom door.

It was a mistake to come here. He should have trusted to luck in the office.

One by one, he extinguished the lights, all but a small lamp that stood on the massive antique chest just inside the entry door. He positioned it so it illuminated the El Greco reproduction that hung above it, and went back and sat down.

It had all begun with that, hadn't it? At least, the awareness had started there. It may have started before, but that's when he began to wonder about himself, to suspect. That look of hers as she contemplated that painting, there at the Civic Museum . . . it had filled him with awe— and fear. He'd never seen that in her before. Something drove him that day to honor it . . . and to make it stop.

He'd stopped it, all right. He'd halted it cold with his flippant talk of buying the painting for her. It shamed him to recall how solemnly he'd made the offer. She had understood what a foolish thing it was and immediately put him in his place.

But he couldn't let it lie, could he?

So he'd bought her that poster. Had it framed. Presented it to her as a kind of afterthought. A joke. A clever, artistic joke, but a joke nonetheless.

But it wasn't a joke, it was serious. It was so serious he'd been running the past three months from the immensity of it. Maybe, if he tried hard enough, he could keep running still.

Go to bed, Baumann. You got nothing done today. You'll need to make up for it tomorrow.

In the bathroom he washed and changed into his pajama bottoms. Pausing at her door on his way back to the living room, he marvelled. How unaware she was of the conflict within him, how oblivious, how . . . *innocent.*

What must it be like to have so much power and never know? But she had it, and to fight it he was treating her in ways that made him cringe. O god, what a pathetic excuse for a man he was! What was he afraid of? He knew the pleasures of passion and had even called it love. But at the thought of the girl behind that closed door, such emotions shrivelled, grew pale and grotesque, and skittered away like last years' leaves.

He turned out the lamp and sat hunched on the couch, his head in his hands. The waving branches of a sycamore outside the window intercepted the rays of the streetlight, conspiring with the blinds to cast weird patterns on the furniture and walls. More haunting still was the utter uselessness of all he had done to ward off what couldn't be stopped. Stop it? He suppressed a sardonic laugh. He may as well put up his hand to halt the cascade of Niagara!

Sometimes lately he'd thought he could stop it. He could go a whole day, maybe two, and things were as they'd been before. He could take her and all she was to him for granted, and never think how shaky the ground was under his feet. Then, when he least expected it, all she had to do was say his name or look up with that smile of hers, and he had to hold on to everything that was solid and sane to keep from being swept away.

He shouldn't have come. Tomorrow, he'd . . . do what?

He didn't know. For several minutes he sat in the darkness, trying to think of something else, anything else; trying not to think at all. But it seemed that a keen-eyed goddess loomed over him, her gaze piercing into his very soul, commanding his attention, compelling him to accept what his fate decreed.

It's impossible! She works for me!

The thought, far from saving him, pushed him into an abyss without bottom or bounds. O god, she did work for him! Her skill, her experience, her intelligence— all that he could compensate her for. Though not enough. Not half enough. But she gave him more than that. She was his patience, his wisdom, his conscience, his hand. Freely she gave to him, courageously, from her heart— and he'd thought he could keep her in her place.

Her place? Better she should keep me in mine!

Falling, faster and faster he was falling, and the well of undeniable knowledge grew wider and fuller with his descent.

It wasn't from mere love of architecture that she did it. It wasn't for the sake of her career.

It was for him.

She works for me, she risks her life for me, and I should serve her!

But what of the office? What about his work?

Their work! What was it without her? Horrified, he saw what he had nearly done. Shutting her out wasn't the key to all he hoped to accomplish, it was letting her in!

And more than what she meant to his work, far more than that, was who she was in herself. "Sandy," he breathed out her name in the darkness. "Sandy." So precious, so dear, that diamond in the sand he'd overlooked and stepped over and even— fates forgive him!— stepped on time and again.

Baumann, you fool! You stupid, blind fool! You'll never make it up to her. She's giving up on you already, you're already driving her away, can't you tell?

The very fact she could invite him so coolly to stay under her roof proved it. *"You're kind of like a brother to me."* It had been more than that once, he was sure. But now? An invisible steel band bound his chest and against it his heart beat in desperation.

Do something. He had to do something.

What could he do? Was it already too late?

From somewhere within him came a word like an ordering hand in the chaos:

Tell her.

He got to his feet, a little unsteadily.

Go to her. Yield to her. Tell her. Tell her now!

A golden ribbon of light lay faint and serene along the threshold of her room. He knocked gently, almost fearfully. "Sandy? Are you awake?"

"Sure, Eric," her voice came lightly. "Do you need anything?"

Trembling, he opened the door.

HE WAS STANDING just inside her room, indistinct in the semi-darkness beyond the glow of the reading lamp. He gulped down a breath, and it struck her ear like a strangled sob.

She closed her book in alarm. He didn't look at all well. He was bare-chested, despite the chill of the night, and much paler than mere winter time could explain.

"Are you cold?" she asked anxiously. "Can I get you another blanket? If there's anything I can do—" She broke off as her mind hinted at the implications of the offer. She climbed out of bed, glad of the dowdy flannel nightgown that covered her, neck to toe.

HOW BEAUTIFUL she is in that white gown! She shines like a diamond in the lamplight . . . like an angel from heaven . . . no, angels aren't real; she is real, she is warm and real and precious to me!

He stood still, taking in every line of her form, and veiled as it was, it filled him with a piercing delight.

He wasn't too late. The soft wonder in her warm brown eyes steadied him. Whatever came next, it would be the right thing for him to do.

She stepped towards him, searching his face, then gasped and halted as his emotion seemed to affect her as well.

My diamond, my shining star!

It's time. Tell her.

"WHAT'S WRONG, tell me!" It came out in a whisper; she couldn't sustain more. She took another step towards him, then stopped.

Why had she thought the rest of the room was in darkness? She could distinguish every line and plane of his face, and in it was a look she'd never seen there, a look that left all her foundations undermined.

"I wanted— I needed— I mean, I've taken you for granted for so long and I had to tell you that— that— I need you."

She wouldn't interpret that the way her heart prompted her to. She didn't dare. "I'm glad I could help you out tonight," she said, her voice trembling, "but I would have done it for almost anyone."

He can't mean more than that. That's all, it has to be.

"No, that's not it! I—"

"You mean the office," she hurriedly countered, closing the floodgates against the coming tide. "I just do my job, you know that."

"No, no, you don't understand! For everything! I *need* you. I need *you!*"

She stared at him blankly, afraid of what thought might admit.

He seemed to collect himself, then said more calmly, "Let me see your wrist."

She raised it to him like one hypnotized. He took her hand and ran his fingers lightly over the scarlet, forming scar.

"My fault," he murmured. "My own terrible fault."

He retained his hold and gazed intently into her face, so that she recalled Ophelia's lines from *Hamlet* she'd been reading just moments before:

> He took me by the wrist and held me hard;
> Then goes he to the length of all his arm;
> And . . . he falls to such perusal of my face
> As he would draw it.

She tried to look away but could not.

I wonder what I'd look like with no face? her frantic intellect gibbered. *Or is that "draw" like an artist?*

It was a last absurd, desperate effort to master the moment— but the moment had overmastered her. She gave a soft moan, as one who sees the approach of welcome death, and her Shakespeare slipped unhindered to the floor. She stooped to retrieve it; he stooped with her; his hand was over hers on the slim volume, arresting her as his gray eyes plumbed her and knew her.

"Sandy," he whispered, "I love you."

I am lost! she cried within herself as his arms went around her, his lips met hers, and she felt herself borne again to her bed. It was over, all over; all pretending and defense fell in ruins as she welcomed the fierce joy of his mouth on her eyes, her face, her shoulders . . . And oh! his hands, his beautiful artist's hands! Without hesitation or thought she yielded to their caresses, opening and responding to him as she gave him what so long had been his own. Jeff's cruelty, Marvin's drunken pawing, Werner's slow artistry— the memories flashed into her mind and like a vapor were gone.

For this at last was *he*: his mouth, his hands, his body; this was Eric, *her* Eric, and now, and now—

"No!" she wailed, sending him unceremoniously to the floor. "No!"

From the carpet, he gaped at her, dumbfounded.

"I can't, I just can't!"

"But— but—" he stammered, "I thought you loved me!"

Her soul groaned within her. "Eric," she cried, desperate with agony, "I can't, because I do love you!"

There. She'd said it. He knew her now more thoroughly than if he had partaken of her body for a thousand years. Clutching the neck of her nightgown closed, she tried not to weep.

"I don't understand," he said weakly as he pulled himself to his feet. "If you love me, then why—?"

"I'm not sure I understand either. Something tells me we both need to try." She gave him a trembling smile. "Maybe if we move to neutral ground . . . unless you've already . . . ?"

"No," he said, "I never opened the sofa up. I've got a tee shirt in there somewhere . . . " Like a man in a fog he disappeared into the other room.

Oh gosh. Oh gosh. Did we really do that? Did that really happen?

It had. And she couldn't find it in her to be sorry.

CHAPTER B.22

HE TURNED ON ALL THE LIVING ROOM LIGHTS, closed the blinds, and waited. She emerged a few minutes later in a pair of acid green tracksuit bottoms and an oversized, paint-splattered Blakewell Academy sweatshirt. An attempt to discourage him? It wasn't working. She was still beautiful.

And he was still a blundering, selfish jerk.

She sat down beside him on the sofa and laid a hand on his shoulder. "I'm sorry," she said. "It's my fault. I shouldn't have let you think . . . I shouldn't have taken advantage like . . . " She gulped.

"You? Take advantage? I'm the one who invaded your bedroom when you only meant to give me a place to crash for the night!"

"No, I—"

"You don't understand! After you went to bed I got to thinking and, oh god, it hit me, I finally realized what I've been so afraid of, what I've been fighting against all this time; I knew at last that I love you, and I had to tell you, to convince you in any way I could." He drew a breath. "And then I ruin everything by marching in and practically raping you!"

"*Rape?*" she repeated, and on the word her voice went up at least an octave. "Rape? Oh, Eric, you don't know the first thing about it!" Her whole body trembled, she covered her face with her hands and laughed bitterly. "You just don't know . . . "

His jaw dropped in horror. "No! You? When? Who?"

She wouldn't look at him.

"Not Al McNair?" He'd feared something like that.

She shook her head. "No. He— he said he was going to. He put his hand on my leg. That was all. No," she said, shaking her head again, more violently this time, "not Al McNair."

"Then . . . ?"

"Ah!" It was a cry of hopelessness and pain. Her body slumped, as if she'd been fighting something for a long time and just couldn't fight anymore. Softly at first, in fits and hiccups, then harder and more steadily, she began to cry.

"Come here," he said, drawing her close in his arms. "That's better. Hush. You don't have to say anything. Just rest."

She let him enfold her, but for a long time rest was beyond her. Sobs wracked her body until he thought she might be ill. But whenever he felt he should let her go, she said, "No, please, hold me, hold me!" and he, obedient, would clasp her tighter.

She feels safe with me. The thought brought him relief and joy.

Eventually her tears were less agonized; her body grew still. "Please, Eric, keep holding me, please," she said, her voice muffled against his shoulder. "But I don't want you to get the wrong idea." She looked up at him. "He— that one— didn't succeed either. I stopped it in time. God helped me." Her tremulous pride tore at his heart. "There was an X-Acto knife I could grab . . . "

"Another architect?" he blurted out without thinking.

He felt her head nod.

Wait a minute. What was it that Mike Laurence said, how she'd gone all satirical and self-loathing the end of their freshman year, and she was herself again in the fall?

She was like that after McNair assaulted her.

As if by revelation he spoke: "During architecture school? In the architecture building?"

He felt the nod again. "Yes . . . down in the store. I— I stabbed him, and someone in the hall heard him yell. I hid, and he left with whoever it was. To go get doughnuts, can you believe it? Doughnuts!" She let out a sound between a laugh and a keening cry.

There was a good chance he'd been in the building that night, and he'd never known.

"But—?" *But who?* A scene arose to his memory: just last month, Sandy advising him not to hire a certain candidate because the man couldn't be trusted. Like an arrow his conclusion winged towards the target. "Jeff Chesters?"

She sat up in astonishment. "How did you know? I never told anybody. Nobody. Until you." The fact that she had admitted it to him seemed to amaze her all the more.

"I didn't know. It was what you said about him when we were going over résumés that day. Now I know why. No, don't apologize . . . I'm just sorry I didn't keep his address. I'd like to know where to find him."

"Oh, no, please don't, nothing like that! I forgave him, a long time ago. Please don't dig it up again! God will take care of him, you don't need to."

"If you say so . . ." Once more he pulled her close. "But Sandy, tonight, if— if you wanted me— if you loved me, and I loved and wanted you, why stop? Was it because of that?"

"*O Domine!*" she said, low, and it sounded like a prayer. She pulled away and looked him in the face. "No, it wasn't that. It wasn't that at all."

HOW TO TELL him? Would he laugh, give her a lecture about entering the twentieth century, think she was preaching at him and despise her for it?

She took a deep breath and concentrated on his hands, which were holding hers. Such beautiful, effective hands . . . "*De sa main la caresse . . .*"

"Eric," she said, "have you ever . . . ?"

No, she should just tell it. Tell it straight.

"Eric, you know I went to Blakewell Public Academy. I may've said something about the classical education I got there. But I don't think I told you about the attitudes we graduated with, especially we girls."

She glanced up at his face. He was listening.

"We had pretty high standards about, about men and women and staying pure till marriage."

His right hand gave a sudden twitch, and was still.

"A lot of us were Christians, but it wasn't just that. We saw ourselves as knights— the girls, too— and we were going to serve God and our professions and to do that we had to stay pure. So we could concentrate on our work and not lose focus. Some of us girls the summer after our senior year even formed an order and swore to do that in college."

"Really?"

"Really. We called it 'The Knights of the Single Eye.'"

"Like Cyclops?" he asked, mystified.

She laughed. "No, 'single' is the old King James word for 'healthy' or 'whole.' We weren't going to stay virgins forever. Just until . . . until God sent us the Christian boys He wanted us to marry."

His face was veiled at this, but he held her hands a little tighter, as if to prevent her from pulling away.

"Thing is, most of us had never been tested." She shook her head at the irony of it. "We socialized in a crowd, and we didn't date. 'Honors monkeys run in packs,' is what the other kids said about us. I got up to Mount Athens, and well, you know how it was in the early '70s, with Women's Lib and the sexual revolution and all. Things were changing. And I changed, too."

"Yes?"

"I— I decided that since God is love, love was enough. That if I loved a guy at the moment, it would be all right to sleep with him, never mind if we ever got married. Then . . . something happened, and I changed my mind again."

"What Chesters did?"

"Yes . . . " Would he conclude she had loved Jeff in that heedless way? Probably. It was in God's hands. "Anyway, after that I went back to thinking marriage had to come into it somehow. I decided being engaged was enough. That made it okay to sleep together beforehand and nobody else could say anything about it."

He said nothing.

"It almost came to that. Once."

"You've been engaged? You never told me!"

"It wasn't . . . it was for a very short time."

But why would he want to know about Werner? He'd never cared about her personal life before.

Of course he cared now. He loved her.

"Did you love . . . uh, I mean . . . ?" He didn't finish.

"Yes, madly. Breaking up with him was the hardest thing I've ever had to do, until . . . " She searched his face: would he understand? "I found out he wasn't faithful. And probably couldn't be. I couldn't risk it. I just couldn't risk it.

"But . . . I kept on thinking that way. That true love— and the intention to get married someday— was enough. Up until tonight I did. You love me— is it true?"

"It is."

"O heavens! And even though I've tried to hide it and make it go away for the sake of our work, I love you too. Tonight I was even willing to forget the part about needing to be engaged. All I wanted was you!"

He tilted her face up to his and gently kissed her lips.

"Yes," she said. "All I want now is you . . . But maybe that's just it. Because in the middle of it all, when we were in there— it hit me that the way I used to think back in high school was right. Not for the same reasons, but right anyway. That all the old stuff about standing up before God and all the neighbors and making promises first is how it has to be. For me, anyway. It has to mean everything. Eric," she cried, "if I had you only part way, it would kill me!"

"I would give myself to you, Sandy. I would. Totally."

"Totally?" she said quietly. "I know how you feel about marriage. I don't want to get so I'm pushing you into it."

Should she mention his not being a Christian? No. Not here. Not now.

"Sandy, I . . . Are you sure it's necessary? Marriage, I mean? When I think of all the time I've wasted . . . god! Tell me, when did you first start to love me?"

"Since I came to work for you. Maybe before."

"See? All these things I never knew about you, never cared to know. I want to know you now, completely. I won't push you till you're ready, but someday I will know you, body, mind, and soul."

This time it was she who took his head between her two hands— oh, the joy of having the right to do it!— and looked deep into his eyes. "Eric," she said, "listen. You have known me."

"How?"

"Like this: I love you. *I love you.* I've never said it before. It meant too much. There was always some reason not to say it, always something holding me back. Until tonight."

"Not even to Ma—?" He stopped, embarrassed.

She smiled at the mistake. Of course, he'd seen her with Marvin the night they met. She'd have to straighten him out on that later.

"No one. Not even the man I was engaged to. I held back: maybe I knew it didn't belong to him. For you, only, first, last, and forever: Eric Edward Baumann, I love you. I love you!"

He took her hands and brought them to his mouth and kissed them. "Sandy— Alexandra Marie Beichten, I love you."

Our hands, our names, like vows. Then their lips met and for a long, long time there was no thought; only swimming, breathing, blissfully existing in the eternal sea of his kiss.

But thought would intrude, and deeper desire. O God, why couldn't they? Why not why not why not?

Trust. Wait. My way is best.

Yes, Lord.

She opened her eyes and caught sight of the clock. "Good gosh, look at the time! It's after 1:00 a.m.!"

"I guess we do have things to do in the morning," he said, in a kind of groan.

"Yeah . . . " she said regretfully. "What is that poem, by Wordsworth I think, 'The world is too much with us; late and soon . . . '?"

"'Getting and spending, we lay waste our powers,'" he took up the lines. "I know."

"But we're not wasting our powers. We do beautiful work," she pronounced. "At least, you do. I just get to help and admire."

She slipped out of his embrace and stood up. He caught hold of her hand. "No, Sandy, that's just it. I can't do it without you. I'm nothing without you. That's what I want you to understand."

Kissing the top of his head, she whispered, "Bless you. . . . Good night."

She was in the bedroom brushing her hair when he called to her.

"Yes?" She regarded him from the hall doorway. He'd extinguished all but one of the lamps and sat on the sofa, his face illuminated by the streetlight glowing through the reopened blinds. "Do you want me to help you pull out that hide-a-bed now?"

"No, leave it." His eyes held hers and she was amazed anew by their command and strength. "Sandy, turn off the light."

She stepped over to the lamp under the El Greco poster and switched it off. "Good night, Eric."

"No. Come here."

"I trust you. I'm not sure why, but I do."

He held out his arms and she nestled into his embrace.

"Pull your legs up here . . . yes, like that. No, you're not too heavy. There."

His arms held her close as they lay on the sofa, her head in the crook of his shoulder, his body a warm, living rock curved around hers in the dappled darkness.

He reached for the blanket and spread it over them both. "Somehow or other," he said, his voice shaking with merriment, "tonight, you're sleeping with me."

CHAPTER B.23

THE PALE GRAY LIGHT of a winter's dawn was glowing faintly between the slats of the blinds when he awoke, stiff but inwardly rested. He looked down at the young woman still sleeping trustingly in his arms.

My star at night, my sun by day.

"Hey, Sunshine," he cajoled her softly, "it's time to get up."

She stirred. "Wha—? Oh, gosh," she groaned, eyes still closed, "I don't want to get up, I want to finish my dream . . . "

"Don't worry," he said as he kissed her forehead, "I won't dock your pay if you're late."

"It wasn't a dream!" she exclaimed, now fully awake. "Oh, Eric, this is terrible! I look awful in the morning."

"Do you? I hadn't noticed."

She struggled upright, pulling down her sweatshirt where it had ridden up. "Did we really sleep like that?"

"Guess so! I've got a muscle or two that's forgotten what it's for, but it'll be okay once I move around a little." He rose and stretched.

"I'll give you first turn in the bathroom," she said, combing out her hair with her fingers.

"Oh, no, ladies first."

"No, you're the guest."

"I hope I'm more than that."

"You are." She reached her arms around his neck and kissed him. A simple good morning salute, but it sent the fire of a hundred comets through his body.

Damn. If only.

Controlling himself he said, "All right, I'll go first. But after I'm out, just point me towards the kitchen and I'll get us breakfast. I'm not a bad chef, really."

"Oh, no, Eric, I couldn't let you do that!"

"No, I want to help you. The way I see it, I'm the boss in the office but you're the boss here. Your wish is my command."

"In that case, you'll let me do it," she replied, and yawned off to the bedroom.

WHEN SANDY took her turn in the bathroom it pleased and amused her to see how neat he was. Razor, soap, toothbrush— everything placed just so, as if he'd lived there forever.

She emerged to the sizzle of frying bacon. She found him in the kitchen, mixing up pancake batter.

"Eric!"

"My grandmother's recipe," he said, proffering the bowl.

"But I told you—!"

"Okay, I'm incorrigible."

"You sure are. You don't mind if I put some syrup on to heat, do you?"

"Oh no, not at all."

"Face it, you run things no matter where you are."

"You don't mind, do you?"

"No, and that's the obnoxious part about it!"

"Sandy," he said, grinning at her, "you are a throwback. But I like you."

"Last night you said you loved me," she said, hoping it sounded like a ribbing. He didn't seem to be having second thoughts, but you never knew.

"I do," he answered firmly, "and in a few minutes I'm going to drive you to work and you'd better wear something warm because I'm going to roll down all the windows and shout to everyone I see, 'I love Sandy Beichten!'"

Alarm seized her. "Do you have to?"

"What? Roll down the windows?"

"No. Do the Paul Revere thing."

"Well, I was exaggerating . . . a little . . . " he said, lifting the bacon out to drain, "but that's the way I feel. Don't you feel that way, too?"

"Yes! But . . . do we really have to let people know?"

He stopped, bacon and tongs in mid-air. "Why not?"

She hardly knew, herself. Because this was all so new and she was afraid publicity would jinx it? Because there were people at her church who might question her loving an unbeliever? (She didn't want to look at that too closely herself.) Because his friends would think they were "doing it" and her friends might, too? Or they'd be bothering her about when were they getting married? She wouldn't be able to bear it.

"Because . . . because of the clients," she said. Yes. That was the way. "Some of them might think . . . might be afraid . . . " Of what? That they'd be so wrapped up in each other they'd get no work done? That lovers' quarrels— and she just-barely admitted to herself that they might have them— would disrupt the design process? Yes. All that and more. "If we missed a deadline they might think it was because we . . . I'm sorry, I'm not expressing myself very well."

He relaxed and poured pancake batter into her other skillet. "I understand. You and I are a great team already, but we'll have to show them that this'll make us stronger still. At least I think it will."

"So do I. Like Denise Scott-Brown and Robert Venturi." She'd long been impressed with the collaboration of that famous Philadelphia architect couple.

Oh-oh. The Venturis are married. Will he think that's a hint?

If he did, he gave no sign. "Are those pancakes done enough for you?" he asked a minute later.

"Just right. Here's a plate."

He flipped the pancakes onto it, re-oiled the skillet, and started the second round.

"We'll take it slow," he agreed. "We'll act like you just work for me and that's it."

"Does that mean you behaving like you did out at the site that time? In that case, uh, *no*."

He bowed his head. "I'm so sorry about that. I was afraid I was falling in love with you, and I thought I had to make myself stop. That's my only excuse. Can you forgive me?"

"Yes, Eric."

"Really?"

"Will this convince you?"

The pancake turner clattered to the countertop as she pulled him to her and his mouth met hers with a hunger that matched her own.

"Sandy. My diamond. My precious, precious love . . . "

"Oh, Eric, I love you. I'll say it, and say it, and say it: I love you! I love you!"

The food's getting cold.

I don't care. He is my food, my drink, my life . . .

As if he could read her thoughts, without ceasing to kiss her, he reached over, whipped the plates of food into the oven, kicked the door closed, then renewed his hold on her body. Pressed fiercely to his broad chest, she could feel his heart beating strong and fast. Her lips burned, her arms ached from holding him tight, yet she clung to him all the more. Oh, that they could both find relief in one another, if only, if only!

Not yet. Wait!

Eternity in his arms . . . *Forever and always, mine. Mine.* Mine.

Hers? Really?

She wriggled out of his embrace. "No, Eric, stop. Wait."

"What's wrong?" he said, alarmed. "Are the pancakes burning?"

"No," she said. "I've just thought of something."

"Don't think. Kiss me again."

"No . . . don't." Again she escaped. "No. It's Leah," she said urgently. *"What about Leah?"*

He did a double-take, then too quickly said, "That's over."

"Really?" she said, stepping out of his reach. "It's been over before. I know. Did you two settle that this time it's for good?"

"No, but it doesn't matter."

"It does matter. I love you, but I can't—"

"I haven't seen her since New Year's Eve," he said with an air of grim finality. He went back to the stove and turned the pancakes.

It might be gossiping to encourage him to go on. "And?" she said, nevertheless.

"It was midnight, and I was going to do what you always do at midnight on New Year's Eve, kiss the girl you came with. I reached out, and Leah wasn't there. You know where I found her?"

She waited.

"In the kitchen, talking shop with the caterer. That wasn't so bad. Maybe I should have expected it, these days. But you know what she did next?"

"What?"

"When I told her I'd come for my New Year's kiss, she asked me was I crazy, she didn't have the time, she wasn't going to miss the chance to pick this woman's brain. She made me look like a fool!"

Sandy squeezed his hand.

He pulled the food out of the oven and added the fresh pancakes to the stack. "Don't feel too sorry for me. My pride was hurt, not my heart. It hit me right then that everything we seemed to have in common had been just that, things. Being with her just didn't matter anymore. I dropped her off at her place and haven't seen her since.

"Yes," he said, more to himself than to her, "it's definitely over."

Sandy took a deep breath. "I believe you. But it would help me if— if you could tell me it's official. She might be waiting for you to come back to her, just like before . . . "

"Precious love, would my settling things with Leah make you happy? I see it would. All right, this very day I'll call and tell her we're officially through."

She kissed him gently to seal the agreement.

"Here's the pancakes," he said, "and I think they're edible."

"They're fine. I've got the butter and the syrup. Bring the coffeepot, and we'll eat."

She put the food on the table and sat down opposite him. He had his first forkful to his mouth when she said, "Wait a minute. I say grace."

He shrugged and smiled indulgently. "Go ahead."

She rushed through the prayer.

What am I afraid of? I'm sorry, Lord. I'll do better next time.

Eric cleared his throat and said, "Okay, let's eat."

For a while they breakfasted in communal silence. Outside, it promised to be a beautiful day. Inside herself, she seemed poised on the verge of something frightening, amazing, yet overwhelmingly good.

"Eric," she said, "you're right. You *are* an excellent chef."

CHAPTER B.24

"YOU KNOW," ERIC SAID Friday evening, "that phone hasn't rung once since I got here."

"That's the beauty of an unlisted number," Sandy replied. They were eating supper, and she rejoiced over how much better it was than the movie he'd suggested they go out and see. "And I've noticed that you haven't had many meetings to go to the past two days."

"No. And I'm glad." He reached across the table and squeezed her hand. "Aren't you?"

"Very. It's almost like . . . "

"Like it was meant to be? I was thinking that, too." He chased down and ate the last strands of spaghetti on his plate. "Amazing," he said, putting down his fork, "how when I came here Wednesday it was only to lie low for a night or two."

"The man with the green ring."

A shadow passed over his brow. "Yes. . . . Sandy, if I weren't so damned happy being here with you, it might scare me to think of all the trash we've had to face lately. As it is, I simply can't be bothered."

Her heart turned over with pleasure at his love for her— and with disquiet at what had brought them together. She said, "I just wish somebody would clue McNair in on who really is working with this Rutherford guy so his lackeys will stop bothering us. Oh, gosh, he's not out on bail, is he?"

"No, I checked today and they've sent him down to Kentucky on that gun charge. But didn't you say McNair heard about us from some source on the street? Maybe they got Rutherford and Hardt confused. Or they were in it together? Maybe McNair was just too stupid to know."

"No idea. Do we have to think about it?"

"I'm sorry," he said, his expression contrite. "I didn't mean to remind you of what happened."

"It's not that. It's just that I'd rather . . . " She felt herself blush.

He stood. "Come here." He drew her towards him and sat down again, pulling her onto his lap.

"Eric, I don't know, these bentwood chairs . . . "

"It'll be fine. Let me hold you. Ah! That's better." He cradled her head against his chest, smoothing her hair and planting kisses on her crown.

After a few minutes she said, "Eric, what do you want to do tonight?"

His only response was to hold her closer.

"I know, but besides that?"

"Hmmm." His mouth found hers, and under his kiss there was no question what she wanted to do, tonight and for always.

If only . . .

"Eric," she said at length, smiling, "you're not making things any easier for me." She slid off his lap and began clearing the table.

They fell into the task of doing the dishes without talk or negotiation, easily, naturally, as if they'd been sharing a kitchen half their lives. It'd been that way since they'd come home— come home!— together the evening before. This, right here, was the real beauty of it.

"Don't laugh," he said suddenly, "but I'm enjoying myself. This is much better than seeing a movie. We make a good team."

"That's what I was thinking. Literally."

"I don't get it, though," he said, putting the last saucepan into the cupboard. "It's not any different from how we work together in the office, but it is different."

"I know. It's like— it's like I've got on a pair of old, comfortable, broken-in shoes and I'm walking along, just living life and doing things in it, and I look down and there I am, walking in mid-air! And I can't come back to earth even if I wanted to."

He bent down, and kissed her forehead. "Sandy, my precious love, I couldn't describe it better myself."

TO ERIC, everything in Sandy's apartment was an object of magical wonder, telling a story he was eager to hear. That framed photograph that stood on the bookcase across from her sofa, for instance. It showed a middle-aged couple, the man's eyes candid and bright through gawky hornrims, the woman sporting a well-sprayed hairdo just as a matron of her mother's generation would have flaunted her best Sunday hat.

"Sandy," he said Saturday afternoon as she entered the living room carrying a full basket of laundry, "are these your parents?"

She set the basket down. "Yes. Taken for their twenty-fifth wedding anniversary, back in '69."

Never could his own mother and father have had such a portrait taken. The couple stood with their arms around each other's waists, both smiling, both comfortable with the camera and with themselves. They appeared to be deeply in love.

"They look like nice people. I think you told me your mom's in Florida; what happened to your dad?"

A shade passed over her face.

"If you don't mind, that is."

"No, that's okay, it's nothing you shouldn't know. It's just that sometimes I still feel guilty. I shouldn't, since I've been forgiven, but it's easy if I let myself."

"Guilty? What do you mean?"

"My father died of a heart attack just before Christmas my junior year in college. Friday of finals week, in fact. He was only fifty-two . . . "

"Oh, Sandy, I'm sorry!" he said, taking her hand.

"Thanks. I— I wasn't there when it happened. I hadn't come home from Mount Athens . . . "

"Why the guilt? You had finals. You couldn't have known."

"But I did. My mom called me the beginning of the month to say he'd been having chest pains. The Monday of finals week she called again and told me he was in the hospital. She begged me to come home, but I said no, Daddy was always having these episodes and he'd want me to take my exams."

"That's understandable."

"Yes. But I wasn't telling the whole truth. The truth was that's when I was dating Marvin Jansovic— you remember him, he's the one I came to—"

"Yes," he said, cutting the explanation short.

"Anyway, I was pretty well up on what I needed to know for the tests, so between exams we were out drinking and dancing and having a jolly old time. I was enjoying myself so much I didn't want to come home until I absolutely had to. Christmas break was going to be three weeks of boredom. I didn't want the fun to end."

"You wouldn't be seeing . . . Marvin . . . " He found himself reluctant to say the loser's name. " . . . back home?"

"No. My family didn't approve of him. I thought I'd show them . . . I could have postponed my exams, but I was going to get my way regardless. And then— Daddy died." She put her fist to her mouth and gave a low groan.

"I'm sorry . . . That must have been a hard Christmas."

She grimaced. "My own fault . . . But your parents. Is your dad still alive?"

Damn it, my father is my own business! Next thing, you'll be telling me he did the right thing, putting his religion first!

She gasped. "Eric, what's wrong?"

"I— I got a stitch in my side." He put his hand hard to his waist, pretending it hurt.

"Poor love!" She massaged the place. "There, is that better?"

"Oh. Yes. Much better."

"But your dad?"

Better tell her something.

He made his voice sad but resigned. "I don't know. The church retired him back in '75 and two months later he told Momma he had to get away for a while. To find himself, he said. He left the next day, and we haven't heard from him since." *"Hopped that midnight freight train, Said he'd ride it down the line . . ." And thank— whatever— for that.*

"Oh, Eric! How terrible for you!"

He gave a mournful shrug. "We manage."

"But—"

"I never pegged you for the rebellious type," he said quickly.

"What?"

"About Marvin. So dating him was just about having fun?" An awkward question, but safer than anything to do with his father.

"No," she said bitterly. "I thought I was going to rescue him. Develop his talent, save him from himself. I can't count how many times I gave him my class notes or cleaned up after him or nursed him when he got one of his cases of the flu!"

"He got sick that much?"

She snorted. "Hung over. Sometimes for three days running. I had no illusions about being in love with him. That made me feel more virtuous about it."

The more he heard about the guy— he couldn't call him a man— the more coldly angry he got. "So you broke up with him after your father died?"

She turned away and stared out the window. "No, heaven help me, I didn't. That didn't happen till spring break when *I* got the flu for real. I—" She faced him, lifting up her hands in appeal. "He told me he'd take care of me if I was ever in trouble! Be there for me, 'like white on rice' is how he put it! And I believed him!"

"Of course you did. So what happened?"

"Monday of spring break, my housemates are both gone, everybody I know has left campus, and Marvin's supposed to take me to a stock car race that evening. But there I was in bed feeling like I was going to die. I could hardly move! Marvin calls and I think, good, he'll keep his promise and come over and take care of me. But no! He tells me he and some other guys have rented a cabin on the lake and are going fishing till Saturday. And he had the gall to tell me he wasn't coming over first because he didn't want to get the flu himself!"

Appalled, Eric took her in his arms. "Poor precious love! What did you do?"

She looked up at him. "I called my mother and she drove up and brought me home. The doctor said it was a good thing she did. I could have ended up in the hospital, or worse."

He held her tighter. Yet one more time he could have lost her, and he never would have known. Damn that Jansovic! Sometime he'd make him pay.

She gently pulled free. "I really shouldn't get all heated about it. I've forgiven him for the way he treated me."

"If forgiveness means going out with a creep like that again," he said stiffly, "I don't think much of it."

She didn't rise to the provocation. "If you mean the party at Leah's, I was interviewing at Speedwell Associates a few days after I got back from Boston and Marvin stepped off the elevator just as I was leaving. He was the first familiar face I'd seen, and it's silly what a comfort that can be, even if it's someone you don't really like." *Please understand,* her eyes pleaded.

"It happens," he allowed. "So he asked you to be his date then dumped you for the Bacardi."

"Something like that. And then this tall dark handsome stranger came along and rescued me."

"He'll keep on rescuing you if you'll let him," he said, drawing her to him again and nuzzling her slender neck with his lips.

"That'd be bliss . . . but it won't get the laundry done." She ducked out of his embrace and picked up the clothes basket.

"I'll get that," he said. "It looks heavy."

She beamed that thousand candlepower smile he was growing to love so well. "I'd be happy for you to carry it down for me. But you're lying low, remember? As much as I'd like to show you off to the neighbors, I'd better hold back."

"All right. But don't be long, okay?"

The door closed behind her. He picked up a book he'd found lying on her nightstand, but didn't open it. She'd had to forgive Marvin for neglecting her; she'd had to forgive Jeff Chesters for assaulting her. There was that other man she'd been engaged to and he'd needed forgiveness as well. Would he do anything she'd have to forgive him that much for?

Other than taking so long to know my own heart?

He didn't claim to be perfect, but when it came to Sandy he'd say his conscience was clear. Far from having anything to feel guilty about, he felt more at peace with himself than he had in years.

He contemplated the poster of the El Greco saint.

"Man, I feel sorry for you," he addressed it. "Getting yourself martyred like that with your whole life ahead of you. You can keep your heaven; this life is just fine with me."

Really? After Hardt and McNair and all?

Yes, even with all that.

And even with helping Sandy keep that sweetly foolish pledge. It was damned hard, going so far and no farther in their lovemaking, but he could do it. It hadn't been easy the last two nights, lying alone in the darkness in the living room. While there she was, just a few feet away from him, behind that closed bedroom door . . . His lips tingled with the memory of her sweet soft flesh. She must ache for him, too. But until she gave the word, he'd keep himself under control.

She's scared, poor girl.

Who wouldn't be, after what she'd been through? Damn that rat Chesters! If only he knew where to find him. What would he do if he had the louse here, face to face? He looked at his hands. In Vietnam he'd discovered what they were capable of. Now? When it came to doing the right thing, civilization could really get in the way.

God! Were those guys all crazy?

He'd do right by her, he swore it. He'd get her past it. The fact that he wouldn't enjoy waiting made the prospect of waiting ironically enjoyable. It'd be his gift to her. But whether the interval was long or short, they would come together. She'd follow his lead and in the end she'd see how happy she could be.

You haven't talked to Leah yet.

No, but that wasn't his fault. He'd finally gotten her on the line last night, but she'd curtly said she was up to her eyeballs in paperwork; call back later. He'd called the store again this morning and only got the clerk. According to her, Leah was too tied up to come to the phone.

He'd keep at it for love's sake, but no need for it to affect what he and Sandy had together.

The door opened and Sandy came in, empty basket under her arm. She looked at him, her expression disturbed.

He glanced at the book in his hands. Shakespeare's *Hamlet*. Had he done wrong taking it out of her bedroom?

"Precious love, what is it?"

"My neighbor who lives under me was down in the laundry room."

"Yes?"

"She said— Wait, did I tell you what happened here the Friday before Christmas? No," she interrupted herself, "that was the night of your fire. I guess I didn't."

"Something happened here, too?" he asked uneasily. "What?"

"I didn't see it first hand," she began to explain. "I was out."

Oh, yes. That was the night she had that date. At least nothing had come of *that*.

"Anyway, she saw a guy hanging around in the shrubbery across the street. I was afraid he was lying in wait for a woman who lives over there and I got her— my downstairs neighbor, I mean— to let me call the cops the next day. But after they came nothing happened and I forgot all about it. But now my neighbor tells me he's been found."

"That's good then."

"Maybe . . . but he was dead. Execution-style. Shot between the eyes."

A strange apprehension crept in. "Did they ID him?"

"Yes. From his fingerprints on the cigarette lighter the cops found in the bushes. Something like Vendham or Ventnor. But they looked up his arrest record, and . . ."

"What did it say?"

"He'd done jail time for attempted homicide . . ."

"Oh no!"

"And he'd been convicted of arson. Twice."

CHAPTER B.25

SUNDAY MORNING, and Sandy was driving to church. By herself.

She hadn't expected Eric to come with her. But what just happened back at her apartment made the aloneness more lonely still.

Last night had been so wonderful. He'd gotten a design bug on the FirstCon project and she'd set up her portable drafting board on the breakfast room table. They'd worked at it till after one in the morning, when she'd kissed him goodnight. How long had he kept drawing? Till very late, she was sure, but when she got up this morning he'd cleared away the drafting equipment and laid the table with placemats and napkins, ready for their next meal.

He was still sound asleep. Even if he might consider joining her for the service, she didn't have the heart to disturb him. She'd found out he never wore a shirt to bed, and the morning sight of his bare shoulder and arm lying over the covers never failed to unsettle her heart. In spite of the beard, he looked boyish then, the worry lines relaxed, the tensions of the day smoothed and eased. Eric vulnerable in slumber moved her to a tenderness that made her whole being ache.

She had her coat on; she'd left him a note; all she needed was her Bible and keys and she could slip out and go.

Where was her Bible, anyway? Yes, over there on the windowsill. Gingerly, she skirted the foot of the sofa bed and retrieved the book. Just as carefully she made her way back towards the door. But as she rounded the corner of the bed, *crack!* went her shin against the metal frame.

"*Ummph!*" she suppressed her cry.

Vain effort. Eric awoke and raised himself up on his elbow. The formidable vision of his naked chest in the mid-morning light, the glow of his good morning smile as his eye first fell upon her: these impressions withered away as his gaze turned somber and even grim. He was assessing her from the hat on her head to the boots on her feet, not missing the Bible in her hand.

"So you are serious," he said at last.

"Serious?"

"About this Jesus stuff."

Her mind went blank. "What?" She gaped at him, confused.

"You're going to church, aren't you." It was an accusation.

"Oh. Yes. I am."

"You were going to spend the whole day with me." His eyes fixed her in their gaze, defying her to contradict what he'd said.

"Eric, I'm sorry, I didn't— I mean, I always go to church on Sunday morning." She searched his face for a sign that he understood. "I thought you knew."

"Surely you can skip it this week at least?" His tone took it for granted that of course, she could.

She hesitated. Would it hurt?

He is so beautiful.

"I was going to take you to brunch at the Hotel Cranbrook."

If Paradise could be said to materialize in Wapatomekie, it did so from 9:00 a.m. to 2:00 p.m. every Sunday at the brunch buffet at the Hotel Cranbrook. She'd never yet had the chance to go, but her friends who'd partaken of its delights had given her such descriptions that her mouth began to water just picturing it.

It's a special occasion. Skip church and go.

No! Remind him we don't have the money. That'll end it.

Her better instincts kept her from wounding his pride.

So why not go?

The image of Esau selling his birthright for a mess of pottage came into her mind. Would it be any different if she were to rob God of His due worship for a slice of truffle-flavored quiche?

Lord, You're right.

She straightened her shoulders and looked him frankly in the eye. "No, Eric, thank you, I can't. I'm sorry. I just can't. I—" How to explain it without sounding preachy? "God has been so good to me— He's given me you—" He grimaced, but she went on. "It's the Lord's Day. I have to go."

"You weren't that religious about it the other night when you were telling me why you wouldn't sleep with me. I almost *expected* you to tell me it was against the Bible or something. But you didn't. It was all about you."

O Domine, I'm sorry. Help me.

"I— What I told you is true. Every word. But I didn't bring all that up— about what the Bible says— because I didn't want you to think I was trying to push anything on you. I'm sorry."

"Aren't you pushing it on me now?"

"I— What? No," she said, bristling. "I'm not. Unless you'd *like* to come to church with me?"

He shook his head emphatically. "Come to brunch with me," he said. "You know you want to."

Oh, how she wanted to! But if she gave in today, where would it end?

She glanced at her watch. She could still get to church on time.

Frowning at the gesture, he said, "I think you love your invisible Jesus more than you love me."

"Eric!" That was unfair. Lord help her if she didn't love Jesus most of all. But put that way it sounded so harsh, so cold.

She was clutching her Bible so hard the marks of her fingernails were impressed into the leather cover. Carefully, trying not to reveal how agitated she was, she laid it on the chest by the door.

Above it on the wall, the El Greco martyr cast his eyes to heaven, looking smugly sanctified.

Easy for you.

"Eric, Jesus loved me and died for me. Of course I love Him most of all. If I didn't love Him first I couldn't love you half as much as I do."

He shook his head skeptically. "I should have known." He hadn't heard a word she'd said. He didn't believe she loved him at all.

"Listen, I'll be home by fifteen till one. We can go to brunch then, okay?"

"And get the leavings after everything's been picked over? No, thanks."

"Sorry, you're right."

"Come on, Sandy, just this once. Your God will understand." He was smiling again now. So beautiful, so beautiful . . .

She picked up her Bible. "I have to go."

His face fell.

Turning back in the doorway, she said, "I . . . I love you, Eric. See you later. We'll discuss it this afternoon, okay?"

As she closed the door she caught one word: "Maybe."

SHE WAS nearly to church but her mind was still back at her apartment.

Lord, please have mercy on me. Of all the things for us to fight about!

What else?

What else indeed?

To agree on nearly everything and to be at odds on the most essential point of all was nearly too much to bear. Maybe it was a sign, maybe God was testing her to see if she'd give up everything for Him, Eric included. *Be not unequally yoked . . .*

But we're not yoked together. Not the way it counts.

And never can be? Everything that had Eric so opposed to Christianity, it had an iron grip on him, and what hope did she have of breaking it? And she couldn't change her belief in Christ . . . *Dear Father, why did You have me meet him in the first place?* Or was it her own fault for allowing herself to fall in love?

She turned into the church parking lot. Other members were hurrying from their cars, eager to get into the service on time. What would they tell her to do? Would they tell her to stop loving him?

I can't. Loving Eric Baumann is a fact of nature, like that bare tree over there. For all I know, it's dead . . . But my love for him just is. It won't die. Whatever he is. Whatever he meant by that word "maybe."

Lord help me, I might be better off if it would!

BY THE TIME Dr. Kennerdene finished his sermon, Sandy felt much better. It reminded her that being a Christian meant not giving up hope. If God was in it, it would come to pass.

When the service was over she didn't linger to talk to anyone. She headed straight home, stopping just briefly at the grocery store to pick up a couple of steaks for dinner. He'd like that. They'd have their usual friendly discussion, they'd come to an understanding, and things would again be fine.

And next week she could go to the early service. They could meet up around 10:30 and have plenty of time for the buffet.

A perfect solution. But when she opened the door to her apartment and stepped inside, Eric and all his belongings were gone.

CHAPTER B.26

She still had to go into to work Monday morning. Until she quit or he fired her, she was his employee. Besides, she had clients depending on her.

The office door was unlocked, his coat was on its hook, the radio was on— tuned, unusually, to an alternative hard rock station— but Eric himself was nowhere to be seen.

Sandy took a deep breath. She'd see him when she'd see him.

But she'd barely hung up her coat and picked up the tea kettle to fill it when he came through the door.

His face was haggard and drawn, and despite her fears it tore at her heart to see him like this. "Eric! You look terrible!"

"Gee, thanks, what a compliment," he said, his tone subdued.

"What have you been doing to yourself? How long have you been here? Where"— she was almost afraid to ask it— "did you spend the night?"

"Here." His voice was flat.

"*Here?* But I thought that would jeopardize the lease."

"I wasn't sleeping."

She looked at his table, covered in a billowing yellow cloud of tracing paper. "Oh."

"Concept alternatives," he said dully. "FirstCon." He dug through the pile and handed her several sheets. "Take these. Compare them to the square footages on the program. See if they work."

Was his laconic manner due to exhaustion, or did he simply not want to talk to her? She couldn't allow it to matter.

"All right. I'll let you know how it's going before lunch."

"I've got a meeting at the Weismans' at 10:00."

"Oh." Stubble pinpointed his cheeks. "Not before you've shaved, surely? Did you bring your kit up?"

He shook his head. "No. DeeDee Weisman can put up with it for once." He put on his coat and cast around listlessly for the things he needed for the meeting.

They could talk this afternoon, then. Assuming he got his second wind?

But as if determined to contradict her hopes, he said, "After the Weismans I'm going over to my new apartment. Doubt I'll be back before tomorrow."

Please, no! All pretense at detachment blew away like dust. She couldn't let another night pass without knowing where she stood with him, or all love was a lie.

"Eric, please. DeeDee won't mind if you're a little late. I need to talk to you before you go."

"About what?"

"About yesterday morning."

"Oh. That. It's your decision."

"To talk about it?"

"No." His demeanor remained detached, apathetic. "About your religion. It's up to you."

He was washing his hands of the whole matter— and of her. Funny, she'd always thought that if she ever gave up something she really loved for the sake of Jesus she'd be luxuriating in virtue as in an exquisite warm sea. But all she had was a hollow void— and the doomed awareness that if she had the moment back she would do the exact same thing.

This is why I didn't want to tell anyone about us.

"Eric, please, it's not that I don't . . . " Her voice trailed off. In his eyes was that same inscrutable look, and it struck her dumb.

It was over. Over like it had been with Werner seven years ago. But this time she would not cry. She refused to cry. She turned back to her drafting table and with a shaking hand began to sort the sketches he'd given her. He still lingered in the doorway. Blast it, why didn't he leave?

"Sandy," he said. Against her will, she looked up. "You've made your decision, and I've made mine. As soon as that meeting is over, I'm calling Leah."

She sucked in her breath. "You still haven't— she's still—"

"Yes," he said grimly, "I haven't. Whatever I do, I'm talking to her . . . and telling her I'm breaking it off with her for good."

DIVISION C

THURSDAY, 25 MARCH –
MONDAY, 16 AUGUST 1982

The LORD is in his holy temple,
the LORD'S throne is in heaven:
his eyes behold, his eyelids try,
the children of men.

–Psalm 11:4

CHAPTER C.1

"SANDY, YOU THINK WE'LL MAKE the shortlist?" Ruth Parrish, their firm's new draftsman, nervously pushed her straight brown hair back behind her ears as the two of them passed through the heavy oaken doors of the Fort Randolph City municipal building.

"No way to tell for a few weeks," Sandy replied. It had been overheated and close in the board room, and she drew in a deep lungful of the cool, damp spring air. "A lot of other firms are interested in the job, too. But Phil Duggins the planning director is behind us, I could tell from his face." She unlocked her Civic and held the door for Ruth. "He was smiling and nodding the whole time."

"He couldn't help it," Ruth said. "Your presentation was great."

"Thanks. But this was only the planning board. If we go on to the next stage we'll have to impress the whole city council."

As they drove through the town she pointed out the neighborhood they'd be dealing with if they got the commission for the redevelopment study and master plan.

"Uh-huh," said Ruth, then both were silent for several miles.

Sandy was glad of the respite. The adrenaline that had her in top form during the presentation was subsiding and for a while it was nice to be calm and think of something else.

Outside the car windows, the trees raced by, their stark black branches still leafless on this gray late March afternoon. But the sides of the two-lane highway were tinged with the green spears of crocus and early daffodils pushing their way through the thawing earth, and Sandy revelled in the exhilaration of love and spring and the open road.

Absurd, how last fall she'd hated the idea of having her own transportation. She'd been so afraid it would drive her and Eric apart. Ironically, it was bringing them closer than ever.

If it weren't for these runs, I'd spend all my waking hours with him. Or I'd be marooned in the office eating my heart out until he came back. "Je suis à ma fenêtre, ou dehors, tout le jour ... I sit at my window all day ..."

She smiled inwardly. *Yes. Like that.*

Being inseparable sounded good in romance novels, but spending time apart then coming back together was, she'd discovered, much better for a relationship. It was the same with it no longer being just the two of them in the office. The new people gave them more to talk about, more to enjoy together.

Didn't somebody say love's the one thing that gets bigger the more you spread it around?

Still, she was grateful they'd had the first half of February to themselves. They'd put Ruth off another week to make sure no more strange visitors showed up. None had, but the wait was a good thing even so. How awkward it would have been, how unbearable, adjusting to a new colleague so soon after their argument that Sunday! So much was hanging over them ... And thank God, they'd had time.

Eric had left for the Weismans' that Monday morning and hadn't reappeared till around noon the next day. When he'd looked over the work she'd completed, his tone as he pronounced it satisfactory was purely professional. Then he'd gone back to his table and put his head down to draw. But something had been vibrating in the air between them, a silent sound, a barely-felt sensation, that grew in intensity as the day went on. Occasionally at first, then more frequently, he'd come to look over her shoulder, then wordlessly returned to his board. Of the two, she'd minded the departure more. The fourth or fifth time he'd done it, he'd stood there for a long time, watching. Not watching her draw, but watching her.

He needed me. He was yearning for me. And I was glad.

Finally, she'd decided to speak. "So," she'd asked casually, keeping her eyes on her work, "what did Leah say?"

It had been exactly the right thing.

"She wasn't surprised."

"About us?" The idea of Leah knowing had alarmed her.

"No, I thought you didn't want to publicize that yet?" (Her heart had surged within her at that word "yet.") "No, that she and I were through. Or do you *want* me to tell her how much I love you?"

"Do you?" she'd whispered shyly, rotating her chair to face him.

"Come here."

He'd kissed her then, tenderly at first, then fiercely, triumphantly, welding their bodies together in what seemed like an unbreakable bond. When his lips had finally released hers he'd kept her in his arms, murmuring, "Want to knock off early and come over and help me paint my apartment?"

"Is that a pickup line?" she'd replied, her voice muffled in his sweater.

"If you want it to be."

By the time she'd gone home to change and driven to his place, they'd both managed to get themselves under control.

Though sometimes I wish ...

No. Waiting was better.

Waiting for what?

For things to work out. Somehow.

Since then they'd managed to behave themselves in the office. It would have been necessary in any case, as first Ruth Parrish the draftsman, then Neil Hughes the specifications guy, joined them. The others' presence was just what she and Eric needed to keep them on the straight and narrow.

Well, we behave ourselves mostly ...

She darted a glance at Ruth to see if she had noticed the grin that kept spilling out onto her face. Her new colleague was gazing out the side window. Sandy went back to her thoughts.

Now when Eric's leg pressed against hers under the drafting table they both knew what it meant, and they both thrilled to the sweet misery of hiding that meaning from their colleagues. Sometimes his long hand would rest ever-so-casually on her shoulder as he discussed her work, or she'd suppress a sigh as his fingers played stealthily with a lock of her hair. As she passed him— more closely than strictly necessary— her arm would brush his, or she would reach up, ostensibly to extract the occasional stray crumb from his beard. It couldn't hurt: Ruth and Neil were in the drafting room most of the time, and it was kind of a game between them to see how well they could share their affection while concealing it from the others.

Other than that, that one kiss was the single time they'd allowed their passion any kind of free rein in the office. It wasn't just Ruth and Neil: that space was for work and it was best to keep it that way, even after the junior members of the firm put on their coats and left for home.

Nor did he spend much time at her place or she at his; that was safer, too. That left those brief, bright, mad periods riding down the elevator (usually way after hours), and walking to their cars in the parking garage. Sometimes he'd pick her up in the morning and when he'd drop her off at night they'd sit in his Ford Galaxie for long minutes on end (discreetly parked around the corner on the side street, away from the eyes of nosy Mrs. Lopez), but their communication was frequently the kind that had no need of words.

She had never yet asked him why he'd reacted so strongly against the idea of her attending church their first Sunday together. It was the one subject she was afraid to raise. It was enough that when she'd suggested getting together after the 9:15 service he'd embraced the idea avidly. They'd gone to brunch at the Hotel Cranbrook the very next Sunday, and she hardly knew which was more ambrosial, the food or sharing it with him.

Sandy slowed down as they passed through a hamlet on the way. At the one stoplight she pointed to a restaurant on the opposite corner. "They have really good lake trout there."

"Sounds yummy. I'll have to see if Harley wants to try it sometime."

Ruth didn't ask her how she'd found this place, so far out of Wapatomekie. Everything in Sandy wanted to exult, "Eric took me there two weekends ago!" But her pregnant colleague, busy telling about her own recent trip to a seafood restaurant, unknowingly saved her from herself.

Carole knew about her and Eric, of course. It would have been disloyal to keep it hidden from her best friend, and having her know kept her accountable for keeping her physical relationship with him under control.

" . . . and of course," Ruth was saying, "I didn't think to tell the waiter to take off the tartar sauce— it's never given me trouble before— but that time, whoa, Nelly! morning sickness doesn't always come in the morning! So up I got to run to the ladies' room, and Harley— you should have seen his face— he said, 'Oh, no, not again, sweetie!' So there's this other waiter coming through with a tray of food and he's . . . "

Sandy laughed at the story. They fell silent, and for the next few miles both watched the road.

Presently, Ruth spoke up: "You know, I like Phil Duggins."

"What?" said Sandy, startled out of her thoughts.

"I like Phil Duggins." She sounded surprised at herself.

"Uh-huh?"

"Yes. They didn't allow col— Afro-Americans in our school down in Payne County."

Payne County? Wasn't that in the far southeastern corner of the state? Redneck country anyway. Not a nice thing to say to somebody born there.

"Yes?

"My daddy used to say Afro-Americans were no better than man-grown babies, or they were good-for-nothing ni— bums. So we didn't have much to do with any of them. Not unless we had to."

Sandy waited.

"But Mr. Duggins is different. Smart. Classy. I like him."

"Well, maybe the Afro-Americans down in Payne County were like him, if you'd gotten to know them."

"Maybe . . . Sandy, I don't want you to think my daddy's a racist or anything."

He isn't? "Oh, no, of course not."

You hypocrite!

"He was just going on facts. It wasn't like old Mrs. McCool, around the other side of the mountain."

"Who?"

"Oh, a terrible old woman! She positively hated colored people. When the store in her town hired a colored clerk, she drove twenty miles out of her way to shop someplace else. Momma said she'd-a been up a creek for real if the rains got hard enough."

"Wow."

"She carried a Colt .45 revolver with her, and said God's law permitted her to shoot any colored person she saw because they got that way because of sin."

"You're kidding! Why wasn't she put in jail?"

"She was stinking rich," Ruth said, as if that explained everything. "And the colored folks kept out of her way. She drove around in this old Model A jalopy and you could hear it coming for miles. At least, that's what my daddy said. She died when I was two, I never knew her myself."

"Wow. Well, God's dealing with her now. Hopefully there's nobody like that down there anymore."

"Don't know. We moved up here when I was thirteen. But Mama told me Mrs. McCool got mad at her only daughter and son-in-law because they were soft on the coloreds. So she cut them out of her will and left everything to her grandson. Daddy said he was just as cockeyed about the coloreds as his grandma was, except he was a better shot."

"What happened to him?"

"Don't know that, either. The way I heard it, he turned twenty-one, sold up, and left the county. Don't know if he's even been back. People wouldn't talk about him much around us kids. Guess they thought he was a bad influence."

"Well, maybe he's changed his mind about these things, too."

"Maybe," said Ruth.

Sandy waited a little, then said, "So you like Phil Duggins. What about Neil?"

"Oh, yes, Neil's great, too."

"You're getting along well in there?"

"We sure are. Sometimes I think if Neil doesn't know how to put a detail together, nobody does." She paused. "Funny how things change. My daddy says he never pictured his little girl sharing an office with a black man . . . But it's better this way."

"I think so, too. We lost out on a lot of talent in the old segregation days. Putting people in boxes hurts everybody." She had a thought. "What did your preacher say?"

"He used to say God put us all where He wanted us to be and it was a sin to change it. These days, I don't know."

"Well, I'm no theologian," Sandy offered, "and it's true that God orders everything by His providence"— *including Eric and me?*— "but I don't think the Bible says anywhere that anybody should look down on anybody else because of how much skin pigment they have. Some people used to think slavery was God's will because the Bible allows it, but my pastor always said that was something He was going to change when the time was right."

"Hmmm. You know, that reminds me of something. I was— *watch out!*"

A blur of blue roared up on her left, with a truck coming straight at it over the crest of the hill. Sandy slammed on the brakes, reflexively flinging out her right arm to keep Ruth in her seat. With hardly an inch to spare, the passing car slipped into the gap at her front bumper and sped away.

"You okay, Ruth?"

"I think so. Yes. Whew."

"And the baby?" Blast. She should have been watching. Anybody could have seen that driver was cutting it too close.

"Far as I can tell. Whew. You've got good brakes. Wow."

When her own heart rate had returned to normal she asked, "But your story. You were saying?"

"What?"

"Just before the guy in that blue car decided to impress us with his driving."

"I don't know. I forgot. Whatever it was, it wasn't important."

CHAPTER C.2

THEY FELT AS WELL AS HEARD the upbeat, percussive music throbbing down the corridor from their office, even before they made the turn from the elevator.

"Gee whillikers, Sandy, what's that?" said Ruth as they drew closer.

"I think—"

Footsteps from within moved to the front room and the radio was switched back to the classical station.

"Hi, Neil," Sandy greeted the dark, chunky young man who was just moving away from the radio shelf. "Any calls this afternoon?"

"Oh, hi, Sandy, Ruth. No, just a drywall accessories rep. He'll call back tomorrow." In his face was a mixture of caution, bravado, and something else she couldn't define. She decided to confront the issue head-on.

"Hey, Neil, I don't blame you for wanting to play the music you like when you're here by yourself."

His expression cleared. "Well, I—"

"And I wish I could say it's first-come, first-served."

"Yeah," said Ruth. "It'd be nice to have some easy listening music sometimes. Or some country and western."

Sandy suppressed the urge to wince. "Problem is, Eric and I think having the classical station going says a lot about who we are as a design firm. So this radio in here . . . ordinarily, during the day . . . Do you two have portable radios with headphones? No harm in listening to your own music on that. That's what I do when I want to catch the news on NPR."

From their expressions, neither Neil nor Ruth was totally satisfied. "We can take it up with Eric later," she offered. "He should be back around 6:00."

"Got you," said Neil. "Though if you really want this firm to be on the cutting edge, people should hear us playing jazz-funk and Afrobeat. There's a super def station on the AM dial that plays those grooves all the time."

"Really?" she said, not comprehending.

"Hey!" cried Ruth. "I just remembered!"

"Huh?" said Sandy. "Remembered what?"

"What I was going to tell you in the car!"

"In the car?"

"You know, we were talking about—" She cast an uncertain glance at Neil. "Neil, we were talking about Phil Duggins and you and what nice people you are"— she glanced at him again— "and about how some people don't like Afro-Americans, and it reminded me of a really weird thing I heard on the radio the other night."

Neil remained impassive. Sandy merely said, "Yes?" and hoped Ruth wouldn't embarrass herself, or her.

"Yeah. I couldn't sleep— that's what a bun in the oven will do to you— so I went down to the kitchen and started washing up some pots I'd left in to soak and all. I turned on the Christian station, and there was this preaching program— at least, I think it was a preacher; anyway, I hadn't heard it before, and it seemed pretty weird."

"Weird like how?" asked Neil.

"Well, he was talking about the Noah story, not the part about the Flood; the part afterwards when Noah gets drunk and his sons find him in his tent buck naked."

"Right, fine," said Sandy, hurrying her over that part.

"So he was going on about the curse on Ham, about how all Ham's sons were supposed to be servants and slaves to the sons of Noah's other sons."

"And he said the sons of Ham are the Negro race," Neil said drily.

"Yes, he did," said Ruth, apparently not picking up on the sarcasm. "But I've heard that before; that wasn't the weird part. The weird part was that he said the reason America's in such bad shape is that the white people aren't keeping the sons of Ham in their place. He said Negroes running companies and being professionals and government officials and all was against Nature and white folks letting them do it put them— the white folks, I mean— out of the will of God. Seemed weird to me, but I don't know the Bible that well."

"Typical white thinking—"

"That guy doesn't know the Bible, either," Sandy broke in over him. "Genesis doesn't say all of Ham's sons would serve the sons of Shem and Japheth, just Canaan, his firstborn. 'Canaan,' sound familiar? As in the people the children of Israel drove out after the Exodus?"

"Oh, that's right," said Ruth.

"And it didn't have anything to do with skin color, it had to do with *sin*." It shocked her how vehement she felt about it. "Dr. Wallace at my church made sure we all knew that. Back when I was a kid, we almost got our first Afro-American members. But then some people started up with that sons-of-Ham nonsense and drove them away. I remember how he let us have it. My dad said it was like John Knox with a dose of John Brown thrown in. I was impressed, I remember that."

"Well, your preacher was radical, that's all I can say," said Neil. "Did the deacons fire him for it?"

"The elders. We're Presbyterian. No, they wouldn't do that. Dr. Wallace was the next thing to God. With a Scots accent.

"Anyway, Ruth, that's interesting, but we've got a meeting memo to write. You have your notes handy?"

"Yeah, but actually, I wasn't finished telling you guys about that program."

"I'm sorry." *Please, God, don't let her say anything awful. It'd upset the whole office.*

"I was going to say I don't think the preacher was from a regular church, more like an organization. And here's the really weird part: He was saying that America is God's true chosen people and all white Christians who wanted to bring the country back in line with the Lord's will should sign up and join him."

"Really?" It sounded way too much like the flyers at the FirstCon site. "Did he announce a meeting place, a time, anything?"

"No, just gave a post office box where people should write for instructions. Don't remember the number or the town, but it wasn't Wapatomekie, I can say that."

"So it's nobody local," Sandy said, trying to reassure herself.

"Why does that matter?" Neil objected. "Racism is racism."

"I know, but . . . " She didn't want to tell him about the flyer. They had too much to do to get into a debate over race.

"Hey!" said Ruth. "I just remembered what that group was called. White Way Ministries. I think so, anyway."

Sandy gasped. "*White Way Ministries?* Are you sure?"

"Yeah," said Ruth, looking at her curiously. "Have you heard of it before?"

"Maybe— I'm not sure. Um, what time was this program? How long has it been on?"

"No idea. Sometime after 3:00 a.m., but I wasn't paying attention."

"Is it on every night?"

"Why, you interested?" Neil joked cynically.

"Neil! Are you crazy? No, I'm thinking I should write a letter to the station and complain. Ruth, you should, too. That crackpot has his freedom of speech, but decent people do too. It makes me sick."

And scared. But she wasn't telling them that.

"No idea about that, either," Ruth responded to Sandy's question. "I really prefer to be asleep that time of night." She looked down and patted her belly. "You hear, Junior?"

"But what night was it?"

"Sunday going into Monday. Yeah."

Meaning she'd have to set her alarm this weekend to catch the garbage. Should she tell Eric? Not until she'd heard it for herself.

But the following early Monday morning, though she made herself get up and listen to the station from 2:40 to 4:00 a.m., no program sponsored by "White Way Ministries" or anything like it was aired. It was all Christian pop music.

No doubt other people complained and it was taken off the air. No, Eric didn't need to know. He might say that was what Christianity was about. They hadn't fought since the first time; she didn't want to go through it again.

Something told her she was being unfair, but she couldn't risk being wrong.

CHAPTER C.3

THE HARSH FLUORESCENT LIGHTS glared off the peeling photo-veneered surface of the conference table, giving Eric a headache. Through the exterior wall of the cramped, windowless room he could hear the racket of an early-April rain, while on the other side of the thin interior partition sounded the footsteps and voices of various FirstCon employees passing in the corridor. Those same employees no doubt could hear everything he was saying in his meeting with Jacob Ryerson and Sam Delkirk if he raised his voice at all.

All these problems would be solved with the new building. He studied Jacob and Sam's expressions as once again they looked over the latest version of the preliminary drawings. The meeting had gone well so far, allowing for the inevitable changes, additions, and second thoughts. None of it would compromise his overall design. That was, if he'd planned correctly for what he was beginning to think of as The Elephant in the Room.

Or rather, The Elephant Not in the Room. "The new corrugating machine," he asked. "When can you get me the final size requirements on it?"

"Oh, yes, about that," said Sam enthusiastically. "We were thinking you should leave that open until I can get you up to Michigan to talk to the design engineer. And see machines something like it in person."

It made sense. The corrugator's design was being custom modified for FirstCon and he couldn't rely on the standard literature. "Sounds good to me. How soon can we go?"

"I'd say in two weeks; three at the most. I'll call the factory and let you know when."

"Sam's dying for an excuse to go talk to that engineer." Jacob laughed. "He's been drooling over that new corrugator for months. You'll have to design in a special trough to drain off the slobber, once it's in."

Sam gave a self-deprecating shrug and said, "It'll increase productivity by twenty-five percent. At least. Well, gentlemen, the plans are coming along fine. Will you excuse me? I have a little issue to deal with in Shipping."

Once Delkirk was gone, Jacob lit a cigarette and paged through the prints again. "I have to say you've put a lot of work into this."

You expected anything less? he nearly said, but the door opened and Jacob's secretary walked into the room carrying some papers.

"Yes, Georgia?" Jacob said.

She placed the documents on the table, indicating with a well-manicured digit where he was to sign. Ryerson couldn't seem to keep his eyeballs from dropping into her cleavage, and Eric steadfastly examined the advertising poster on the wall past Jacob's head so his wouldn't do the same. As she left with the signed documents, her boss tracked her retreating form.

The door closed, the spell broke, and Jacob leaned back in his chair. "So how soon can you work in the changes we discussed today?" He grinned and waved the cigarette towards the drawings, gray ash flying.

Eric restrained himself from snatching the cigarette from between his fingers. "Would a week from now be soon enough? Barring any we might make with the new machine, of course."

"Oy!" said Jacob. "You can take care of it that quick? I swear, do you do anything besides work?"

Sometimes, thought Eric, remembering two nights before when he'd "kidnapped" Sandy on their way home and whisked her out to a blues joint in a distant suburb. "Well, this project is so absorbing . . ."

"You need to get out more. I saw that poor girlfriend of yours the other day—"

Dammit, stop underestimating her like—

"—at that store of hers and mentioned you."

Oh. Leah.

"What did she say?" he asked, trying to sound casual.

"That she hadn't seen you in weeks. What the hell are you doing, Eric? Making yourself into a real troglodyte?" Jacob chortled. "You've even got the whiskers for it." Eric winced as his client reached over and gave his beard a tug. "Our project can wait a day or two. Call that girl up and take her out," he said, smirking. "Show her a little action— *heh, heh*— if you know what I mean."

So Jacob thought he and Leah were still dating. Might come in handy, with Sandy and him keeping their relationship secret. He doubted they needed to, but—

"Neglecting a babe with legs like that— *um, um!*" Jacob shook his head in mock regret. "And *stacked?* Whoo!"

Scratch that. It was one thing to stay out of the public eye. But to use Leah as a blind? Not fair, to either woman. Eric cleared his throat. "Actually, Leah and I broke up. Several weeks ago."

"Well, I'm damned. Sorry I mentioned it." Jacob took a pull on his cigarette. "How come? You two fight?"

"No," Eric replied, making his tone as repressive as he could. "We just grew apart. Different interests."

"Well, well. Sheila and I'll have to introduce you to some nice girls. There's a beautiful *zaftig* girl at our temple—" he gestured an hourglass figure— "or do you only date *shiksas?*"

"Shiksas?"

"Christian girls. Gentiles."

Was Jacob hinting something about him and Sandy? No, it was just Jacob being Jacob. "Don't worry," Eric said, standing and gathering the drawings and tools, "I can take care of myself."

Ryerson accompanied him to the parking lot, keeping up a flow of nonsense interspersed with a cogent comment or two about the project. Thankfully, Eric thought as he drove away, Jacob hadn't mentioned Sandy at all.

If he brings her up in relation to our work, I'm fine. But when he's going on about women like that . . . He could just see himself, red to the roots, and Jacob flying salaciously to the right conclusion.

Amazing how things had changed. The way he reacted last November when Ryerson implied they were having sex . . . now he wished they were. And so did she, probably, if only . . . But it was different then. Then he would have been using her. Now . . .

Oh, Sandy, how long will you make me wait?

Hell. He knew how long. Until he could see his way clear to marrying her. She wasn't holding out on him. It was just something she needed and he couldn't give. Maybe he could bring her to the place where she wouldn't need it. Patience.

In the meantime, abstinence might have something to say for itself. If Sandy got pregnant? The thought was appalling. She wasn't on the Pill, and he'd heard of too many failed condoms. The last thing he needed was a baby she'd certainly want to keep.

Marriage, though. Maybe she wouldn't even if he asked. Didn't he get that back in his Lutheran high school, about not being "unequally yoked" with an unbeliever? Ha. If his teachers had known what an unbeliever he was even then. Sandy was probably infected with the same thinking.

Her religion was the real problem, wasn't it? When they fought last January, he shouldn't have been surprised that she wanted to go to church. But she could do that any week; why couldn't she have given up that one Sunday for him? Inexplicable kind of god that would make a demand like that.

He drew up to a stoplight. A blonde was crossing the street in front of him, tall and curvy, her raincoat collar open and her dress cut low to flaunt her ample breasts. *Zaftig,* as Jacob would put it.

But she walks like a cow.

Flirtatiously, she caught his eye as she passed, and on reflex he smiled back.

Overbuilt. And why did some girls stump along like that, especially the tall ones? Sandy never dragged her feet or slouched. And throw a challenge at her, she'd stand up straighter still.

Come to think of it, that's what she'd done during their dispute. She'd stood there in her burgundy coat and darker wine-red hat, feet planted, with that big black Bible of hers clutched to her chest, calmly arguing back at him (against her real wishes, he wagered) and never once backed down. "Like a mule," he'd thought at the time. But now he had to admire her determination. Maybe Sandy's Christianity was different from his mother's. It never made her cringe in fear.

But why did a sensible person like Sandy Beichten believe there was some Big Man in the sky she was accountable to? She was a good person. She'd be the same if she weren't a Christian at all. But when he tried to envision her without her religion he couldn't do it. He shook his head to get it clear.

Enough of that. Let's see what's on the radio.

Within a block or two he switched it off again.

Maybe he was thinking about this the wrong way. It'd been a struggle to admit she was right about Nick Hardt, but if her moral compass gave him clear direction in a matter like that, it was something to be supported, not suppressed. And since they weren't living together, what she did on Sunday mornings was her own business. Her going to church didn't hurt him. In fact, a big, well-off congregation like Fourth Presbyterian was just the place to make contacts.

As he waited for the light to change at a downtown intersection, his eye wandered to the Roman Catholic cathedral on the corner. A signboard erected on the tiny patch of lawn next to the front steps read "HOLY WEEK SERVICES."

An idea emerged full-blown in his mind. Why not? God didn't exist, so it wouldn't hurt him. And it would please her.

He could hardly wait to find out what she would say.

"GOODNIGHT, RUTH," Eric said as she headed out the door. Neil had left fifteen minutes earlier.

"Bye, Ruth," said Sandy, "see you tomorrow."

For about two minutes he deliberately went on working. Then he turned his chair and said, "Sandy?"

"Yes, Eric?"

God! What she could put into just his name! "I was wondering. Easter's coming up. Would you like Good Friday off?"

"What?" The idea seemed to startle her. Good.

"With pay, of course. Maybe I should give everyone Good Friday off, what do you think?"

"Well, since we don't really have an Easter break . . . and if you think we can afford it . . . ?"

"I think we can."

"Yes, I'd appreciate that. I've never had a chance to go to the Good Friday service at my church, I've always had to work."

"All right, that's what we'll do."

She turned back to her drawing, and again he spoke: "I imagine having Friday off would give you more time to prepare for Easter Sunday. Unless you're going to somebody's house?"

"No, actually, this year I'm having Carole and George and Robbie over to my place."

Here was an opportunity. "Any chance you have room for one more?

I can bring my own chair."

"Oh, Eric!" She rose from her table and approached him. "I'd been wondering if you'd be willing to come, considering what day it is. Oh, yes, please do!"

"All right, I'll put that on my calendar. What time?"

"Oh, you don't need to come until 2:45 if you don't want to. Dinner won't be on until 3:00."

"Maybe I might come earlier? I like Carole, and I'd like to meet George."

"Would you? They'll be arriving around 2:00. Come around then. They'll both be glad to see you." Her face was suffused with real pleasure.

That's nothing. Just wait.

"Actually, I was thinking I'd come sooner and help you."

"Would you? That would be wonderful! I should be getting home from church a little after 1:00. The service will go longer that day."

"Hmm. Well. What time does your Easter service begin?"

"Eleven o'clock, same as always."

"All right," he said, holding back his smile, "I can come by your place around 10:30 and drive you to church."

"No, Eric, that wouldn't be convenient, you making two trips," she said in confusion. "I can drive myself."

He laughed. "No, you silly girl, I'm coming to Easter service with you. What do you think of that? . . . *Sandy!*"

She looked as if she was about to faint.

CHAPTER C.4

Eric waited tolerantly for the pastor to finish the benediction.

" . . . Take the good news into the world!" proclaimed the black-robed man at the chancel steps. "Alleluia, Christ is risen!"

"He is risen indeed!" the people around Eric chorused back. "Alleluia!"

"And the blessing of God Almighty, the Father, the Son, and the Holy Spirit, be with you and remain with you always. Amen."

The organ began to sound and the packed congregation surged to their feet, singing along with the choir.

Hallelujah! Hallelujah!

Cheerfully, Eric rose too, and finding the bass line, joined in. At his side Sandy momentarily faltered in her part, then, quickly recovering, she went on more strongly than before.

For the Lord God omnipotent reigneth!
Hallelujah! Hallelujah!

Her hand stole over and found his as their voices blended in Handel's immortal anthem. *I've got this,* he thought. He twined his arm through hers and sang on.

Walking down the block to where they'd parked the car, Sandy couldn't get over what she had just heard. "You never told me you could sing parts," she said happily. "Or that you sang at all."

"You never asked."

A lemony April sun was peeking fitfully through the wet clouds. Together they laughed as a wanton gust shook droplets of last night's rain off the budding branches of the trees, sprinkling them as they passed below.

Lord, it's perfect, just like this. Or it would be if he believed in You.

"I wish I could have heard you take the bass on the hymns as well," she ventured.

He gave a careless shrug. "I don't sight read. The 'Hallelujah Chorus,' I've got that down."

"I noticed. From where?"

"High school choir."

"Of course. It would have to be."

He unlocked the car door and held it open for her.

"Thanks."

"You've got a good choir at your church there," Eric said as he swung his long body into the driver's seat. "How come you're not singing in it?"

"Well," she teased, "I tend to get a little tied up at work on practice nights . . ."

"You could go if you wanted. I'd hate to think I was keeping you from anything you wanted to do."

She considered the idea. "No . . . not right now. Maybe sometime later." If by some miracle he came to church again, she wanted to sit in the congregation with him. It was bound to raise friendly questions if he did: a single girl like her next to a beautiful man like Eric. But she'd deal with that when— if!— it happened.

"Eric?"

"Yes, precious love? Something you want to ask me?"

"The house I grew up in isn't too far from here. Want to drive by and see it?"

"Sure." There was puzzlement in the word.

That wasn't what he was expecting. He knows I want to talk about the sermon. He'll see I can control myself.

"Some other people own it now. My mom sold it the fall after I graduated from college."

They pulled up in front of her old home and got out.

"Nice," Eric said at last. "I like that stucco English Cottage style. Very organic lines. Do you miss it?"

"Sometimes."

"You've got a beautiful church," he commented as the car pulled away.

She glanced sidelong at his profile. *That's nice, but what did you think of the service?*

"I generally don't think much of twentieth-century Gothic," he said, "but that was very sensitively done. Who was your architect?"

"Merritt Greene. Grandfather of your old boss."

"Ah. Yes. I should have known."

"Reg Fyfield did the education wing, back when I was a kid."

"He did a good job tying it in. You didn't always get that in the 'Sixties."

"No."

Silence for a mile or two. Already they were on Meyers Trafficway. Low-built office buildings and 1920s-era brick hotels, restaurants, and shops were passed and left behind. Would he bring up the sermon, or wouldn't he? Should she just come out and ask?

Finally, he spoke: "Your pastor."

"Dr. Kennerdene."

"He seems like a reasonable and intelligent man."

You're surprised? "Yes, he studied at Princeton and Edinburgh."

"I liked the way he gave evidence for the resurrection of Christ."

She forced down her excitement. Pointedly studying the cracked vinyl on the Galaxie's dashboard, she said, "Yes, that's his way."

Silence again. A splatter of rain and the squeak of the wipers as they swept across the windshield.

"You know," Eric said slowly, "I think he convinced me."

"He *what?*" she yelped.

His eyes met hers frankly. "Assuming the evidence he gave is correct, and I expect it is, Jesus rising from the dead is the only thing that explains it."

"Eric, that's wonderful!" Was it possible that now, already, he believed? The sun, which had gone behind a cloud, shone out in all its brilliance, seeming to lavish the rain-wet pavement with loose diamonds. Symbolic?

"Don't get me wrong," he said repressively. "I'm not saying there was anything supernatural about it."

Oh. The sun was still out; the diamond effect remained. No. Not symbolic.

"Or that there's anything to the idea about him dying for anybody's sins."

Crumb.

"But he had to be dead then alive again. There's some scientific explanation for it, but I'd be an idiot to deny it happened."

She stared out at the stores that lined the street, their windows decorated for Easter. Bunnies, chicks, eggs. Life from the dead, supposedly, but only in Nature's ordinary way. Is that how he saw what Jesus did?

Sandy pushed down her disappointment and said, "So what decided you? The fact that nobody could produce the body? What happened to the guards?"

"No, none of that. What happened to the disciples."

Her breath caught. "You mean what they wrote in the Scriptures?"

"I mean the way they kept on saying they'd seen him alive even when the authorities had a knife to their throats."

Reflexively, she put her hand to her own neck, then grasped her right wrist. Three months later and the scar was still red.

He noticed. "Sorry. I forgot." He laid a reassuring hand over hers.

"That's all right, I forget about it most of the time, too."

"Anyway," he went on, "you've got to be pretty convinced about something in order to die for it. Especially when you're swearing it's something you've actually seen and heard."

"When you could save your skin by rationalizing that you'd made a mistake?"

"Yeah. Or admitting you'd lied."

Amazing. He was making a perfect argument for Jesus' resurrection and he didn't even believe. Unbidden, the verse came to her mind: *The devils also believe, and tremble.*

No, it did *not* apply. Eric was a man, not a devil. A sinner, like her, so there was hope for him.

Please, Lord Jesus, save him. Make him Your own!

"The disciples weren't expecting Jesus to rise from the dead," she offered. "It wasn't wishful thinking."

"That counts, too," he granted, and was silent.

She needed to say something to take him to the next stage. But what? *Holy Spirit, help me!*

She opened her mouth, but he spoke first. "Here's Forty-fourth Street coming up. I'm really looking forward to dinner. Especially that lemon mousse thing you've made." His smile fell upon her and as always its beam warmed her soul. Nevertheless, there was something in his look that told her the former subject was closed.

CHAPTER C.5

"WHAT'S THIS?" Ruth's voice broke into Sandy's thoughts one morning. She looked up from her drafting board. "What is what?"

Her colleague was standing by the pile of mail on the conference table, holding a large, flat envelope. "Something from *Design Mode* magazine. Awfully big for a subscription notice. Boy, they sure pull out all the—"

"Let me see," Sandy said avidly, hurrying over and taking it from her. "Oh, wow, maybe this could be—?" She held it up to the light from the window, trying to make out the contents.

"Are you going to open it? What is it? Is it good?"

"I think we should wait for Eric, but yes, it could be very good."

She managed to keep her hands off the envelope till she could place it into his early that afternoon. He drew out a letter from the *Design Mode* editor and a certificate (suitable for framing) informing them that the office renovation project they had submitted last fall had won first prize in its division and would be featured in the July issue. There was no money attached to the honor; still, exposure in a national magazine meant a lot. Even Neil and Ruth shared in the glow. Eric simply looked modest and told the new employees how much better the design could have been if Lev Eisenbaum had given him more time.

It was funny, Sandy reflected a couple weeks later, how much more gratified he was when news of the award was reported in the local newspaper.

"Hey, people, look at this!" Neil charged into the office waving a copy of the Wapatomekie *News-Herald*.

"Look at what?" Eric asked mildly.

"Yeah, what?" Sandy echoed.

"Here, on page A4! They've got a piece about our *Design Mode* award."
Sandy liked how he said "our."

"Well, I'm damned!" said Eric, his voice warm with pleasure. Sandy winced at the word, but said nothing. "I sent them a press release when we got our notice, but I never dreamed they'd do anything with it. Let me see."

She and Eric crowded around Neil to get a look.

"'Potential Disaster for Region,'" Eric read ostentatiously. "Well, that's a nice thing to say. It may not be Palladio, but it's a damn good office plan, if I do say so myself."

Sandy chuckled. "Uh, Eric, that's about the nuclear power plant." Her eye went to where Neil was pointing. "Our article is just above that."

He skimmed it over. "Oh, this is good. Where's Ruth? She'll want to hear this, too. Ruth!"

"What is it?" she asked, appearing in the drafting room doorway.

"It's the article about our design award," said Neil.

Ruth clapped her hands. "Oh, that's wonderful! What does it say?"

"Well, besides what I put in the press release," said Eric, "it mentions how young a firm we are to have won a nationwide award like this."

"And look," said Sandy, "it says there'll be a picture spread on Sunday. Eric, did you send photos with that press release?"

"Guilty as charged. You think I trust their photogs to shoot my project in the best light?"

"Hey, man, that's the way to do it," Neil pronounced. "Publicity like this should bring us more work, right?"

"Right." Eric reread the article from start to finish, his bearded lips spreading in a wide grin. "This is more than good. I never imagined. Fame and maybe even fortune. What shall we do to celebrate?"

Sandy knew what *she* wanted to do, but it wasn't appropriate for the office. "I can take some petty cash and run down and buy us all Hershey bars."

"Yes, chocolate, that's exactly what we want."

As she headed out the door, Eric said again, "Wow. This is great! They keep this up, I might even subscribe!"

"NEIL," SAID SANDY, wandering into the drafting room a half hour later, "could I see that paper again?"

"Sure." He handed it to her.

"Thanks." Opening it to page four, she read as she returned to the main room, then paused near her chair.

"What is it?" asked Eric, looking up from his table and smiling at her warmly. "Can't get over the shock? I told them to mention you in it, and you see they did."

"No, it's not that . . . " she said, still perusing the page. "It's the article about the Tyler Creek breeder reactor. It says some canisters of plutonium have gone missing over there."

He came over to look. "Really? When was it stolen?"

"That's just it, they're not sure it was. It was there at the last inventory, but now it's gone."

"And when was that?"

"The last inventory? Paper says two weeks ago."

"Damn nuke operators! Why can't they be responsible? Just what we need, Three Mile Island in the Midwest." He shook his head. "Not that I'm really worried. It'll turn up in some storeroom."

"What if it doesn't? I mean, remember those awful flyers we found on our cars last January? The threats they were making—"

"'The White Way'? I haven't heard a peep out of them since then. Have you?"

Had she? That radio program Ruth heard . . . *He'll think all Christians are like that . . .* And she hadn't heard it herself. "No, not really."

He drew her close. "It's probably just some paperwork snafu. Nothing to worry about."

"You're right. You have to be."

"Of course I am. Life is good. Let's just be famous architects and enjoy it, okay?" He smiled at her.

"Okay," she whispered, gazing into his marvellous gray eyes. If she hadn't heard Ruth approaching the connecting doorway, she would have kissed him, in the office or no.

. . . THE OFFICE RENT is paid, and the printer's bill . . . There'll be a bill from the drafting supply store, but assuming Jacob and Sam pay the latest invoice in time, I'll have enough to cover that and the salaries at the end of the month, with something to spare . . .

Behind Eric, the hinges on the men's room door creaked as Neil walked in. Taking his place at a nearby urinal, he acknowledged him with a discreet grunt, then both men maintained the customary silence.

. . . It'd help if Millerson would pay up; he's a quarter past due. Maybe I'll have Sandy try and sweet-talk him into it. After the way he raved about her work on his store design . . .

Eric washed up and threw the paper towel into the trash can. As he gripped the door handle to leave, Neil turned off the faucet and said, "Hey, man, hold on a sec. There's something I need to talk to you about."

"Certainly," he said, as Neil dried his hands. "You can tell me on the way back."

"No. In private. Not in front of—" He cocked his head in the direction of their office suite.

Why the reluctance to discuss whatever it was around the rest of the staff? He wasn't after a raise already, was he? He'd only been there three months. That wouldn't be like him, not unless . . . "Is everything okay at home? Your wife's doing all right?

"No, it's all cool," Neil said, grinning. "Marsha's cool. Doctor says the baby's coming along just fine."

Well, thank goodness for that. But maybe he was asking too much of his specifications guy. It couldn't be easy, coping with a pregnant wife at home and a pregnant colleague at work. He asked, "Is it Ruth? You two getting along all right? Nothing too, um, hormonal?"

Neil laughed. "No, nothing like that. Though she does give me tips on what to expect as Marsh gets farther along. No, Ruth's cool."

"So, what . . . ?"

"It's something that went down this morning, when you were out."

"Something happened?" Eric said, a little too quickly. He stepped away from the door and prepared for the worst.

"Around ten o'clock, Sandy comes in to get me; some new building products rep has just shown up. She says, 'He asked to talk to me, but I told him it was your thing and you'd see him.' So I did."

"What company was he from? Was the product any good?"

"No. He *said* he was from an outfit called HydroHalt— I've never heard of it, have you? Supposed to be a new foundation waterproofing system, but it looked pretty useless to me. I told him we weren't interested, and he left."

For a moment Eric was annoyed. "So what's the problem? I trust your judgement; why tell me in here?"

"Because . . . well, here's where it's at." Neil's broad face clouded. "The dude's trying to convince me to spec this system for FirstCon, but all the time he's whispering that 'Ms. Beichten' really should be the one looking at it, and trying to get me to hand the interview over to her. I figured he had a problem with black folks and let him suffer."

Eric laughed. "Yeah, his problem. You were doing your job."

"Then Ruth comes out of the drafting room and goes to Sandy's table to ask her something. And the dude— he's looking over my shoulder at the girls— his face looks like . . . like a high school kid who's just found out he studied for the wrong test. I could swear he had some kind of card down in his lap and he's reading something off it."

"Really? What for?"

"You want my guess, he was trying to figure out which one was Sandy. I guess she didn't say that's who she was when he walked in, just handed him over to me. But with Ruth there, he wasn't sure. They're both kind of squatty, you know, with brown hair."

Squatty? Eric let that pass. "True, Ruth isn't really showing yet."

"Yeah. I must have blinked because when I looked again, the card was gone."

"What happened then?"

"Sandy got up and she and Ruth went in the other room. And the dude stops talking about the product and doubles down on wanting to know which girl is Sandy Beichten. Gave me a really weird feeling, man. I showed him the door."

Crap, not another fishing expedition from McNair. Kentucky was holding him on that weapons charge, but apparently he could still send his thugs on the outside to do his dirty work. Why couldn't he get it through his head that Sandy had no information to give?

"What did he look like?"

Neil shrugged. "White. Tallish. Cheap navy suit, brown shoes."

Not the short man with the green ring, anyway. "Think you could take him if you had to?"

"Say what?"

"Never mind. Listen, it's probably nothing, but if anyone else comes around that you think is at all off-key, especially anyone asking personal questions about me or Sandy or anyone connected to this office, you do what you did this morning: tell them nothing, get rid of them, and let me know as soon as you can. I'll tell Sandy and Ruth the same."

"Got it. This have anything to do with that dude that was hassling you last fall?"

"Not him, he's dead. Maybe the guy who invaded the office in January. Though it could just be somebody underestimating Sandy, thinking she'd be easier to sell to since she's a woman. Sorry if this puts you in a bad position."

"It's all cool, man. It's not like you didn't fill me in on all that when I was hired."

"I wonder," Eric said, "do you think I was wrong hiring Ruth, under the circumstances? She knew, but . . . "

"It was all trash talk, what that Hardt dude was up to? And the other dude's in jail?"

"Yes."

"So what can they do?" said Neil. "Besides, Ruth's got guts, too. She's told me she wanted to work here just to prove that BS wrong."

"*Did* she?" said Eric, pleased. "Well, just in case, keep your eyes open."

"Right, man. And since you asked, yeah, I could take him."

Back in the office, Neil handed him a glossy brochure featuring a section detail of a typical building foundation and photographs of something purporting to be an innovative waterproofing system. The detail looked valid enough at first glance, but closer examination would have told anyone in the building trades that the product wouldn't keep moisture out for five minutes. It was no compliment to Sandy's professional reputation if this "HydroHalt" guy thought she'd go for it.

Laying the brochure aside, Eric unlocked the tall file cabinet and pulled out the office ledger.

"Everything all right?" Sandy asked. "We're still in the black?"

"We should be fine, once the next FirstCon payment comes in. No, I was just wondering . . . if I should offer Neil a raise."

CHAPTER C.6

RUNNING A LITTLE LATE, Eric dashed down the steps of his apartment building into the gray drizzle of a late May morning. It had been more like six or seven weeks before the engineer in Michigan was free to discuss the new corrugator, and Eric was surprised to see Jacob Ryerson's gleaming black Lincoln Continental idling at the curb, instead of Sam Delkirk's pale blue Caddy. As he reached for the handle of the back passenger door, the tinted driver's side window whirred down. "Around here," said Jacob, motioning with his hand.

"Where's Sam?" he asked as he climbed into the front next to his client.

Jacob pulled out into the traffic. "Family emergency."

"Really? I thought he was divorced, no kids."

"It's the dog." He lit up a cigarette. "Had to take it the vet."

"Really? I would have thought he'd do anything rather than miss this trip. So it's bad?"

Ryerson shrugged. "From what Sam told me, he got up this morning and the mutt couldn't stand up, its *tuches* kept hitting the floor. Not eating. Barfing. That kind of thing."

"Oh." Eric didn't know what to say. He'd never had the chance to own a dog. Not unless he counted the mechanical one Sandy had given him.

"Far as he can tell, it was some caviar the mutt got into last night. Sam'd just opened it for himself, the black kind, like he's so *meshuggah* over. Turned his back a second, and— poor *schlemiel*, he didn't get a bite."

"If that's what made the dog sick, it's probably just as well." said Eric. Hadn't he seen a photo of the pet in Sam's office? "Golden retriever, is it?"

"Irish setter. Poor Sam, that dog's like a baby to him. That ex-wife of his took him for everything he had— not really, but she sure tried— but he fought like a fiend to get custody of old MacGregor."

"Umm," he responded, vaguely. "Well, let's hope the vet knows what to do." The cigarette smoke swirled thickly around his head and he searched a little desperately for the electronic window control. He found what appeared to be a likely button. "You don't mind if I roll down the window, do you?"

"Sure, go ahead."

He took deep breaths of cool fresh air, and Jacob said, "Anyway, the engineer's name we're going to see is Mitchell. We should get up there around 11:00 . . . "

⅄

BARRING THE SIX HOURS spent as Jacob Ryerson's captive audience— and Eric wasn't sure which was worse, the cigarette smoke or the adolescent back-room stories— it was a valuable trip. Without the information he'd gained talking face to face with the corrugating machine's customizer, he could have made errors that would have cost him dozens of manhours in redesign.

By the time they arrived back in Wapatomekie after 10:00 p.m., the morning's drizzle had clamped down into a dark, steady rain. Jacob slowed and put on his left turn signal. "Hope you don't mind if I stop at the 7-Eleven, do you? I'm almost out of coffin nails."

"Of course not." Eric waited in the car as his client ducked in. In a few minutes, he was back, two or three cartons in hand. He laughed. "Sheila says I should stop. Says the smokes will be the death of me."

She could be right, thought Eric. "I don't know," he said. "I wouldn't mind keeping you around awhile longer."

"I'm sure you wouldn't!" Jacob said, and backed out.

From their left came the banshee squeal of tires turning too fast into the narrow convenience store lot. Jamming the Lincoln into drive, Jacob pulled forward so hard the front tires mounted the curb. A shuddering jolt that slammed Eric into the passenger side door told him it hadn't been far enough. His body swayed back against the seatbelt as they spun counterclockwise and came to a halt mere inches from the plate glass façade. Adrenaline surging, he looked past Jacob through the back side window to locate the other car. Yes, there it was, a mid-sized sedan, also black or navy. With the growl of a souped-up engine it reversed, stopped, accelerated— no, impossible, it was coming right at them again! "Hey!" shrilled a woman's cry from the store entry. The dark sedan swerved, roared past, and sped out into the alley, its driver cursing as he went.

"'Silly idiot'?" repeated Jacob. "Is that the best he's got? I'll 'silly idiot' him if he's wrecked my car!"

Their faces blank white and staring, the female store clerk and a male customer stood in the rain in front of the store. "I *told* the manager he should put in speed bumps!" lamented the clerk. "Those damn kids drag race through here all the time!"

Jacob paid her no heed. He looked at Eric and broke out in hysterical laughter. "Whoo! Oy! Wait till Sheila finds out about this! Maybe she's right about the cigarettes! Hee! Oy!"

Eric wished he could laugh it off, too. But the words his client had beard as "silly idiot!" he was sure had actually been . . . *"filthy Yid."*

※

"HI, ROSIE!" Eric greeted the StudioFabrik rep as she sailed into his office, looking prettier than ever. "Looks like being hyphenated suits you."

"What?" said Rosie Crenshaw-Laurence. "Oh! Yes, it does." She beamed.

It hit him that Sandy might think he'd just said something positive about marriage. If so, she didn't let on.

"I'm looking forward to seeing what you've got," she told Rosie. "We'll be thinking about the FirstCon offices before long."

"Ooh, I've got some great Jhane Barnes menswear fabric lines that'd be perfect for the side chairs."

"Great, let's see them!" At his gesture Rosie sat down, opened her case, and arranged the tempting new samples on the white surface.

"But first," she said, "tell me what's happening with you. Last time I was here, things weren't going so good. But now, look at you. Bigger office, bigger staff, big job— Hey, Eric," she said slyly, "you sure I can't sell you something for yourself? What about you, Sandy? There's always discounts!"

"Things *are* better," he said, taking his usual seat. "But we had a close one a couple weeks ago."

Sandy nodded, and Rosie said, "What happened?"

"Couple of close ones, actually," he said, "and both of them on FirstCon. One of the owners, Sam Delkirk, his dog died."

Rosie looked blank.

"It wasn't that," he hurried to explain, "though of course Sam is upset about it. But it was food poisoning, botulism, in a jar of caviar that Sam was going to eat himself. They sent samples from the dog and the jar itself to the vet lab, and both were full of it."

"That's terrible!"

"Eric," Sandy reminded him somberly, "tell her what else happened with that."

"Oh, yes. Seems he gets his caviar shipments sent to the office, and he keeps a jar or two in his private office fridge. Well, apparently his personal assistant, his male secretary or whatever, sometimes got in there and helped himself to a spoonful or two. Because after the dog died, but before the cultures came back from the lab, the PA came down with botulism poisoning, too."

"He died," Sandy said. "The caviar came from Iran, and the Board of Health is following up on it, but they doubt they'll get far with it, the way things are between us and the Iranians."

"That's awful!" said Rosie. "That was more than a close one!"

"No," Eric said, "I meant the other partner, Jacob Ryerson. He and I were coming home from a business trip late one night and some kid came roaring through the parking lot of the convenience store we stopped at and hit us on the back left fender. That Continental of his is built like a tank, but if he didn't have such good reflexes— 'good reflexes for an *alter kocker*' is the way he put it—"

"'*Alter kocker*'?"

"Yiddish for 'old fart,' though Jacob's not that old, fifty-two at the most." Should he tell her about the racial slur? No. He hadn't mentioned it to Jacob, either. It was probably just his imagination. "Good thing he moved fast or they would have hit him in the driver's side door, broadside. Good thing for me they didn't, right?"

"You're kidding," Rosie said.

"Not at all. The FirstCon job could have been history. If Jacob or Sam had shuffled off this mortal coil, you might have come up here and found a FOR RENT sign on the office door." He looked at her, expecting to see shock, sympathy, and relief in her face.

Shocked she definitely was— at him. "God bless America, Eric, you should hear yourself!" Her voice shook with disgust. "You sound like Whatsisname from Watergate, the one who said he'd walk over his grandmother to get Dick Nixon reelected!"

"Charles Colson," Sandy said quietly.

"Yeah, him. God bless America! Two of your clients— your friends, really— nearly get themselves killed, one man actually is killed, and all you can think about is what it means to your practice! There's a time and a place for business, but—"

"I was hurt, too," he said coldly. "I had to go to the chiropractor, several times, which I didn't have time for."

"The chiropractor! Oh, poor you! A man is dead, and you're moaning about the chiropractor!"

She's right, whispered his conscience. It only made his rage more frigid and deep. "Shit! Why am I wasting my time looking at fabric samples?" He pushed back his chair and strode to the drafting room door. "Ruth!" he shouted at her. "Get out here!"

Wonderment in her face, his junior draftsman complied. He brusquely gestured for her to take his seat.

What now? Oh, crap, he'd sent Neil out an hour ago to meet with the mechanical engineer. He couldn't sit in the empty drafting room waiting for Rosie to leave, and there was no way he could tell her to go; he needed the fabrics she represented to make his projects complete. Besides, as the wife of a close friend . . . Stolidly ignoring the three women at the conference table, he flung himself out the door and down the corridor.

It was ridiculous. He was the principal of the firm. Why couldn't he be alone if he wanted? Dammit, as soon as he had the money he'd see about renting a private office for himself, one of the empty rooms across the hall. In fact, that was where he was going now. Down to Building Management to see what it would cost.

"You sound like Dick Nixon's hatchet man." Who the hell did Rosie Crenshaw-Laurence think she was?

IT WAS A STRAINED and silent walk to the parking garage that evening. He'd been sulking the past three hours, and maybe, Sandy debated inwardly, she should keep quiet and let him work it out by himself.

No. This has gone on too long.

"Eric," she spoke up, "Rosie didn't mean what she said."

Three grim flights of stairs up to her parking level. He made no response.

Try again. "Okay, maybe she did. I don't know. What I do know is that you didn't mean it the way it sounded when you were telling her about Jacob and Sam."

He stopped still, a cynical smile distorting his face. "Oh, didn't I? Maybe I *am* just a cold-hearted bastard who only cares about making money."

"She didn't say that! It's just that, well, sometimes you come off like, well, like nothing matters in life but architecture and you doing it. Not money," she said, biting her lip. "It's never about the money."

"Well, thank you for the vote of confidence," he said in that same hardbitten tone. "But I'd run over my grandmother to get my work into *Architectural Record.* Is that what you're saying?"

"No, Eric, I—" *All right. You want a frontal assault, I'll give you one.* "Eric, I know your heart. I know you'd lie down and die if it meant doing the best for your clients. But sometimes you give the impression—"

"That what?"

"That everyone else should lie down and die for Architecture, too." Breath held, she peered into his eyes, searching, hoping for some sign he was about to yield.

"I thought you'd be willing to do that with me, at least."

O Domine! Help me say what I need to before we get to my car.

Only tonight he was hurrying, not slowing his long-legged stride to accommodate her.

"Hold on! You're going too fast for me!"

He stood and looked back at her, and she couldn't read his face. She couldn't let that matter. Not now. "I am devoted to Architecture. You know that. Except, some things are even more important than that."

"Oh, yes. I forgot. Like God." He resumed his quick pace along the aisle of cars. "Well, I'm not perfect like you."

How could he say such a stupid thing? It made her want to stomp and cry.

Oh, yeah, go ahead. That'll really make Jesus attractive to him.

"Eric, I'm not—"

"All I have is what I believe in, and that's my work. And if I come off as singleminded about it, that's nobody's business but my own."

"Eric, dearest—" Catching up, she laid a hand on his arm, and thank God! he slowed down and didn't shake her off. "I like to think it's my business, too. And maybe if you could focus first on Jesus, like me, you'd see that—"

"Dammit, Sandy, I'm not like you! I can't believe all that stuff! Or keep all those religious rules! Isn't what I do enough? You sound like my mother, on me to memorize Luther's *Small Catechism!*"

Deliberately, she focussed not on him as she answered, but on the far end of the parking garage. "Thank you for the compliment— I think." She tried to keep her tone light. "But you seem to have a strange idea of what Christianity is about. I wish you would read the Bible and find out what it really is."

"No thanks. If I want a lot of *thees* and *thous* I'll read Shakespeare. Here's your car."

She fumbled a little with her keys. "There are modern translations. I keep one at the office."

"You do, do you? You'd better not be reading it on company time."

"Of course I don't! That wouldn't be Christian. Just at lunch."

"I see. And I suppose you pray for your own personal Charles Colson, the architectural hatchet man."

She took a breath. "Eric, Chuck Colson became a Christian. I thought you'd heard."

"I guess you don't want to kiss me goodnight."

She shouldn't kiss him, should she, not the way he was behaving.

Maybe you should say you'll do it only if he promises to read the Gospels with you.

Good heavens! What kind of thought was that? It'd be spiritual blackmail— or something even uglier and worse.

She put her car keys back in her purse.

"Eric?"

"What?"

"I love you." She reached up and wrapped her arms around him, pulling him close. With a surprising eagerness he responded, his lips meeting hers, his arms locking her in their embrace. *For better or worse, faults and all.* And soon nothing mattered in heaven or on earth but how incredibly dear he was to her.

Until— "Eric, I think there's someone over there, on the other side."

"It's no one. Kiss me again."

Her mind told her he was wrong. The rest of her told her mind to tend to its own business. Her mind had said enough.

CHAPTER C.7

"R UTH," SANDY SAID, poking her head into the middle room. "Have you seen my New Testament?"

It was a beautiful day in early June, and the windows stood open to the breeze. Out on the window ledge beyond the adjustable screens Eric had brought in, pigeons strutted and preened, while inside on Ruth and Neil's throw-off shelf neat piles of tracing paper sketches were weighted down with marble samples to keep them from drifting to the floor.

Ruth looked up from her table. "The *Good News* version? No, you loaned it to me that one time, but I put it back. Have you lost it?"

"Not sure. I wanted to read it over lunch, and I thought it was in my drawer."

"Maybe Eric's seen it. Did you ask him before he and Neil went to the meeting?"

Don't be silly! Sandy nearly snapped back. Her office New Testament was the last thing he'd keep track of. He'd made that very, very clear.

"I'll help you look for it, okay?" Without waiting for a response, Ruth got up and followed her into the front room. "Where did you see it last?"

"I could have sworn it was in my drawer. But maybe I left it on the throw-off."

Ruth surveyed the chaos on the shelf under the windows. "Gee whil-likers. Then it could be any place under here."

They rummaged through piles of canary sketch paper and dog-eared, marked-up whiteprints. They lifted up samples, manuals, and drafting tools. They looked on the floor and in the space beneath the slant of Sandy's drafting board. They found Corb the mechanical dog, shamefully neglected behind a stack of architectural magazines— *Poor dog, and he's really a hero. He may have saved my life*— but no *Good News for Modern Man.*

"That's all right, Ruth, it'll turn up. I may have taken it home."

"Hey!" the younger woman exclaimed. "Isn't this it?" She held up a gray paperback.

"Yes! Where did you find it?"

"Over here on Eric's side."

"Really? That's—" She broke off. *Weird.* An intimation of what it might mean, of what she dreamed and prayed it could mean, flashed into her mind.

It was too much to hope. The book had just gotten itself submerged under the flood of paper and was pushed over until it ended up next to Eric's board. "Well, thanks. Though," she said, glancing at the clock over the door, "I don't think I'll get much reading done today. Lunch break's almost over."

MORE THAN ONCE after that she found her New Testament missing from where she thought she'd put it last, then it would mysteriously reappear. She came up with every logical explanation she could: The shelf was such a mess. She was so busy she was getting forgetful. Somebody had mistaken it for another kind of book. Every reason except the one she dared not entertain.

Why not? "Everything is possible with God." Wasn't that verse talking about Him saving people who might seem impossible to save?

I know. But I don't want to get my hopes up.

This isn't about you. It's about Eric. And God's glory.

Yes, Lord. But it's still too strange to believe.

THINGS GREW stranger still.

One Sunday morning, later in June, she felt a disturbance as she stood in her usual pew singing the first hymn. A low murmur of "Excuse me, excuse me" rippled down the row in her direction, and presently a familiar hand took most of the weight of her hymnal and a beloved baritone voice began to sing lustily. He said almost nothing to her all through the service; he held her hand and appeared to be paying attention. With her emotions in turmoil, the only thing that kept her mind on the sermon was the chance that he might ask her about it. But he excused himself just after the benediction, and the next day at work it could have been a dream.

It didn't happen again. But at intervals over the summer— usually once he'd pulled up in front of her apartment on those rare days he drove them both— he'd grill her about her faith. She did what she could, but it was never enough. It didn't help that he'd usually bring up the topic at the last minute, then stop her in mid-sentence, saying he had an evening appointment to make. Sometimes she wondered if he wanted answers at all.

CHAPTER C.8

"I HAVE TO GO DOWN TO CITY HALL to meet with the Codes guy," said Eric one afternoon. "You'll hold the fort while I'm gone?"

"Against all challengers!" Sandy said blithely.

She tilted her face to his as he bent over her shoulder (to look at her drawing, of course!), and his lips stole a surreptitious kiss. "That's my girl," he whispered in her ear. His hand lingered on the nape of her neck, his fingers doing something that could have sent a rocket into orbit. Then he was off.

"Sandy?"

She jumped, the heat rushing to her face.

Ruth stood peering at her from the drafting room doorway. "Are you and Eric courting?"

"Goodness, no! I mean, it's not like . . . That's kind of an old-fashioned term, isn't it? Like you're on your way to being married."

"Sorry if I was butting in," Ruth said. "That's how we'd put it in Payne County. It's just seems there's something between you two, something I felt when Harley and I were going together."

"You don't think it's disrupting the office, do you?"

O Domine. Now I've totally given myself away.

"Oh, no, no! In fact, if anything is going on—" Ruth looked embarrassed— "it's helping the work. I think I can recognize your design styles when I see them separately. But you two get working together and I can't tell what's Eric and what's Sandy. It's a blend of both and better than either."

"I hope it's good enough to get this manufacturing plant built the way it needs to be. I can't help feeling we have to prove ourselves on this project."

"I think you will— way more than either of you expect."

The following Saturday was the third of July, and that night she and Eric watched the city fireworks from the hood of his Ford parked among the trees down at the riverfront. It was dark where they'd pulled in and with every spectator's eye on the display, it was doubtful anyone could have recognized them. But if someone had, would that have been so awful? Maybe they didn't have to hide in the shadows— or in their office— any longer?

The next few days, the thought was never far from her consciousness. Sometimes it brought refreshment and delight, like a warm summer breeze. Other times, fear of it tore into her like the whip of a tornado. What if he was worrying that everyone expected him to marry her? What if people thought she was compromising her Christian beliefs being involved with him?

Was she compromising her beliefs?

I love him. That's the long and short of it. I won't do anything irrevocable. I promise. If he wants to send me away, that will be the sign. Until then ...

Still, the idea that their love was known and accepted by Ruth— and by Neil?— who saw them every day gave her a peace that wasn't disturbed even when the phone rang one morning and it was Leah Matthews on the line.

"Hey, Sandy, it's for you," Neil said, holding out the receiver. "Some chick named Leah."

"Leah Matthews?" she said casually. "You sure it's not for Eric?"

"No. She asked for you. Specifically."

"Hmm." She took the receiver with sedate confidence. "Hello, Leah," she said. "What can I do for you?"

"You can get out of that office and come to lunch with me tomorrow, that's what," Eric's ex-girlfriend replied.

"I can't do that. We've got a big deadline coming up."

"When?" Leah challenged. "Day after tomorrow?"

"Beginning of September."

"Hell, that's what? Two months off? That's what I want to talk to you about, anyway. I won't take no for an answer."

"But I can't—"

"No. Tell that workaholic boss of yours you have to buy some new shoes. Meet me at Spruce's Café. Tomorrow. 12:30."

And before Sandy could object further, Leah hung up.

Her curiosity was piqued. It might be interesting, even instructional, to spend a lunch hour with the woman he'd dated (and presumably, loved) for so long. All right, she'd go.

SPRUCE'S CAFÉ, with its discreet sage-green and creamy-white decor, struck Sandy as a sunny, neutral venue for an encounter that could go anywhere. *Good choice, Leah.*

"Okay," said the waitress, "here's the ham and Swiss on whole wheat for you and the pastrami and mushroom on Italian roll for you." She set down their orders. "Enjoy your lunch."

"I'll get to the point," Leah said once the waitress was gone. "Eric was in my store on Monday and I thought he looked terrible." She fixed her eye on her as if waiting for a particular reaction.

Sandy hid her smile. His shopping there was no news to her. Last week she'd mentioned how handy a garlic press would be, and Tuesday, after the Independence Day holiday, there on her table sat the bag marked with the familiar shop logo. "Preliminary birthday present," he'd remarked, his tone leaving the possibility open for something more to come.

Or was Leah hoping to alarm her by commenting on his looks? To her eye he always looked wonderful. But then, she saw him every day.

Blast it, she did see him every day. What was his old girlfriend trying to prove?

"What is wrong with the man?" Leah demanded. "Is he really spending all his time working on this project?"

Sandy collected her thoughts, glancing up at the ribbed glass globes of the light fixtures hanging from the ceiling. "As far as I know, he is. By his count he hasn't gotten to bed before 5:00 a.m. any night this week."

"But is he designing all that time?"

"I think so. No, I know so. He said it."

"You're not sure?"

"I know he's coming up with the final details to get this project out on time."

"You aren't there?"

Leah's black and white striped boatneck shirt made her look like Marcel Marceau. Appropriate, Sandy thought, the way she seemed to have dragged her into some elaborate duo mime, only with words.

"At his place? How could I be?" she answered lightly. "I have my own schedule to keep." If she was going to be open and casual concerning her relationship with Eric, it wouldn't be with Leah Matthews. "Besides, if I were babysitting him, who'd get in early and crack the whip at the office? The boy rarely appears before 1:00 p.m."

"He'll burn himself out. I know him. He looked halfway to it the other day."

Did he? "I don't think so," she said. "He's more likely to make a religion of it."

"Really?" Leah shrugged as if the concept was foreign to her. "At least you can tell me if he ever gets out."

"Gets out?" She got a cartoonish mental image of Eric frantically tugging at the handle of the office door, unable to escape.

"You know, to a movie, concert, whatever."

Did a quick run to the all-night taqueria count? The indigestion that had produced still burned in her stomach's memory. But how was that Leah's business?

"Look, I know you and Eric are . . . " she chose the word carefully, " . . . friends. And you're concerned about him. So why ask me? Why not ask him yourself?"

"Because," Leah said, her eyes riveting Sandy's, "he broke up with me last winter. Or didn't you know?"

She knows I know. She looked down at her sandwich, anywhere, to break that gaze. *And I bet she knows why I know.*

"Yes," Eric's ex said grimly. "He said things hadn't been working out between us for a long time. I don't know what his problem was; we would have been fine if he hadn't been so obsessive about his job." His job? Was that how Leah saw Eric's work, as a mere job? "Then he said he had to be honest with me, there was someone new. He wouldn't tell me who she was"—again, the piercing dark eyes grabbed her and would not let her go— "but I could tell she wasn't making him happy."

Sandy's jaw dropped open in indignation. "That's a— How interesting. You could tell all that from a phone call?"

"Ah," said Leah, settling back in her chair and folding her arms. "So I was right."

"About what?" She tried to sound casual.

"Did I say he called me? Never mind. I told him he was making a big mistake, whoever she was, but you know Eric. If he thinks a woman can give him what he thinks he needs, he'll latch onto her no matter what. Until . . . " She made a fluttering gesture with her hands. " . . . until he decides he doesn't need that thing anymore." She paused. "That's what happened with me. It was good. We were there for each other. Then he opened that office of his and he changed."

What about that store of yours? You weren't exactly there for him anymore, either.

Leah paused, then said, "He'll change again, I promise you."

You think this'll make me doubt him? I know more than you think I do, Miss Matthews. "Did he say he was—?" *No. Be assertive.* "What made you so sure he was unhappy?"

"Last winter? Oh, no, he didn't say a thing about it to *me*. It was the tone of his voice. And it hasn't gotten better, has it?" she challenged. "The way he looked the other day . . . I've picked up some information here and there, so I know what's going on. That haggard look, it's not just from working too hard. Eric's a man with passions. He's got real physical needs. This new girl of his, she's holding out on him, isn't she?" Leah looked straight at her. "*Aren't you?*"

Blast it to hell! What right did Leah Matthews have to butt into what she and Eric did— or didn't— do?

She reined herself in. "I'm sorry, why do you think I—"

Leah shook her head. "You probably hit him with your religion and told him you couldn't sleep with him before marriage," she said bitterly. "So what's the point? Eric's never going to commit to you, any more than he could commit to me."

"Really, I don't know why you're bringing me into this. I only work for him." *Forgive me, Eric, I have to.* She focussed not on the mocking face, but on the stylized spruce tree stencilled on the chair back beyond Leah's left shoulder. "Besides, I already know Eric doesn't believe in marriage; something to do with his parents. He told me himself."

"He did? Now, why would he mention that?" She took a drink of her Coke and in a hard voice said, "Oh, just cut the crap, would you?"

"What do you mean?"

"You're acting like this has nothing to do with you. Sorry, Beichten, it's no secret. I've got a friend who parks in the garage down from your building, and he's seen a thing or two. He said if his girlfriend got him that worked up then just drove away, he'd knock her silly." Leah sniffed. "Why don't you come clean? I thought you Christians were big on honesty, but I'm beginning to wonder."

Maybe I should "just happen" to remember a prior commitment and rush out.

Faker. Coward.

"All right," she said defiantly. "I love him and he loves me. We're keeping things private for business reasons. Okay?"

"That's no excuse for being a tease. I bet you like seeing him suffer. Suppose he changed his mind and asked you to marry him, I bet you'd say no and put it down to your stupid religion."

O Domine, help me. "You don't understand. Eric's not a believer. Marrying him wouldn't be an act of love, it'd be selfish." Inwardly she braced herself. "We'd be miserable together. I need a husband who'll be the spiritual leader in the family, and Eric can't do that. Or else he *would* lead me, and I'd end up turning my back on Christ. I don't know what's the most important thing to you, but what if the man you married thought you were a fool to love it and wanted you to stop?"

"Why couldn't you do your thing and he could do his? It wouldn't kill you. You say you love him. Ask him to marry you. It might be the best thing for him. That way he gets what he wants and you'll have him where you want him. He'll be singing 'Here Comes the Bride' in no time."

Why was Leah suddenly eager to get the two of them together? This conversation was going totally backwards.

"No, but it would probably kill our marriage. Jesus my Savior"—it amazed her how fearlessly the Name fell from her lips— "is the most important thing— Person, I mean— in my life. In marriage you become one flesh with your husband; it's an image of Christ and the Church. If I were joined like that to somebody who was indifferent to Him, even opposed, I—"

Leah brought her hands together in a slow, sardonic clap . . . clap . . . clap. "Brava!" she said. "You get a gold star for that?"

"What?"

"Great job parroting what they fed you in Sunday School. *Civilized* people compromise. It happens all the time."

Around them their fellow lunchers were happily consuming their meals. No one else was being forced to justify her basic principles over the ham-and-cheese. Sandy took a deep breath and ignored the inner voice warning her not to give too much away. This wasn't about Eric anymore. It was about Christ. "No," she said, as firmly as she could. "That's not just something they taught me. I learned it first hand."

"Really?" Leah's eyes narrowed. "You've been married before?"

"No, but— there was this guy I went steady with back in college. He claimed to be a Christian, just not the Christianity I was raised with. He was into Transcendental Meditation and Eastern religion all mixed up with Jesus and the Bible. It was a little weird, but I compromised like you said. Or I kept my mouth shut. I thought it didn't matter, since I wasn't really in love with him. But then—"

She took momentary refuge in an examination of the café's sheet-vinyl flooring, then steeled herself to look at the woman across the table. "Only reason I'm telling you this is so you don't get the wrong idea about my faith." Leah's face remained impassive. "I did fall in love with him eventually. He asked me to marry him, and I accepted. I told myself none of it mattered, all his talk about each human being a spark of God and us all being connected in one Universal Soul. Like you said, we were civilized and our differences wouldn't matter."

Leah took a bite of her sandwich, which may or may not have been a signal for Sandy to go on.

"Actually, the way I felt about him, I told myself they weren't really differences. I wanted him and all he was. I was ready—"

"Ha!" said Leah, as if she'd heard something that amused and pleased her. "You mean you wanted him to screw you. Nothing wrong with that; I hope he did." She sounded almost friendly. "I'd believe you were human."

"I didn't say that," Sandy protested, annoyed at how accurately Leah's mind was working. "We didn't— I said no in time. Anyway, before that, he said certain things. I had to stop pretending his beliefs didn't make a difference. He was living by them, and if I married him I'd be living by them too."

"Nothing wrong with that, either. Plenty of people are into TM. They bliss out and life is good."

"Not," she replied earnestly, "if bliss means him sleeping with ten other women and saying since everything is connected it's as good as sleeping with you." Even now, seven years on, her heart still felt the rage that nearly drove her to kill Werner with his own Buddhist idol. "We broke up. And I promised myself— and God— that I'd never put myself in that position again."

"I don't see how that applies," objected Leah. "Eric's not into sleeping around, I'll give him that. He's too deep into his work for his own good, but otherwise he's the most decent man that ever lived."

"I know," she said, gripping her glass so tightly the beads of sweat on it rolled over her fingers. "From the perspective of this world, he is. But Wer— the other man— only wanted me to compromise my marriage bed."

She put the glass down and wiped her hand with the napkin. "But if I were married to Eric, he might want me to compromise my relationship with God!"

Leah's face was grim. "So why are you stringing him along? Seems to me that could happen the way things are right now."

Sandy stared at her, not comprehending.

"I mean it," Leah said bluntly. "If that's how it is, cut him loose. You're so all-fired concerned about your stupid Christianity, you don't even care about him. I had to tell you how strung out he's looking, you're too high in your holy clouds to notice or care! Cut him loose before you kill him! You love him, don't you? At least, you claim to."

"I do love him," she said, her voice miserable and low. "More than anything. But—"

"Oh, don't worry about your job," Leah said spitefully. "I hear you're good enough, six firms around here would snatch you right up." Some expression on Sandy's face must have made her pause, for she said, "No, I'm not trying to get him back, I know better. Just set him free and let him find someone who'll appreciate him and won't think he's inferior because he refuses to believe a lot of myths!"

On Sandy's plate lay her sandwich, with only a few bites taken out of it. Never mind. She wasn't hungry.

At her elbow the waitress said, "You ladies be wanting dessert?"

"No thank you," she said stiffly. "Separate checks, please."

The two of them sat there saying nothing. After what seemed like ten eternities, the waitress returned. Sandy didn't wait for Leah to accompany her to the cash register. Quickly, she paid her bill and left.

Curiosity killed the cat? I guess so.

CHAPTER C.9

SOMETHING WAS WRONG with Sandy.

He'd wanted to take her out the previous weekend, but she'd begged off, muttering something about them both needing rest. And the past few work nights she'd been awkwardly silent and pulled away from his kiss when he walked her to her car.

And then, her eyes followed him in the office. Nothing unusual about that; he liked it even though he knew it meant she wasn't giving full attention to her work. It made him glad he hadn't done anything about adding on a private room for himself alone. But lately when he turned around and met her gaze, it wasn't the breathtaking glow he'd come to rejoice in since last January. Her look now was perplexed, anxious, even sad.

"Sandy, what's wrong? You're staring at me like I was growing another arm between my shoulder blades."

"Was I? I'm sorry." Her tone was subdued, not like her at all. "I— I won't do it anymore."

"Won't look at me? Hey, I like you to look at me. I just want to know what's wrong."

"Nothing," she said curtly. Then, "No, it is something. Eric, I'm worried about you, and I'm kicking myself that I didn't notice it before."

"Notice what? Why?"

"You're not getting enough sleep. Your eyes . . . "

"Oh, you don't have to tell me. I look like Rocky Raccoon. Or a bandit. Should I tell people you punched me out?"

"Eric, it's not funny! And your hair, so much more gray than before . . . "

He poufed it up on one side, making a show of preening himself. "You don't think it looks distinguished?"

"Oh, no, of course it does! It's just . . . it feels like it's my fault."

"Your fault?" It was his turn to be perplexed.

"Yes. Because I won't—" She hesitated, and started again. "Because I haven't urged you to take care of yourself better."

He got the distinct impression that was not what she had started to say. He looked at her closely, but she added nothing.

"Now look," he said. "If I stay up working it's my decision. Don't be getting maternal on me." The distress on her face grieved him. "Hey, come here. I'm sorry, I know you care. I just don't want you taking all that on yourself."

He took her hands between his and kissed them.

"Eric, they're filthy! They've got graphite all over!"

"So now you're on me about my diet? Precious love, if there weren't two people in that other room I'd kiss you several other places as well. Now get back to work and save your worrying for Jacob and Sam."

"Yes, sir."

"Yes, sir"? She hasn't called me that since . . . well, since Before.

"Sandy?"

"Yes?"

"Don't 'sir' me. I'm not a knight. Call me by my name, or what you usually call me when we're alone together."

"Yes, Eric . . . dearest." But the word was forced out, and the slump of her shoulders as she bent over her table filled him with apprehension.

But Sandy had an appointment in an hour with the FirstCon department heads, and he had some paperwork to go over for the Fort Randolph City master plan submission. No time to probe into it now.

THAT EVENING when he stepped into his apartment, his foot crackled on a folded piece of paper that had been pushed under his door.

It was a plain, letter-sized sheet. Neatly centered on it, in 10-point Courier type, was the message

```
         Never forget
       you've always
          been mine
```

Was that how she was going to be? Maybe it was a good thing they weren't sleeping together. Hadn't they settled all that at the office?

As the evening wore on his attitude softened. Maybe he needed her concern to keep him from running himself into the ground. Leah had never seemed to care how tired he was as long as he could take her out on the weekends. And Sandy must really be worried, since she'd driven out of her way from the present FirstCon office just to leave him a six-word note.

He wished she'd written it by hand and signed it. It would have been more like her. Still, he got her point. Tonight he'd make himself go to bed early— right after he got down his latest idea for the desk in the FirstCon lobby.

THE TIMING was perfect, if the concept of perfect timing could apply to a dread necessity like this. Neil was at the structural engineer's and Ruth was out having lunch with a girlfriend. Still, Sandy couldn't be too careful. Reluctantly, she had prayed that Eric would go into the back room; the fact that the prayer had just been answered told her that what she had to do was predestined.

She gave him a minute. Then quietly she passed through the drafting room and through the open door of the resource library.

He stood by the window, a binder spread open under his hands on a bare stretch of shelving. He hadn't turned on the ceiling fixtures and the light from between the half-closed vanes of the blinds appeared to cut him into strips of color and shadow. He turned toward her, smiling. How tired he looked, how thin and pale! The silver stars in his hair were merging into clouds, and how could she have missed those new lines etching his face?

"I was thinking curved glass block would look really good for the main reception desk." He gestured at the catalog. "Did you see these units VitroBlok has come out with? With any luck they'll have the radius we'll need."

"Eric," she said, "I need to talk to you."

"About what?" he said as she closed the door behind her. His tone was light, but apprehension flashed across his face.

Do I really have to do this?

Yes, if she loved him.

"Eric, I need the professional photos of our earlier jobs. May I have access to the negatives?"

His brow furrowed.

"For my portfolio."

"For your portfolio?" he said in mild astonishment.

"Yes."

"Of course you can. I want all of you to have your portfolios up to date for when we go out to interview with new clients. But is this really the time? In September, after we've got FirstCon put to bed, there'll be plenty of time for that."

"No, Eric." She straightened her shoulders and steeled her voice to be firm. "I need them now."

"But why?"

"Because—" She hitched in her breath. "I have to look for a new job."

He stood there, his expression blank, as if she were gibbering in an alien tongue. Then, an incredulous whisper: "You what?"

"I have to look for a new job." She'd better say it all at once, before she lost her nerve. "I'm not good for you, Eric. I'm wearing you down. You admitted it yesterday."

He made a gesture of denial, but before he could speak she said, "I can never be the woman you want me to be. Too many things about me get in the way. My beliefs, my . . . ideals. It's hurting you."

"It's what?"

"Yes. I have to go away, so you can find someone you can be happy with." She gulped back a sob. "I'm not the right girl for you; I never was."

"So you're breaking up our relationship, and breaking up the firm, too? Whatever happened to you've always been mine?"

The words made no sense. She said, "I won't leave until after the FirstCon docs are in."

"Because I'm miserable with you because your religion won't let you sleep with me?"

She could only nod. She couldn't bear to look at him. Her eye fixed on the spine of a brightly-colored binder. "New Horizon Lighting," it said. Ironic, how her horizon was contracting in on her, old and limited and dark.

"Where will you go?"

"I don't know yet." she said, struggling to keep down the despair that was forcing its way up from her heart. "I— I thought I'd ask Reg Fyfield. Unless you know of someone who needs a project architect?"

He was staring at her as if she were out of her mind. "Sandy, you could ask me that? Don't you love me at all?"

Jesus help me, he's right. One more reason he'll be better off when I'm gone.

"Eric, dearest," she nearly wailed, "I love you more than life itself! That's why I have to leave you, for your own good! Please tell me you see that, please!"

He did not touch her. He remained at the window, his left hand on the sill, his head down, the bizarre shadows from the blinds making it difficult to read his face.

"Was this your idea, or did someone put you up to it?" he demanded, his voice grim.

"Did somebody . . . ?" she faltered. "I didn't— I mean—"

"Someone put you up to this. Who?" he insisted roughly. *"Who?"*

"Leah Matthews. She told me that—"

"Leah. I should have known."

The room felt chilly, even in the heat of a July day. Was it the coldness of his tone, or was it her heart that was refusing to send the blood through her veins?

"Yes. She made me face up to—"

"Alexandra Marie Beichten." She stiffened at her full name. "Did it never occur to you that Leah Matthews might not have your best interests at heart?" It came out as a suppressed roar. "Or mine, either?"

O Domine! Was it a trick all along? And now I've fallen for it, and it's too late!

He crossed the room and took her hard by the shoulders. His voice shook with the violence of deep pain. "Did it never occur to you that *I'd rather be miserable with you than happy with anybody else?"*

She startled. *What?*

"Which I'm not! Miserable, I mean!"

She gasped.

"Do you *want* to leave me? Aside from all this useless altruism you're dumping on me today?"

She bowed her head. "No."

"All right. Now never say such a thing to me again." He gave her a little push towards the door. "We'll talk about it later. Okay?"

"Yes—" *Yes, sir,* she'd been about to say, but stopped herself in time. "Yes, dearest."

He went back to the glass block catalog, then looked up and gave her an encouraging smile. She was still too dazed to return it. Her eyes were drawn to his, even as she put her hand to the knob behind her to open the door.

Then, with no interval of time or space, she was across the room and in his arms. Tightly she clung to him; more tightly he clung back; they were kissing one another, greedily, ravenously, conscious only of something precious they had nearly lost and didn't dare let go.

"Don't ever leave me don't ever leave me don't ever leave me," a fierce voice was saying over and over; with a shock she realized it was hers. "Don't let me go, Eric, don't let me go!"

"O precious love, I need you, I want you— god, how I need you!"

Their voices soon were lost in their kiss, its force pushing her under like an earthmover, pouring through her like golden sunshine and the rich silver starglow of passion's night. He had her up against the wooden edge of the shelf, his body hard and triumphant against hers, and she didn't care, she welcomed the pain in her back, it was proof she was alive and living and loved.

"Eric, I want you so much, please, please . . . " Oh, if he would only take her now, just as they were, with her body willing clay under his beautiful artist's hands!

In another universe a voice was screaming, *Wrong! This is wrong! You're not married, what would your Lord say?* But the voice of her earthly lord was the only one she could heed.

"My diamond, my star, let me— now— o god! now, please!"

"Sa voix enchanteresse, dont il sait m'embrâser . . . " His voice, his magical voice, *he knows it sets me ablaze . . .*

An ear that hardly seemed to be her own picked up light footsteps entering the office and the sound of the radio station being switched. An announcer was talking: the fact registered itself in a remote part of her brain. Ruth, and the one o'clock news.

It made no difference. If anything, they devoured each other more voraciously. "Shhh!" was all he said before finding her mouth again. Her breath came faster and faster, or was it their breathing together? louder and harder their hearts beat, nearly drowning out the cry that came from the other room.

Footsteps approached the closed door and a woman's urgent voice called, "Eric? Sandy? Are you in there?"

Ruth, of course it was Ruth, but neither of them cared. Sandy guided his roving hand in defiance of heaven and earth while he whispered, "I'll never let you go, never, never!"

A knocking now on the door, which grew to a pounding. "Eric, Sandy, if you're in there, open up! Something's happened! Open up, please!"

The insistence in the cry finally got through. Alarmed, they sprang apart and hurriedly straightened their clothes.

O dear Lord, I'm sorry, I'm sorry, forgive me! What was I doing?

No time to consider. She pulled a catalog off the shelf and pretended to be searching it. Eric went to the door to admit Ruth.

"Why . . . didn't you . . . just come in?" he said, his breath still coming in short gasps. "It wasn't . . . locked."

Sandy ever-so-casually turned around with the binder, just in time to realize she was holding it upside down. The shocked expression on Ruth's face stopped the pretense immediately.

"No!" she cried, "You have to listen to me! On the radio, just now! Phil Duggins has been stabbed in his office! He's dead!"

CHAPTER C.10

HE HAD TO CALL the Fort Randolph City planning division, if only to confirm the evil news.

"Sandy," he said eventually, "I've got Roxanne on the line, Mr. Duggins' secretary. She's the one who found the body, and she wants to talk to you."

She took the receiver. "Yes, Roxanne? . . . Oh, gosh, how terrible for you! . . ."

A minute or two later, Neil burst into the office, his face set like grim death. "Did you hear—?"

Sandy held up a hand for silence, and Eric said, "Yes, we know. Sandy's on the phone with his secretary right now."

"The note was— *what?*" For a long stretch she paid quiet attention, her hand clapped to her mouth. *She's good like that,* Eric reflected. *The woman probably met her three times and now she's the one she turns to in this crisis.* "We're just devastated here; I can't imagine how awful it is for you. . . . Can you go home and get some rest? Do you have a friend who can stay with you? . . . Well, anytime you want to talk to me, just call. All right? . . . You take good care of yourself, Roxanne. All right now. Bye."

She hung up the phone and shook her head.

"What did she say?" asked Ruth.

"It's worse than we thought. I couldn't imagine why anyone would want to kill Phil Duggins, a nice man like that. Well, they weren't out to kill him, exactly."

He asked, "What do you mean?"

She turned to Neil. "It sounds like they wanted to kill the entire black race."

"I knew it!" he exploded. "It's like the other ones!"

"What other ones?" Eric and Sandy said together.

"The other murders. That's what I was trying to tell you. The radio station in the car said Phil Duggins' killing resembled four or five other murders in various parts of the state the last few months. All unsolved."

"But I never heard of them," Sandy said.

"I didn't either," said Ruth.

"Of course you didn't," said Neil, bitterly. "It was *only* random black and Chicano dudes getting bludgeoned over the head then knifed to death in small towns nobody ever heard of. Nobody thought to wonder about the racist notes pinned to the bodies, the ones with the letters cut out of newspapers!"

"Lord have mercy!" Sandy exclaimed, and Eric thought of the threatening message he'd received the previous December.

"Yeah," said Neil. "It took the death of somebody high profile to get the honky cops off their lazy white asses and make some kind of connection. *Shit!*" He hurled his tube of drawings to the floor and looked as if he wanted to cry. Silently, Ruth retrieved it and placed it on the conference table.

"Sandy," Eric said quickly, "there was a note in Phil Duggins' case?"

"Yes."

"Did Roxanne see it? Did she tell you what it said? I think we should know."

"Are you sure, Eric?" she said, glancing over at Neil who had found Corb and was artificially busy winding him up.

"Yes. Neil, leave that damn dog. If this is the kind of world we live in, we all have to face it. Sandy, what did it say?"

"*ARF-ARF-ARF! ARF-ARF-ARF!*" clamored the toy.

"*I'm* not the one who's avoiding reality," Neil said under his breath, but to Eric's relief he rejoined the group.

"*ARF-ARF-ARF! ARF . . . ARF . . . ARF . . .*" No one spoke while the incongruous noise ran down.

Sandy took a deep breath. "Well, it was what Neil said. Cut-out letters from newspapers and magazines, just like— um, just like people do when they don't want their handwriting identified. It said, 'True men won't be ruled by ni—'" She grimaced. "I'm sorry, I don't use words like that."

"'Niggers,'" Neil supplied.

"If you say so. 'True men won't be ruled by nigger slaves.'" She winced again. "Then it said, um, 'The swaggering ape is dead. All niggers will die.'" She bowed her head. "I'm sorry."

"Not your fault," Eric said, irrelevantly— though from the way Neil was glowering he could almost think he thought it were. "If you want to rinse out your mouth after that, go ahead."

She looked at him gratefully, but stayed in the room. "I just can't believe it," she said. "Anyone saying something like that about Phil Duggins."

"Me neither," echoed Ruth.

"So they could say it about the butchered college student and the business owner and the young doctor in those other towns?" Neil inquired acidly.

"Oh, no! Oh, gosh, no! It's just that— well, we *knew* Phil." She paused. "All I can say is, thank God he was a Christian."

"What?" Eric exclaimed. "'Thank God he's a *Christian?*' Isn't that rooting for the other team, to want your people dead?"

"I don't want my people dead," she said patiently. "You know that. But if people have to die suddenly, it's a comfort knowing they're safe in the arms of Jesus. We'll see our brother Phil again, won't we, Ruth?"

Ruth's hesitation annoyed him. Dammit, was she doubting Sandy's Christianity because of what she'd walked in on in the resource library a half hour ago? She'd damn well better not!

The warm soft skin under her blouse . . . the memory lingered on his fingertips, threatening to shake him into desire even now.

Baumann, focus!

But Ruth must have remembered about forgiveness or some such thing because she gave a firm "Yes. 'Blessed are the dead which die in the Lord. Their words follow after them.'"

Both the girls seemed to think the prospect of life beyond the grave gave Duggins' death meaning. But the Christian resurrection wasn't for him, Eric Baumann. When it was his turn, would his death mean anything?

"All right," he said, shaking off the thought, "at least we could pitch in and buy flowers. Sandy, will you find out who's handling the funeral arrangements?"

"Yes. And I think I should go to the funeral. Or . . . ?"

"I think we should all go," said Ruth.

"So do I," said Neil.

"I'm not so sure," he countered. "I doubt that master planning project will go away just because the planning director is dead. If we all show up, it might look like we're using Duggins' death to influence the commission to give us the job. We've got more pride than that!"

"Pride's overrated," Sandy said bluntly. "Especially when it keeps you from doing what's right."

"Damn straight," said Neil.

"Phil was a great guy," Ruth put in. "We should go and honor him."

"Exactly what I was thinking," Sandy agreed. "It's not like we're going to jump in his grave like Hamlet and yell 'Hire us!'"

It was three to one— but it was his office and his decision.

"All right," he said, "I'll think about it. And children, I hate to say it, but life goes on and we've all got work to do. Get done what you can, but . . . get back to it."

IN THE END, all four of them attended the funeral the following Monday at the A.M.E. church in Fort Randolph City, crowded into an old pine pew with Carole and George Fenton. The building was packed with mourners, most of them black, who swayed to the music of the gospel choir and cried out their *Amen!*s and *Lord have mercy!*s to the brown-stained rafters above. As different as the worship style was, it reminded Eric of enthusiastically singing hymns at his mother's side in their Lutheran churches in Wisconsin and North Dakota.

Then the preacher mounted the pulpit and began hammering away about the resurrection. Deluded as the man was, Eric had to admire him. He certainly was fond of the phrase "eternal life." He used it over and over, approaching it like an Olympic long-jumper gathering momentum through the word "eternal," then making a mighty leap onto the word "life." "E— ter— NAL— *LIFE!*" was how he said it, and with the power he put behind the final word Eric could readily imagine how it could stand against all the terrors of Death.

Imagined terrors, because after this world was only oblivion. But, he reflected, it must be refreshing to believe like that.

During the prayers he came to a decision. He'd call the police detective who'd interviewed them after Sandy's assault last January, tell him about the note and his fire, and see if he thought there might be a connection between that and what happened to Mr. Duggins.

The man he wanted was out by the time they got back to Wapatomekie, but the desk sergeant said he'd pass the information along.

The next day, his detective called back. Communications made up of cut-out letters were common as dirt. Between Eric's lost note making vague threats and the message rammed with a knife into Phil Duggins' dying chest, the police could see no connection whatever.

CHAPTER C.11

ERIC STOOD HESITATING in the produce section of Carpese's grocery. The strawberries looked good, but they'd had them last week. Why were raspberries always so high? You'd think, with them being in season . . . But Sandy liked them. Raspberries it was. They'd have them for dessert after their take-out supper in the office tomorrow evening.

Better get another carton, in case Neil or Ruth could stay. Since the day Phil Duggins died, he'd asked them to work late whenever they could. His official line was that it was better they put in the extra hours now, instead of getting into a panic in August. In reality, what happened in the resource room had put the fear of God into him and Sandy both. They'd barely touched each other during working hours since then: no words were needed to convince them the barest stroke of a finger might set them off. Hot sex in the office looked exciting in the movies, but if that's how they ended up, how could they get any work done?

But who would have thought he had it in him? Or that she did, either? Both of them planners and designers— so intellectual, so logical, so orderly . . . Many times he'd envisioned what it would be like when she surrendered to him, and it never included tearing up the office library. If Ruth hadn't returned to the office just then . . . if the appalling news had been broadcast later . . . The possibilities filled him with both exhilaration and deep fear.

They'd get past it. They were sensible people, after all. But right now the more the others were around, the better. And someday, soon, he hoped, she would give herself to him totally— but it would be in his bed or hers, not in the back room amid the catalogs and samples.

But to think they both had it in them! No woman had ever aroused him like that; no one, not even Leah, had driven him to abandon himself in that way. No other woman—

"Hey, Sexy," said a female voice at his elbow, "fondling the peaches?"

Speak of the devil.

"Oh, hi, Leah. How's it going."

"Fine. Hmm, what's this? You don't like raspberries," she said, picking up one of the cartons. "You always griped they had too many seeds."

"People change. I like them fine now." He took it from her and replaced it in his cart.

"Hmm. Should I also congratulate you on the change in your office?"

"Change? What do you mean?"

"Isn't that woman draftsman of yours leaving?"

"Yes, we'll miss her, but we always knew Ruth would be quitting when her baby got near due."

"That's not who I meant. The other one."

You bitch.

"If you're referring to Sandy Beichten, she's let me know about your concern for my well-being, and she's not going anywhere. Is that understood?"

She picked up a plum off the display and took a bite out of it, her eyes laughing at him as the juice dribbled down her hand. "Don't look so shocked," she said, licking her fingers. "I'll pay for it." She wiped her mouth on her sleeve, threw the half-eaten piece of fruit into a plastic bag with a couple others, and wrapped the twist-tie around its neck like she was garrotting the head off a small bird. "So she told you all that, did she? Did she also tell you about the old boyfriend she all but slept with because she was stupid enough to think he wanted to marry her? I'll bet it was that drunk Marvin Jansovic, and she did sleep with him. And now she's playing professional virgin and holding out on you."

"Shut up. I don't have time for this."

"She *is* holding out on you, isn't she! Ha, goes all the way with Marv Jansovic and you've hardly gotten to first base."

"Leah, let go of my cart. I've got business to take care of, and it doesn't include trading bullshit with you."

"You know what?" She swung the bag of plums casually in his direction. "She told me she wouldn't marry you even if you asked. You're not holy enough for her, you know that?"

"I told you, that's enough!"

"You don't want to hear what a hypocrite she is, do you? Sandy Beichten, the perfect little Christian!"

Suppressing a cold inward rage, he steadied himself and said, "Last time I checked, Christianity wasn't about being perfect. It was about being forgiven because we're not!"

Her eyes widened with glee. "Ooooooh, who's the missionary now? Just like dear old dad!"

He took a deep breath and counted to five.

Impudently she grinned at him, shaking her curly head. "Shit, Eric, you should see your face! You'd think somebody had threatened to cover one of your designs with mirror tiles. Face it, you're just putting up with her being a Christian and hope she'll drop it so you can get a hand in her pants!"

He drew himself up to his full height. "On the contrary. I might have thought that once, but lately I've found her Christianity to be one of the most refreshing things about her!"

She stood stark still, mouth gaping in astonishment.

"Leah?" he said patiently. "Please move. I have shopping to do."

"Um, excuse me?" said a mousy woman in pedal-pushers. "I need to get some berries?" She maneuvered her cart in towards the display, forcing Leah to step aside. Eric steered his cart by his ex-girlfriend. At the end of the aisle, he glanced back. She was still staring at him, the bag of plums dangling from her hand.

Shaking his head, he left her behind. Truth was, he was astonished at himself.

"THESE ARE WONDERFUL," said Sandy, spooning the last bite of raspberries and canned whipped cream out of a Styrofoam coffee cup. "Thanks." Her smile made last night at Carpese's worth the hassle.

"Thought you'd like them." Eric licked his fingers. "Perfect finish to fast food chicken."

She shook her head, eyes wide in mock wonder. "Ruth and Neil don't know what they're missing."

"Well, I *did* tell them they could stay . . . with overtime, too."

"But for some strange reason they decided to go home. Do you think they might have lives outside this office?"

"Really? Is there any world beyond this?"

"I've heard rumors of it. But I think it's a figment of someone's imagination."

They both laughed, and she gathered up the empty containers and threw them in the wastebasket. "Back to the salt mines!"

"Not so fast," he said. "Your birthday's next week, isn't it?"

"Yes, Tuesday the twenty-seventh."

"Hmm. It might not be a bad idea if you and I explored the wide world of Wapatomekie for a change, just to celebrate. Not that evening; we've got a meeting first thing the next morning. But this weekend. Or the weekend after. Preferably the one after."

"You have something in mind?"

He gave her what he hoped was his most cryptic smile. "Maybe I have." He reached under the papers on the throw-off shelf. "Damn, I thought it was here somewhere . . . oh, well."

"What is it?"

"I got the notice in the mail a couple weeks ago, but I can't lay my hand on it just now. You've heard of the Rothspieler Chamber Orchestra?"

"Authentic Baroque ensemble, conducted from the first violin. I got the notice, too. I'm afraid I didn't look at it. I threw it away the moment it came."

"But why?" he said, his heart sinking. "Don't you like them?"

"I love them. I have all their recordings. I just couldn't bear the thought of there I'd be"— she raised her left hand— "finally getting to hear them in person, and there you'd be"— she gestured with her right— "way on the other side of the concert hall, with both of us pretending you're only my boss."

"I think we can rectify that . . . I assume you're free on Friday the thirtieth?"

"Yes?"

"I've got us tickets. Together."

"Oh, Eric! That's wonder—" Her look of joy collapsed into doubt. "Do you really think we should?"

"Which? Leave the office for an evening or hear us some good music?"

"Be seen out together here in town."

"Let's not worry about that. Not anymore. People close to us probably guess already"— *including Leah, unfortunately*— "and if they're not close to us, they either won't notice or we don't care."

She sat considering. "Yeeess, I think Ruth knows."

"And by now the clients know we're a great team. All right, then. Besides, it's a good-sized hall and the seats are in the balcony."

"The acoustics are better up there."

"That's what I think."

"Well, I'll be happy to go. Thank you." She went back to her drawing and he indulged himself contemplating the shining brown waves of her hair as she bent over it. After a minute or two, she turned and said to him, "I'm curious. Who's the concertmaster-conductor these days? Last time I heard it was Claudius Bamberger, but he was talking about retiring."

"Yeah, they've got a new guy. Funny, I can't remember his name. It's on the notice, if I could remember where I put it."

"Wait a minute." She went over and slid a book off a glossy piece of paper on the conference table. "Is this it?" She took it back to her chair. He came and stood next to her, giving himself the pleasure of watching her as she read. To his amazement, disbelief overspread her face, supplanted by something like fear, which gave place to ironic resignation.

"You really want to go to this?" she asked, her eyes searching his.

"I told you, I've got the tickets."

"Well," she said, blowing out her breath a little, "don't expect me to introduce him to you."

"Who?"

"The new concertmaster of the Rothspieler Chamber Orchestra."

"What? You know him?"

"Do I know Werner Edelstein?" She pronounced it the German way, "Vairnair Edelschtine." "Very well. We dated all my senior year in architecture school, when he was finishing up his Master's in performance and composition."

Werner Edelstein, the violinist? Good lord, was *he* the one she was engaged to? A sickening fear of being outclassed made war with the mercenary yen to be close to a celebrity. *His* Sandy knew someone like Werner Edelstein, and was in a position to introduce him if she chose! The moment passed and, self-chastened, he said, "We don't have to go if you don't want. It's your birthday present."

She shook her head. "No, it's been long enough. I can go and appreciate him for his artistry. And so can you."

He laughed mischievously and said, "In that case, shall I change the tickets so we're sitting front and center?"

"So he can see how well I'm doing now? No . . . that won't be necessary. We'll enjoy ourselves in the balcony."

He guffawed.

"Not that way!" she protested. "Unless you want to set the whole concert hall on fire!"

"Maybe I do. And if I catch him with his beady German eyes on you, it'll be the start of World War III!"

CHAPTER C.12

IT WAS A LOVELY WARM SUMMER'S NIGHT, and she was glad they'd walked over to the ice cream stand across from the park near the music hall for a late dessert.

"That'll be one blueberry and one rocky road, please," Eric said quietly.

"Far out," said the kid at the window. "Here ya go."

Cones in hand, Eric led her across the street to a park bench under the trees. "Here's yours. Happy birthday."

"Thank you. Searight's always has the best ice cream, don't they?"

To this he gave no reply. Since the concert he'd spoken but little, except to suggest coming here. He sat next to her on the bench, but he could have been miles away.

She waited a few minutes while they finished their ice cream. Then she asked, "What did you think?"

Trust him to know she wasn't asking about the rocky road. "Oh, the orchestra was wonderful. Marvellous ensemble. I've never heard that Pergolesi sonata done so well."

"Werner had a couple of solos. I figured he would." Better to mention him now and get it over with.

"He was very, um, *effective*."

No need to ask what he meant by that. "I know."

"I couldn't help wondering if you wanted—"

"No, Eric. His playing *is* very effective. It made me want *you*."

He pulled her toward him but a footstep sounded nearby on the path and he let her go. "It's just that I can't help thinking that you could be married to him right now," he said, keeping her hand in his, "and I never would have met you."

"No, I doubt that." She gave a little laugh. So he had guessed who her one-time fiancé had been! Sometimes it seemed her mind was his as much as it was her own. But this he had wrong. "More likely we'd be divorced."

"What do you mean?"

"It's what I told you last January. He couldn't be faithful. It was— well, maybe I should tell you how it was.

"You said his playing was effective. He didn't develop that power overnight, good thing for me. It wasn't until his master's recital in the spring that I got hit— *whap!*— with the full force of his musicianship. And it wasn't till then that I gave in to being in love with him. He'd been courting and wooing and trying to get me into bed the whole year, but I was happy with things the way they were. Hugs and kisses and not much more." She sighed.

"But that evening, I fell, hard. You would have laughed," she said, purposely making her tone light. "I went from 'Let's just be really good friends' to 'Please ask me to marry you!' in the space of one recital. We went back to his place afterwards and had a romantic supper and too much wine, and when he proposed, I accepted."

"He must've been pretty sure you'd— no, never mind."

"So it seemed logical to, well, act like we were married. That same night, I mean." She glanced at him. "I told myself we'd made our vows and were husband and wife in the eyes of God. Who cared what anyone else thought?"

She realized she had her fingers intertwined and was making bird wings with them. Deliberately, she pulled them apart and wiped her palms on her skirt. "Funny, I still didn't tell him I loved him. He was making love to me and meanwhile I was orchestrating the whole thing in my mind, how I'd wait until things got— things got—" She broke off, embarrassed. "Well, all fireworks and glory. And *then* I'd say the magic words." She paused. "I guess all that planning should have told me he was the wrong guy to say it to."

"All right," was all Eric said.

"Anyway, all through the process he's been saying these romantic things in German—"

He laughed sardonically. "Romantic? In German?"

"You'd be surprised. Anyway, like an idiot I thought I understood it all. Finally he said something I couldn't work out and I went, 'Werner, speak English!' And he started babbling on about 'Love' being too big to be confined to just one woman, and how he was thinking of me when he made love to 'the others,' and, well, that stopped things cold. I put it together with some other things that'd been happening, weird phone calls from girls who'd hang up when I answered, and— turns out he'd been seeing a couple of other women for months, and when I confronted him with it he didn't think he'd been doing anything wrong at all!"

"He was a damn fool."

"Or I was. Well, we fought. At least, I did. He stayed calm while I nearly tore his head off. Eventually, he apologized and said he'd give the others up." She looked in his face anxiously. "Maybe I'm a hardhearted you-know-what, but I said we were through even if he did. He wasn't sleeping with them just because he was— he was—"

Eric supplied a vulgar term.

She smiled and shook her head. "No, it was way more 'exalted' than that. It came out of his beliefs. *'Diesen Kuss der ganzen Welt,'*— *'this kiss for all the world,'* as it says in Beethoven's *Ninth Symphony*. He actually played that piece for me that night, the Georg Solti recording, even while we were—"

"He didn't!" Eric burst out, barely-suppressed laughter twitching his lips. "Well, scratch that idea!"

"Eric! This is serious!"

"Of course it is, precious love. Go on. What was that all about?"

"That having Beethoven on his side would convince me he was right? But he wasn't; he couldn't be. And as long as he kept believing love was like that he'd be spreading it around to anything in a skirt." She gave a tentative laugh. "Last I heard, he was married to someone back in Germany, but I wouldn't be surprised if he's got a girl here in Wapatomekie right now too. Or two or three."

"He wasn't a Christian either?"

"Oh, no, he claimed to be, but—" In her eagerness to tell the tale she had, for a moment, *forgotten.* "Either," Eric had just said. "Not a Christian *either.*" "—I'm sorry. You're wondering how it's different with you— when you're—"

It was hard to read his expression, but she went on. "Call me an idiot, but maybe it's because I didn't really love him."

"But you said you did. Madly. You admitted it yourself."

"Yes, I did use that word, didn't I? Out of my mind for about five hours. But it wasn't like I really loved *him.* I think— yes, it was his talent I loved. His effect on me."

Was that really true? What about her utter misery after she and Werner broke up? The weeks before she was willing to listen to Beethoven's *Ninth* again? In a way, she had loved him. But— "Not like I love you."

"He is damned talented. And I'm not?" The envy in his voice shocked her.

"You know better than that," she rebuked him. "You're the best architect in this city, and I'm not the only one who says so. And pretty soon they're going to hear about you in the rest of the country, too.

"What I want to say— what I want you to know, is . . . Eric?" She touched his face, the texture of his beard under her fingertips arousing sensations that tore at her heart.

He captured her fingers and kissed them.

"Eric, you are talented, and brilliant, and beautiful, and I admire you more than you'll ever know. But if something happened and you couldn't draw another line, I would still love you. If something— God forbid!— happened to your mind and you couldn't put two sensible words together, I would still love you. If something came between us and we had to separate, maybe for years, I would still belong to only you. I'd go on loving only you and praying for you and wanting only what was best for you. Now do you understand?"

His hand trembled as it held hers, but his voice was resolute and firm. "Would you? Sandy, precious love, I'd do anything, give up anything, for you. If it came to it— I mean it— I'd die for you."

The thought of Eric dead or compromised for her sake was appalling. "Oh, no, no! There's only one thing I'd want you to give up, but please, don't do it for me. Do it for yourself. And for God."

He released her fingers with a groan. "Oh. That. I'm sorry. I can't see my way clear to it now. There are too many—"

"Questions?"

"Yes. Maybe I can explain it someday. Not now. Right now, let's just . . . oh, damn it, why does life have to be so complicated!"

A remarkably adolescent lament coming from a man in his mid-thirties, and she couldn't help but laugh.

"What's so—?" he began. Then his lips twitched, he put his hand to his mouth as if to hold something in, but it wouldn't be suppressed. "Oh, Sandy, I—!" and both of them laughed uproariously until the people going by on the path began to stare.

But even under the merriment, the relentless fact of his unbelief tugged at the hem of her mind. *"I'm still here,"* it whispered. *"And you can't do a thing about it."*

Lord, You can. Please do something, soon!

CHAPTER C.13

SANDY SHADED HER EYES against the bright August sunshine as she and her co-workers emerged from the Dragon Palace.

"Hey, Ruth," joked Eric, "want to come back to the office and get some more work in?"

"Oh, I'd *love* to," Ruth teased back, "but Junior here's been pushing me away from my drafting table the past two weeks. Besides, I took my tools home on Friday, remember? But thanks for the nice going-away lunch. I'll miss you all."

"I'll miss working with you," said Neil. "Even with the Dolly Parton music leaking out of your headphones."

Ruth laughed. "Hey, Neil, you've broadened my horizons, too. Tell Marsha I expect to hear when your baby is born."

"Sure thing." He gave a thumbs up.

"Is your husband picking you up here?" Eric asked.

"Yes," said Ruth, looking at her watch. "Any minute now. Sandy, keep me posted on the Fort Randolph City job, whatever happens. If I thought I'd have time I'd offer to help out on that from home."

"If we get it," Sandy said. "The city council presentation last week went okay, but I could have done better . . . "

"Don't underrate yourself. Take it from me," she assured the others, "she bowled them over. And such a nice tribute to Phil at the end."

"You don't have to convince *me*," Eric said. "Though with politicians you never know."

They stood chatting on the sidewalk a minute or two longer until Ruth's husband, Harley, pulled up and drove her waving and smiling away. Neil said, "Hey, man, I've got an errand to run before I come back to the office. Do you mind?"

"Go ahead." Eric grinned at Sandy and her heart rejoiced. "Come on," he said to her, "let's get back to work."

"It doesn't seem like a Monday," she commented as they turned to walk the few blocks to their office building.

"More like a Friday? Maybe because it's mid-month payday. I did offer to keep Ruth on till the twentieth, but the baby said otherwise. I'm glad I've got you to myself because I wanted to tell you about the party I went to Friday night."

"The one that business school buddy of Sam Delkirk's gave?" she asked as they stood waiting at the corner. "Thanks for letting me off going. I'd hardly seen my friend Pat since the summers after high school, and Friday was the only night Carole could join us. We had a great time."

"Glad to hear it. Come on, the walk light's on." He took her arm as they crossed.

"So how was the party?" she prompted. "Any new work, do you think?"

"Maybe, but it's play I'm thinking about now. After I did the rounds with Sam, I got to talking with a guy. He didn't strike me as the type to show up at an affair like that, but you don't get anywhere being prejudiced."

"Why, was he a minority?"

"Oh, no. Just the opposite. A real live hillbilly scrubbed down and wrestled into a three-piece suit: drawl, bad grammar, the works. But after two hours of trying to impress all those deadly-earnest potential clients, he was—"

"Refreshing?"

"Yeah. Genuine, somehow. He's from McAllister County, and he was telling me all about the great hunting and fishing down there. Made me realize how long it's been since I've been out of the office. Funny, he said he could tell I needed a break. If you'd been a fly on the wall you would have laughed."

"How's that? Whoops!" she said as they dodged a kid skateboarding on the sidewalk.

"You okay? He kept telling me it was a great place for us guys, especially if we wanted to get away from 'those naggin' females.' He seemed adamant about it. 'Leave 'em home,' he says. 'They mess up the fishin'.'"

She gave him a doubtful look. "Okaaaay. And to this you said?"

"I told him I didn't have any 'nagging females' in my life. But the place sounded like fun."

"Really? I never saw you as the big outdoorsman."

"Oh?" he said. "Should I grow the beard longer and convince you?"

"No, no, it's fine as it is!"

"Actually, I haven't been fishing in ages. Didn't tell him that. The thing that really interests me is this little town up in the hills down there, on the west fork of the White River. Rains Overlook, it's called."

"I've heard of the place."

"Thought you might have. Good nineteenth century Victorian architecture all hanging off the sides of the hills. But kept up over the years, with no ugly plastic and aluminum façades— like *that*—" He gestured towards the building they were passing— "and no cutesy restoration. Not real touristy, either. I said I'd been thinking of visiting down there someday, and you would have thought I'd handed him a birthday present. He said in that case I should go soon, it's beautiful this time of year. You know, I may just do that."

"You mean a vacation?" It took effort to keep the shock and disappointment out of her voice.

"Sure, why not? Do you realize I opened the office over two years ago and except for Christmas at my brother's I haven't taken a day off since?"

"You do work too hard . . . " She looked away, pretending to admire the Back-to-College outfits in a store window as they passed. He deserved some time alone. He had no obligation to spend every waking minute with her.

"You haven't taken any of your vacation time either, last time I checked."

"Oh. I haven't?"

"No, you haven't." He laughed. "You need to get away, too."

"If you say so."

"Hey, such enthusiasm! What's the matter?"

She tried to keep her voice even. She was not going to make a fool of herself right there on the street. "I was thinking I'd miss you. But that's all right. Maybe we need some time apart."

He stopped stone still. "What do you mean? You're coming with me!"

"Oh! Really?" Her spirits lifted in amazed gladness— then fell into stark sobriety.

Where would they stay? And how?

Face reality. He might have hopes . . .

And so do I . . . In an absurd flash she was again in that alternate universe where she could yield herself utterly to the man she loved without displeasing the God she served. Impossible. The Lord was God over all. Hadn't she committed herself to obey Him?

Yes, but I want to be happy and make Eric happy, too.

Not in that way she couldn't. Not the way things were.

"Of course!" he was saying. "You think I'd abandon you in the hot smelly city while I'm whooping it up in the mountains? You know me better than that."

"Oh! I just . . . when did you have in mind? Who's going to watch the office?"

"We send out the bid sets on FirstCon on the third. I was thinking we'd go that next week, while the prospective bidders are looking things over. Nothing much will be happening then. If there are any Requests for Information, Neil can take care of it."

He held the door of their building open for her.

"Thanks. Yes. Of course he can."

"And I'll give him a contact number in case any design issues come up."

Standing next to him in the elevator up to their floor, she kept silent. "Not touristy," he'd said about Rains Overlook, but she had no idea what that meant for costs. Single rooms could be pricey, but if she mentioned the added expense, would he think she was complaining about her salary? And what if he was assuming they'd share a room . . . and a bed?

"The mail's here," he commented, picking up the letters scattered on the floor under the office mail slot. He examined one piece in particular, a brown envelope, hand-addressed. He extracted several glossy brochures. "Looks like my new friend from the party hasn't lost any time. Here's one for Rains Overlook," he said, handing a brochure to her, "and one for McAllister County in general, and look, here's some information on the annual persimmon festival. That's not till October; we'll give it a pass.

"My new friend Pratt— that's his name, Pratt," he said, glancing up from the enclosed note, "tells me to get off State Route 46 just south of Hendricks-burg. He's drawn me a sketch map of a scenic route I should take instead."

"Oh?" she said, going through the rest of the mail.

"Yeah. He admits Route 46 is the fastest and easiest way to Rains, but for a long stretch around Belham City it is— and I quote— 'uglier than a boar-pig in a flounced petticoat,' and I wouldn't like it."

She laughed. "He's got you sized up pretty well."

"Nothing wrong with that," he said cheerfully. "We'll take Mr. Pratt's advice."

"Sounds good." *Though it's too soon to be saying "we."* She examined a large, flat envelope. "Eric, look. It's from Fort Randolph City. And it's thick. Should we open it now, or wait till Neil gets back?"

He considered. "Let's wait for Neil."

Good. Anticipating the news about the master plan would distract him. And give her time to work out just what she needed to say.

"RIGHT ON, Sandy!" said Neil when the Fort Randolph packet was opened on his return. "I knew you'd land the job for us."

"You had a part in it, Neil. The planning area takes in some black-owned shops, and I made sure they knew we had somebody like you and could keep that perspective in mind."

Eric's forehead wrinkled in doubt, and Neil gave her a quizzical look.

"Oh! I'm sorry," she said, clapping her hand to her mouth. "That was rude of me. I shouldn't assume just because you're black that you know everything about what other black people are thinking."

"No sweat. Nobody understands a brother like a brother."

You put your foot into it there, kid. If Neil wasn't such a nice person . . .

"Sandy, I figured you'd impressed them," said Eric. "Fortunately this job doesn't start till mid-September. Finishing FirstCon comes first."

"YOU GOING HOME tonight?" Eric's joking voice startled her out of her focus on her drawing.

"What?" She glanced up at the clock. Nearly 9:00 PM. "Oh! Sorry, there was that expansion joint system we had to change out. I'll have the detail redone in a half hour or so."

"That's fine, but pull off for a second. About our vacation. I was thinking we wouldn't go till Monday the sixth. That's Labor Day, but the traffic should be in the opposite direction. That'll give us the weekend after the deadline to recover. What do you think?"

"Eric, I . . . "

"Is something wrong? I thought you'd be happy to get away."

She fiddled with her pencil. "Of course I am . . . it's just . . . I think you've forgotten something."

"What? To let Neil know he'll be flying solo for a week? Or two?" he added, his eyebrows raised hopefully.

She shook her head.

"Oh! Al McNair!" he exclaimed. "I forgot all about him. The police did say we should check in before we left town."

"Yes, that, but—"

"I'm sorry. You've been so strong since then, I let the scumbag slide right out of my mind. You're still doing all right? Sleeping okay?"

"Yes, Eric, but it's—"

"You're right, it is late, but there's got to be somebody at the desk at the police department tonight we can run this by. Why not do it while we're thinking about it?"

He looked up the number and punched it in. He must have got someone who could answer his query, for he brightened and winked at her. Then as he listened, a disturbing blend of emotions flashed over his face: shock, disgust, and what looked like relief.

"What is it?" she asked as he hung up. "What did they say?"

"We're free to go."

"The trial's been put off till sometime this fall?"

"There won't be a trial."

"*What?*" she cried. "They let him plea bargain out and didn't talk to me?"

"No. Al McNair is dead."

"Really?" *Lord, forgive me. I shouldn't be glad.* "What happened?"

"They set bail so high for him in Kentucky he couldn't even post bond—"

"Another inmate killed him?"

"No. About two weeks ago somebody finally put up the bond money. In cash. He was supposed to report in in person every week."

"And?"

"This last week, he didn't. They found him Friday night— trussed up on the riverfront down in Sykesburg. He'd been shot between the eyes."

She gave a short painful cry. *Like that arsonist. A sinner like me, and I stopped praying for him.*

For a somber moment neither of them spoke.

"Damn, it is terrible, but there's nothing we can do about it," Eric said. "And it takes a load off us both. If we'd had to testify the publicity wouldn't have done us any good."

"True . . . " she responded, her tone subdued.

"So everything's taken care of."

"Not really. It's still bothering me that, well, that . . . "

He looked at her with amazement. "Listen, don't take that Christian love of yours too far. Sykesburg's less than twenty miles from here. What if he wanted at you again? The creep got what he deserved. 'Live by the sword, die by the sword,' isn't it? If your religion is right he'll pay for what he did to you in Hell. Let's go enjoy ourselves; he's not our concern anymore."

She braced herself. "Eric, I'm sorry, it's not Al McNair, or Neil, or anybody else that's bothering me. It's you. Something you've forgotten to do."

His eyes went wide in panic. "What is it? I thought I had everything arranged."

"That's the problem! You're not one to find the 'wimminfolk' superfluous, but you've settled everything without me. You've assumed— oh, everything! Maybe I was saving up my vacation time to go see my mother in Florida. Or to take another trip to Europe. But you never asked."

His face went blank. He sat down at his table, picked up his pencil and triangle, and without another word began to draw.

O Domine, have I overdone it? He's closing me out. He hasn't done that since . . . oh, for months.

But the frost lasted only a minute or two. He muttered something that sounded like, "Man, don't be an idiot," laid down his tools, and got up to face her again. "I just wanted to surprise you," he said. "With this deadline, I thought it'd be a relief to you if it was all arranged. Besides, we seem to think alike on everything . . . "

Headlong, she took the opening he gave her. "Mostly we do. The original Vulcan mind meld. I just don't like the idea it's got to be *your* mind."

A look of anger or frustration flashed over his face.

Now I have done *it.*

He groaned. "Oh god, I'm doing it again, aren't I? My brother Paul yelled at me about this. Sandy, I'm sorry. We can go somewhere else if you like."

She hurried to reassure him. "Rains Overlook is fine. A week in the mountains is what we both need. No, the real problem is . . . " She took a deep breath. "You seem to be taking for granted where we're going to stay. And how. Do I need to book myself a room somewhere? Because I can't have you checking me into some motel as Mrs. John Smith."

In his eyes a light dawned. "Is *that* what's worrying you! Actually, I arranged that already." He gave her an apologetic smile. "Sorry, it's what decided me on going. I have some married friends with a summer home about fifteen miles from there, near Osceomenie Falls. They have *two* spare bedrooms. I've already talked to Jen and they'll be glad to put us up the whole time. That is, if it suits you?" he offered. "I'm sorry, I should have discussed it with you first."

"And this Jen and—?"

"Allen."

"They'll be there, too?"

"Yes, fair maiden. He's a novelist and she's a graphic designer. They work at home. We'll be properly chaperoned and your virtue will be preserved."

The look on his face made it impossible not to laugh. "Oh, Eric! What's left of it. But I approve. Bless you. Say what you like, you *are* my knight."

"At your service, my lady." Bowing over her hand, he kissed it with a flourish. But instead of releasing it, he pulled her into his arms.

I don't care, she thought, yielding to his embrace.

The janitor's cart squealed in the corridor. They jumped apart.

"Hey," said the custodian, poking his head into the room, "mind if I take out the trash?"

DIVISION D

MONDAY, 6 SEPTEMBER,
LABOR DAY –
WEDNESDAY, 8 SEPTEMBER 1982

And if thy right eye offend thee,
pluck it out and cast it from thee:
for it is profitable for thee that one of thy members should perish,
and not that thy whole body should be cast into hell.

—Matthew 5:29

But seek ye first the kingdom of God, and his righteousness;
and all these things shall be added unto you.

—Matthew 6:33

CHAPTER D.1

ERIC DID HIS BEST to sound utterly serious. "I'm glad we're getting an early start."

Sandy locked her apartment door and put away the key. "Yes, you're right," she answered, equally deadpan. "For us, 2:00 p.m. is a *very* early start."

"Absolutely." He picked up her suitcase and backpack, and they headed for the stairs. "I just *had* to stay up till 6:00 sketching for that new house we've just gotten in."

"You didn't!"

"You're right. It was only till 4:00. Hey!" he protested (as she shook her head and mouthed, "You're crazy"), "I had to leave Neil something to do. Let's give him some design work to chew on while we're gone. I think he'll enjoy it."

Outside, the weather was warm, blue, and breezy, with just a hint of high cloud. Just what he liked for a long drive.

"Is this everything?" he asked, fitting her bags into the trunk of his car.

"Think so— unless I should bring my portable drafting board? It'll be a *whole week,* after all."

"No, you can use mine!" The Galaxie's bumper clanked as he closed the lid.

"Sure that thing's wired on tight enough?" Sandy asked, eyebrows raised in good-humored skepticism.

"It's held on so far! All ready?"

"Ready."

She looked so beautiful standing there next to his car, her sweet legs bare in blue shorts and her curves tantalizing him under her comfortable old architecture school tee shirt. Her shining brown hair was tied back in a single long braid. . . . Later, she'd undo it— no, maybe she'd let him release it, let him spread the rippling strands over her shoulders, let his hands stroke down the sweet softness of hair and skin, let him—

Baumann, you promised. Not till she's ready.

But maybe she would be, soon. This trip could make all the difference.

She smiled up at him, her face open and eager.

To Rains Overlook? To the ends of the earth!

"You want to drive first, or shall I?" she offered.

"Oh! Sorry, yes, I slept enough, I— Yes, I'll drive." He paused. "Unless you want to? You don't mind navigating?"

"Not at all. My privilege."

As he started the car, she twisted around to look into the back seat. "Did we forget something?" he asked.

"Well," she said brightly, "here's the fishing rods, you're wearing your cargo shorts with the million pockets, but you didn't bring your gun."

"Don't have one— as you know. Had enough of guns in 'Nam. Funny, that reminds me. Friday after you ran the drawings over to the printer's I got a call from Pratt."

"Uh-huh?"

"Said there was somebody I should get in touch with if I ever came down to McAllister County. Jones, Johns, something like that. I said I'd be coming down on Monday— by way of his scenic route— and he was thrilled. Said he wished he could be there to welcome me, but I should call his friend and he'd do it for him. But it nearly made me laugh, he was so solemn about me not bringing my gun."

"Did you tell him you don't have one?"

"Heck, no! With my he-man reputation to maintain?"

"Eric, you're terrible!"

"He said it wasn't hunting season and if the local authorities saw me with a firearm they might think I was poaching."

"Weird. I thought everyone in places like that drove around with a gun rack in the back of their 'pick-'em-up' truck."

"Now *you're* being terrible," he teased. "Well, not quite, but they might make a distinction between the locals and strangers. It happens."

"True. Uh, are we going to look up this friend?"

"Probably not— unless you get bored with me and want a change?"

She met that with a gratifying silence as he made the left turn onto Meyers.

"Uh, Eric? I know you're dedicated, but this is the way to the office."

"I know. I have to leave these sketches and some instructions for Neil."

Downtown, he pulled into a parking place in front of their building, conveniently empty due to the holiday. "Coming up?" he invited.

"Sure."

He nearly had the note finished when the phone rang.

"Should I get it?" she asked.

"Up to you. Though who'd be calling on Labor Day?"

Shrugging, she picked up the receiver. "Hello, Eric Baumann, Architect; Sandy Beichten speaking . . . Yes?" She turned to him and mouthed, "Are you in?"

He shook his head so emphatically he could feel the breeze in his hair.

"Sir, Mr. Baumann isn't available today . . . No, he's gone on vacation. . . . No, I'm sorry, he won't be back for at least a week. . . . Yes, well, normally I wouldn't be in on Labor Day either, but something came up. . . . Yes, sir, that does sound interesting. . . . Yes, I understand. Would you like to leave your name and number so I can have him call you back when he returns? . . . All right, you call back in a week or so. He'll be glad to talk to you then. Goodbye."

"Who was that?"

"Potential client? Said he had a new job he wanted to discuss with you. Wouldn't leave his name or tell me what it was about. Have I been naughty not putting you on the line? I was afraid if I did we wouldn't get away till midnight."

He was tempted to say, "Yes, we need all the work we can get." But he checked himself. "No," he told her, "anyone who really appreciates our design will be willing to wait."

"Sounds like somebody who knows your reputation as a workaholic."

"All the more reason for us to get out of here. Let's go."

"YOU PICKED a great day for driving," she commented, pleasurably contemplating his strong hands on the steering wheel. He smoothly merged the car onto the trafficway leading out of town.

"Perfect weather made to order, precious love. I heard it's been kind of wet up in the hills, but it stopped a few days ago."

"So it should be nice and green."

"That's what I thought. It's around 270 miles to Osceomenie Falls; the turnoff for Rains Overlook is about twelve miles before that. We'll take our time . . ."

"See the sights along the back roads? Perfect."

"Jen and Allen don't expect us till 9:00 or 10:00 at the earliest."

After a mile or two more she turned on the radio. "Let's get the traffic report. Oh, it's the news. Gosh, is it three o'clock already? They should have traffic after this."

They listened to an item on the day's parade, and another on plans to make off-season renovations to the city's largest swimming pool. Then, "In regional news, police in Fort Randolph City have issued a warrant for the arrest of Jonas Kramer, age thirty-seven, of the Pike Creek district, for the July fourteen slaying of city planning director Theophilus Duggins. Kramer, who has been missing since shortly after the murder, was known to have blamed Duggins for his failure to be hired for a job with the city's planning department. Any information on his whereabouts should be reported to the Fort Randolph City police.

"In Shawnee Township, residents should be on the alert for an apparently rabid dog sighted on—"

Sandy shut the radio off. "So it was only personal," she said soberly.

"You were inclined to link it to those White Way flyers, too?"

"Yes. It seemed even more likely after what my friend Pat told me."

"Pat?"

"The friend from high school Carole and I got together with the night you went to that party. She's a county commissioner down in Tennessee, and they've been having trouble with threats and attacks on minorities, especially Afro-Americans. One or two people have been killed, and it's getting tense."

"Ku Klux Klan?" said Eric, horrified.

"If it is, they're leaving the sheets and the burning crosses at home. This seems to be a new group, but they don't know who. That's the trouble."

"You'd think people could grow up and enter the twentieth century." He put on the signal and took the exit for Route 46 South.

"I know. But I guess Phil's murder was only ordinary jealousy after all. Even with that—" she shuddered— "disgusting racist note. Poor Phil. And his poor wife and little girl."

"Yes," said Eric, shaking his head. "But we can honor his memory by doing the best job we can on that plan."

"True, we can," she said, and fell silent.

"*But the righteous souls are in the hands of God,*" she inwardly sang from the chorus from the Brahms *Requiem*. "*Nor pain, nor grief shall nigh them come.*"

Brother Phil, rest in peace.

CHAPTER D.2

"IT MIGHT HAVE BEEN DIFFERENT," said Eric, glancing over at her, "if he'd remained a civil engineer. But I suppose he thought my sister Addie died because he hadn't been good enough and he had to pay God off. And then Lou-Lou died, and that *was* his fault. That's how it looked to me, anyway."

Outside her car window the sunlit landscape flowed by, peaceful with fields, cows, and old barns. The shadows were beginning to lengthen towards the east, but there was plenty of daylight left.

In her heart Sandy blessed the Lord. It was the first time Eric had trusted her with any of this. She hadn't even known he'd *had* sisters!

"I'm so sorry!" she said. "I can see how that might make you mad at God. They say we get our first idea of Him from our fathers. If your dad was like that . . ."

"He was. Though lately I've started to understand him better. There's no excuse for what he did, but at least I know he wasn't a jerk just to be a jerk."

"The beautiful thing," she replied, "is that even if our fathers are jerks, our heavenly Father loves us and will give us everything we need. Starting with Christ."

He was listening. Miraculously, he was listening. Today it was somehow easy to talk to him about these things.

Holy Spirit, thank You.

"I can see how it might work like that, if that's how God really is . . . " he said at length. "If he exists, anyway." He looked her way and smiled. "I said, '*if.*' But your father, Sandy. What was he like?"

"Wonderful. Smart, funny, supportive . . . I'm almost embarrassed to say so, when I hear about yours."

"Don't be. I'm happy for you. Sounds like you had the ideal home."

Odd how she felt she had to disabuse him of this idea. "It was very good, thank God. But he wasn't perfect, no human is. He . . . Well, I was a surprise. My brother Mark was eight when I was born and Larry was seven. Then there I came, and I always got the feeling Daddy expected another boy. He never made me feel he was disappointed in me, just the opposite. It's just that he was proudest of me when I was doing traditional guy things— like wanting to go into architecture.

"Sometimes I wonder what it would have been like to be Daddy's little princess." She gave Eric a wry smile. "But I was too busy trying to be just like my big brothers and make my dad proud of me. You know," she said, surprising even herself, "you remind me of him sometimes."

"I do?" said Eric, sounding a little startled. "That's good . . . isn't it? It's not like I love you only for what you do in the office. I mean—"

"It's very good, and no, my dad didn't love me only for what I could do, either. He was very happy I was a girl . . . Forget I mentioned it. It was probably just me putting something on myself."

She looked out the window, her gaze but half-focussed on the rows of corn whirling away on her right.

Maybe that's why I've never really been in love before. I was waiting for a man like Roderick Beichten.

But Daddy was a Christian. Eric isn't.

I know. But here we are and I love him so terribly and he loves me . . . It's so messed up, really: where can we possibly go with it? But if I ever lost him I don't know what I'd do.

"However it was, it worked out well for me," her lover said. "If you'd been raised all girly you might be some housewife somewhere and I never would have met you. Sandy," he said, his eyes intent on the road ahead, "when I think of that possibility, it frightens me. If you ever left me I think I'd die."

"Don't say that!" she cried out in dismay— but hadn't her thoughts been nearly the same? "Well, in that case," she said in a lighter tone, "I'll make sure you're stuck with me for a good long time."

"Even I," he answered, "can say amen to that."

THEY STOPPED to eat in Hendricksburg, a pretty, tree-shaded village, and he easily found the turnoff for Pratt's scenic county road a few miles to the south. The terrain was rising now, growing steadily steeper. The two-lane road twisted and turned, and where a slower vehicle blocked their way it could be awhile before he could find a place to pass. But he was more than repaid for the inconvenience by the beauty of the landscape around them. They'd be driving through a belt of trees, the verges sunlit with black-eyed Susans and chicory, when suddenly on a height the woods would part to reveal the green and golden countryside spread out for miles below. On the western horizon the evening star— Venus, he believed it was— hung glowing like a lamp in the crystal-blue sky. He sighed with happiness and began to hum.

"Sing it, Eric," Sandy said.

"Sing what?"

"That tune you're humming. '*Nature immense.*' I know you know it."

Is that what it was? Faust's paean to Nature from *La Damnation;* how appropriate. "Are you sure?" he half teased. "It's got that line about 'boredom without measure.' I don't want to imply . . . "

"I don't care. Sing it."

"What'll you give me if I do?"

"My full and undivided attention?"

"How about you sing me Marguerite's aria first?"

"Which one?" she teased back.

"You know which one."

"If you're sure . . . " She lifted up her ravishing sweet voice and began to sing. "'*D'amour l'ardente flamme consume mes beaux jours!*'"

His heart swelled within him. There was nothing in the world but her and that song.

"*Eric!*"

"What? What?"

"You've let the car drift over the line for the second time now!"

"Oh! Have I? Maybe," he said hurriedly, "you'd better sing the other one."

He controlled himself and the car better as she spun out the ballad of the King of Thule, that legendary monarch who was faithful to his late queen unto death.

The song ended. "Eric, dearest, that makes me wonder."

"What, precious jewel?"

"Whether I could keep faith like that."

"To me?"

"Yes . . . and to Jesus."

Discontent mingled with guilt roiled in the pit of his stomach. Always God and Jesus! She must have sensed his reaction, for she said. "I wouldn't be the same person if it wasn't for Him. I doubt you'd find much in me to love."

"I doubt that."

She shook her head. "If you only knew . . . but I was thinking of Faust too. Such a disappointment to poor Marguerite. And to God."

"He goes to heaven in the end," he pointed out.

"In Goethe's poem. Not in the Berlioz. Wer—" She stopped, and hesitantly met his eye. He nodded for her to go on.

"Werner said that was because the French were fatalists. I'm mostly German with a good dose of English and Belgian on my mother's side, but on this I'm with the French. Faust made a devil's bargain. It wasn't enough for him to have his brilliant career as a scholar. Or his faith. He had to connive with Mephistopheles to get everything else as well."

"So I'm a will-o'-the-wisp your personal tempter has conjured up?" he teased. He glanced over. Her head was bent down and she was making fans with her entwined fingers, a childish gesture he found endearing.

She looked up. "Oh, no, Eric, no, no! I thank my God every day for you! . . . it's just . . . I wonder if I had to give up architecture . . . or my life . . . or you . . . for the sake of what Jesus wanted, if I'd be able to do it. Would I really be faithful unto death?"

"Well, I doubt your God would ever demand you make a choice like that," he said heartily. "Now aren't you forgetting something?"

"What?"

"I owe you a song."

"Oh! Yes! Let's hear it."

And having chosen a key to fit his range, he began to sing. *"Boundless Nature, inscrutable and proud . . ."*

CHAPTER D.3

SANDY OPENED HER EYES to near-darkness. "What time is it?" she asked, stretching.

"A little after 8:00."

"I missed the sunset."

"Yes, I didn't want to wake you," said Eric. "I've got one on order for you tomorrow. Will that serve, my lady?"

"Yes, my lord, it will. And you've done a great job with the starlight. Look!" She pointed out the front windshield towards the wash of filmy-white brushed vertically down the night sky. "Isn't that the Milky Way? I haven't seen it since Girl Scout camp when I was a kid."

They settled into an appreciative silence, happy to have the quiet nighttime highway to themselves. Sandy watched for crossing deer and idly made note of the roadside features that came and went in the glow of their headlights: A tiny cabin with a mailbox shaped like a chicken on a post out front. A ramshackle store with a placard at the road's edge advertising "Far Wood." A bullet-riddled sign reading "WELCOME TO PAYNE COUNTY."

"What?" she exclaimed, sitting bolt upright.

"You see something?"

"That sign back there. The one the locals have been using for target practice. It says we're in Payne County. I thought Osceomenie Falls was in McAllister."

"It is. They're next to each other."

"I didn't know that. I guess with this road having so many curves, it's not surprising we cross into Payne. That's where Ruth's from."

"Really? I didn't know *that*. You should have told me. I could have called and asked her about things to do down here."

To this she said nothing. It had never occurred to her to call Ruth to say she and Eric would be going away together. She hadn't even mentioned her plans to Carole. Neil was the only one who knew where they were going. If anything happened to them down here . . . and something happened to Neil . . . it could be days, even weeks, before anyone back home discovered where they were. Were there still people like old Mrs. McCool living in these hills? People who hated blacks might not take kindly to "Yankees," either.

She shook her head at her foolishness. Nothing was going to happen to Neil Hughes or to them. That vicious old biddy was dead and in her grave twenty-five years ago, and her fanatic grandson had disappeared from the area for nearly as long. Things were different now. She and Eric would have a good time soaking up Nature and history and return to Wapatomekie refreshed.

Even now the light of the stars flowing into the car was invigorating. It fell lambent on Eric's face as he steered the car up and down the difficult road, stars and man two ineffable beauties, each complementing and affirming the other.

Her poetic mood shattered as he braked suddenly and hard. "Screw it," he said, "there's somebody in the road! Idiot! Could get himself killed!"

She peered ahead. There *was* a human figure standing in the middle of their lane. It held what could have been a radio in one hand and a flashlight in the other and seemed to be staring intently at their car.

At last the form detached itself from the shadows and came within range of their headlights. It was a man, dressed in some kind of uniform, khaki or olive drab, she couldn't tell in the yellow glare. He approached the Galaxie on Eric's side. "Sorry, sir," his drawl oozed through the open window, "but the bridge just ahead is out. Bad rains night 'fore last."

"What?" Eric objected. "Man at the filling station in Stringerville said it hasn't rained around here for days."

"Well," he said, pronouncing it "Wal," "they get them different weather down in Stringerville than we do up here. Regular gully-washers one place, dry as a bone the other. Ya'll a tourist?"

Sandy hated to be called a tourist, but no way this redneck would appreciate a debate about words.

"Yes," Eric said for them both.

"All the way down from Wapatomekie, I bet."

"Yes," said Eric, "and it's getting late and we're tired. Are you sure the bridge isn't passable? I don't see any barricade."

"You shouldn't stand in the road like that," Sandy said.

The man jerked back; he must not have seen her in the passenger seat. That's what she got for being short.

"You— you brought a girl with ya'll?" he asked Eric, as if she were dangerous contraband.

Good gosh. If that's how they feel about women down here, maybe we should go home.

"What business is that of yours?"

"None, sir. I, um—!" The uniformed man squirmed.

"You could get yourself killed," Sandy said ruthlessly. "Why not just post a sign?"

"A sign? Oh!" He recovered himself, and came around to her side of the car. "Why, miss, there is a sign. See?" He waved the flashlight's beam over vacancy. "Well, look at that. It fell over."

He righted an easel that held a large triangular metal placard, phosphorescent yellow with black printing saying "BRIDGE OUT AHEAD." Below the triangle was affixed a rectangle directing them to "DETOUR LEFT."

He came back to the car. "Well, sorry about that. Wind keeps knocking the gol-darned thing over. They got me here 'cause a lotta you tourists been missing the detour and getting all stacked up down at the bridge. I'll show ya'll which way to go."

"Oh," said Sandy, "you're with the county sheriff's department?"

"Not exactly, miss."

"Probably with a local volunteer patrol," Eric surmised. "Right?"

"Yeah, mister, I reckon you could say that. Well, folks," he said briskly, "the detour's round the bend a ways. Just follow me slow and I'll show ya'll where to turn."

Eric looked at her. "What do you want to do?"

"Do we have any choice? There's no place to pull off and read the map. He's local, he knows the roads . . . "

"All right," Eric said to the man, "you lead, we'll follow."

Ghostly in headlights and starlight, the uniformed man walked before them for about a hundred fifty feet, then stopped where a large beech tree on the left side of the road marked the entrance to a dark lane. On the tree's trunk another

DETOURLEFT sign was barely visible in their headlights' beam; at any speed over twenty-five miles per hour they would have missed it entirely.

Again their guide leaned into Eric's window. "This here's a gravel road, but it's a good one. It'll take ya'll around to the cross highway and over another bridge. Shouldn't be more'n ten, twelve miles out of your way. Ya'll be sure'n watch for the signs. Nice evening, now!" He tipped his hat, grinned, and stepped away. They turned left onto the gravel road.

"IS THIS GOAT TRACK on the map?" Eric asked her a half-hour later.

"I'm not sure." She peered out the front window into the shifting gray of the starry night. "I can't keep the flashlight steady with the car jouncing around. Lot of dotted lines on this Geological Survey map, but which one this is, God only knows."

"I haven't seen a detour sign in miles."

"Me neither. Did we miss a turn? Were we supposed to get onto the cross highway he mentioned, or was the bridge past it?"

"We probably went over it. I never saw it, myself." He leaned forward for a better view. "Hope we work it out soon, or you'll have to spend a long night with me in the deep, dark woods. Grrrrrowwrrrl!"

"Animal!" she said happily. They'd figure it out. Besides, she couldn't think of any place nicer to find herself than lost with him. But Allen and Jen would be worried. She checked the map again. "Hey, Eric, see that high hill sticking up over there?" She pointed, then put her finger where the map showed a brown place with close contour lines. "I think it's this one here, Bennett's Knob. If I'm right, in five miles or so we should hit a county road that'll bring us into Osceomenie Falls from the east. I'll watch and tell you where to turn."

But the road they were on refused to match what appeared under her joggling flashlight. It was an endless succession of identical windings, right, left, up, down, its darkness never yielding a sign of any road that was paved.

"It's been more than five miles already," said Eric.

"I'm sorry."

"Not your fault. I should have called Allen before we left and found out about that bridge."

They drove on.

"I'm starting to feel we're entering the Twilight Zone!" he said several minutes later. His tone was light and joking, but a trickle of worry ran beneath.

"Think we did several miles back," she agreed. "We've already had the mysterious stranger appearing smack in the middle of the road."

"Different episode. I'm thinking of the one with the driver doomed to travel the same stretch of highway throughout eternity."

"Well, it can't be that, because it isn't the same stretch of road," she pointed out. "It's not gravel anymore."

"You're right. Only dirt now. Funny, if it's rained that much up here you'd think it'd be mud. Whoops! Spoke too soon!"

They had been travelling down into a long shadowy depression, and as he spoke the dirt road gave way to a two-wheeled wagon track, rutted and increasingly plagued with mire. The woods crowded in closely, the undergrowth and vines at the lane's edge catching at the Ford as if to impede its progress. The overhanging trees loomed eerie and malevolent; anything could emerge from among their blackly-shifting limbs.

"Eric, this is giving me the creeps. We can't be anywhere near where that guy said we'd come out."

"No kidding. Have you seen any cross roads since we saw him? I haven't. I think he had his head up his rear. Keep an eye out for a place to turn around. I'll get us back to the county highway and cut over to Route 46. We'll get into Rains Overlook from that direction and I'll call Jen from there. If it's really late we'll book a couple of rooms in a hotel."

"Eric, up ahead. I think the trees are thinning out."

He inched the car forward. "Good. We can turn around in a minute."

It was a good-sized clearing, thank God. No, more like a field.

He was maneuvering the car into turning position when "Crap!" No need to ask what was wrong: the Ford was sinking hubcap-deep into wet, sticky mud.

Rrrowwwwwhirrrrrr! went the rear wheels until the transmission stank. "Crap!" he said again. "I can't get us out without burning up the engine. What do you think, precious love? Should we stay here and wait for daylight, or take a nice walk under the stars and find someone with a phone?"

"My dad always said if you're lost in the woods, stay put. Especially at night."

"We'll take your dad's advice. But you're freezing."

"I—" She hadn't till then noticed the goosebumps on her arms. Of course, the temperature had dropped; it couldn't be because she was afraid. With the Lord and Eric with her, she refused to be afraid.

"I'm afraid I can't run the heater," he said. "The tailpipe's probably down in the mud. Tonight we'll have to keep each other warm. Do you mind? I'll behave myself."

The arrangement went without saying. She said so. "There's a blanket," she reminded him, "but I put it in the trunk. Didn't think we'd need it."

"And we'll have to clear this gear out of the back seat. It's a clear night; we can leave the trunk lid open if we have to. You stay put and I'll take care of it." His shoes squelched noisily as he stepped out into the mud.

"No," she said. "I'll have to get out anyway. I can't go over the seat." Before he could object, she climbed out and sank nearly to her knees.

"Sandy!"

"I'm all right. I'll hold onto the door handles and meet you at the back."

Laboriously, they each made their way around to the rear of the car. "There's kind of a higher place back here," he said. "Too bad I rolled the wheels off it, but it should make it easier getting that stuff into the trunk." He reached out and pulled her to him. He had just raised the lid when she grabbed his arm.

"Eric, look!" she said, pointing to the edge of the field. To their left, about a hundred and fifty yards away, lights, several of them, were bobbing and flashing among the trees.

Thank God! People! We can ask them for help!

All at once the lights went out. Without a word, he took her around the body and slammed them both flat to the muddy ground.

"Eri—?" she started to say, but he clapped his hand over her mouth and shook his head. But his eyes spoke, and the word they uttered was "fear."

CHAPTER D.4

PRIVATE FIRST CLASS ERIC BAUMANN LAY still and wary in the stinking mire, rifle bullets whizzing over his head. Holy Rolly had trusted him to lead this recon, and he'd effed up and run his men smack into the enemy. Not too many, and for the moment, somebody else was drawing their fire. If none of his own squad panicked and stood up, the Viet Cong might overlook them in the darkness and his men could pick them off as they passed. This new kid he was holding down with his body seemed to have a level head, but it was the cherry's first firefight and you never knew.

Crap! He bit his lips to keep from swearing aloud. Some fool near him had turned on a searchlight and it was bound to give their position away. He raised his eyes. The gooks, all carrying Kalashnikovs, were coming closer. Eight or ten of them, out of the jungle now, wading into the rice paddy.

Turn it off! Turn the damn light off!

The kid stiffened under his hold. He must have seen them too. PFC Baumann did his best to make his grip reassuring. But the young man's body was softer and more pliable than any soldier's had a right to be. Five little fingers found his other hand and held it tight.

He turned his head slightly and stared into the cherry's muddy face. The gunfire faded into the crying of a lone owl.

Sandy! And dammit, my own headlights.

He knew where he was now, but he remained silent and down. The men with the AKs were no flashback, they were assuredly there and drawing nearer by the second. If only he could creep around and kill his stinking lights . . .

He made a sign to her that he would try. Stooping low, he began to pull himself towards the open driver's side door.

His basketball shoes were no match for the high boots the men with the rifles wore. Faster than seemed possible, they were upon him, hauling him up, pinning his arms. He barely had time to take in the khaki uniforms, pale in the starlight, the unlit headband lights on their foreheads, and, most ominous of all, the little grayish masks over their eyes. Then two or three of them turned on high-powered battery lanterns and shone them full in his eyes.

"*Whooo-wheeee!*" whistled one of them. "Whaddya think, boys, we hit the jackpot?"

"Better make sure he's the one the colonel wants," said another voice, sharp and vicious as a punji stick. "You Eric Baumann?" he demanded.

Despite his light-blindness, despite their hands on him, he stood proudly, mouth firmly closed. Name, rank, and serial number? Whoever they were, these masked assholes weren't even getting his name.

"Is that how it's gonna be?" another voice snarled. "I'll show you!" A rifle butt flashed towards him and he threw up his hand to ward off the blow.

But someone pulled the assailant back. "Hawk One-Four-Three, no," said the calm, cruel voice Eric identified with Punji Stick Man. "The colonel will be real upset if we damage the goods. Do it *this* way."

A hard blow took him full in the gut. He bent double with the pain and a hand reached into his back pocket and extracted his wallet. "Yep, this is him, all right," said the thief. "'Eric Edward Baumann, born June 9, 1947, six foot four inches, 214 pounds, brown hair, gray eyes.'"

They searched him, emptying every pocket, then lowered their lights. The after-orbs danced green on his outraged retinas but he could still pick out Punji Stick Man when he said, "Good. Tie his hands and we'll get back to headquarters." He seemed to be the leader of the group, and Eric doubted the men followed him out of gratitude for his kindness.

He can't weigh more than 150 pounds. I could take him . . . if I weren't outnumbered.

His hands were yanked behind his back and a cord tightly knotted around them. Someone roughly pushed him away from the car, poking the barrel of his AK-47 into the small of his back.

"Want me to call headquarters?" The speaker was holding what appeared to be a two-way radio. "Tell 'em we got him?"

"You can try," Punji Stick Man answered him, his tone cynical.

" . . . Naw, signal's dead."

"'Course it is, fool. Mountain's in the way." The leader spat on the ground at Eric's feet, but he couldn't move away. "Heard nothing since we got word from Hawk Seven-Three-Eight down at the roadblock. And he cut out halfway through."

"Better shut off them car lights," one of the men growled. "There's a cabin up on that there ridge and we don't wanna attract no attention."

Behind him, the headlights went out and the driver's side door slammed.

"Hawk Two-Five-Four! Close them other doors, too," ordered Punji Stick Man. "No use running down the battery. This car might come in real handy later."

Oh god. Sandy. She'd stayed wonderfully quiet so far, but if one of them went around to close the trunk they'd find her for sure. *Please, Sandy, lie low. Get away, go for help!*

Slam! That was the door on the passenger side. He could hear the mud sucking at the boots of the man slogging around to the rear of the car.

"You don't need to close the trunk," Eric said, doing his best to sound helpful. "There's no light in there."

"Shut up!" said the leader, striking him a blow across the face. "I can gag you, too, if you don't keep quiet."

Slam! went the lid of the trunk. Some object hit the muddy ground with a soft, wet, metallic thud.

"Sonovabitch!" Then a floundering noise as the man apparently lost his footing.

"*Yiiiii!*" a feminine cry went up. "My hand!"

O god. O god. For the first time since they'd seized him Eric's mind went blank in panic fear. He was nothing but an ear, straining to catch every sound.

"Let me go!"

"Shut up, you!" The man charged with closing the doors dragged Sandy, filthy with mud, into the circle of lights. Massaging the fingers of her left hand, she had no chance even to raise her eyes to Eric's before the man called Hawk Two-Five-Four practically picked her up and shook her in the face of his leader.

"Falcon Oh-Three-Seven, sir, lookee what we got here," he crowed. "A filly!"

Punji Stick Man— or Falcon Oh-Three-Seven, as he apparently was known— wasn't pleased. "A girl! The colonel said they were supposed to make sure there weren't no girl. He's gonna be mad. Real mad." He spat.

Even with the lanterns down Eric could read the dread on the men's faces. Somebody, he was sure, would pay.

"What do we do with her?" one of the men said in a tone that nearly made Eric retch. "Have us some fun then drown her in the swamp?"

For a second Sandy's eyes went wide with terror, then her face shut down and communicated nothing at all.

"No," decided the leader. "We got her now. The colonel'll deal with her back at headquarters."

They tied her hands behind her as well and the two of them were marched stumbling at gunpoint across the swampy field and into the trees.

CHAPTER D.5

ONE FOOT IN FRONT OF THE OTHER. *One foot in front of the other.*

Sandy cycled the phrase over and over in her mind as she and Eric were forced through the darkness of the woods. Two of their captors went first in this nocturnal parade, the repellent little man who seemed to be in charge taking the lead. She came third, prodded along by two of the thugs, one of them a very smelly individual who took a sadistic joy in jabbing her with the muzzle of his gun when she least expected it. He liked nothing better than to make her trip over obstacles in the path, and though she did her best to fall on her hip and shoulder and not on her face, her whole body was mud-soaked, bruised, and sore.

After her guards, they'd put Eric next, secured from behind by more of their tormenters, and then, she guessed, the rest of the troop. It was impossible to turn around to see.

She hadn't expected this much discipline when they'd first accosted Eric back at the car. Despite their masks and the uniforms that matched the one she'd seen on the man blocking the highway, they'd struck her as a gang of rural hoodlums: mean, dangerous, but not at all organized. But as soon as they'd filtered into the trees, without a word they'd extinguished all but one of their high-powered lanterns. And it they hardly needed, finding their way unerringly along the woodland track and hesitating only a little when she or Eric tripped up or fell.

She'd been praying ever since Eric had pulled her down in the clearing; she was praying now.

"Deliver me from mine enemies, O my God: defend me from them that rise up against me . . ."

It had all been a trap, a conspiracy to get Eric down here— without her. But why? Why did they want him to be alone?

She'd nearly gotten away. She'd scrambled under the rear of the car when Eric was rushed, but she'd had to hold onto the metal of the frame to keep from sinking too deep into the mud. When that thug slammed the trunk closed, the stupid loose rear bumper had fallen off and she'd had to let go. That was when her captor's big clodhopper foot found her fingers.

It could have been worse. He could have slipped all the way under and his boot would have been in her face. And at least she and Eric were together.

She stumbled a little over a root, then quickly recovered.

"He will not suffer thy foot to be moved: he that keepeth thee will not slumber nor sleep…"

Lord my Father, watch over us tonight!

She tried hard to pick out landmarks in case they got free. But with the speed of the march and the nightmare quality of the light it was difficult to get a fix on anything in particular.

The terrain grew steeper and their captors were forced to untie their hands or carry them up bodily. She didn't need the cold steel of the gun between her shoulder blades to tell her that any attempt to run would be futile.

I'm not leaving without him anyway.

At last, they gained a plateau with higher hills rising above it; mountains, really, their trees a dark blur in the starlight. They trudged across the tableland, into a little gully concealed by underbrush, up a ravine, and from there to the foot of a steep rocky hill. The leader, the one known as Falcon Oh-Three-Seven, called a halt and stood to one side. "In!" he ordered.

As if by magic, the man ahead of her disappeared into the mountain. Without warning she was pushed into a man-sized crevice, its opening turned towards the face of the rock. Behind her Eric exclaimed, "A cave!" and her stomach lurched at the thud of fist on bone as his guard enforced his silence.

O Lord, protect him, help him; save us both, please!

The crevice opened to a kind of shallow flat area with blackness just beyond it. The man in front of her switched on the light on his headband, then, absurdly, turned and disappeared feet-first into the void. Before she'd had time to understand what she was seeing, one of her guards, the big smelly one, hoisted her up bodily, tucked her under his arm, and swung over the edge as well. By the light of his headlamp she saw they were on a metal ladder bolted into the rock. Surprise was enough to keep her from struggling; even so, "Hold still," he said. "I could drop you just like that." He would have enjoyed that, no doubt, and she wouldn't gratify him by giving him the excuse.

At the bottom was a passageway, its walls scarred by the marks of picks or drills, she couldn't tell which. It had been smoothed and enlarged, at any rate. Once everyone was down the ladder she and Eric were forced downward through passages, some natural, some man-made, glistening in the light of their captors' headlamps. The leader seemed to check for signs or marks to tell him which way to go, but she couldn't tell what they were. At least twice more they made their descent by ladder, and she was allowed— or made— to climb down under her own power. Occasionally they splashed through water up to their ankles; other times they hurried by what might have been openings once, but had been blocked up with stones and hydraulic cement.

When it seemed they couldn't descend lower, Oh-Three-Seven gave the order to halt. They were in a smallish natural chamber, formed in the dripping rock of the mountain. A strange smell drifted in from an opening on the far side, like road tar or something burning. The men seemed not to notice it. Rather, as if it was standard procedure, they took off their headlamps and stuffed them into their pockets. All but one of the battery lamps were extinguished and placed in plastic milk crates near the wall. Then to Sandy's confusion (and to Eric's, too, from what she could see of his face in the semi-darkness) they picked up what seemed to be long wooden clubs from a pile on the ground.

O Domine. They aren't going to beat us to death, are they? In the dark? But what about the colonel the leader had spoken of? Weren't they to be taken to him?

Before she could piece things together, one of the men pulled out a cigarette lighter and touched it to the end of Oh-Three-Seven's club, which burst into flame. He in turn lit those held by the others. Not clubs, then. Torches, old-fashioned torches, long branches of pine with their ends steeped in pitch.

It still made no sense. Why fire torches when they had battery power? The flames gave a lurid, infernal shine to the dank cavern walls, but how could their captors see by them? In such a confined space, how could anyone breathe?

The leader called one of the men to him. Whatever the directive was, the second man didn't like it. "You trying to get me killt?" he complained. "He'll have my head for that!"

"I'll make damn sure he has your head iffen you don't!" was the rejoinder, and the second man slipped through the opening and out of Sandy's view.

After a few minutes he reappeared, shaking his head with disbelief. "Colonel says bring 'em both in."

With one guard gripping each of them by the arm and two more keeping their guns at their backs, she and Eric were hustled down a passage into a vast and lofty subterranean chamber.

High as a cathedral, its outer walls were hidden in gloom, while its center was lit by nothing but pine torches. Massive stalactites and stalagmites loomed eerily in the flickering glow, and the stifling odor of pitch evoked incense offered up in worship to some unspeakable demigod. The orange light fell upon a wide semicircle of pale faces, at least a hundred or so she could distinguish, but she sensed that a great multitude stood waiting behind them in the shadows. Like their captors, every man wore a gray or white mask, some covering his eyes only, some concealing the top half of his head, and through them the glittering eyes were rapt with expectation, as if some hellish sacrifice were about to begin.

On the thought, the terror she'd been too distracted to feel during the march began to trickle in.

Stop it, Sandy! Stop it now! Things are bad enough without your imagination making it worse.

But that rock formation in the middle of the hall, surely it had been carved to bring out its natural resemblance to a throne? The cushioned seat was empty when she first laid eyes on it, but as she watched, a procession materialized from out of the shadows behind the chair. Six men in formation, carrying large menacing guns, then six more, then six more— and between the last two ranks of six, a man strode, individual and alone. Of average height, he wore an ordinary dark three-piece suit like a robe of state. His mask was chalk-white and stretched over his entire head, leaving only the eyes, nostrils, and lips exposed.

The cavern exploded in a profound, echoing din of male voices. "The White Way is the right way! The White Way is the right way!" "Colonel! Our great colonel!" The fully-masked man, who appeared to be in his early forties, seemed to absorb the plaudits into himself while acknowledging them not at all. He took his seat on the throne. His glance fell upon her. His eyes, there was something not right about his eyes—

This time, she could not maintain control. Above the clamor, her appalled soprano voice rang out: "It's Mephistopheles! He's alive!"

CHAPTER D.6

THE CHAMBER AROUND THEM went deathly still. Nick Hardt— even with the white ski mask, Eric knew him now— rose from the stone chair, cocked his ear, and chuckled, as if he'd heard something that amused him. "Yes, here I am," he declared, "alive and risen from the dead!"

He turned to Punji Stick Man. "I see our special *guests* have arrived."

"Yessir, Colonel," the lieutenant replied.

"Well then, bring them to me!" He waved in a lordly manner and sat down. Eric and Sandy were pushed forward.

"Mr. Baumann!" the man on the throne exclaimed. "It's been so long since I've seen you!"

O god, yes, he should have known. The car crash in the Black Hills— of course it was a lie. Unless Hardt really had died and come back to life? In this torch-lit hell anything seemed possible. Sandy had complained about the man's eyes— why hadn't he noticed them before? Seeing them through the mask made their horror all the more apparent. By the flaming glare of the torches they gave Eric the queasy impression of some strange inhuman but sentient creature loose by night in an old abandoned city warehouse, pelting up and down the stairs, joyriding the freight elevator, peeking out of one glassless window and then another. A trickle of sweat took its slow maddening course through the dried filth that covered his forehead, and he wondered what the guards would do if he tried to wipe it away.

"And your delightful assistant, too. Such a surprise to see her here! I'm sorry, I forget her name?"

"'Alexandra M. Beichten,'" one of the raiding party read off Sandy's driver's license.

"Miss Beichten! But then, you are such a dedicated employee. Observant, too." To Eric's right, kept just out of his reach, Sandy stirred uneasily. "Very impressive.

"But what's this?" Hardt said, giving his head a shake. "You two don't look comfortable at all. Men," he commanded, beckoning to a pair of guards who stood nearby, "our guests have come hundreds of miles to see us, but they've had no chance to refresh themselves. Do better by them, right away."

"Yessir, Colonel," said the men, saluting. And with the guards still at their backs, he and Sandy were led from the hall.

HE'D HAD worse.

After the initial shock, the frigid wash water, presented in galvanized tubs, was tolerable. There wasn't much he and Sandy could do about their clothing except to crack the now-dried mud off it, but he felt better with his skin somewhat clean. The meal was coffee and pork and beans out of a can, both hot. Could it have been poisoned? He felt all right so far.

Shouting and applause rolled up from the great chamber even from several passages away. As their guards brought them back in, someone, not Hardt, seemed to be giving a presentation.

Hardt must have been watching for their arrival. "Wait," he said, holding up his hand for silence. "Our guests have returned. I trust you found everything to your satisfaction?" he inquired.

"Yes, thank you," said Eric, trying to placate him. Sandy looked at the ground and kept silent.

"You understand, I hope," said their jailer-host with deceptive mildness, "that the primitive conditions you've had to endure— that we *all* have to endure— are largely due to your own failure to play your part in the building of this organization?"

Eric made no reply.

"I brought you here so you could rectify that omission. But you must pardon me. You're not the only one who has come a long way." Hardt stood once more and motioned with his hand. When all attention was on him, he shouted, "Let the convocation of the Order of the White Way proceed!"

HE CAN'T be alive. We aren't really here.

But the aches in her shin and shoulder where she'd tripped on the way were real, and so was the chill of her hair that hung dripping and loose (the elastic band long gone), and the gritty sensation over her skin from the dirt that cruel excuse for a wash hadn't taken away. Just as cruelly real were the iron grip and stinking body odor of the guard who held her and the petty sadism of the other with the gun at her back.

And Nick Hardt was undeniably in the land of the living and, bizarrely, was exerting himself to be nice to them. She had no chance to unravel this, for once he shouted for the rally to go on, somewhere in the cavernous hall a giant drum began to beat and the chanting rose up again: "The White Way is the right way! The White Way is the right way. *The White Way is the right way!*" Louder and louder rose the tumult until she thought she would go deaf or run mad.

It was like some monstrous annual meeting. Various men in half-head masks, all of whom were referred to as "Eagle-this" or "Vulture-that," gave reports. One referred to partisans having come there from over ten states, including Tennessee— oh gosh, were they causing the trouble Pat told her about? Another encouraged the crowd with news of the acts of sabotage, arson, and other mayhem committed in the name of the group. Yet another spoke on progress made getting the White Way message out by flyer, radio, and other media— including, to her chagrin, Christian stations like the one in Wapatomekie.

Only the guard's grip on her arm kept her from collapsing to the floor. Eric took a half step her way and was pulled back. She forced herself to detach, to breathe, *breathe*— then coughed as her lungs rejected the smoke-filled air.

She had to keep herself steady. When they got out of here— she refused to consider the alternative— they'd have to report all this to the police.

But even when one man, by his half-mask apparently a captain of very high rank, started handing out awards and promotions for the assassinations the organization had carried out in the last year, it was impossible to tell who had been killed and where and when. It was a garble of code. The captain read off number after number, and every man who stepped forward was masked. How could she hope to identify any of them again?

But then a victim was referred to as "the swaggering ape." And his murderer was commended for putting a stop to his "unnatural pretensions to public office."

O Domine. He's talking about Phil Duggins.

A thin-legged, balding man with a beer gut approached. Grinning under his eye mask and pumping his fists in the air like Sylvester Stallone in *Rocky,* he received congratulations from the captain and from Hardt himself. Jonas Kramer, that's who it had to be. No wonder the police in Fort Randolph City couldn't find him. He'd fled to his "colonel" right away.

Stay still. Don't react. She memorized as much about him as she could.

At last the travesty of an awards ceremony was over. Another captain stepped forward and read the Roll of Shame, and this time, no one was called out of the massed ranks. Every man on this list had either been disciplined for his failure already— and it took no imagination for Sandy to know what that meant— or had committed suicide before Hardt or his loyal followers could get their hands on him.

"Finally," said the captain, "the rival element Albert McNair has been neutralized."

Albert McNair? What does Nick Hardt have to do—

"He did not understand our aims," said Hardt. "The White Way must maintain focus on the one and only goal."

—with Al McNair?

"*. . . you just gotta tell me where Cole Rutherford's setting up his operation . . .*"

Blind, blind, *blind!* How could she not have *seen?* It was Nick Hardt all along— whatever his real name was— that's who McNair wanted, that's who she was tortured over, and she'd been blind to it the whole time!

But I thought he was dead!

You could have urged the police to look into him anyway.

But out of a foolish desire to believe that all that was over, all she'd done was tell them repeatedly that he was dead. And now Phil Duggins and a lot of other people had been murdered, she and Eric were kidnapped, and this vicious organization was growing and spreading and committing crime after crime for the sake of its cause.

Was Eric also wishing he'd questioned Hardt's death that January night? Sidelong, he caught her eye. But all possibility of communication or even thought was swallowed up in the appalling noise that once more rose to the heights of the cavern:

"The White Way is the right way! The White Way is the right way! The White Way is the right way!!!"

IT HAD BEEN, Eric was sure, over forty-five minutes since Hardt had taken the floor. He thanked his stars that the sardonic voice had at least put a stop to the mindless chanting.

He's brought us here to rectify some omission . . . what? Not working for him before? And he expects us to do it after hearing this?

Through the vast chamber Hardt's tones rang out unaided, exhorting, encouraging, rallying his troops. Without moving his head, Eric tried to observe the reactions of the men he could see. That it was all men, he'd grasped shortly after he and Sandy were brought in. Only a few individuals standing at the front of the crowd were distinct in the torchlight, but on every masked face the expression was the same: transfixed, focussed, committed, and the gaze of every man was riveted on his colonel.

Except for one. It was a member of Hardt's honor guard, thirty-ish, a little under six feet tall, with an athlete's body that had run to fat and a bald head surrounded by a clownish ring of thick reddish hair. This man was staring at Sandy. His lewd greedy eyes seemed not so much to be undressing as dissecting her.

O god, and I can't do a thing about it!

"MEN, THEY CLAIM the USA is a land of opportunity, a place where a free white man can get a fair shake. I say bullshit! The socialists and the Communists are taking over, and the Demo-cans and the Republi-crats are helping them right along . . . "

Anger drove out her remorse and fear. If only she could shut him up somehow! Only a hedge of remembered hymns and Scripture verses kept her from breaking loose and doing something that surely would get her killed.

"And who's behind the corruption of white America?" Hardt roared, waving his arms. "It's the niggers and the kikes and the spics, every last one of those filthy, impure breeds that our enemies imported to bring America down!"

The worst thing was how like a revival meeting it was. Every time Hardt made a statement, no matter how false, offensive, or inane, the *Amen!*s and the *Preach it!*s roared up until she could swear the stalactites were crumbling from the vibration and raining dust on their heads.

"Some of you are new to our organization. If you had the balls you would ask your colonel, 'Why do we need the White Way revolution? Why must there be violence to bring about change? Why not—'" He spat, and affected a high, effeminate voice— "'work through the system?' I will tell you why we can't work through the system! Because the system is corrupt to the core! Because the system is in the hands of nigger officials and kike judges and soft Commie sympathizers who unite to take away what belongs by right to hardworking honest white men who God Almighty created to have it!"

The alien force behind the uncanny eyes seemed to aim his glance towards every man in the crowd, individually and all at once. But at these words, the eyes seemed to pierce into Eric alone. Why? *O Domine*, why?

"Men, America is yours! By right, by justice, by destiny, by . . . "

His cadence was hypnotic, and she shifted her attention away, lest she fall under its spell. As she did she noticed there was one man in the chamber besides Eric who was not staring at the "colonel" transfixed with joy. He'd marched in with Hardt, but now through his mask his eyes were homed in on her, crawling over her body, taking possession of it, telling of unspeakable things he'd do to her if he could.

Ignore it. Some men are like that. It's not personal. He doesn't know me.

But against the denial a sickening conviction stole in. That flabby body was once muscular and trim. The hair had covered the whole skull and had been a mane of auburn curls. The arrogant mouth was the same, and the Grecian profile nothing could alter, short of breakage or surgery. She was transported back to a night over ten years before. Herself alone at the wooden sales counter of the student store in the basement of Mahony Griffin Hall. A senior architecture student, young, virile, classically handsome, lounging against the door he'd closed and locked, taunting her fear.

She closed her eyes tight, but could not shut out the memory of the marijuana-slurred voice: "*Well, well, well. If it isn't little Sandy Beichten.*"

Again she saw him flaunting the cartridges of drawing leads he'd stolen from her table to force her to go down to buy more the night before the big deadline. Again she felt the panic that had her willing that early April morning to do anything, to say anything, to try to keep the situation normal.

But between him and her, the situation had never been normal.

I thought I loved him I thought I loved him I thought I loved him! Like a speeded-up recording, the old shame speared through her without relenting or relief.

Lord help her, her eye had once fed on him, consumed him, devoured him! No, rather, it had fed on the *idea* of him, on the fantasy being he never was, could never be. *I didn't know him. I never even spoke with him. Not till that night. But that's over. It can't be happening again, it can't be, it can't be!*

She forced her eyes open. His were still devouring her body, just as they had ten years before. Horribly compelled, she looked him in the face.

"*Little Sandy Beichten,*" his stare repeated, "*I've seen how you look at me. You're horny for me. You want me, don't you?*" He'd pinned her against the counter back then, just as his eyes were pinning her down now. "*You want me, and tonight I'm going to give you what you want, right here, right now!*"

No. I won't look at him. I won't think about that anymore. Lord, help me. Lord, help me think of something else!

But she couldn't think of anything else. She couldn't think at all. More than anything that had happened to her this evening, the revival of the old horror threatened to shake her into ruins.

Still smirking and trying to arrest her eye, he moved his hand to his crotch and began to rub it.

Have to get away. Now! I'm going to scream, O God, I'm going to scream! Help me! Help me . . .

And by the most unexpected of means, help came.

The man-at-arms next to her tormenter gave him a slight shove. The hand dropped to his side and the crawling eyes refocussed on Hardt as if they'd never strayed anywhere else.

"I'LL TELL YOU what happens when you work through the system. I had a woman once. She was a good woman. She didn't talk back, she put the meals on the table on time, and she knew it was my job to keep her in line. A good wife, I say."

Sandy was calmer now. She could detach and thank God her father never treated her mother like that.

"But twelve years ago she was murdered. Raped and butchered, I tell you, by a sex-hungry shithole of an eye-rolling nigger. No dog should suffer what she did!"

Was this true? If it was, it might explain . . . But no, nothing justified the campaign Hardt was waging.

"They arrested the coon that did it. But the damn pig Jew of a judge declared a mistrial. Said important evidence had been suppressed. Then they tried him again, and he got off! Freed, when he should have gone to the chair and fried! I tell you I saw him on my street the day my woman died, and they refused to take the word of a free white male!

"That's what the system does, and why it must be destroyed and rebuilt from top to bottom! And with it we must search out and destroy everyone—" His voice dropped menacingly— "*everyone* who infests and infects our great America. Not just the colored cockroaches, not just the Hebrew bloodsuckers, but also," he finished with a roar, "the pansy-assed, bleeding-heart artificial whites who support and promote them!"

People like us. She hoped she was ready. But how could Eric be? But her deep exhaustion and the mind-insulting foulness of Hardt's rant made it hard to get her mind around the prospect of death. If death was anything like sleep, the faster it came, the better.

"So now they put this ac-tor"— that was how he pronounced it— "in the White House. A 'man'—" Hardt gestured satirical quotation marks— "who puts on makeup and prances around in front of a camera! He may play real men in the movies, but he isn't one. He talks about improving the economy for everyone when he should be attacking the problem at the root!

"Well, men, the ac-tor isn't part of the solution, he's part of the problem. *You* are the solution! *You* are what will restore America and make her supreme over all! Every act of sabotage, every confiscation of the enemy's ill-gotten loot, every secret chapter meeting held, every white baby conceived, every police and fire department infiltrated, every piece of human trash removed, every scum of the opposition taken out— that was how the kingdom of God comes on this earth!"

That was how the— what? She glanced over at Eric, standing stock still with his guards. *Please, God, don't let him think this has anything to do with Christ!*

She couldn't catch his eye.

Hardt spoke in the same manner at least twenty minutes more. Long before he concluded she nearly buckled again from exhaustion and dread. But the crowd was in such a frenzy she doubted anyone would have cared.

CHAPTER D.7

RAINED, HARDT FELL BACK onto the cushions. He mopped his brow and took a drink of something he was offered.

What time was it? Eric wondered. Down here in the dark, it could have been nearly midnight or well into the next millennium.

The uproar died down. Maybe Hardt would dismiss the assembly and he and Sandy would be taken somewhere they could sleep and it would all be worked out in the morning. But their captor called out, "Men, an item of special business has been added to the agenda tonight. Prisoner Baumann, approach!"

Rough hands pushed him forward. But Hardt's voice grew warm and confidential. "Did I say 'prisoner'? I'm sorry, you're my guest. Baumann, I've been watching you since last year. Testing you. You took everything I threw at you and came through it all."

"I don't know what you mean." It sounded shamefully like bluster, even to his own ears.

Hardt chuckled. "You have loyal friends, don't you, even if they are kikes. I understand you're more prosperous than ever? You have me to thank: I could have stopped that in a heartbeat had I wanted to.

"You even passed the trial by fire in your apartment." Hardt sounded like a coach whose protégé had run a record-setting race. "You and everything in it should have gone up in flames." The strange eyes probed his, and Eric turned away. So that gut feeling he'd had about it had spoken true. Too late now.

"You're a cool one, aren't you? You outwitted one of my best men. He has been disposed of: I don't allow failure. He claimed you were there on the couch, asleep. He *claimed* he thought he could just throw in a pop bottle bomb and knock your space heater to the floor." The voice went high and sarcastic. "He even took the time to close the window so it would look like an accident. I didn't care if it looked like an accident!" Hardt's volume increased till his words echoed off the cavern heights. "*I just wanted you dead!*"

Eric clenched his teeth. If only he could tell Sandy she'd been right all along.

"Pardon me," Hardt said, dropping his voice. "I mean, I wanted to make sure you were the man I took you for. I had purposes for you, Baumann. I always have. You'll serve me better alive.

"You went to earth like an old fox and even I had trouble finding out where you were. I flushed you out of your den a time or two, didn't I? In the dead of winter, too, and I admit I enjoyed the thought of you sleeping in some fleabag motel. Or in your car? You endured some cold nights, I imagine."

The memory of Sandy's body warm against his that January night eased into his mind. He stolidly pushed it back: it was a soft distraction he couldn't afford.

"You are fortunate: I could have had you out of your new apartment as well, but I had other matters to attend to. But I did not forget you. Not once did I forget you!

"I saw you had balls, Baumann. I wanted you with me." Again Hardt's tone was soft, insinuating. "You've let yourself be contaminated too long. Break loose and be the free white male you were meant to be. The White Way really is the right way," cajoled the voice. "I can offer you wealth, opportunity, fame, everything I know you want. Join us. Join us now."

Why was Hardt so fixated on him? He'd told him no a year ago; what would happen to them both when he said it again? Even now the man was regarding Sandy as if she were an insect he might need to squash. Maybe he could mollify him, play along till he knew how she fit into his plans, put him off until he could figure out a way to escape.

"Mr. Ha—"

"Silence!" he roared. "You will address me as Colonel, like everyone else here."

Eric's Adam's apple felt like a rock. He gulped and tried to think fast. "Y— yes, Colonel. Thank you for— for your high opinion of me. But I'd need to know exactly what you want me to do. I can't really help you unless—"

"Eric, no!"

"Quiet!" shouted Hardt again. "Baumann, you were not to bring this *assistant* of yours with you. I thought I made that clear. Do you need a nursemaid? Aren't you a man?"

The united breathing of the unseen silent assembly made the cavern seem as if it were alive. In, out, in again: it was hard not to be sucked into its rhythm.

"What *is* she to you, Baumann? *What?*"

Eric did his best to sound detached, even patronizing. "You don't need to worry about her. She's just my employee." *Please, Sandy, I have to do this. For your sake.* "My *subordinate*. Nothing more."

"It's true," she spoke up in a calm, controlled voice. "I'm here to do some research while he has a break. On Victorian architecture. I'm his assistant, that's all."

"Is that so? A mere functionary." Hardt motioned to her guard. Viciously twisting her arm behind her back, the man shoved her down, her scream of pain cut off with a grunt as her face and body hit the rocky floor. His booted foot swung back to kick her head.

Tearing himself loose from the man holding him, with all his weight Eric threw himself against her assailant. The man rolled aside, and he bent over her prone figure.

"Are you all right?" he pleaded, searching her stunned eyes as he raised her to her feet.

"I— I think so—" She put a hand to a bleeding cut on her cheek.

Violent hands tore them apart and held them firmly.

"I thought as much," Hardt said, satisfied. "Wish I'd known earlier. Never mind. I can still use it."

"Hey!" Eric protested. "Any civilized man would protect a lady— oh, *hell!*" It was no use. "Colonel," he said, bracing himself, "Do whatever you want to me, but let her go. She's no good to you. Let her go."

"Really? No, I think we'll keep her for awhile— to ensure your good behavior. We don't have much use for women in our organization, not yet, but for this one we'll make an exception."

He turned on Sandy a look that sent Eric's heart into his throat. "You," Hardt said to her, venom in his tone. "You've been trouble since the first day I came to his office."

Legs shaking, she stood straight as she could and said nothing.

"You *bitch*," he spat at her, "you've been in my way from the beginning. I'll give you credit. I've tried to keep you from interfering, in more ways than you'll ever know. But here you are with him, and closer than ever, eh?" He gave her a syrupy smile. "*You weren't supposed to be here!*" he bellowed. "*Somebody failed!*"

He glared around at the silent assembly. "You heard it before, but all of you need to *see* what happens to members who fail. Bring in the prisoner!"

ANOTHER PRISONER? Sandy's mind reeled. Who? What? Someone else like them?

The guard holding her arm tightened his grip. "You watch this."

A man around thirty years old, thin, unmasked, with hangdog features and a dishwater-blond mullet was hustled protesting into the hall and flung down at the foot of Hardt's throne. No, of course not an outsider, this had to be one of his own men. With his hands bound behind his back the prisoner couldn't catch himself and tumbled face-first onto the unyielding ground. Sandy couldn't help but sympathize.

"Kneel!"

The guards hauled him to his knees.

"Please, Colonel!" the young man pleaded in a raspy drawl. "I did what you said, all of it!"

"Shut up! Hawk Seven-Nine-Eight, your orders were to get Baumann down here, and to make sure that female stayed home."

"But— but—" A note of hope emerged in the prisoner's voice. "She's here now, you can deal with her—"

"I was planning to deal with her there *in my own time!*"

Now it all made sense. The convicted arsonist lurking outside her building, later found dead. The obscene phone calls last winter. Maybe the man who'd come to their office looking for Eric. All designed to get her out of the way, probably for good.

He knows we're stronger together. He—

"I told him not to bring no women!" The prisoner's wail echoed off the cavern roof. "I called their office this afternoon, she was there, she said he was gone!"

Was this the man Eric met at the party? Pratt? She glanced over at him. Yes.

"Shut up!" Hardt said again. "You failed. You know the penalty for failure."

"No, Colonel, please!" The man Pratt grovelled before him, trembling. "I don't want to die! Have mercy, for God's sake, have mercy!"

Hardt regarded him for a moment. "Yes . . . " he said slowly. "I think I will have mercy. I won't give you to *them.*"

"Oh, thank you, Colonel, thank you! I promise I'll—"

"No," Hardt said grimly. "I'll execute you myself."

Pratt went rigid with terror as Hardt casually extended his open hand to one of his honor guard. The man-at-arms put a black, long-barreled revolver into it, like something out of an old Western. Without a word, he clicked back the hammer and shot the prisoner square between the eyes.

EARS RINGING, Eric watched in fascinated horror as the body was dragged from the chamber feet first, a trail of blood glistening in its wake. He'd seen men die in combat, but this callous slaughter of a hapless ally shook him to the core.

"Men, failure is not an option!" shouted Hardt. "You're doing the work of God!"

With another speech— thankfully brief this time— he dismissed the assembly. Not a word had been said that could tell Eric what Hardt's actual plans were, only that something horrifyingly big was to happen soon. All he'd picked up for certain was that most of the men were from outside the area, and they'd start leaving two hours before sunrise.

"You have your orders. Be in place. Be ready. The White Way is the right way!"

The chanting started up again, a little less energetic than before, but just as fanatical. "The White Way is the right way! The White Way is the right way! *The White Way is the right way!*"

Every man put on his head lamp and turned it on. Shouting their slogan, in wave after wave Hardt's partisans swarmed out into the passageways like an endless cloud of infernal fireflies. Hundreds of them, well over a thousand, maybe more. At last no one remained, except themselves and their own guards, Hardt, and his armed escort.

He had to get Sandy out of there. He drew in a determined breath, forced himself to unclench his fists, and spoke: "All right, Colonel. You have the power here, we understand that. But we can't help you. Tell us what your ransom demands are and I'll put you in touch with my attorney. He'll see you're paid whatever you want."

Even through the mask, the astonishment in Hardt's face was almost comical. "Ransom?" he exclaimed, throwing himself back onto the cushions and laughing. "*Ransom?* Don't you understand by now? I don't want any ransom, I don't want just your work, I want *you*."

"Me? I don't—"

"You, Baumann. Since you were twenty years old"— the man's teeth gritted and his voice grew grim— "you've been mine. Never forget it: you've *always* been mine."

He snapped his fingers. "Escort our *guests* to my private quarters. Baumann, you will hear your fate from The Book of Life."

CHAPTER D.8

"**N**EVER FORGET IT, *you've always been mine…*"

Eric stumbled as the guards forced him and Sandy up the passage. He'd saved that note. Let it inspire him. He'd even— fates help him!— *kissed* it. Now if only he could rinse the poison of it from his lips, scour away its memory, howl to the stars his horror at allowing himself to be so violated.

Hardt's quarters came as ironic relief. The walls had been stuccoed smooth with foundation cement and painted a stark white. On them hung skilled copies of iconic modern paintings. The green-tinged fluorescent lighting (the first he'd seen in these caverns) did no justice to the colors, but at least the room had electric power. The furniture? That low-slung chaise behind Hardt was by Le Corbusier. To Eric's left stood a pair of sleek stainless steel and leather Barcelona lounge chairs, designed by Mies van der Rohe. Eric clung to the sight of these familiar objects as to a life preserver.

Hardt gestured towards the chairs. "Sit."

Eric eased his aching body into the leather seat, catching Sandy's eye as he did. Where had Hardt gotten them in that light brownish tan? Each tufted square of the upholstery was made of a separate piece, as if it came from beasts with hides too small to cover the whole chair. Natural calfskin, most likely. Eric allowed himself to admire the subtle and pleasant variation in color it produced, running his fingers in desperate gratitude over the butter-soft surface.

"Guards, wait outside." Hardt removed his mask with a grateful sigh, and the White Way partisans— three captains and two lieutenants— who remained with him followed suit.

The naked face of his enemy recalled Eric to himself. With veiled eyes he glanced around. The room was small, irregular in shape, and offered no place to hide. Hardt and all his attendants were armed, the men with their AKs and Hardt with his Colt. At least six more guards waited out in the passage. No, fighting their way out was not a plan.

"Vulture Oh-Six-Eight, bring me the Book."

The lieutenant slipped into an inner chamber, presumably Hardt's sleeping quarters. Could there be another way out through there? He doubted it, and the door closed before he could get a look.

"Colonel." Vulture Oh-Six-Eight handed him the book, saluted, and rejoined the men beside Hardt's chair.

What Hardt was calling "the Book of Life" appeared to be nothing more than an old-fashioned photo album, the kind with hardboard leaves and some kind of medallion, plated to look like silver, adorning its dark leather cover. As Hardt sat on his ponyskin-upholstered chaise and opened the album on his knee, Eric's impression was confirmed. It was full of clippings and photographs, but its homey look did not reassure.

Their captor found the page he wanted. "Baumann," he said, "a year ago I offered you the chance of a lifetime. I intended to fulfill all your dreams, if you would use your talent to serve me. Due to the influence of that female there, you did not."

That was what Sandy was now, Eric reflected bitterly: "That female." And a man had died because Hardt considered her a threat.

"I'm offering you another chance. But given your prior refusal, I'm thinking of reducing your fee. This time, it might be only my permission to keep your life."

Eric stiffened his nerve. "Colonel, I will not—"

"Silence, Baumann! I'm not finished. You have strikes against you. You have Jew clients, a great many of them, not to mention clients that might as well be Jews. Oh, did I hear something about *accidents* happening to a couple of them?" He sniggered. "You *had*—" He emitted a stomach-turning laugh— "a nigger client."

Whatever was behind the abandoned warehouse eyes peered at Eric as if gauging his reaction. "Then there's that nigger employee of yours. I suppose you've left him in charge while you're gone. I know you left him alone with the females when you weren't there. Very foolish, Baumann. Your woman there, she just might be comparing that coon's equipment to yours, and maybe you come up short."

Eric gritted his teeth, then relaxed. "Actually, I trust Mr. Hughes. Without reservation. Apparently you sent your agents around. I'm glad he was there to head them off."

"The modern tolerant liberal animal. I'm touched. Not a whiff of race prejudice about you."

Eric couldn't help returning a nod, brief but proud.

"But I know you better than you know yourself, Baumann. Underneath that liberal façade you're just like me. Underneath, you *are* me."

The man had to be crazy. Eric even felt a little sorry for him, sitting there with the skin of his face creased from the mask, fatuously smoothing down the leaves of the scrapbook.

"I have here," their captor began in a detached, offhand manner, "a letter printed in the October 12, 1967, edition of the Burleigh County *Thursday Advertiser*. It is signed 'PFC Eric E. Baumann.' Shall I read it to you?"

No! Shame slammed its hot sickness through his body. That? Impossible. How had Hardt laid his hands on *that*?

I can't let her hear it. "That won't be necessary."

"I think it is. Don't interrupt, or I'll dispose of you immediately."

Clearing his throat, he read:

> To the Editor:
> I'm writing to voice my outrage about a
> shameful injustice that has been done to
> me, a returning veteran of the Viet Nam
> war. When I was drafted two years ago,
> I had a scholarship to Yale Architecture
> School. But I didn't run to Canada or go
> for a student deferment. I proudly did my
> duty to my country, and if that duty
> didn't cost me my life, it's only because
> I was skillful enough to keep my head
> and outwit the enemy and make him give
> his instead.

Hardt looked up. "Stirring stuff, Baumann. You should be proud of your exploits."

O god. Shut up. Just shut up. Now!
But Hardt read on, remorselessly.

> When I reapplied to Yale I wasn't really surprised that an Eastern liberal university like that would refuse to renew my scholarship. We Viet Nam vets are used to being spit on and treated with disrespect by Red sympathizers. What I didn't expect was the obscene treatment given me by the Architecture School here in my home state of North Dakota. I applied well within the deadline, and what did I get for my service and sacrifice? A form letter telling me that every place that could have gone to a white male American had already been filled, and the remainder were all being held for Indians off the reservations! All thanks to some anonymous bleeding-heart private donor and the greed of the university administration.
>
> Ask yourself, what do red Indians know about Architecture? When our white ancestors came over from Europe we found this great continent going to waste. The Indians of North America never built anything worth mentioning and I doubt they're going to start now. Even if they stay sober, they don't have the incentive, the brains, or the skill.

Hardt grinned. "A man after my own heart, Baumann. I agree with you. Totally."

O god, what must Sandy think of him? He'd changed since then, surely she saw that. Those insults, that bigotry— that wasn't who he was now.

> Redskins are nothing but parasites on this nation. They couldn't recognize effective design if it fell on them, they're good only for childish tricks with feathers and beads.

He'd changed since then? Really?

What about that Sioux guy, Whatsisface, you refused to interview last year, even when Sandy asked? You hated his guts, just hearing his Indian name. Which you don't even have the decency to remember.

Hardt's right about me. And Sandy probably despises me. I despise myself.

He gave her a fearful sidelong glance. She sat with her eyes cast to the floor.

Hardt read the letter through to its bitter end.

> America would be better off if all red-skins were allowed to die of disease and alcoholism. North Dakota State University in its shameful mistreatment of me, a white American veteran, has shown that it is beyond the call of decency. Don't go there, don't send your children there. This so-called university should be ridiculed and ignored.
>
> Sincerely yours,
> PFC Eric E. Baumann

"The same letter," said Hardt, closing the scrapbook and laying his hand on the cover, "was also sent to the Bismarck *Tribune* and the Fargo *Forum*. They both refused to print it. But the Burleigh County *Thursday Advertiser* wanted to boost circulation. They figured a little controversy would do the trick. And it did. There was quite a war of letters after they printed yours, Baumann. But you didn't stay around to see it, did you? You shook the dust of North Dakota off your feet and moved down to Wapatomekie.

"But this letter came to my attention. I saw you could be useful to me someday. And I promised myself that once you came into your own, I would claim you as mine.

"The time has come, Baumann." He smiled grimly. "I'll even pretend you have a choice. Decide!"

HOW COULD her Eric write such a thing? How could he even think it?

Earlier today— an eternity ago!— when he'd finally opened up about how bad it had been between him and his father, she'd never imagined that his resentment spilled over onto the people his dad had served. The words he'd written were shocking, repulsive, hateful. The fact they were Eric's didn't excuse them, it made them worse.

She'd heard other women, friends of hers, announce proudly, "If my man ever did—" and they'd name some terrible thing— "it'd be all over with us. I'd tell him to leave." And now she knew Eric had done— no, had been— something like that. But she couldn't reject him. She couldn't even look down on him in virtuous pity. She loved him, she was part of him, and she shared in his crime.

Lord have mercy upon us, miserable offenders!

But what if Eric kept refusing God's mercy?

She bowed her head. *Please, Lord, soften his heart. We may not have much time. Soon? Now!*

"That was a long time ago," said the man she loved. "I've changed." He hesitated. "I've— I've rejected all that. I could never . . . " His hands gave a gesture of futility. "Please, we're tired. Release us. We don't know anything about your plans. We don't even know where we are. Let us go home."

Hardt's features twisted up in a sinister grin. "Great suggestion!" he said. "I send you and that woman back to the city and give up all claim to you. Say I trust you to keep your mouths shut. Good. But let me warn you: if you go home, this letter will follow you. Your clientele won't be as understanding as I imagine she is. And wherever you go, I will make sure everyone knows what you are."

Eric hunched over, looking drained and defeated.

"But I don't think you want to go back," Hardt went on. "I think you'll find it's safer here with me. After all, I have the Bomb."

CHAPTER D.9

IF HE TRIED HARD ENOUGH, he would wake up. "That can't be— You don't mean a real—"

Hardt's leering smile broadened, like a searchlight that could discover all his weaknesses. "That's exactly what I mean. A real, live, functional atomic bomb. All armed and ready to go. It'll make a good-sized dent in a city like Chicago or New York. And that wouldn't count the radioactive fallout." He cast his soulless eyes to the ceiling as in contemplation. "Or maybe Wapato-mekie? That'll scare the complacency out of the blind, lazy population of this country."

"But that's impossible!" he heard Sandy say. He himself was beyond speech.

"Or maybe we'll detonate it at one of those big nuke plants," Hardt mused. "More bang for our buck, you might say." The pale eyes locked in on his. "Impossible?" their owner said. "No, it's not. Did you hear about the plutonium missing from the Tyler Creek breeder reactor?"

Eric and Sandy both nodded their heads, as if they were marionettes.

"Another White Way success. We got it, and we're using it."

"I don't believe you," Eric made himself say.

"O ye of little faith!" Hardt beckoned to Vulture Oh-Six-Eight and whispered in his ear. The man and his fellow-lieutenant replaced their masks and slung their weapons more squarely on their shoulders. They moved toward him and Sandy. Reflexively, Eric threw up his elbow to protect his head. The man grabbed his arm and pulled him to his feet.

"Men, take our *guests* to see my baby. Tell no one where you're going, or it will be your lives."

"Yessir, Colonel."

"When you come back to me, Baumann, I expect you'll have changed your mind."

IF SANDY had found Hardt's personal quarters hard to believe, the laboratory they were admitted to via intercom and fingerprint scanner astonished her even more. It corresponded with nothing she'd seen in this subterranean hideout so far. Brightly lit, clean, and modern, with a dropped acoustical ceiling, it would not have been out of place at her father's old chemical firm. Even the white-coated, bespectacled man who emerged from a glass-windowed office at the rear of the room would have reminded her bizarrely of Daddy, had it not been for the pale half-mask he wore.

"Oh, hello," he greeted Vulture Oh-Six-Eight, who was the only one of Hardt's men to come in with them. "Brought me a couple customers for the nickel tour?"

"Colonel says they're to see *It.*"

"Really? That, too?" The man shrugged. "What the colonel wants, the colonel gets."

As the lieutenant covered them with his rifle—*in case we go berserk and try to take this scientist guy hostage?*— the man in the white coat took them to a door in the side of the room and drew a strange-looking key from around his neck.

"Lead-lined chamber. I'm working to solve the problem, but this is our first working version and it leaks a little."

"Leaks?" she asked. The normality of the surroundings lulled her into relaxing her guard.

"Radiation. Here. Put on these lead aprons and hoods."

They donned them, and it alarmed her to see how mechanical, even clumsy, Eric's movements had become.

"I guess you're like me," said the man in the white coat, his voice muffled through the clear face guard. "The colonel likes to collect men with expertise. Not women, usually, but I guess he'll make an exception if you're outstanding in your field.

"Oh! Let me introduce myself," he said, sticking out his gloved hand to each of them in turn.

"How do you do?" Sandy responded out of sheer habit.

"Fine, thanks. Around here I'm known as Eagle Two-Oh-Four, but Out There"— he dropped his voice, as if he didn't want the lieutenant with the gun to hear— "my name was Turner. Dr. Ivan Turner. I'm a nuclear physicist. I used to hold a professorship at Harvard, but there was a little, you know, *misunderstanding* . . . So," he said brightly, "what's he got on you two?"

"What?" said Eric, speaking for the first time since they'd left Hardt's room.

"You know. Blackmail. That's how he generally does it. Picks out guys like us, saves up some dirt, then when he's ready, comes in for the kill."

Sandy gaped at him.

Hurriedly, the scientist said, "Figure of speech, figure of speech . . . It's not bad around here, once you get used to it. You're an architect, I hear?" he said to Eric. "Yes, word's gotten around. We could use your services. Lot of things need redesigning. Not that he hasn't snagged an architect or two already. For some reason we haven't had much planning out of them. Waiting till he got you, maybe?"

Eric stood there mutely, his eyes wide, reminding her of a punchdrunk boxer tottering on his feet in the ninth round.

"Oh, don't worry. Once you're in and pass probation, the colonel keeps his side of the bargain. You won't be made to dig latrines. He won't kill you, either, as long as you do your job. And I imagine you'll have even more latitude for that when the dust settles after the big mobilization. I don't concern myself with that side of it, though. Just leave me in peace to do my research."

Behind them, Vulture Oh-Six-Eight pretended to cough.

"Oh! I suppose we should get a move on." He unlocked the door and ushered them through.

Lying on a bed of Styrofoam on a cart in the middle of the eight by eight room was something that looked more like an oversized steel breadbox than a nuclear weapon. Except for handles at each end, its outer casing was smooth, devoid of wires or switches.

"I don't believe it," said Eric. His voice seemed to come out of the dead walls rather than from living human lungs.

"Yes, sure is a beauty, isn't it?" said Turner.

"No," Sandy interpreted, "we don't believe it's a real atomic bomb."

"That's because it's not designed to be dropped from an airplane," said the physicist. "More likely it'll be slipped in in an ordinary freight truck. Maybe packed with fertilizer to make it really go."

"Fertilizer?" responded Sandy, confused. She pictured giant nightmarish radioactive flowers sprouting out of the roof of a tractor-trailer.

"Sure. Fertilizer makes a perfectly effective conventional bomb," said

Turner, like a college professor explaining a problem in Physics 101. "So, put it together with a nuclear warhead, and *ka-boom!* You can get a lot done. Strictly-speaking, it's not the structural damage we're after, it's the fallout. But that's a minor point.

"Now, take a look at this." With a flourish all the more unreal for seeming so normal, the physicist inserted a key and slid the trapezoidal top to one side. Crammed inside were canisters, wires, dials, and other machinery her outraged mind refused to grasp. "Lovely, just lovely!" he breathed.

"But how do we know that's really what it is?" she insisted.

"Either of you wearing a watch?"

"A watch?" said Eric. "Yes. But—"

"Let's see it."

Eric held out his left wrist.

"Beautiful," said Turner. "Old, isn't it? Perfect."

It had belonged to Eric's grandfather. Dully he answered, "Yes."

Turner brought an instrument with a wand off a side table. "Geiger counter." He ran the wand over the watch. The counter gave off a faint ticking and on its face the needle went up the meter a little way. "Radium," he said. "Used to make watch dials luminous, up to 1970 or so.

"Now watch." He passed the wand over the open device on the cart. The clicking went manic and the needle swung over into the red zone.

"Sorry I can't demonstrate our baby for you," he said cheerfully as he closed and locked it. "That might prove awkward. But it's simple, really. An undergraduate at Princeton did the library research and built a working atomic bomb not too long back. For a term paper. FBI confiscated the device and the paper both, but not before a friend of mine sent me a copy." He gave them a sly look. "I figured it might prove interesting. And so it has."

"Hey, Eagle Two-Oh-Four?" said the lieutenant from the outer door. "The colonel's waiting."

"Oh. Sorry." Turner led her and Eric out and relocked the chamber. "Good meeting you," he said. "Be seeing you around, I hope? I don't get much of a chance to talk to really intelligent people around here. Looking forward to it."

"I think it's real," Eric whispered before the guards separated them again. "O god, I think it's real!"

TOO MUCH TO THINK ABOUT, too much he didn't want to think about. This time, two of the guards from the passage came into Hardt's room with them and held them in restraint. This time, he and Sandy were not allowed to sit, on the Mies chairs or anywhere else.

"Are you pleased with our laboratory? Did you speak with our nuclear physicist?" Hardt and the others had re-donned their masks, and the friendly tones through the blank white fabric made the undercurrent of malice all the more chilling. "I'm sure you admired my baby. I predict he'll make quite a bang in the world." He laughed, and the noise of it made Eric retch. "And his brothers, too," Hardt went on. "They're already in gestation! My baby and his brothers are the key, Baumann. I'm going to remake America the White Way. Break the eggs first, then make the omelet. And you're going to help me. Aren't you?"

Eric avoided meeting the pale eyes. Perhaps if he hit just the right note of self-deprecation, he might, even now, persuade this madman to let them go. "Colonel, I couldn't— That's too big for me— I never pretended to think that big. We just want to make a living and—"

Hardt cut him off with a chuckle. "You know, Baumann," he said, his tone so disarmingly confidential it threw him off guard, "I read that article in the Sunday magazine of the *News-Herald* last May. I saved it, too." He flipped to another page in his scrapbook. "Yes, here it is: 'I believe architecture is the most powerful force there is for the shaping of society. The built environment affects everything we do as humans, and I aspire to use the power of design to help our culture achieve its highest ends.'"

He closed the album and fixed Eric with his alien eye. "Your own words, Baumann. Now I'm giving you the chance to do it. Complete charge of all planning and building for the new society. Think of it! The architectural destiny of America will be in your hands! Free rein, Baumann, free rein! I have great plans for you. You shirk your destiny, it will be your own fault, not mine." His mouth twisted up as if the prospect made him infinitely sad. "Your blood will be on your own head.

"You," he said, turning to Sandy. "I'm feeling generous. I extend the same offer to you."

"Colonel, I . . . what are our alternatives?"

"Damn you, Baumann, you heard your alternatives!" At the shout even the partisans standing around him quailed. "You've worn out my patience! I'll give you 'alternatives.' Say no to me, and your deaths *might* be quick and clean, like Pratt's." He pointed the Colt revolver at him and pretended to fire. "*Or* we can make an extra-special example out of you. We can drag it out so long you'll be begging to die. That woman first, I think. And you can watch. And every man here." He paused. "I think I'll let them help."

Eric gasped, and Sandy made a noise like a little sob.

"However . . . " The lips in their frame of white cracked into the parody of a smile. "You'll be happy to know your families won't be at any expense for your burials. We're very ecologically-minded here. We can make use of every scrap of your dead bodies. And we *will*."

"Tell me, Baumann," Hardt said, his tone suddenly warm and conversational, "did you like those Barcelona chairs you were sitting on? Have you ever felt leather as soft and supple as that?"

No! Every part of him that had come into contact with the chair burned with a horrified revulsion.

Hardt laughed. "I have other things that would look good in leather. Which would you rather be, a jacket or a sofa cushion? Maybe that female would make me a nice briefcase?

"*Now choose!*"

Eric stood swaying, knowing nothing but terror. He himself *was* Terror, and terror was everywhere, filling him, obliterating the world, engorging the universe entire. He was chewing frantically on his mustache; he tried to make himself stop, but the sensation was something to hold onto; if he let go he would dissolve into chaos.

I can't do it. I can't do it.

Do what? Work for him, or die?

Both! Either!

You can't? Why pretend you're too good for him, Baumann? You're corrupted already. You heard what you are. Your own words proved it. Live. Do your architecture. So what if it's for him? If it's any good, your miserable life might be worthwhile.

No! It's not true! I'm not perfect, but I'm not that bad. Never that bad. You think I'd give up my honor—

What honor?

All right, dammit, what's left of it— to be his flunky, his slave?

You're right. It was a new inner voice that spoke now, calming, insidious, and seductive. He could hardly accept that it spoke from his own heart, yet it did. *You don't want to dance to his tune, and you don't want to die. Why do either? You're in charge here, really. He's desperate to get you and your work. Think of all the trouble he's gone to to get you down here. Once you start, he'll be in the palm of your hand. You could enlighten him. Architecture is a strong force for good. Play your cards right, there's nothing you won't be able to get him to do.*

Vision, money, the ideal patron . . .

You've dreamed of this since you were a boy. Isn't it everything you've ever longed for and desired? Think of it . . .

To his mind's eye arose a vision of street after street, city after city, all built up anew with shining white structures, all of his design, all constructed with him in charge. And in those streets, inhabiting those buildings, thronged millions of happy, productive human beings, living lives of fulfilment and peace through the power of Architecture to make society new . . . Throngs of happy, productive, fulfilled *white* people, thronging the bright, clean, shining white streets lined with his bright, shining, pure white buildings . . . streets ankle deep, knee deep, neck deep in the sick red gore of all the non-white people and all the people Nick Hardt didn't think were white enough . . . victims of his *vision* . . . the blood of Jews, blacks, and Chicanos; of Asians, Arabs, and American Indians . . . of American Indians, who'd make America better off if they'd all die of alcoholism and disease . . .

But they'd deserve it! Rage like dark lava welled up in him, transforming him into a hard, hot mass of bitterness. *They stole my father from me!*

Hardt's eye was upon him. His mouth, framed by the white mask, curled in a sardonic smile.

He knows, you fool. He's always known.

O god! I am as bad as he is! I'm as bad as he is!

It was no use fighting it, no use at all.

I. *Give. In.*

His mind froze, appalled at the decision he had just made. Then from within him came a silent scream of defiance. Damn it, maybe he was that bad. In a way, maybe he was. But he knew he was bad, and that meant he could fight it. Just because he had been a bigot in the past didn't mean he should keep on being one. And Hardt's plans weren't merely bigoted, they aimed at mass murder. He could never be part of that, never. And— and— damn him to *hell* if he'd prostitute his art or himself to help that demon creature carry them out. He'd die first. He would.

You'll be tortured . . .

Who gave a damn? In 'Nam they all knew what the Viet Cong would do to them if they were captured. He'd been prepared to face that, even though that was a war he'd only been drafted to fight. Architecture— architecture for human benefit— was something he believed in. If it took shedding his blood to keep his principles clean, he'd do it.

Bizarrely, the memory came to him of his conversation with Sandy the previous Easter. So Christians could die for what they believed? They weren't the only ones! She'd see that he put his faith in something just as real. No, more real. She'd see—

Shame, horror, and excruciating love crashed over him like an avalanche, nearly felling him to his knees.

O god. O god. Sandy. He'd actually forgotten Sandy.

He took one ragged breath. Then another.

He choked down his fear. "Colonel, sir. I— I need to know something. So I can give you my . . . so I can decide if . . . " A curt nod of the masked head gave him permission to speak. "Suppose . . . just *suppose* I say . . . I say no . . . " Hardt's eyes narrowed, but Eric went on. " . . . and suppose . . . Miss Beichten says yes." He avoided looking her way. "Would you— will you— allow her to, to live and . . . " The thought of Sandy body and soul at the mercy of that creature and his henchmen nearly gagged him, but the question had to be asked. "Would you—"

"Baumann!" Hardt's disdain saved him the trouble. "Let me give *you* a 'just suppose'! *Just suppose* you're a car dealer and I want to buy a brand-new, fully-loaded BMW from you. And *just suppose* you offer to throw in the floor mats for free. And *just suppose—*" His voice rose higher and higher— "the next day you refuse to sell me that car. *Am I going to want the goddamned floor mats?*"

The image ripped through his consciousness like a fragmentation grenade: Sandy, his soul, his life, his precious love, slowly being tortured, brutally raped, and finally killed, and he'd be dead or forced to watch, unable to make a single move to prevent it.

Oh, but he would prevent it. To keep her from that horror he would gladly hurl himself and all he believed in straight into the abyss.

The empty eyes were assessing her with cold malice. "Colonel," Eric said, drawing the creature's attention back to himself. "You win. I'll—"

Over his, Sandy's voice rang out. "Mr. Hardt, I refuse!"

CHAPTER D.11

Hardt hadn't looked at her once since they returned from the laboratory. She knew what that meant. The only one he valued here was Eric. He'd dispose of the garbage later.

" . . . I'm going to remake America the White Way. Break the eggs first, then make the omelet. And you'll be helping me . . . "

In a wave of nausea it hit her: He didn't want Eric dead; he wanted him to be just like him.

" . . . free rein . . . if you miss your destiny, it will be your own fault . . . Your blood will be on your own head . . . "

"You," he said, turning his pale eyes on her, "I'm feeling generous. I extend the same offer to you."

What? Astonishment, shock, and a crazy relief swirled through her, the very offer of Not-Death ripping down her defenses. Right behind it came the terror of Death itself, flooding over her, nearly carrying her away. She wanted to scream, to run, to flee from this man and from the horror of her own desires. At the same time she desired nothing more than to throw herself at his feet and sob out her gratitude for his willingness to spare her life. To her shame, only the guard's iron clutch on her arm kept her still.

In his mask, with those eyes, Hardt looked artificial, scarcely human at all. He peered at her a moment longer, then turned back to Eric.

I don't want to die, I'm scared to die, don't make me die! her frantic soul gibbered out to the unhearing universe. *I'll do anything not to die.*

Had she compared the man with the tempter Mephistopheles? God help her, that was exactly what he was, and her own traitor soul was pleading with her to do what he wanted, to save herself, to take what he offered and live.

"Colonel, what are our alternatives?" her lover said.

Oh, Eric, didn't you hear him? We don't have any!

"Damn you, you heard your alternatives!" Hardt raged, pulling his gun. "You'll be begging to die. The woman first . . . I think I'll let the men help."

Oh, no. Not that too. Everything she'd been running from the past ten years; everything she thought she'd overcome since then and been so terribly wrong about, it was all here, waiting, closing in. Like a maelstrom, the fear of violation and death sucked her further and further into its cold, black, irresistible vortex, and the terror was worse than death itself. From inside the shell of her body her mind gibbered at her, repeating, *"You heard what you were sitting on. If you die, that'll be you!"* And before they finally killed her, before that—

She had but heart enough to send up one feeble prayer: *Dear Jesus, help!*

And help came. *"Jesus rose from the dead. Jesus rose from the dead."* That was all she could remember. It was enough. Gradually, just in time, her heart was calmed, her mind was still. Whatever happened to her in this place, however afraid she was, eternally she was safe.

She focussed on a spot in one of the Modernist paintings on the wall behind Hardt and made herself breathe. Death was only a portal. Christ would bring her through it, and she would be okay. *"Absent from the body, present with the Lord."* She would be fine.

The real danger was to Eric. He stood gripped by his guards, wavering and diminished. His shoulders were hunched, his fists nervously clenched, his brow sweating and furrowed in struggle. Depleted he was: dejected, nearly defeated. But still he was Eric, and in spite of her fear she was nearly overwhelmed with sorrowing love.

I almost hope he says yes.

Had she actually thought that?

Yes, she had. And she was willing to think it again. It'd give him more time. If he died now, he'd be out of an earthly hell and into the one that would never end.

Apparently Hardt had again forgotten her existence: all the power-lust of those uncanny eyes was directed towards the man she adored. She gazed at him too, her eyes caressing him in loving despair.

Lord, is this really Your will? I waited! I wanted him so, and he wanted me. But we held back. Is this our reward? Please, Lord, it isn't fair! I love him. I need him. I want him! You can't end us this way, please, Lord, You can't!

Stop it! The inward rebuke brought her to her senses. *Don't think of yourself. Do what's best for him.*

Of course, Eric's salvation. That's what mattered most. If she was gone, he'd never be saved. That made it her duty to say yes. This wasn't like playing missionaries when she was a kid. Nobody here was ordering her to stop telling people about Jesus. God would understand if she worked for Hardt for awhile. He would forgive.

Eric seemed to be standing straighter . . . gathering his courage to die?

Quickly. You know what you have to do. So he can be saved.

But as she opened her mouth, the ear of her heart was arrested by a new voice that was not her own. Eric's image wavered and dislimned, as if Someone were standing between her and him, Someone whom only the eyes of her spirit could see. The Presence spoke, Its voice overflowing with love. "Don't be afraid," It said. *"All that the Father gives Me shall come to Me; and him who comes to Me I will in no wise cast out."*

But Lord, how can he come, if I'm not here with him?

Her lover broke the terrible silence. "Colonel, sir . . . " His voice was humble. Was he giving in? Should she be appalled— or rejoice?

"I need to know something . . . so I can decide . . . Suppose I say no, and Miss Beichten says yes."

Her heart lurched.

Hardt's reply ended in a scream of rage. " . . . and next day you won't sell me the car, do I want the *goddamned floor mats?*"

That was the verdict. Only if Eric said yes, could she live. And beyond certainty he would sacrifice everything that made him human to see that she did.

My child. The Voice was gentle. *Do you want to save him?*

Yes, Lord, more than anything on earth!

You must trust him to Me. In life and in death.

I know, but—

Listen to Me: "If your right hand causes you to sin, cut it off."

Cut him off? I couldn't do that! How can You ask me to— Oh!

Her lips moved in silent acceptance: *"Be Thou my Vision, O Lord of my heart"!*

Eric was not her right hand. She was his.

CHAPTER D.12

"M R. HARDT, I REFUSE!" The words rang out over Eric's without hurry or fear, as if it was no longer she, but some Other who spoke. "This is a great wickedness you do here. You commit blasphemy against Almighty God. You commit sacrilege against men and women made in His image. Repent, or share the fire reserved for the Devil and his angels."

"Sandy!" Eric sucked in his breath. "You don't know what you're saying! He'll kill you!"

"Eric, I know that. It's all right. In Christ I'm already dead, and my life is hidden with Him in God. I'm only going to claim what's already mine."

She seemed to be standing behind and above herself, watching herself, hearing herself speak. Nothing on earth could touch her now. This wasn't the detachment she'd called upon when she'd suffered at the hands of Jeff Chesters and Al McNair. It wasn't even the objectivity she'd mustered earlier this evening. It was wholly different, something miraculous and new that came from outside herself, filling her with peace and power and awe.

"Mr. Hardt," she said, turning to their captor, and she was amazed at the love she felt even for him, "I don't answer for Mr. Baumann. Only for myself. I can't share in your evil. Do to me what you will."

The man had sat dumbfounded, but now he gave a derisive, raucous whoop. "Shit, Baumann, you brought me a little religious fanatic. I should have suspected as much." His tone went cold. "She bores me. Hawk Two-Five-Four," he addressed the guard holding her, "have her taken her away."

"Do you want her reserved for the persuasion squad, Colonel?" one of the captains asked.

"No, I've changed my mind. Finish her before I turn in tonight. Now."

"No!" cried Eric. He pulled away from the men holding him, pushed her astonished guards aside, and seized her in his arms. "No! Colonel, please," he said, his breath labored. "You want me. But if I come to you without this woman you only have half of what you want. Less than half. She's my right hand, my creativity, my— my—" He faltered for the words, and her heart ached with tenderness for his struggle.

Eric, Eric! I love you, but please don't hold me back. You should be happy for me!

"Very pretty," Hardt said, sneering. "Strange, that's not what you told me an hour ago. I suppose you'll say next she's your inspiration. Or your muse?" His teeth clenched. "Now back off before I shoot you both myself!"

His face wrung with misery, Eric let her go. "No, Colonel, I mean it. I lied before. We're a team. We have been practically ever since I opened the office. Without her skill, her knowledge, her— her— creativity, we couldn't do what we do. Without her I'm useless to you." He was looking their captor full in the face. "You say you've claimed me. That I belong to you. All right. But this woman is part of me. Don't cheat yourself! Let her live!"

"And?" inquired Hardt. The eyebrows behind the pale mask lifted in sarcasm. "She refuses to work for me. You heard her. Let her die."

"No," Eric insisted, "I can convince her to change her mind. I know how. Please, Colonel, give me the chance to talk to her!"

"All right. There she is. Talk to her."

"No, Colonel, I can't do it here. In private. Just the two of us."

"Oho! I catch your drift," Hardt replied salaciously. "She's a woman, and you're a real good convincer of women, aren't you, Baumann?

"Hawk Two-Five-Four, call in Falcon Oh-Three-Seven."

Once more she was faced with the cruel, wiry man who'd taken them prisoner at the car. But to her wonder, this time her heart greeted him with pitying love.

That isn't me feeling like this. I could never . . .

"Falcon Oh-Three-Seven!" snapped Hardt. "You and your men take the prisoners to that cell in Quadrant C. You know the one, in Passage C2."

"But Colonel—!" objected the little man, drawing back.

"You obey my orders, Falcon!" He looked at his watch. "That's a ten minute march from here . . . Yes. Baumann, you've got another ten to do your 'convincing.' Fifteen, if you make good time on the way. You have a half hour total to come back and tell me you're both with me, no pulling back. Otherwise . . .

"Falcon Oh-Three-Seven, if either of them gives you any trouble, follow the usual procedure. If they don't see reason, report back here in an hour to let me know the matter's been disposed of. Oh-one-hundred hours and no later, or you'll get what's coming to them. Do you hear?"

"Yessir, Colonel."

"Excuse me," said Sandy, and still her voice seemed hardly to be her own. "Please don't hold Mr. Baumann responsible for any decision I have made. If he desires to live, please grant his request."

Hardt waved his hand and turned away. Eric stared at her, astounded. Only for a moment, until their guards swarmed in and removed them from the room. The procession reformed: Falcon Oh-Three-Seven with his rifle, a man with a battery lantern, herself covered as before by Hawk Two-Five-Four and his smelly colleague, Eric with his guards, then another lantern holder to bring up the rear.

At first the lamps weren't needed: the passage was illuminated, though dimly, by low-wattage bulbs on wire strung along the dank walls. Eventually the way darkened and began to slope upward, at times steeply so. Upward and higher it wound, perhaps bringing them toward the surface.

> *High King of heaven, my victory won,*
> *May I reach heaven's joys, O bright heaven's Son!*

Her heightened senses picked up the scent of shale and earth amid the prevailing odor of dripping limestone. Behind her Eric was fretting to himself that the guards were going too slow. And yes, they weren't moving along as smartly as they usually did, though the passage was open and clear. Falcon Oh-Three-Seven and his light bearer, who'd drawn abreast of one another, seemed to be dragging their feet as if they were reluctant to go where they'd been ordered.

"Why *that* cell?" the lantern carrier griped. "Got plenty others."

"Maybe to put the fear of the devil into them," whispered the leader. " . . . the old McCool place . . . haunted . . . "

The old McCool place? Isn't that the name of the bigoted old woman Ruth told me about? I wonder if it's the same family.

The man with the lamp shuddered, and the light wavered on the glistening stone walls. "Faster we get them in there, faster we can get away ourselves."

She felt a lively curiosity, but no fear.

Falcon Oh-Three-Seven picked up the pace, moving them along in double time. Suddenly, the lantern light behind her went crazy, one body thudded against another, and Eric gave a cry, instantly cut off.

Lord, please, no!

The whole company halted. The men at the front turned around to look past her. Dismayed, she tried to turn as well— but the gun at her spine kept her eyes forward.

"Colonel's orders, Falcon! Change of plans!" The voice was oddly familiar. "You, Hawk One-Four-Three, come with me!"

A scuffle, and Eric was no longer behind her.

Sovereign Lord, help him!

Their group hurried on. In another two or three minutes, they stopped at a crude, barred wooden door, livid in the bluish electric light. This was opened, and behind it, for all she could see, was a high, deep kennel barely six feet wide.

Her guard roughly took her by the shoulder. "You know what's in there?" he asked, his own fear communicated in his grip. "Haints! There's upwards of four-five people buried in that there floor. Get friendly, you hear? You probably goin' to join 'em soon!"

He shoved her inside and the door was slammed and barred. The men's footsteps, dulled now by the barrier's bulk, hurried away.

The cell stank of urine and wet soil. The darkness was nearly complete. She was alone.

Alone? No.

"Yea, though I walk through the valley of the shadow of death, I will fear no evil. For Thou art with me."

Were people really buried here? It could be, whatever Hardt had said about using corpses. The floor beneath her feet was earth, not stone. But the dead could not harm her.

"Thy rod and Thy staff, they comfort me."

As her eyes grew accustomed to the darkness, a pale glow suffused the narrow space. Spiritual light? She laughed at herself and went to investigate.

Yes, there it was. An aperture the size of a baby's face, in the wall maybe fifteen feet up, with the barest glimmer of moonlight filtering through.

She felt the surface below it. Rough wet shale. There must be some spring that had cut its way through the clayey soil and made the opening.

Lord, are You offering me a way of escape?

But the gap was too high and the shale surface under it too firm to dig through for that to be a possibility. Not in the time Hardt had given them.

But where was Eric?

Please, Lord, protect him. If I could tell him goodbye? But Your will be done.

A disturbance in the passage. The door was opened and a body was flung in, to the laughter of the guards. It hit the ground face down at her feet, the left side of the dark head flowing with blood, and lay there, deathly still.

CHAPTER D.13

"DON'T MOVE," SAID SANDY, probing the wound at his temple delicately with her fingers.

Eric lay wincing, his bleeding head cradled in her lap.

"Well," she said at length, "it doesn't *feel* broken. More like a bad cut. Oh, Eric, what happened? Who did this to you?"

"Bozo the Clown." He groaned.

"Who?"

"Bozo. That fat balding red-headed creep that was giving you the eye during Hardt's speech. He and the guy covering me grabbed me and Mr. Gunman held my arms behind my back while Bozo worked me over." He put a faltering hand to his temple. "God! It hurts!"

"Shh. Rest while you can."

"What the hell was that all about? The bastard acted like it was personal."

Her soul sorrowed for him. "Maybe it was. You didn't recognize him?"

"Well, except for looking like Bozo in a stupid little mask, no."

"Eric, that was Jeff Chesters."

"What!" He sat bolt upright, but dizziness overcame him and he subsided back into her lap.

"Oh god. Oh god. And I've always wanted to pound the crap out of him. It's not fair." He balled up his fists and pounded his knee. "It just isn't fair!"

"Hush," she said, stroking back his hair and kissing his forehead. His blood was salt on her lips and she wiped it away reverently. Moving carefully, so not to jostle him, she stripped off her tee shirt.

He struggled to sit up. "What are you doing?"

"You need a bandage. There's plenty of hem on this thing. I hope it's not too dirty." She started a tear with her teeth and ripped four or five inches of the cotton fabric loose.

"I can't let you—" he protested.

"I have to stop that bleeding. Now hold still," she said, wrapping it around his head and securing it with a knot. "That will have to do. Now lie down."

"No, I'm better now. Put your shirt back on and let's both sit against this wall." He pulled her into his arms and held her against his heart. "Sandy, listen. (God, my head hurts!) Why don't we pretend to work for him and use it to defeat him? We can put little things into the designs so they'll fail and collapse. He'll want a big rallying hall, that's for sure."

"But how do you know—?"

He put his finger to her lips. "Listen. Remember the skywalks that collapsed at that hotel in Kansas City last year? The connections were under-designed. We could work something like that into every building we do."

"No, dearest. Don't you think he's heard about that? You and Turner and Jeff can't be the only experts he's coerced into working for him. He'll have the drawings checked over. He'd find anything like that right away and kill us."

"Yes, but if we don't try, he'll kill us tonight, and what good would that do?"

"For me, the highest good: obedience to my Lord."

"Oh, Sandy!" It came out in a wail. "You don't really mean it, do you? You won't really die for . . . I mean, how can you die for a god that allows this kind of crap to happen to us?"

"Eric, love, I'm willing to die for the God who allowed all kinds of bad things to happen to Him. That's why He died, to save us in spite of it. Not just me; you, too." She took his hand. "Remember last Easter when you said you believed Jesus rose from the dead? You're right, He did, and there was nothing earthly about it. The grave simply couldn't hold Him. I trust in Him, and it's not going to hold me, either."

"But Sandy, would your god— Jesus— really mind all that much if you compromised, for a good end? He's reasonable, isn't he?"

She measured her small hand against his great one. So dear to her, so dear . . .

"We could undermine him," he urged. "Be like secret agents. Isn't that better than letting him go on doing what he's doing?"

Lord, he's not thinking clearly. Help me help him. Be Thou my Wisdom, and Thou my true Word!

"Eric, Eric, my dearest love! I know you. You worship Architecture. You could no more do bad design on purpose than you could walk through these walls. Whether you wanted to or not, you'd be sucked in."

"But don't we already work for people whose principles we don't like? Jacob Ryerson is a terrible chauvinist. The way he talks about you and other women makes me sick. And here we are, building him a factory and office block!"

"I know he is," she said patiently. "I wish he weren't. But FirstCon isn't the headquarters for a movement to keep all women barefoot and pregnant."

He groaned. "I'm sorry. I'm sorry. You're right. But I— Sandy, I can't help it. I don't want to lose you. If you have to work for Hardt to stay alive, that's what I wish you would do!"

"Oh, my dear, my dear!" She stroked his face gently. In the pale illumination the bruises stood like deeper shadows on his skin. "Please don't say that! If I did that, I wouldn't be the person you love anymore."

"But you have principles. You wouldn't let it touch you."

"It would. And how could I want to live, knowing every day I'm purposely doing things that displease my Lord? I'm gaining Christ by choosing death now, Him and everything He is. It's better this way. It really is."

"Do you have to go?" His voice broke on a sob.

"Yes," she said. "And I'm not afraid. Jesus has prepared a place for me and I'm going there to take it up." She looked into his eyes. So much distress there, so much sorrow! "Eric, you were baptized. God has claimed you for His own. May He remind you of that and give you strength to join me where Jesus is. Oh! I love you so much; God grant I'll see you again!"

Her emotions were barely controlled; his gave way completely. "Oh, Sandy, hold me, hold me!"

He pulled her tightly to him in the gray darkness, and where her head lay against his breast his heart beat like a great captive bird. He did not speak. His body quaked with fierce masculine sobs that seemed to shake the foundations of the world, and his tears flowed profuse and heavy, running down onto the crown of her head.

Anointing me for my burial . . . Her own tears welled over more quietly. "*I am poured out like a drink offering and the time is come for my departure . . .*"

The door was jerked open and the silhouette of the guard loomed against the lantern light in the passage.

"All right, break it up. You might just make it back to the colonel to say yes if you run."

Sandy rose to her feet, leaving Eric slumped against the dank wall. "My answer is the same," she confessed firmly. "I'm ready to go."

"You are, are you?" The guard gave a morbid chuckle and grabbed at her arm.

She eluded his grasp. "Eric," she said, stooping down to him, "the Holy Spirit has led me to this. It is good, it really is. Please, give Him a chance to show you that Christ is true, please!" He caught her hand and kissed it, wetting it with his tears. Lightly, her lips caressed his forehead. "Eric, remember me. I love you."

She turned to the guard. "When you will."

He yanked her out of the cell. To her surprise, he was by himself.

"I should have known!" she gasped. *Father in heaven, I should have known.*

CHAPTER D.14

"Y̶OU EXPECTED ME, DID YOU? Yeah, it's me. In the flesh." Jeff Chesters sniggered, and the old fear and loathing came flooding back.

Only for a moment, then the incomprehensible peace drove it out again. She stood still before him, waiting to see what he would do.

"Wonderful what a bribe can accomplish in a place like this," he said. "Sandy Beichten, you and I have unfinished business." Slinging the strap of his rifle over his shoulder, he shoved her against the rough passage wall, the butt of the gun grazing her side as it swung loose.

"Jeff, don't. For your own sake. Don't." Her pushing arms were like rotten straw against a column of lead. She opened her mouth to scream.

No. Eric mustn't hear. I won't leave him with that.

No one would come to help her. If anyone heard, most likely he'd want to join in.

Jesus, spare me this. Please!

One fat sweaty hand crawled up under her shirt while the other— the other, God help her!— circled around and ground her hips hard against his groin. "I saved that for you," he muttered, the sick words poison in her ear.

"Please, no!" She twisted away, frantically digging her nails into his arm. He didn't seem to feel it at all.

"Oh, yes! You've wanted that for—"

"Hey!" Their heads snapped towards the sound. Another White Way partisan stood at the bend of the passage, of Vulture rank by his half-mask, his feet doing a nervous little dance as if duty alone kept him where he was. "I *thought* I heard something!"

Jeff let her go and hitched up his rifle. "Sorry," he said to the man, "I had to— she wasn't cooperating—"

"Stop wasting time. Falcon Four-Two-Two, isn't it? You got execution detail?"

"Uh, yeah. Yes, sir."

Her heart beating wild with relief, she stepped just out of his reach. It was useless to try to flee, but still— *Thank You, Jesus. Thank You for sending someone, again.*

"Where's your partner?" demanded the newcomer.

"Uh, partner, sir? Oh, yes. He's sick. Sudden attack of nausea. Told him I could handle this one on my own."

"Well, stop handling her—" the Vulture gave a cynical laugh— "and dispose of her, quick. Outside. Colonel's got a bug tonight about not setting off vibrations."

"Yes, sir."

"The other one gonna need it, too?"

"Probably."

He'll kill Eric whether he agrees to work for Hardt or not. Father in heaven, do Your miracle. Make him ready!

Ready to defend himself and escape, or ready to die? Even she didn't know.

"Well, make damn sure to get back by oh-one-hundred hours and tell him the job's done, like he said. Or it'll be your neck, too."

Jeff looked at his watch. "Shit!" he said under his breath. "Asshole didn't tell me there was a deadline." Then, "Yes, sir!" he spoke up, and the man disappeared back the way he had come.

"Now move!" Jeff ordered, prodding her with the barrel of the rifle. Calmer now, she obeyed.

The passage was steep and at times she needed her hands to negotiate it. "You're out of luck tonight, Sandy Beichten. I was going to give you a treat before you died. Better than that baby killer back there ever did. Bet you're sorry you ever picked up that knife down in the student store."

There was no need to answer that. *Lord Jesus, thank You for your mercies. Heart of my own heart, I'm coming.*

"Jeff," she said, marvelling at the benevolence she again felt towards him, "what happened? Why are you here? You were so gifted, we were all sure you'd be famous some day."

"Shut up!" he snapped, shoving the gun into her back. They marched onward a few yards. "Pansy East Coast liberals," he said eventually, almost as if he was talking to himself. "Don't understand a real man has needs. Besides, I was doing those women a favor. A little extra service for the lady clients." He laughed. "And for women 'colleagues' like you!" He gave her a push, but she managed to keep her footing. "The bitches enjoyed it! How do I know? They never told. Like you!"

"Somebody must have."

"They had no right to keep me in the office writing specs! I'm a designer! I'm a better architect than all those losers at AGI put together! They had no right!"

"And Nick Hardt somehow found out about you and made you an offer you couldn't refuse."

"Who? Is that who he said he was? Yes." He said it with the barest note of shame. There was silence as they made their way around a difficult turn. Then, "God damn it, I'll be glad when you and Baumann are dead and doubly glad I did it! He promised me I'd be in charge of his rebuilding program! 'Probation,' my ass!"

He spat, and it made no sound against the slippery, clayey soil. On either side and overhead, timbers shored up the passage roof. Were they in an old mine? The humusy odor she'd detected in the cell grew stronger. They must be approaching the surface.

"What the hell does he mean making me stand around all day with a stupid Russki gun making him look macho?" Jeff broke the silence. "Then bringing in you two to push me out of my place? When I tell him what I've done he'll have to give me what he promised."

Lord, Eric is in Your hands. May they be Your hands of love, not Your hands of judgement!

Her heart was at peace about it. All would be well in her Father's good design. Still, it would be a satisfaction to learn one thing more:

"Last fall, did he tell you to apply for the job with us?"

Behind her, Jeff chuckled. "That's something you'll die not knowing, isn't it?"

Lord, You're right. Only thing now is being with You.

They came up against a locked and barred wooden door.

"Don't you dare budge."

He pulled a ring of keys out of his pants pocket. But when the door was unlocked and open, all she saw was another wood plank barrier. Inserting a different key released some mechanism, but nothing happened. "Dammit," he said, pushing at the wood. "Screw you, thing, *move!*" Finally, with a screech like the cry of a lost soul, the barrier slid to one side and stopped.

"Go," he ordered her, and with his gun waved her through.

The battery lantern's beam revealed a low, dirt-floored space, hardly seven feet across. Along the walls to the right and the left stood crude wooden shelving, empty, festooned with cobwebs and black with age. The barrier that had taken so much effort to move turned out to be a great, tall, closed wooden cupboard reaching floor to ceiling, but now it was halfway concealed in the side wall.

Like Grandma Fleming's root cellar. With a secret passage?

He turned the key on the heavy door to the cave but left the cabinet where it was.

At the opposite end of the root cellar was an ordinary interior door, closed, its cracked panels curled with peeling paint of various colors. He unlocked this, too, and pushed her through to a dirt-floored basement room. They took the steps up to a side exit, which he left open.

Outside, the moon had risen and hung huge, somber, and misshapen just above the trees. "The locals think this place is haunted," Jeff said with a satisfied chuckle. "Came in handy for me, none of those hicks in your detail wanted to stay anywhere near it. Above ground *or* below."

He forced her at a quick march downhill away from the house, through a thicket, then into a small clearing. Somewhere nearby a stream trickled. Around them the tall solemn trees stood silent, ready to bear witness to what was about to occur. It comforted her to think they'd be here still, long after she was gone.

"Turn around."

The house, now she could see it, was a ramshackle Victorian, abandoned for who knows how many years.

"The old McCool place," he said. "Belonged to the colonel's grandma. Full of ghosts— nasty ones!"

He positioned her against a broad oak, its pocked, dark-stained trunk nearly three feet wide. "You probably believe in ghosts, too. If I had time I'd tie you up, but you're too chicken to run. You're scared of dying, aren't you?" He smirked at her.

"No, Jeff, I'm not," she replied, pulling herself up straight and bracing her feet. Again she seemed to be watching herself saying and doing things that amazed her. *It's You, Holy Spirit, isn't it? Praise You!* "I'm only afraid for you," she said. "I thought I loved you once. It was only lust and pride, and I ask your forgiveness for thinking of you that way."

"Shut up. You're crazy."

"But now I really do love you, with the love of Christ. Jeff, I've forgiven you, even for this. For Jesus' sake, for your own, repent and accept His grace. He died for you. Don't tell Him no."

He gave a derisive snort. "Trying to get out of it, are you?" He backed up, his rifle pointed at her form, now mercilessly exposed in the moonlight. "That's all BS and you know it."

In the tall growth under the edging trees he halted. She heard him release the safety and watched him sight down the scope. It was the last thing she would see on earth.

"Still be my Vision, O Ruler of all."

"Lord Jesus, receive my spirit!"

There was a sickening crash and a strangled cry as the world exploded in gunfire.

CHAPTER D.15

S HE WAS GONE. Through the thick door he'd heard low, indistinguishable noises, then nothing at all.

"I'll kill him," Eric whispered into the semi-darkness. His head ached badly; his heart ached worse. "They can't do that to her. I'll make him pay."

He'd pretend to agree to Hardt's offer, then wait for his chance. Steal a weapon, waylay him in some dark passage. Strangle him with his bare hands. They could do what they liked to him after that; his life would have been worthwhile.

He rose to his feet and began to pace the narrow, urine-reeking cell, luxuriating in all the hate and power of his plotted revenge . . . until it ebbed out of him like the ash-polluted water that has quenched a fire.

They'd never let him anywhere near Hardt alone. He was a fool to think it.

But wait. Why not—? Yes. Grab one of the White Way partisans as a hostage. Maybe Bozo himself. Threaten to kill him unless—

Unless what? Hardt himself would happily put a bullet into him and the hostage both, just as he had with Pratt.

Which left sabotage. Sandy was wrong there. He could do it. He could design in those little flaws that would bring everything tumbling down.

But the objecting voice refused to be still. *When?* it asked. *Baumann, are you deluded too?*

He'd never design Hardt's new society. However much damage the White Way did, the federal government would push back and stop them from taking over America before they even got close.

Meanwhile, he'd be here, stuck in these sun-abandoned caves, or in some other hideout. Dependent on Hardt for the basic necessities of life. Working for him, doing his best for him— for him only, since he'd betrayed true architecture— influenced by him, growing more and more like him—

No. He'd rather die.

Or would he?

His splayed fingers grasped the wall of his cell, but he drew no resolution from its rough solidity. Above him gray light filtered through a fist-sized circle high in the wall. His eyes strained towards it, as if through that portal his soul would pass once his body was killed. He wrenched in a breath.

Out into oblivion. Eternal, dreamless sleep. Nothing he hadn't known and accepted since he was a child. Nothing he couldn't . . .

Nothing. Nothing. It was *all* Nothing! Meaninglessness and chaos and disorder and formlessness and negation and horror! He doubled over, about to be sick.

No. Stay calm. Breathe. Think.

Think about architecture . . . about the meaning it brought to the world . . . about the beauty that rose out of form and order . . . about everything that was the opposite of what that piece of inhuman crap stood for . . . Remember how he, Eric Baumann, had done his duty to his art, how his work in its service would live on after him, how it—

O god, his art was the very thing that— *devil*— had perverted to lure him down into living death!

Actual death would be better. It had to be. Whatever else they took away from him, he would hold onto meaning. And love. For love he'd been willing to sacrifice his art . . . He could die like a man in her memory. He let the vision comfort him for a moment.

Oh hell, what good would it do? His death wouldn't avenge her. It wouldn't stop the White Way from carrying out their plans. Hardt would start his race war, and his own friends would be just as dead.

Meaningless, meaningless, meaningless! He collapsed to the floor, his throbbing head in his arms.

Why aren't I dead already? Why didn't that bastard Chesters finish the job? I told her if she ever left me I'd die. Why am I still alive?

He pulled himself to his knees, his fists clenched.

"Let there be Nothing!" he roared into the darkness. "Death take me! I can do it. I can do it!"

Silence. His ear strained at it, till he seemed to hear a whisper spoken out of the stillness around him:

Liar.

A cry of misery escaped his lips and he smacked the wall.

"All right! I *can't* do it! I'm not ready, I don't want to die! I just don't want to die . . . Sandy, help me, please!"

On his forehead the impress of her last kiss yet lingered. She was so fragile and small . . . How could she go to her death like that? She hadn't flinched once since her declaration in Hardt's room. It was different this time, not like after McNair. She'd had every excuse to fall to pieces, and she'd walked up to her executioner as if he were an usher at a concert she was excited to hear. "I'm ready," she'd said.

She had been ready, and he was not.

But Sandy's hope wasn't for him. Sure, he'd admit that the man Jesus somehow rose from the dead. And suppose the Catechism was right and the God Sandy called her Father in heaven really did make him and all creatures. What help was that to him? God must hate him now. He was on his own.

Is that true? Is that what Sandy told you all those evenings you grilled her about her faith? Is that what you read in that New Testament you kept sneaking from her drawer?

He pressed his hands over his ears.

Is that what you learned about Me in the Catechism when you were a boy?

Almost without thought, the remembered words fell from his lips: "He defends me against all danger and guards and protects me from all evil. All this He does only out of fatherly, divine goodness and mercy, without any merit or worthiness in me.'"

"Without any merit or worthiness" in you. My son, stop working. I've done the work for you already.

But all the bad things Poppa did in Your name?

Your earthly father is the only Christian you know?

No, but— but if he gave in to God now, he'd look like a fool. He'd be proving he couldn't die on his own, admitting that everything he'd lived for wasn't enough. What would people think? What would he think of himself?

"Pride is overrated. Especially when it keeps you from doing what's right." Sandy's words after Phil Duggins was murdered.

"She's right, she's right," he cried. "But I can't do it! I just can't do it!"

It was true. He *couldn't* do it. It wasn't death he had to embrace now, it was Life. But between him and Life lay a great bottomless pit he had no way to bridge, no way even to make himself jump into. If only there was someone who saw what he had to do and would help him do it in spite of himself! But no, that could only be the Christ he'd been rejecting, been running from for years, had long fled— the Life wasn't for him— not for him . . .

Past endurance, he buried his head in his arms and bowed himself to the earth, willing the hardness of it to shield him from all feeling, all sight, all sound. Even so, through the aperture above penetrated the muffled but unmistakable burst of an automatic rifle. Three close, quick shots, a high-pitched cry, then silence.

"It's over! She's— Oh, God!" Suddenly his fear and pride were more accursed and contemptible than anything Hardt could ever force him to do. He began to shake and sob, rocking back and forth in his misery. "Lord Jesus Christ, have mercy on me! Have mercy on me!"

"You have been baptized. God has claimed you for His own."

As the noonday sun explodes through a high, broad window when a smothering drape is pulled away, his soul's eye beheld the One whose nail-pierced hands were extended to him in forgiving love. He bowed his head.

"I *am* Yours, Lord Jesus. Forgive me. Take me home."

CHAPTER D.16

HE WAS AT PEACE when they came for him. "I am ready to die," he said calmly to the indistinct figure in the doorway.

"Eric!"

So angels are real!

"Hurry!" the voice whispered, and a very solid hand tugged at his arm.

"Sandy, is it really—? Thank God! But how—?"

"Shh. Explain later. Let's go!"

She closed the door behind them and relocked it. "We'll keep the lantern on low."

"But all that way to the entrance, how can we—?"

"Not that way. Closer. I didn't see anybody on the way back, but we won't take chances. Here, you take the gun."

"Is the safety on?"

"Safety? Probably not. I just kept my hand away from the trigger."

He rectified the matter.

"Pretend to cover me, just in case," she said.

It wouldn't have fooled even the stupidest White Way militiaman for a second: no uniform, and they'd all gotten too good a look at him in the great cavern. But no one appeared, and they made it safely past a heavy wooden barrier into—

"What's this? It looks like a root cellar. With a— what? A sliding cabinet to cover the entry?"

"It is," she said, locking the cave door behind them.

"We should try to close this, too," he said.

"I don't know how to lock it, but let's try." But even with their combined strength, the cabinet wouldn't budge. "Let's leave it," she said. "Through here."

Out in the moonlight he took in the dilapidated Victorian house and the massive bald knob of rock looming over it like a golem in a nightmare. *What place is this?*

It could wait. "Sandy, what happened? Where is the guard?"

"Ohhh . . . " For a moment she clutched at him, her head buried in his chest, then looked up, sadness, horror, and sympathy mingled in her eyes. "Oh, Eric, I think he's dead! It was terrible, I had to get the keys out of his pocket . . . "

Her canvas shoes were wet. "Where?"

She led him down into a moonlit clearing ringed with trees, one of them a large oak scarred with bullet holes. The sound of running water rippled the stillness.

"There," she said, pointing to a spot a few yards opposite the oak. "Be careful, there's a bad drop."

Rifle at the ready, he looked over. About twelve feet below him, in a rocky streambed, lay the body of a balding, red-haired man. Through the gray mask its eyes gaped wide and unseeing at the heedless moonlit sky.

"Wait here," Eric told her. "I'm going down."

A tinge of scarlet was still visible in an eddy by the jagged rock on which the head lay. It was Jeff Chesters, and he was assuredly dead.

"*Vengeance is Mine, saith the Lord,*" he thought soberly. *I remember that one.*

Quickly, he searched the corpse. A couple of chocolate bars, wrapped in foil and mercifully unopened, a small flashlight, too wet to use, an empty pocket flask, and a pornographic novel. He tossed this last into a deep-looking pool, then walked upstream a little way, wiped the mouth of the flask, and filled it with clean water.

Having secured the chocolate bars and the flask in the pockets of his cargo shorts, he clambered back up to where Sandy waited.

"We'd better get out of here before they miss me— and him," he said. "Which way?"

"There's got to be a driveway around front. That'd be fastest, wouldn't it?"

"They'd look for us there first. Ordinarily I'd say we should follow this stream down, but . . . No, better go through the woods."

She hesitated a second, then said, "Towards the river, do you think? The roads generally follow them around here. It's over there," she said, pointing, "to the west of us. I mean, if the moon's in the south. I could see it— the river— from up by the house."

"Good idea." He wheeled around, searching the sky. "Yes, there's the Big Dipper, and the Little Dipper with the North Star. We'll keep that to our right and the moon to our left."

He still ached from Jeff's beating and Sandy seemed to be operating on nervous energy alone. There was no help for it; they had to put miles between themselves and Hardt's hideout as fast as they could.

"Tell me what happened. If you want," he said once they came to a place where they could slacken their pace and catch their breath. He searched her face in the moonlight. "My poor precious love, I heard the shots and was sure you were dead!"

"He must have stumbled when he was pulling the trigger. All the bullets went wide, thank God."

"Amen."

"Funny thing, I wasn't scared at all until I realized they hadn't hit me."

"It takes people that way." He looked around. "Here's a trail," he said, gesturing. "I wonder how much experience he had with that rifle."

"Not much, from the way he was talking on the way out." She paused to extricate herself from a thorn bush, then, swiftly and silently as they could, they hurried on.

HOW LATE was it? She tried to take a look at her watch, but it was too dark among the trees to make the numbers out.

"Eric, can you see the time?"

He swung up his wrist to look even as they hurried along. "After 2:00."

"I think it was a little after one when I made it back to you. Any sign of pursuit?"

"No, not unless they have night vision goggles."

Her stomach turned over. She remembered how well the patrol that captured them had raced through the woods by the light of a single lantern. If it was because of night vision . . . "I didn't see any on that gang that abducted us."

"Then let's hope none of them do."

"SO TELL ME about that house," Eric reminded her several minutes later. They were skirting a broad level place now, probably where crops were raised when the land was a working farm. He'd avoided the easy walking directly across the field, leading her instead into the shelter of the trees on its fringe.

"Oh, yes. Jeff said it was the old McCool place, and everyone around here thinks it's haunted."

"McCool place?" The name seemed to mean nothing to him.

Wait a minute. Why should it?

"I'm sorry, you don't know. It's something Ruth told me once and I didn't tell you because it was just us talking and I didn't think it was relevant."

"It is now. Let's hear it."

"... I DON'T THINK I'm jumping to conclusions," she said once she'd related Ruth's story about Mrs. McCool, her grandson, and their hatred of blacks, "but I think Mrs. McCool was grandmother to Nick Hardt."

"Or to Cole Rutherford, since it looks like they're one and the same." He paused. "Come on. We'd better pick up the pace."

They continued in the inner edge of the woods, keeping the open ground on their left.

"I wonder," she said a little breathlessly, "which is the alias, or if they both are. I mentioned Nick Hardt to . . . to Jeff . . . and for a second he didn't know who I was talking about. But if they call him The Colonel and not Colonel Hardt or whatever, doesn't that mean most of the White Way gang aren't locals?"

"Not necessarily," said Eric, using a long stick he'd picked up to hold back the undergrowth so they could pass. "With all of them wearing masks, and his covering his whole head . . . And the way he insists on the title by itself, 'Colonel,' like something out of the Old Confederacy. Maybe even the locals don't know."

"True. Nobody has a name in there. Just a raptor name and a number."

He gave her a hand to help her around some thorn bushes.

"Still, Ruth told me he'd sold up his inheritance and left back in 1961 or so," she said. "How could he buy it back without anyone knowing it was him? I mean— *yii!*"

"What was it?" he whispered, alarmed.

She put her hand to her pounding heart and kept moving. "Nothing. Just some animal."

"Maybe he didn't sell up right away," Eric took up the question. "Maybe an agent took care of the whole deal, and the man we know as Nick Hardt never showed up back here at all. I'm betting that Rutherford's the real name, by the way."

"You're probably right. Which might explain why Al McNair didn't know where the operation was. He thought all this property was out of Rutherford's hands years ago."

"Yes. I bet McNair knew him in Kentucky under his real name, maybe sold him some—"

"Shh," she said, grabbing his shirt. She pointed back the way they'd come.

Just the barest pinpricks of light dotted the middle reaches of the slope at the far margin of the field. At least two dozen of them, maybe more, were fanned out at regular intervals like dew on the web of a stalking spider, a spider moving straight towards her prey.

"I don't see anything," said Eric.

"There. Those lights?"

"That's not moonlight on the trees? . . . no, they're coming this way. Listen. If I say 'Hit the ground,' do it, no questions."

There wasn't time even for her to nod yes before he took her hand and fled with her deep into the woods. Though maybe "fleeing" (the thought flashed through her mind) wasn't quite the word for it. The very moon that lit their way rendered every bush, every dip in the ground, every fallen log weird and unfathomable. If they made little noise it was because every step had to be gauged, and it was a miracle her wet tennis shoes hadn't yet betrayed her into turning an ankle. Weeds and thorns grabbed at their bodies as they passed as if they were in league with their hunters. Long before she expected it, she could glance back among the trees and see not only the high-powered lights, but the shadowy olive-clad forms of the men carrying them.

She groaned inwardly. *Locals or not, they know these woods.*

Two or three of them disengaged from the group and came running their way.

"Hit!" Eric breathed in her ear as he grabbed her around the body and pushed her down into a stand of laurels. He lay over her, both of them silent and heart-racing like hunted animals in the grim night. Hardly three yards away the men could be heard crashing through the undergrowth, with someone talking breathlessly into a two-way radio, followed soon by the rest of their squad. The glare from the lanterns flashed in through the leaves above them, then swung away.

The footsteps faded; the lights disappeared.

One minute. Two minutes. A lifetime and a half.

"Come on," he whispered, and she followed him on a new course perpendicular to the track they'd been taking, but always, she hoped, towards the river and maybe— just maybe— a major road. Her legs and lungs ached, she was bleeding from a hundred cuts and abrasions, and something irritated her skin like she'd lain in poison ivy. Perhaps she had; time and again they went to ground and she thanked God every minute that Eric seemed to have an instinct for best knowing where.

In the sky to the south the wild white Huntress laughed at her exhaustion and drove strange delusions into her mind. Or was that Mab, the Queen of the Fairies? Something untamed and dream-inducing at any rate, for hadn't she just heard Eric say, "Don't worry, Jesus will get us out of this"?

This is surreal.

Surreal was good. It kept her from questioning him when he persistently pulled her to the left, more south than west. The main body of the search seemed to have swept past on their right, to the northwest, as if certain that was the way fugitives would take.

Maybe the ground's easier there. Maybe there's a good open trail. Maybe nobody with any sense would head the way we're going.

They emerged from the wood. *O Domine.* She was right.

Before them lay a fantastic vista of silvered, folded hills. At their feet, a sheer rocky cliff, its foot drowned in darkness. Behind them, the searcher-ridden woods. Brief flashes of light showed between the trees, distant still, but undeniably sweeping their way.

He did his best. That's all he could do.

Eric gestured for the lantern; mechanically, she surrendered it into his hand. Creeping on all-fours, he approached the brink. Careful to shield the light with his body, he switched it on low and flashed it down the rock face. "Here," he said, beckoning her towards a bush growing at the cliff's edge. "Come on."

"What? Oh!"

The bush concealed a crevice like a large, angular smokestack, studded here and there with shrubs hanging on for dear life in fissures in the rock. Though the moonlight was shining full on it Sandy could see few or no foot or handholds.

"What—?"

"Like this," he whispered. He wedged himself into it, his back and shoulders against the rock wall on one side, his feet against the other, and the rifle on his lap. He began to work his way down, then stopped. He motioned for her to do the same.

Positioning herself the opposite way so she'd be able to see his face, she eased herself into the crack. She'd been afraid her legs wouldn't be long enough to reach across, but it was just possible.

So far, so good, so far, so good . . . Please, God, don't let me slip and fall down on him!

Below her, she could watch his dark head descending by jerks and stops lower and lower. It scared her less if she kept her eyes on him rather than focussing on what her own body was doing.

"Eye—!" she bit off a yelp. Eric looked up.

Her right foot trod out into emptiness. Her back had lost full contact with the rock behind her; her right shoulder and left foot alone kept her suspended. She teetered between them, her hands groping wildly to seize on anything they could.

Jesus, don't let me fall don't let me fall—!

A bush! Tiny, but she grabbed it.

He shook his head, hard. "No bushes," he breathed. "Not safe."

"Then what am I—?" she protested. But her fingertips found a hold in the rock below her rear and she wriggled her way past the difficulty.

The crack bottomed out onto a narrow ledge with a steep rocky slope below. Faces sideways, their bodies flattened against the cliff face like figures from an Egyptian tomb painting, they stepped along the edge until it terminated in a shelf just wide enough to hold two people standing. Ahead of them the hillside slanted down like an eyelid; above them the rock canted outwards to cover them with a hood of living stone.

Her arms flew around him as he enfolded her into his own. "Oh, Eric!" she said, her mouth at his pounding heart. "Oh, Eric!"

"Shh . . ." They listened. Not a sound but the innocent noises of a forest at night. His touch was gentle as he brushed her hair from her forehead. "Can you hold up? We may be here for a while . . ."

She smiled up her yes.

They shared a chocolate bar and a drink from the flask. Then, "Tell me, precious love," he began, keeping his voice low, "were you really ready to die for Christ back there?"

"Yes, Eric, I was. Only don't think that makes me noble or anything. It was the Holy Spirit doing the work, not me. And it's fairly easy to die for Christ. It's living for Him that's hard."

"If we survive the night, I'm going to have to do that harder thing, too."

"What?" she gasped, staring up into his face.

"After you were gone, I . . . well, I came— or was driven— to the conclusion that I had a lot of bad reasons to live, but Jesus was the only good reason to die."

If he had not been holding her she would have lost all strength and rolled off the ledge. "You mean you—? Really?"

He nodded. "Yeah, I'm kind of astonished, too. I wonder if Jesus knows what a load He's taken on with me."

"Oh, He knows, He knows, and He'll carry it gladly!" She embraced him all the harder. "Welcome home, my brother, welcome home!"

"Be it ever so humble," he returned, suddenly distracted. "Or insecure. Shh. Listen."

Through the woods above them boots sounded heavily in the undergrowth. Eric and Sandy clung together, fearing to breathe, as the footsteps halted on the grassy summit, scarcely thirty feet over their heads.

"You think they went this-a way?" one rough voice said.

"Hard to tell," another replied. "Gotta look, anyway. What's down there, over the cliff? Gimme the light."

She thought her teeth would crumble, she was gritting them so hard.

The beam of a lantern caught the top of a tree whose roots clung to the side of the hill a little way down from where they stood. "Rock face," said the apparent holder of the lantern. "Steep."

"What's this here?" said the other. "A crack below this bush."

Eric's arms tightened on her body.

"Hold the light out farther and lemme see."

The shadows wheeled crazily just within her field of vision.

Please, Father, don't let them see—!

"Think they coulda got down that way?" the voice with the lantern said.

"Naw . . . " the first voice replied. "They're a coupla yuppies. They'd gone down that way, all them bushes'd be tore out and broke."

So that's why . . .

"And they'd be all broke to pieces at the bottom," his partner agreed, laughing maliciously. "Don't care to try it myself."

"Me, neither. Hell, it's late and I'm tired of this wild goose chase. Get on the radio and ask Falcon Seven-Eight-Nine if we can come in."

Her ears picked up the sound of a hand knocking against plastic.

"Damn thing won't work," said the second voice.

"It's the hills. Well, let's hoof it back and tell the squad they ain't here." The footsteps began to move away.

She nearly laughed with relief until, with the soft, surreptitious sound of a mouse in a cupboard, a tiny stone rolled loose under their feet.

The footsteps halted. "What was that?" The voice was sharp, suspicious.

"Sounds like it came from over there."

"No, dammit, it was down the cliff. Something's down there. I'm goin' to see."

At Eric's sign, Sandy pressed herself to the wall. Swiftly and silently he bent down and picked up a stone. Leaning out from the face, he hooked the missile across and up the hillside to fall somewhere with a crash, among thick vegetation, from the sound of it.

"There it went again!" said the first voice. "Dammit, it was over there, in the trees! Let's go!" The boots pounded off.

Eric and Sandy remained where they were. For what seemed an eternity they stood, pressed together, staring, listening, saying not a word.

"Come on," he whispered at last. "You're not too stiff, are you?"

"For what?"

"Straight downhill. It's steep but I think we can manage it. I could see the river from the top, so we're headed in the right direction."

"Oh! . . . Well, *excelsior!*"

"I said *down* hill." And to hear him dryly correcting her Latin was the second-happiest thing she'd heard all night.

CHAPTER D.17

OW DID ERIC MANAGE with that gun slung over his shoulder? They were picking their way along the slope sideways as much as down, to avoid crashing to the valley floor in an avalanche of scree. But he appeared to take handling the weapon as second nature.

Praise heaven, the next rise turned out not to be as steep. After wading a small stream, they plunged into the trees. The slender trunks didn't provide much cover. She prayed it would be enough.

"Sandy, I'm thinking," he said after a while, "when we get to the road, we need to find a phone and call the police as soon as possible."

"Do you think they can stop those guys before most of them head home?"

"Don't know, but we have to try. Here, this way. It's not as blocked."

It was still demanding. Not for the first time she was grateful that a lifetime of singing had developed her lungs.

Apparently he'd developed a few skills, too. "Eric," she whispered, "where'd you learn to throw like that? That rock must have gone over a hundred feet. High school center fielder?"

"No. Vietnam. Hand grenades."

Oh. Simple as that.

ERIC STOOD motionless in the dark behind a slender maple, the AK-47 cradled in his arms. Down the slope a little way Sandy was concealed in the undergrowth, attending to the call of nature.

"Thanks for standing guard," she said as she rejoined him.

"Don't mention it."

She took a step to continue up the hillside but he touched her arm and brought her back beside him. "Look over there," he said, indicating the ridges over which they'd fled.

"Yes?"

"See anything?"

"No . . . not really."

"I've been watching those hills the past three or four minutes and I haven't seen anything either."

"Do you think Hardt's called off the search?"

"Not permanently, but for tonight, I think so."

"Waiting for daylight to pick up our bodies, maybe."

"Maybe." He glanced down at the rifle. "Thank God if it's true. I was afraid I might have to use this thing."

"Could you if you had to?"

"Oh, yeah. We captured enough of them off the Viet Cong . . . Let's get moving." He laughed, low. "We're not out of the woods yet."

JUST A HUNDRED *feet more.* Panting, Sandy raised her eyes to the top of the hill. *And the rate we're going, it'll take the rest of the night.* The moonlight, now coming more from the west, didn't reach this side of the mountain, and they had to do their best relying on whatever skyshine filtered through the trees. It was just possible their pursuers were simply lying low, waiting for them to use the lantern.

Wait a minute. Was that an actual track a little above them?

It was. And though it crisscrossed the hillside at least they could walk upright side by side for a while.

They split the second chocolate bar, then for several minutes Eric kept silent. It wasn't caution, she felt. Something else.

"Eric, are you all right?"

"Yes. Just thinking."

"About what?"

"My dad. And Jesus."

She waited.

"You know how they say, 'Jesus died for your sins'? I always resented it."

"Uh-huh?"

"Yes. Like Jesus was saying, 'See what you made Me do?' Mean and vindictive. Like the time Paul and I were arguing in the back seat and Poppa reached over to smack us and ran the car into the ditch. All our fault. If we'd gotten allowances I'm sure he would have made us pay for the damage."

"I see. Just more guilt and no good news."

"Right. Who needs that? But now I'm wondering if Poppa ever knew Jesus at all. I wish I knew where he was. I'd tell him what I know now."

"And maybe forgive him?" she hazarded the question.

He took a deep breath. "Yes. Even maybe forgive him." He shook his head. "Unbelievable. I never thought I'd say that."

"That's the Holy Spirit at work."

He squeezed her hand as they topped the hill and came out onto a grassy plateau. The westering moon sailed above the opposite ridge, penetrating the spaces between the thinning trees with a dull silver shine. Curtains of cloud, drifting in from the northwest, reflected the moon's glow like a portent. She hoped they didn't mean rain.

She glanced back. Still no sign of search from the hills behind.

"Just a second," Eric said, slipping into a clump of bushes. Discreetly, she walked on a few yards and waited. It was a good time to remove the sliver of rock that had worked its way into her shoe.

Presently he emerged. Signaling her to stay where she was, he turned back the way they had come and looked first one way, then the other.

Blast it, that pebble or whatever it was was still in there. Standing on one foot in the turf, she took the shoe off again and emptied it out, keeping her eyes on him to help her maintain her balance.

Apparently satisfied with what he had seen, he came towards her, his form distinct in the moonlight. Ages ago he'd lost the bandage she'd made him, and the wound in his left temple was beginning to bleed. On his right cheekbone sat an appalling bruise, murky and swollen. His dark hair stood out from his head pollen-streaked and twig-torn, and his beard was dusty with broken leaves. What color his tee-shirt had been that afternoon she couldn't remember and couldn't tell from the way it looked now, and his calves and arms were so marked with lacerations he looked as if he'd been scourged. He held the automatic rifle loosely, as if he would gladly have surrendered it to his would-be executioner, now lying dead a few miles away.

I probably look as bad. I—

She stopped herself in wonder, put her foot to the ground, and dropped the shoe.

What? His face. His eyes. He looks just like— Oh, thank You, Lord Jesus, You've given him that look!

"SANDY, WHAT'S wrong?"

Beside her on the grass lay her tennis shoe, a pale dot dropped and disregarded in the fitful moonlight. She was staring at him, her hands to her mouth.

"What is it?" he whispered. "What do you see?"

His impulse was to turn and see if he'd been wrong, if a pursuer was coming at them after all. But something in her eyes kept him absolutely still and focussed his whole attention on her rapt countenance.

That's it again! That look I saw at the Civic Museum. And when I gave her the El Greco poster. What does it mean? What does it mean!

He shook off the spell and approached her. Laying his hands on her shoulders, he searched her face. "Sandy, tell me, what is it?"

"Eric," she said, taking a deep breath, "has anyone ever told you . . . you look like an Old Master?"

CHAPTER D.18

"LOOK, THERE'S THE RIVER," Eric said. In the valley not far below them a plume of mist shimmered over the surface of the water like the tail of a long-haired cat, welling up in places to cover what had to be a two-lane highway. Next to Sandy's appearance back in that cell, he doubted he'd been this glad to see anything in his life.

"Thank . . .. God," she panted. "And . . . the road. Thank God."

"And praise God it's on this side of the river." He took her hand. "After that bridge over there," he said, pointing a little to the north, "see, it veers off."

"Is that . . . the highway . . . we were on? Is that . . . our 'washed-out' . . . bridge?"

"Probably not. Ready for the homestretch?"

She took a ragged breath, as if she couldn't get enough air into her lungs. "Eric, I . . . I don't want to be a wimp . . . but I'm not sure. Really cold . . . and tired . . ."

She was swaying where she stood. Alarmed, he drew her to his side. "Don't! It's only—"

Was there any place they could rest? Yes, down the slope a little lay an area of deeper darkness where they might be able to hunker down and hide.

"Can you make it down there?"

"I think so . . . Yes."

In the little hollow, they nestled into a pile of last year's leaves. Pulling her onto his lap and circling her with his arms, he said, "Sleep, if you can."

"But we need to tell . . ."

"Shh." He stroked her dirt-smeared face, gently, so not to give her pain from the cuts she had suffered. "We can't do anything if we run ourselves dead. Sleep."

She tucked her head into the hollow of his shoulder and closed her eyes. In a few short minutes he felt her body relax.

He remained awake and vigilant, his gaze patrolling the road and river below them and the slopes of the opposite hills. The moon had disappeared behind the bank of clouds creeping across the sky from the northwest. Never mind, he'd long since gotten his night eyes, and there wouldn't be any moving for them for a while.

He looked at the woman in his arms and softly kissed her tangled hair. Years since, his mother had held him so, safe and protected, before everything changed, before he had to grow up quickly and be Momma's Little Man.

Before I started running from You, Lord. I'm not running anymore.

On her smudged cheeks her lashes fluttered, soft with dreams. How beautiful she was! His diamond. His star. Love like a wall of water from a broken dam thundered through his being, till he was certain she'd feel it surging from him into her and surely wake. But she rested quietly, at peace.

For the first time since they'd been taken captive he allowed himself to consider what would happen after their ordeal was over. He'd just as soon hand the whole mess over to law enforcement and walk away. It wouldn't be like that, of course. There'd be questions upon questions, from state and local police, probably from the ATF and the FBI. They'd be called on to testify at Hardt's— Rutherford's?— trial. And publicity. Whoa, would there be publicity. Ruefully, he shook his head. Notoriety was great when it came from having a project featured in *Design Mode* magazine. But the kind of exposure they'd get now … Oh, well. There was nothing for it but to brave it out.

We did it last fall, we can do it again.

With God's help, he realized. Of course, now he'd have God's help.

In his arms Sandy mumbled something in her sleep, then once more was still.

Their relationship wouldn't be a secret anymore. Would she still want it to be, after the change that had been worked in him tonight? *I'm a Christian now,* he thought in wide-eyed wonder. *I'm actually a Christian!*

Sandy's joy in the revelation had been unmistakable.

Lord, he admitted, *that's one obstacle down.*

But what would happen after everyone knew they were a couple? Could they go on as they had since January? Or worse, as they had since mid-July? Hardly touching each other, with no hope of ever…

Please, God, no. I'm not that strong. I couldn't stand it.

There was only one solution. Only, wouldn't that be unfair to her? That's what he'd always believed.

If you really love this woman, you'll let her remain free.

The instant the thought came into his mind he recognized it for the cowardice it was. Not only was it cowardly, it was absurd. Free? Her vow that night after the Werner Edelstein concert echoed in his heart: *"If something came between us and we had to separate … I would go on loving only you …"*

She could *never* be free of him, she had no desire to be, and he could not imagine life free of her. Only together did freedom have any meaning at all.

If we did it, it would only be letting everyone know what's already true about us. "Before God and all the neighbors," as she put it …

He raised his eyes to the heavens. Above him the firmament, yet unclouded, was studded with a million smiling stars. Trembling with awe-filled joy, he marvelled at the step he was committing himself to take.

Yes, Lord, he promised, *as soon as this is settled, I'll do it.*

"SANDY, QUICK, wake up!"

A voice from nowhere jarred her. She was in the office, trying to get some work done, but somebody had left a lumpy bag of marble samples on her chair. Phil Duggins was standing near her saying, "You can't move those, it's all part of the plan," and he had to be referring to the study for Fort Randolph City, but that wasn't started yet, and—

"Sandy, please, wake up!" Hands pulled her to her feet. Her eyes flew open. Eric's face confronted hers, his eyes urgent and wide. "Look, over there," he said, pointing to her left. "Is that headlights?"

Fully roused, she looked. It *was* a vehicle of some kind, some two or three miles distant, its lights visible between the trunks of the trees, piercing the mist, creeping downhill along the twisting road. "Yes!"

Eric slung the rifle over his shoulder, grabbed her hand, and said, "Come on!"

It was maybe seventy yards down to the roadbed, and her impression was that they traversed most of it slamming from tree to tree or else sliding on their rears. Why had she thought that car was moving slowly? Now when its lights were visible at all, they seemed to be racing up and down the highway's curves. In a minute it would pass by and be away over the bridge, and if that happened she couldn't take one more step.

"Eric, why are you stopping?" They had reached the rim of the bank above the road; with a scramble of another ten feet or so they could be on the pavement. Down the fog-bound grade the car was quickly approaching, its windshield almost level with their eyes. They'd lose it if they didn't reach the road in time.

"Quick," he said, "the lantern!"

He took it and blinked out a signal.

Miraculously, the car slowed, rolled past them, and came to a stop just short of the bridge. A light on the roof came on and began to rotate, casting a weird scarlet glow through the mist onto the trees at the road's edge.

Disregarding all caution, they slid down the nearly-vertical bank, landing splay-footed on the gravel shoulder.

"Payne County Sheriff's Department" read the legend on the side of the black and white sedan. Eric held her back. "Wait a minute," he said, panting. "We'd . . . we'd better leave the gun here."

He laid it down on the gravel at the side of the road. Then, as if they'd been released by a bow, they pelted towards the patrol car, she nearly tripping over herself with relief.

The officer stood silhouetted beside the vehicle, his handgun drawn, his flashlight shining in their faces. His own face was obscured by the brim of his hat and it was impossible to tell his expression.

"Whoa! Stay right there!"

They halted in their tracks.

We could be anybody. Hijackers. Moonshiners. Anything.

She put her hands in the air. Eric did the same.

Still covering them, the lawman approached. Apparently satisfied that they were harmless, he lowered the flashlight and holstered his gun.

"Sheriff," said Eric, gasping for breath, "so glad to see you— we were kidnapped— up in the hills—"

"—Escaped, maybe three hours ago—"

"—Caves, his hideout, up in the hills—"

"—An atomic bomb, he's got an A-bomb— he'll use it—"

"—Over a thousand men, all armed— automatic rifles, massive arsenal—"

"—You need to— need to—" She put her fist to her side and bent double. Eric's hands were on his knees; his head was down, his mouth open and panting.

"Whoa there!" exclaimed the man in the hat. "Why don't you two get in and catch your breath? Then you can tell me what this is all about."

He opened the back door of the black and white. Sandy, then Eric, tumbled in, and he closed it behind them. The dark green vinyl upholstery was hard and spartan and on the driver's side the back seat was piled with paperwork, crowding them into the remaining space. She didn't care. Resting her forehead against the back of the front seat, she nearly sobbed. "We're safe, Eric, we're safe, we're safe!"

Eric was looking through the rear window. "He's picking up the gun."

The man brought the rifle back to the cruiser and put it in the trunk. He opened the driver's side door, and got in.

"Here's a blanket if you're cold," he said, handing it over his shoulder.

Eric wrapped it around them both.

"All settled?" the man in the front seat asked. He switched on the dome light and consulted a clipboard. "You gave us quite a chase, didn't you? We've been looking for you two all night."

He turned around. Sandy saw his face and screamed.

It was Nick Hardt.

CHAPTER D.19

"*W*HOOOOOOO-WEEEEEE!*" It came out somewhere between a whistle and a laugh. "I've been told my face'd stop a clock, but it's never gotten a reaction like that! What on earth did you do that for, young lady?" The crewcut, blue-eyed man screwed his little finger in his ear and made a show of clearing it.

"You're not—? I'm sorry— I thought you were— you look like—"

My poor Sandy!

"It's true, sir," Eric broke in. "You— you look just like the man we've been running from all night, and now you say you've been looking for us. What were we supposed to think?"

The lawman went sober. "I see." He showed them his identification card. "My name's Ken Rutherford and I'm the sheriff of this county."

"Whew! You've got to help us," Eric rushed to say, "It's like we were telling you, there's a man up in the hills, he needs to be stopped—"

"Hold on, son!" Rutherford put up his hand. "Before all that, who are you?"

It felt strange to be called "son" by someone who couldn't be more than ten years his senior. Odd, and oddly comforting.

"I'm Eric Baumann." He spelled it out. "And this is my girlfriend, Sandy Beichten."

The sheriff checked his clipboard. "Yep, that's you all right. We got a call a few hours ago from the McAllister County sheriff's department, saying some summer people down in Osceomenie Falls were missing a couple of out of town guests and could we keep an eye out for you."

"Jen and Allen Watkins," Eric confirmed. Lord forgive him— He hadn't spared them a thought all night.

"Well, that's one problem solved." He got someone— Eric guessed it was a dispatcher— on the radio. "Yep, Junie, tell John they're kinda beat up but in one piece. Call those summer folks down in Osceomenie Falls, if you don't think they'd mind being woke up at this hour."

"They won't mind," Eric said.

The sheriff signed off. "Got my first aid kit here," he said, turning around again. "That's quite a cut you got there, young lady. And you're no oil painting yourself, son." He tended to their facial injuries the best he could. "Your friends got a doctor here?"

"I think so," Eric said.

"Get yourselves checked out soon's you can." He started the cruiser and drove across the bridge and on down the twisting highway. "I'll take you over to the McAllister County sheriff's office in Zicksburg. They'll see you get down to Osceomenie Falls. Meantime, let's have your story. Maybe that'll help us solve my other problem."

"What's that, Sheriff?" Sandy asked.

"Came on my shift ten last night, picked up a report of suspicious activity in both counties. Fella living along Shucks Lane— it doesn't lead to anything but farm fields— called in saying he'd been seeing heavy traffic along there Thursday and Friday. Cars going in one way and none of them coming back the other. Then down at Osceomenie Falls and over here at Lewis Springs we've had out-of-state fellas checking into motels and parking their cars, but never sleeping in the beds. Parking other places, too, overnight, and the cars just stayed put all weekend. Merchants were getting annoyed, all these fellas who weren't customers taking up their parking spaces."

"So they called and complained?" asked Sandy.

"Yep. Report said folks in town last Thursday and Friday were noticing groups of visitors just standing on the street corners, and somebody'd come by and pick them up and drive off. White Econoline delivery vans, no markings, no windows. And just men, no families like you'd expect over Labor Day. Disappearing into thin air." He shook his head. "Heck, you'd think they'd-a let us know sooner . . . "

"Sheriff," said Eric, taking a deep breath, "we can tell you where all those men went."

❈

DRIFTING IN and out of sleep, every bone in her body its own separate ache, Sandy listened but vaguely, as if from a thousand miles away. "Hold up," Sheriff Rutherford's voice made her pay attention a few minutes later. "You're sure he said they'd *start* moving out an hour or two before dawn?"

"Absolutely sure," Eric said.

Rutherford considered a moment. "Maybe they don't have that many vans, and they have to bring them down in relays . . . Still, we don't have a lot of time. Sun rises around 6:30 and it's nearly 4:00 a.m. now. You think you could remember where those caves are?"

Sandy roused herself and sat up. "The old McCool place. Like Eric said, the leader calls himself Nick Hardt, but it's likely his real name is Cole Rutherford."

Oh-oh. She clapped her hand to her mouth.

"Cole's back? You've seen Cole?"

"Sheriff, I'm sorry if he's a cousin or something," she said nervously. "But it's true."

"Closer than that, young lady. I've got a younger brother named Cole. And Wava McCool was my grandmother. And since you took me for him—"

"I'm sorry. I didn't mean—"

"No need to apologize. I know what Cole was like. And Granny McCool, too. I'm sorry he's caused you two so much trouble. Now I suppose I'm going to have to cause him some."

He picked up the radio microphone and spoke into it. "Lila Rose, it's Ken. Raise every deputy we've got. Tell 'em to swear in some solid citizens; we're gonna need them. . . . No, I don't care when they're scheduled— *now*. And have Junie get John Sturgis over in McAllister and patch him through. And get me the chief of the state police on the horn. And the FBI as well."

"That boy's no early riser," said the woman's voice over the radio. "Not from what I hear." She laughed.

"Well, if he's not up now, he's gonna be."

"So what— tell— Ken?" The voice on the other end was starting to break up.

"That we got us a major domestic terrorism situation on our hands and he'd better pitch in if he doesn't want his name in the papers the wrong way."

A question from the radio. Something that sounded like " . . . in charge?"

"The ringleader?" Sheriff Rutherford hesitated. "Dammit, I know my duty," he said under his breath. He spoke into the mike again. "Lila, the alleged ringleader's Cole Rutherford."

A crackle Sandy couldn't make out.

Apparently the sheriff could. "You heard me, my long-lost black sheep brother."

The radio squawked in reply.

"No kidding. No, I won't be enjoying myself. Out."

The tires squealed as he did a U-turn. "Sorry, folks, but I can't get you to Zicksburg. That's more'n fifteen, twenty miles from here. I'll try and drop you over here in Lewis Springs before the action starts. You can get a motel room there."

"Two motel rooms," said Sandy, feeling prudish as soon as she said it. She changed the subject. "But what will you do? If it's not confidential police business, I mean."

"You leave that to us," the sheriff said grimly. "But you two be careful who you tell about that nuke. Don't want to start a panic."

The dark gray predawn hills flung themselves behind as the cruiser roared up the curving road.

CHAPTER D.20

"**O**W!" HIS TAILBONE HIT the barely-upholstered seat hard as the cruiser bounced through a pothole. It hurt more than it had the right to.

"Eric, what's wrong?"

"You okay back there?" Sheriff Rutherford asked.

"Sure, I . . . well, I hate to admit it, but I think last night is catching up with me."

The sheriff chuckled. "That'll happen when the adrenaline runs out . . . But as I was saying, I haven't seen Cole more'n a time or two since he left in 1960. We heard he'd sold Bennett's Knob to somebody named Hardt a year or so later, but the new owner never did anything with it and the old place went to ruin."

"It's still there, Sheriff," Eric replied. "And there's a door in the back of the root cellar that leads to the caves I told you about."

"With a sliding jelly cupboard to cover it," Sandy put in.

"You don't say! So there *are* caves under the house." Ken Rutherford shook his head. "We heard tell there was, but put it down to family legend. Story goes our great-granduncle Ephraim Bennett hid runaway slaves in there."

"You're kidding," protested Eric. The irony made him want to howl.

"No, son, why should I kid?" said Rutherford, sounding a little offended. "Uncle Ephraim was pro-Union and anti-slavery through and through."

"It's not that, Sheriff. It's thinking what your brother Cole— Nick Hardt— is doing in them now."

"They kept telling me the place was haunted," said Sandy. "Maybe it's old Uncle Ephraim. He'd hate what they're doing in there, it's so . . . so . . . "

"Could be," said Rutherford with a seriousness that surprised him. "Found him murdered right there on the property and they never found out who did it. He never got married— didn't have a will— and next day his younger brother John Joseph marches home from the Confederate Army and the whole property goes to him, no questions asked."

"And he was your grandmother's father?" asked Eric.

"Yep. I got the good Lord's own blessing in advance when my mama married my dad. He's ready to accept anybody, provided they treat him fair. I take after him, I guess. Cole, now, he's more like Granny McCool. Pretty much lived with her once he turned twelve."

"Maybe that's when he discovered the caves," Sandy said. "Must have figured out how that cupboard works."

"Could be." The next few miles, barring brief radio exchanges with other law enforcement personnel, the sheriff said nothing. Outside the car window, the rocky hills faded from black to a chilly gray. Eric checked his watch. Stopped.

"Sandy, what time is it?" he said, low.

"4:26."

Damn, they were cutting it close.

"Eric," she whispered, "how can he get enough men to arrest them all? Won't most of them get away?"

Rutherford had good hearing, apparently, for he answered, "Don't you worry about that, young lady. We'll set up a coupla roadblocks where the road from the farm comes down. Nice narrow place; we won't have to worry about any of them fleeing into the woods. I still mean to get you two someplace out of harm's way first. Which reminds me, son. Why was Cole so interested in you?"

Eric squirmed on the hard vinyl seat. For the first time he noticed there were no inside handles on their doors. The window cranks were missing as well.

Sandy spoke up. "He found out how good Eric is. Believe it or not, your brother's got good taste in design. Only the best for his new society, I suppose."

Gratefully, he squeezed her hand.

"That so? I wondered because Cole was always good at getting other kids to do his dirty work, and generally he'd get something on them first."

"Really? Wow!" she said. "And here's a question I had . . . "

Deliberately changing the subject, bless her. What a relief that Rutherford was content to go along with it.

"What's that?" the sheriff said.

"Nick Hardt— Cole— said he was married, but back in 1970 his wife was killed by a black man. Is that true?"

"Which part? Yep, he was married. A local girl. They eloped after he came home to visit in '63 or so, and I never saw her since. Never knew more about her killing but what I read in the newspapers. According to them, that poor fella was a Federal Census worker and there wasn't a speck of evidence he'd even been in the house, let alone in the bedroom. I guess Cole ruined his life for him, even if he couldn't send him to the chair." He shook his head.

"Any idea who did do it?" she asked.

"None at all."

But there was something in the way he said it that made Eric suspect Ken Rutherford had a good theory, and it wasn't to his brother's credit.

"What's got me wondering," Eric said, "is how he's spending his money."

"What do you mean?" Sandy asked.

"Well, think of it. He's a successful developer, he's got that gold mine in South Dakota—"

"Wait a minute," she interrupted. "Didn't those lawyers say his share in that went to some nephew?"

"Nephew?" said Rutherford. "No nephews on his wife's side, I know that for sure, and my kids are both girls."

"So that was another fake identity," Eric concluded. "Okay, so there's that squirrelled away someplace, and he inherited a good deal of money and property from your grandma. He's got millions to spend, but there's nothing luxurious about the way they're subsisting up there. No electricity in most of it and living on pork and beans and cave water. Their two-way radios don't work in the cave—"

"—They do all their communications by runner," Sandy broke in.

"—and even outside they can't rely on the signal."

"Reception's none too good up here," said Rutherford, "unless you got the right equipment." He gave his radio an affectionate pat.

Eric let that go without comment. "So it's got to mean— Sandy, remember all that storage he wanted for guns and ammo when he first came to us?"

"You're right. Even if he did spend a mint on that lab and the bombs he's building, I doubt he'd hold back on buying those precious guns he was talking about last year."

"Yes. Sheriff, we know he has Kalashnikovs, fully automatic. But besides that, he has to have an enormous arsenal up there. We didn't see it, but it stands to reason."

"You may be onto something," said Ken. "Cole had a real hankering after guns and explosives when he was a boy; wouldn't surprise me at all if he'd bought up a lot of them. We'll come ready for that, never you fear.

"But what I was saying before, he also liked sniffing out dirt on people. Whooooo-wheeee! What that boy could find out!"

Eric's stomach sank. *This is it. He'll do the Lieutenant Columbo thing and make me confess.*

But Rutherford asked him no questions. "There was this one time . . . " and he launched into a story about how Cole had inveigled some other boys into throwing fireworks off the roof of the Negro schoolhouse into the all-black crowd during the speeches one Fourth of July.

"It was after that, Mama and Daddy washed their hands of him." He sighed. "Guess he's on my hands now."

CHAPTER D.21

A FRESH BREEZE DRIFTED IN through the police car's open rear doors. For the tenth time in the past half hour Sandy checked her watch. 7:23 on a chilly, gray, misty morning, and there she and Eric were, stashed in the backseat of a McAllister County cruiser at the diversion point a mile down from the police roadblocks. Out of the action. Chilly, but safe.

Eric was stretched out dozing against the right hand doorpost, his arms folded and his long legs hanging over the seat, competing with hers for space on her side of the car. She didn't mind— much.

She joggled his knee. "How close is the nearest ATF office?"

"Huh?" he said, opening his eyes a crack.

"Alcohol, Tobacco and Firearms. Where are they?"

"No idea. I think they just have to be notified; they don't send anybody to help with the arrests."

"You think he believed us about that bomb?"

He shrugged. "I'd say so. Besides, I didn't really believe it myself, at first." He shifted a little and closed his eyes.

That wasn't the answer she wanted.

She shivered. Her torn-off tee-shirt barely covered her midriff but they couldn't shut the doors: if they did they'd be like prisoners, trapped inside. She pulled up her legs and supported herself against the left side of the car, wishing she and Eric could be holding each other. But there were too many cops around, and he'd said he was in no mood for him and her to be treated like college kids parked in Lovers Lane. She clamped her own folded arms tight against her middle and settled herself to think.

A yellow school bus rolled past, then another, each window dotted with a man's head, White Way followers under arrest and headed to the armory at

Lewis Springs for processing. State highway patrol cars and sheriff's department cruisers marked with the insignia of several surrounding counties raced through, all heading towards the roadblock where, if Ken's plan was going well, Hardt's unsuspecting followers were coming down the mountain and landing in the net of the law. Once, a state car stopped and a patrolman handed them each a sweatshirt printed STATE POLICE BARRACKS. She was practically drowning in hers and Eric's hands and wrists looked huge and knobbly sticking out of his, but at least they provided some warmth.

"Eric, I'm going to stretch my legs a little."

"Okay." He got out and stretched too, then drew her to him, his arm around her shoulders.

Up on Bennett's Knob the low clouds sat askew like a gray Beatles wig. Down the road nearby, a state trooper directed the detour with his phosphorus flare, gobbets of flame splashing off as he waved an oncoming car into a Y-turn and back the way it had come.

What would it take to set off that atom bomb? What if it was a lot less than even Dr. Turner believed?

"Are you hungry?" Eric asked.

She jumped. Recovering, she said, "You could say that. Can't be helped." She addressed her rumbling stomach: "Shut up, you!"

"I'm going to ask that trooper if anybody's got anything for us to eat. Like some d—"

"Don't say it!"

"—drinks of orange juice. What did you think I was going to say?" He smiled mischievously and strolled over.

In a few minutes he was back. "Trooper said he'd radio for somebody to bring something for us."

"Okay."

BACK IN THE CAR, Eric yawned as more school busses, all filled with unmasked men, drove by. His watch said 8:43. Reeling them in . . . Sheriff Rutherford had had a hunch the White Way van drivers would mostly be locals the police could convince to cooperate in exchange for leniency and it looked as if he was right. *"Keep on delivering those out-of-towners down, boys, and keep your mouths shut . . ."* He closed his eyes again and dozed.

"Hey," Sandy said.

He opened an eye. She was on her knees, looking out the rear window. "Car coming."

"Hope it's food," he replied. "I'm so empty my front's saying hello to my spine."

A cramp stabbed through his right calf. He was out of the car rubbing the place when the Payne County cruiser pulled up on the shoulder opposite.

"Morning," the deputy behind the wheel greeted him as he hobbled over. "Sheriff thought you two might be hungry." He passed a white box through his open window, followed by two Styrofoam cups. "Here's coffee, too."

"Thanks. Sandy!" he called. "They brought coffee! And—?"

"Sweet rolls from Emmett's," said the deputy. "Over in Rains Overlook."

"Nice. We'll have to drop by once we get there."

"Did somebody say 'sweet rolls'?" said Sandy, joining him and taking one. "Thank you, I'm starving!"

For a minute, they did nothing but eat. Then she asked, "What's the news down there at the roadblocks?"

"They didn't leave the radio on for you?"

"No," said Eric.

"Well," said the deputy, "we've already sent over five hundred to Lewis Springs for processing, and that doesn't count the ones still waiting in the busses."

"So the locals found out fast where their real loyalties lie?" Sandy suggested.

"Guess so," said the deputy. "We found the field off Shucks Lane where the out of towners' cars are parked and blocked it, so they can't go anywhere even if they come down on foot."

"Think that might happen?" asked Eric. "There's at least one other entrance to those caves, but I couldn't tell you where it is."

"I wouldn't worry about that," said the deputy. "Once these good ole boys hear what they're up against, they're plenty ready to talk. One of 'em's leading a patrol of our guys up there already."

"But what about Hardt— I mean, Cole Rutherford?" she asked. "Any sign of him yet?"

"Nope, but we'll get him. So you've seen him to talk to?"

"Yes, we have," said Eric.

The deputy shook his head. "Some folks around here won't be sorry to see him get his. Especially not the Dozier boys, after what he did to their sister Eileen."

"Eileen?" asked Sandy.

"Cole's wife. If he didn't kill her, it wasn't for lack of trying."

"I got the impression," said Eric slowly, "that his brother feels the same."

The deputy coughed and looked away. "Well, gotta be getting back. You two keep the rest of those rolls."

"Great!" said Sandy. He followed her back to the other cruiser. How cute she looked in that gigantic man's sweatshirt! Going around to her side, she got in with the bakery box and scooted towards him on the seat, reaching out, fingers beckoning. "Hand me my coffee, will you?"

"Here it is," he said, ducking down to give it to her. "Careful, it's—"

Air and ground gave an absurd hiccup and he lost his balance, falling into the car on top of her. The hot coffee flew out of his grasp; she cried out. A pattering like solid rain hit the car roof over his head, struck and ricocheted off the pavement, dug into the backs of his legs like a cat was using them to sharpen its claws. Then, drowning out the drumming of the stones, a deep, earth-engulfing roar swelled around and through him and quickly passed, resolving itself into a dull, ominous silence.

"Whoa," came the deputy's voice from across the road. "Whoa!" A car door slammed. "You two okay?"

Under him, another voice: "Ow! My leg! Let me up, I have to see!"

Grabbing hold of the door frame, he regained his feet, then helped Sandy out.

"Would ya look at that!" marvelled the deputy, pointing.

They wheeled around. The cloud cover over the top of Bennett's Knob had begun to lift as the day warmed. But on the far side of the mountain a thick, churning, black pillar of smoke and dust rose, roiling up and darkening the morning sky. The acrid stink of it assaulted his senses, bringing the water to his eyes.

"Eric, is it—?" Sandy grabbed his arm and clung to him. "It's not a mushroom cloud, is it? Is it?"

"No, I don't think so." He rubbed his eyes and looked again. "Just regular smoke."

"Not a mushroom," she said, slipping her trembling hand into his. "Thank God, that means that bomb wasn't real after all?"

"Or it was far enough from his munitions cache." He pulled her to him and gave a her a comforting squeeze. "It's buried under tons of rubble now, anyway."

"You're sure?" She pulled away and stared at the mountainside.

"Sandy? It's okay. Assuming Hardt didn't blow himself up, too, they'll arrest him and we'll be home free."

"Will we?" she murmured. "I don't know."

"Don't know what?"

But before he could get an answer, the radio in the Payne County cruiser squawked into life and the deputy dived in to answer it. Four or five police cars, all with different markings, roared up from the direction of the roadblock. Grabbing Sandy by the arm, he scrambled to the shoulder as the cars, lights blazing, streaked past them, swerved around the detour car, and sped sirenless down the highway.

The last one, its side emblazoned "PAYNE COUNTY SHERIFF'S DEPARTMENT," screeched to a halt. Both front doors flew open and Rutherford launched himself out of the driver's seat and ran up to his deputy, who sat behind the wheel of his car, open-mouthed in amazement or shock at what he was hearing over the radio. Out of the passenger side of the sheriff's cruiser another deputy emerged and pelted across the road towards the McAllister County car where Eric and Sandy had been sheltering. Before they could react, he slammed the rear doors, jumped in, and in a flurry of gravel tore out and was gone.

"Somebody talked . . ." gasped Rutherford to his deputy. "He escaped . . . back way . . . "

The man gunned his vehicle and tore off as well.

"Hey!" Eric protested. "Where are we supposed—?"

Rutherford sprinted away from them, towards the patrolman manning the roadblock.

"It's okay!" Sandy said, grabbing Eric's arm and tugging him across to Rutherford's vacant cruiser. She yanked open the back passenger door. "Quick, get in!"

"What?"

"Get in!" She scrambled in and, not pausing to think, he followed after. "Shut the door, quick!" she cried.

"I can't," he said, "there's no inside handle! Wait a minute, the armrest . . . " He pulled the door to just as Rutherford flung himself into the driver's seat. The car surged forward like a cougar after its prey. Eric squeezed her hand but neither of them spoke; their ears were tuned only to the exchange going on over the radio.

"Lila, notify all agencies. We think he got away, somebody must have tipped him off . . . yes, before the explosion . . . one of the last suspects down said his Jeep was missing . . . Ten to one he's taking the old Bennett's Knob logging road down, but just in case, here's the description, listen up: 1972 Willys Jeep, dirty white, closed, vinyl top. . . . You know what he looks like."

"Any law enforcement personnel down?" the dispatcher asked, her voice worried.

"No, our men hadn't gotten that close when those weapons went up. Some cuts and bruises, but okay otherwise."

"Praise God!" Sandy exclaimed.

"*Crap!* No, Lila, I wasn't talking to you," the sheriff said into the microphone. "Hold on a minute."

He caught Sandy's attention in the rear view mirror. "Beg pardon for swearing like that, young lady, but it's damn inconvenient having civilians along on a run like this."

Eric's bored his eyes into her but she ignored him. "I'm sorry, Sheriff."

"No, my fault, I forgot," Rutherford said grimly. "I should have got you to someplace safe hours ago. Maybe I still could—"

"No, you have to catch him," she interrupted. "We'll be all right. We just didn't want to be left behind."

Eric raised his eyebrows at her and said, "*We*"?

She smiled.

"Lila," said Rutherford, reactivating the mike, "tell Junie in McAllister I've got our civilian informants with me, in case their friends call. And tell all units my orders are to take Cole alive. He'll come across with what we need to know if I have to get Daddy back from Sun City to wale it out of him."

He signed off and hit the accelerator. Maintaining a silence so heavy Eric could practically feel it, he sped the cruiser along the twisting highway at what must have been over eighty miles per hour, turning the siren on to a lurp-lurp only when another vehicle was in sight. However many questions Eric had, he knew this wasn't the time to ask.

Several minutes later, Rutherford spoke up. "With any luck he won't know we're waiting for him. That logging road isn't only but dirt and gravel and he'll have to take it slow. When I let you out, go down the opposite slope and find yourselves a rock or a good-sized tree to hide behind, well away from the roadblock, okay?"

"Thanks, Sheriff," Eric said. "We'll keep out of the way, we promise. Sandy?" He jiggled her arm a little. "Won't we?"

"Oh! Yes, of course. We'll do . . . that."

He gave her a curious look. She smiled back and said, "Too bad those rolls are in the other car. I'm still hungry."

CHAPTER D.22

"AAA-TSCHOO!" Eric wiped his nose on his arm. "*Stchoo!*"

"Bless you!" whispered Sandy.

The dust and debris from the blast was really getting up his sinuses. It lay much thicker on this side of the mountain, and though the ground was relatively free of it under this massive rhododendron, his elbow must have joggled a branch and sent a shower of it down.

Dust or no dust, from under this bush they had a clear view across the county highway to where a steep, rut-scarred gravel lane met it at nearly a right angle. The lane's mouth was marked by a rusted octagonal sign, and on either side of the junction a wide swath of dirt was cleared, surely to allow the logging trucks with their long loads to make the turn.

But the bush wasn't a rock or a large tree, and there wasn't an officer in sight.

"I don't think we should be here," he said.

"Why not?" Sandy answered. "Ken said we should stay across the road and down the slope a little. That's where we are."

His body slipped a little on the uneven ground. "Come on," he said. "There's a place down farther where we'll be safer. And we can sit."

"You think we can see the logging trail from there?"

"Probably not. But it might be less dusty."

"I'm sorry, Eric," she said, laying a hand on his arm. "It really is bothering you. You go down. I'll stay here."

He wasn't leaving her. Something besides the dust was bothering him, and he could worry it out here as well as down the hill. Something he'd forgotten to say or do, something he should have remembered, but what it was he couldn't recall.

"Sandy," he whispered, "we did tell Ken everything, didn't we?"

"We must have. At least, you did. I fell asleep in the middle of it." She gave him an apologetic smile. "I'm sorry."

"Don't be, precious love. *Aaa-schoo!*"

"God bless you."

They fell silent. The minutes went by.

What is it I can't remember? What is it?

Sandy was too quiet. She'd risen to her knees and had that resolute set to her shoulders. This time, he wasn't sure he liked it.

"Sandy, what's up?"

She jumped.

"Relax, love. Whichever way he goes, they'll catch him. It'll be fine."

"I know they will," she said abstractedly, and went back to scanning the opposite hill.

A few minutes later, she stripped off her sweatshirt.

"Hot?" he asked.

She didn't answer.

What was that, up the slope of the mountain opposite? He rose up, too. "We'd better get lower," he said, taking her hand. "We don't want him to see us."

"He won't," she said, deftly eluding his grasp, "and we need to see him. Why? Is he coming?"

"I'm not sure. Up there. That flash. Your eyes are better than mine."

"Only a bird."

"Oh."

More waiting.

Come on, Hardt, you jerk!

"Do you think he has it with him?"

It was his turn to be startled. "Has what?"

"The bomb."

"I told you, it's buried. And if it isn't, Ken will take care of it."

"Hmm."

His knees were whining in protest, and his whole body wanted to join in. He stifled another sneeze. Then he saw something that made him grab her shoulder and point. This time it was no bird. Something white was flashing between the trees up the mountain, coming lower all the time. It could almost be mistaken for the leaves of a silver maple blowing in the wind. But it was progressing from left to right; barely visible but there nonetheless.

Nick Hardt coming down in his white Jeep.

It was almost over. Thank God.

HOLDING HER BREATH as if Hardt could hear her even from this distance, Sandy tracked the white spot that was his Jeep as it flashed between the slender trees, before being eaten up again by the undergrowth.

The note of the engine, now louder, now softer as it took the switchbacks of the road, seemed off. It wasn't just that the Jeep sounded old; there was a low arrhythmic clunk that made Sandy suspect damage. But what kind? She should have paid more attention back in college when Marvin was explaining the repairs he was making to his Firebird.

Too late for that now. The real question was, which way would Hardt turn at the stop sign? Ken Rutherford and his Payne County forces had set up their roadblock over the hill to her right, while John Sturgis of McAllister County, she'd heard, was taking his stand with his men down the road to her left.

She'd gotten a good look earlier at Sheriff Sturgis: a short-legged, broad-chested man who looked like a bantam weight boxer. He'd struck her as someone who put up with no nonsense and played things strictly by the book. Was there space in his universe for atomic bombs disguised as kitchen equipment? All things considered, she hoped it would be up to Cole Rutherford's brother Ken to confront him instead.

She could see the Jeep now, almost full on, still a ways up the slope but coming down the home stretch. The right front fender was curled back and steam was boiling off the radiator, as if he'd run into something.

Two heads in the windshield.

"Is that Turner without his mask?" whispered Eric.

"I think so. Eric, don't laugh, but I don't think that bomb is buried. I think he has it with him."

"Anything's possible. Don't worry: he won't get far with his Jeep banged up like that."

She waited, everything in her willing him to turn left.

And praise God, at the bottom of the track, he did— straight into his brother's legal arms.

Even so . . . "You're sure Ken understood what that bomb looks like?"

"Good grief, Sandy," he said, exasperated, "he's trained to understand things like that! Just let the police take care of it and stop worrying!"

She closed her mouth on her reply. *Maybe, but what about the rest of them?* "*Is it bigger than a breadbox?*" *Heck, no, it is a breadbox . . .*

He took her hand. "Let's stay here out of the way until it's over. They won't go without us."

"I'm not so sure," she said, trying to keep her tone casual. "We should get back closer to the roadblock. Under cover. Sheriff Rutherford forgot about us before; we don't want him to leave us behind again."

He sighed. "Okay, let's go."

"COLE RUTHERFORD! Drop the gun and surrender!"

Eric could hear Sheriff Ken on the bullhorn long before they drew even with the roadblock.

Now, in the underbrush a little below the margin of the road, Sandy agreed with a nod that they were close enough. The roadblock cruiser on their side of the road was less two car lengths away. Behind it crouched six or seven law enforcement officers, sheriff's department and state police both, their rifles at the ready. Sheriff Rutherford was there with the bullhorn, positioned low at the front of the cruiser behind a trooper with his rifle. Maybe five or six more officers were stationed behind the other car, he couldn't see for sure.

Maybe twenty feet up the slope opposite, the white Jeep hung smoking, its passenger side in close embrace with a tree. Crouched on the far side of the hood was Nick Hardt— or should he say Cole Rutherford?— brandishing what looked like the same Colt revolver he'd used on Pratt. He'd discarded the mask and held a large quilt-swaddled bundle in the crook of his left arm.

"Must have tried to make a run for it back up the mountain," he whispered to Sandy.

If I had my old M16, I could pick him off easily. Twenty-five yards, if that.

"Where's Dr. Turner?" she asked, just audible.

"No idea. Behind the cab?"

"Probably."

"Drop the gun and put your hands up!" Sheriff Rutherford shouted through the bullhorn.

His wayward brother, Eric noticed wryly, needed no amplification. "Oh, no, Kenny-boy," he taunted, "I'm not taking orders from you! You're the same nigger-lover you always were, aren't you?"

"Cole, nobody here wants to hurt you. Surrender peaceably and we can talk this out later."

"Oh, no, big brother. You're going to let me go. Maybe you'll even give me one of those fancy police cruisers and pay me back for how the system ripped me off."

"Cole, drop the gun!"

"I can't, Kenny-boy. How would I protect my baby?"

At Eric's side Sandy sucked in her breath.

"You can drop whatever it is you're holding, too," the Sheriff's voice came over the bullhorn.

"Oh, no, you wouldn't want me to do that. This is a very special baby . . . "

Oh God. Sandy was right.

Several cruisers quietly pulled up from the east and stopped a little distance the other side of Hardt's position. Uniformed officers spilled out and took their stance, cutting off escape. Eric recognized the McAllister County sheriff, John Sturgis; he doubted Hardt could expect much mercy in a shootout with him. He squeezed Sandy's hand and gave her a thumbs up. To his surprise, she shook her head no.

"That was a stupid move, big brother!" shouted Hardt. "If I didn't love my baby as much as I do, I'd put a bullet through that stupid hat of yours!"

"Drop the gun," Ken Rutherford repeated. "Drop the bundle!"

"You don't want me to drop this bundle, Kenny-boy. You know what this is? My own very special bomb!"

"Bomb?" The word rippled from one side of the roadblock to the other.

"Yes, you stupid fools," shouted Hardt, "this isn't just any bomb, it's my atomic bomb!"

"I don't believe you!" a voice yelled from somewhere.

"You! Eagle Two-Oh-Four!" Hardt appeared to kick at something. A yelp, and another kick. "I've got a bona-fide nuclear physicist here! This is Dr. Ivan Turner of Harvard University!"

A chalk-white face popped up next to Hardt's over the smoking hood of the Jeep.

"Is this a real atomic bomb?" Hardt demanded.

"Yes!" squeaked the physicist, in a voice Eric could barely hear.

Another kick. "Now keep out of my way."

The face disappeared again.

"Let's see it," shouted a skeptical voice from among the men who had just come up with the McAllister forces.

"You want to see my baby, do you?" One-handedly, he worked the quilt off and allowed it to fall away. The stainless steel of the casing glinted in the mid-morning light.

"You gonna blow us all up with that?" somebody scoffed. "Where's the fins?"

"No such thing as an A-bomb that little!"

"That ain't no A-bomb, that's a breadbox!"

Mocking laughter rose from the waiting lawmen. Sandy clutched his arm. "Eric," she sobbed, "they don't believe it's real!"

MAYBE, SHE PRAYED, it would still be all right.

"That's enough, Cole," Sheriff Rutherford shouted patiently. "You probably lost over four hundred men in that explosion. Surrender now and there won't be any more killed here today."

Please, Jesus, make him put it down and give himself up. Doesn't he see it's all over?

"Anybody else dies here, it'll be your fault, Kenny-boy!" Hardt raised his voice even louder. "You all with your guns pointed at me, you don't know what traitors you are. Yes! Traitors to your forefathers and the whole white race! You should be helping exterminate the colored vermin and here you are, ready to kill me! If you knew what I know, you'd be begging me to make men of you and lick my boots to let me do it!"

"Cole, it's no use. Give up."

Lord, do something, please. Please please please please please!

"Hear me, all of you! I've got the power you want! Follow me!"

Nervously, she surveyed the officers and civilians on each side. To her horror, two men quietly detached themselves from the contingent that came with Sheriff Sturgis. They wore jeans and red plaid shirts, but they carried rifles. Ad hoc deputies, sworn in for the occasion? If so, they were turning coat already. She couldn't see where they went.

"Cole," Ken Rutherford's voice came again, "stop playing around. That's no A-bomb and you know it. Throw down that contraption and surrender."

Her heart rammed into her throat. She'd been right.

God help us, it's up to me.

Shouldn't she discuss it with Eric? They could plan what to do.

Ridiculous idea. It had to be her and no one else. If he knew, he'd want to protect her; he'd probably stop her from doing anything at all.

She caught sight of the men in the plaid shirts, up in the woodland on the slope above and to one side of Hardt. No one else seemed aware of them. Gradually and silently they stalked downward, screened by the trees. Then they halted, whispered together, and waved the barrels of their guns in Hardt's direction.

O Domine. They weren't out to help him; they wanted to kill him. And if they did, everyone here would die.

Like a rabbit she bolted from Eric's side. "Sandy!" he protested, low. He came running close behind but she couldn't let that distract her. She had to get to Ken.

Down the slope first— she didn't want to be seen from the roadblock— then back up along the line of police cruisers. They'd parked them nearly bumper to bumper to take advantage of every foot of shoulder. That would work in her favor. She stopped dead a little downslope of the cars and glanced right. There was a big knot of law officers down there, covering the rear; what if they saw her and fired?

Catching up, Eric grabbed her hand. "Stop! Where are you going?"

"He doesn't believe— they'll shoot him, it'll go off—!"

"Let the police handle it! Now get down!"

"Let me go!" She was surprised at how easily she was able to twist out of his grasp. "I have to make him understand!"

She dashed up the remaining slope, dropped flat, and wriggled under the nearest cruiser. Her head bumped against the undercarriage as she tried to keep her nose and mouth clear of the dust that coated the shoulder of the road. Stones tore at the skin of her forearms, legs, and belly. The sweatshirt would have been some protection, but she'd left it under that bush back there, no point wishing for it now. At least she was small enough to scrape under. Eric wasn't . . . A sickening picture flashed before her mind's eye of his tall body exposed to Hardt's fire should he try to cut between the bumpers of the cars.

Please, God, no.

She popped her head out on the other side, next to the front tire. From under the car Eric's voice whispered, "Come back!"

"Stay there!" she hissed back.

It was five car lengths to where Ken crouched with his bullhorn. Seventy feet? She darted a glance back down to her right. The police gathered there weren't looking this way, or if they were, they were all focussed on Hardt.

Good, again. They mustn't stop her.

What if the officers at the roadblock turned around in a panic and shot at her? A chance she'd have to take. She wriggled out and got to her knees.

"Call off your dogs and get me go, Kenny-boy!" Hardt coughed from the smoke coming off his engine. "Here's what'll happen if you don't!"

Tchyewww!

What was it? What had happened?

"Hold your fire!" Ken ordered. "We need to take him alive." Only now did she register the swirl of smoke coming from the barrel of Hardt's unbelievable Wild West revolver. Was anyone hit? Couldn't be, for the sheriff only said, "Cole, throw the gun down and surrender! I don't want you dead, but do that one more time, and we'll shoot!"

The silence stretched out like a long, held breath, shattered by the sound of bolts being pulled back on maybe fifty rifles.

Lord help us, no!

As fast as she could, she began painfully to crawl along the line of cars.

"You don't have the guts to kill me, Kenny-boy!" He coughed again. "Not even if I shot one of your stupid deputies. You're too scared of my baby here!"

"Cole, it's your last chance."

She glanced up. Hardt waved the revolver in the air and gave a vicious laugh.

"Men, don't fire till I give the order!" Sheriff Rutherford shouted.

Maybe twelve yards to the right of Hardt, the pair in the red plaid shirts raised their rifles to their shoulders.

Rutherford's head jerked up towards the hillside. "Don't interfere, Ed Dozier, or I'll arrest you and your brother both."

"Might be worth it to get rid of the skunk that murdered our sister," one of the men yelled back.

"We'll shoot him if you won't, Ken Rutherford," growled the other.

Before the words were out of their mouths Hardt whipped around and pointed the revolver in their direction. "You always were stupid, Chuck

Dozier, just like your sister. Everyone's blood'll be on your head if this baby goes off!"

His back was turned. Keeping her head down, Sandy got to her feet and ran.

"Stop!" Eric's voice behind her was breathless, distant, scarcely audible.

Faster! O God, help me run faster! "Sheriff!"

Rutherford spun towards her, staring in dismay.

"Don't let them shoot— that bomb— it's real— it could—"

A snarl of rage from the hillside:

"*You!*"

Her gaze jerked up. Hardt's demon eyes transfixed hers. Time slowed, her body froze. Nothing remained but herself and those eyes . . . and a flash from the revolver's bore.

Something hit her.

She fell.

CHAPTER D.24

"*You!*"

"*Sandy, get down!*" Had he actually yelled it or did the words stick in his throat?

Tchyewww!

The noise split the air like an obscenity. Helpless, Eric watched her crumple to the ground, Sheriff Rutherford on top of her.

No. No no no!

Voices, appalled, yelling: "Ken's hit!"

Don't shoot! Eric wanted to cry out. *She was right, it might explode that bomb!*

Hardt aimed again. He'd seen him.

"Fire!"

A volley from left and right pounded out. What was left of Hardt reeled back. The bomb slid out of his grasp and disappeared.

Under the Jeep? It must be— and the Jeep, to his horror, was on fire. Flames like evilly gorgeous tiger lilies blossomed out of the engine, the passenger cab, from under the chassis, igniting the undergrowth and singeing the tree trunks and the overhanging leaves.

Scrambling between two of the patrol cars, he ran around to the front of the roadblock, his terror focussed on what he hoped against hope would not happen on that hill. Men rushed towards the blazing Willys with fire extinguishers. Eric could only stare.

Appalling, how fast the fire reached the gas tank. As it exploded, the men with the extinguishers were knocked back; he ducked; they all ducked as blazing shrapnel blew towards them; he stared again in fascinated horror as the steel breadbox slid out from under the burning vehicle and tumbled end over end down the twenty-foot bank, bounced, and landed on the pavement.

It lay there, inert.

He ran across the road, frantically waving. "Don't touch it!" he shouted. "It's real! It could still go off!"

Uniformed arms drew him back to the opposite side. "We'll take care of it," someone said. "Nobody else is dying here today."

Nobody else …

With a howl of anguish he understood.

Lord, I've had enough. Take me.

Falling to his knees in the dust, he lost what little breakfast he'd had.

"IT'S ALL OVER." A deputy took him by the arm and helped him to his feet. "Everything's fine."

How dared he? Eric clenched his fist to strike him— but sobbed on his shoulder instead. "I loved her. She's gone, and I loved her."

The deputy swung him around. "Get a grip, son. Look!"

To his amazed ears, from the other side of the nearest roadblock cruiser came the sound of Ken Rutherford's sober voice. "Darn, look at that. Put a hole right through my hat."

Through his hat? The bullet went through his hat! Sandy? He began to laugh with hope and fear. The deputy pushed him towards the front of the car. He ran.

He found her leaning shakily on its bumper, attempting to pull herself upright.

"Precious love!"

She wavered, but he caught her in his embrace. "Thank you, God, thank you, thank you!" he cried. "You're alive, don't ever do that to me again, you're alive!"

But not well. Her skin was burning hot and her hold on him was flaccid and weak. She turned a gray-pale face up to his (he'd never noticed she had freckles), an uncertain smile on her lips. "Ruth said he was a good shot," she said, her voice tremulous. "I'm glad she was wrong"— and went limp in his arms.

CHAPTER D.25

WHY WAS SHE LYING in the back of a patrol car? She bit her lips to hold back a wave of nausea, an effort little helped by the stench of smoke in the air. A cool wet cloth lay across her forehead, but it was about to fall off because someone's arm was lifting her shoulders. A Thermos bottle cup rattled against her teeth.

"Drink this," said a man's voice.

"This" was overly-sweetened iced tea, and it made her queasy stomach churn.

"No," she sputtered.

"Don't fuss now, you need it."

She choked some down, and was allowed to lie down again.

"Rest," said the voice. "We need to get you to a doctor."

"Eric?" she called his name, and was shocked at how little sound she made.

"I'm here," he assured her from somewhere behind her head. The car doors were open; he must have been standing nearby.

"Did I pass out?"

His face appeared inverted above hers. "Take it easy, precious love. You'll be all right pretty soon."

"What happened? Did they arrest him?"

"Sandy, you don't remember?"

"No . . . nothing, since . . . since he and Turner drove down the hill. Is it over? What happened? Did they take him alive?"

"No. He was shot dead. Turner crawled away before the Jeep exploded, but he's in pretty bad shape."

"It exploded!" She struggled to sit upright, but her head was ten helium balloons and her vision was obscured by dancing fragments of red and blue and purple stained glass. She subsided back onto the hard vinyl seat. "It exploded..." she said again to the car roof. "And the bomb? Did he have it with him?"

"He did."

"But it— it didn't—?"

"No, it's safe. They're taking to a lab to have it dismantled."

"Oh, thank God," she whispered. "Thank God. But . . . I don't understand. Why did I faint?" A terrible suspicion loomed in her mind. "Did I do something idiotic? Eric, tell me! *What did I do?*"

She couldn't see him anymore. She only heard his voice, low, and other voices in reply.

"Sandy," he said, taking her hand, "I'll tell you when you're feeling better. Right now you have to rest."

It must be something awful. Oh, dear Father, what did I do?

HE BROKE IT to her once they'd been seen and treated at the county hospital in Zicksburg. She didn't want to believe it, not because Eric would lie, but because she didn't want to think she'd been that stupid.

Nobody could get hold of the Watkinses, so it was decided they should be put up in a Zicksburg motel— something about the officers taking up a collection, since their wallets had been stolen.

But even after they'd had a little more to eat; even after she'd retired to her room, had a long, hot bath, and had put on the State Police sweatshirt Eric had worn all morning; even when she'd closed the blinds and drawn the curtains and climbed— well past noon— into the bed with its orange chenille spread, she still couldn't shake the sick feeling that she'd done nothing but interfere.

Sleep was a long time coming.

AT 3:30 in the afternoon, the phone rang. Sheriff Sturgis wanted to see her and Eric in the lobby lounge in ten minutes.

HE KEPT THEM at it for nearly two hours, writing everything down on forms in a clipboard with a dull metal cover. She suppressed her need to ask her own questions and submitted to answering his. Other guests wandered in to use the vending machines, and even in the orange and gold vinyl anonymity of the motel lounge she had to wonder what people thought they were, sitting there in their stained, tattered clothing being questioned by the sheriff of the county.

"That was a foolish thing to do, young lady," he said regarding her heroics that morning. "The only reason our officers in the rear didn't shoot you or your boyfriend is because a stray bullet might have hit one of our own."

She felt the blood drain from her face. "I'm sorry, I don't even remember doing it, I guess I wanted—"

"You had no call to interfere in police business. You nearly got a good man killed."

"Yes, sir. I understand."

"Wait a minute," said Eric. "I don't remember any of you taking that bomb too seriously. Or wasn't it a threat after all?"

Sheriff Sturgis was silent for a moment, then said, "We talked to Cole's tame scientist."

"And?" asked Eric.

"His credentials check out. He admits that device was 'a little unstable'— that's how he put it. No way of knowing how close it came to going off till we get the report from the NRC, but I gather the threat was real."

Eric squeezed her hand.

"Turner confessed about the rest of the stolen plutonium and we got the Nuclear Regulatory Commission boys up here in their white safety suits; they've been testing the blast site all afternoon."

"What do you mean?" she asked.

Eric's eyes went wide. "That was it," he whispered.

"'It,' what?" she whispered back. His look chilled her to the core.

"What I was trying to remember when we were hiding under the rhododendrons, waiting for Hardt— I mean, Cole— to come down. He said he had more bombs in progress, remember?"

"You're right, yes! If all that plutonium went up in the explosion—"

"—then all that dust we were sitting in was—"

"Oh, Eric! Please, God, no!"

"All right, you two," Sturgis said brusquely. "No call to be making up stories. I was about to say the NRC so far hasn't found a speck of radiation.

No more than natural, anyway. Stands to reason: Turner says Cole kept his lab as far away from his arsenal as he could, a good two miles, and half a mile down. That material is buried deep enough, I wager." He took a sip of his vending machine coffee. "Cole was cutting it close blowing up the conventional stuff, but he wasn't out to commit suicide."

"But he ended up dead after all," Sandy felt forced to say. Stolidly, she pushed down the urge to cry. "Ken wanted him alive so he could get more information out of him, but I came running in trying to fix things and messed it all up."

Sturgis looked at her strangely, then dug a cotton handkerchief out of his pocket and handed it to her. "No call for tears, young lady. I likely shouldn't say this, but you drawing his fire likely ended things a lot quicker, with no law enforcement personnel killed. There was a whole stack of weapons and ammo in that Jeep, and he was ready to use them. And it would have been pretty damn hard for Ken to give the order to shoot his own brother. I'm not saying he wouldn't have, but that's the biggest problem with policing in these parts. The folks you have to arrest are mostly folks you know."

"You're not just saying that?"

"Ask anybody I've slapped the cuffs on: I don't say things just to say them."

"Sheriff," said Eric, "was it you who gave the order to fire?"

"I did. I thought Ken had been hit. Young lady, you're such a little bug of a thing, only Cole saw you. Lucky for you, so did Ken."

"I really am grateful he tackled me and pulled me down."

"He's a man who does his duty. But you be sure and thank him yourself." Sturgis' no-nonsense face relaxed into a smile. "But leaving aside you interfering . . . you two deserve a lot of credit. If half of what the prisoners say is so, there's a lot of unsolved crimes we can trace to these terrorists, and we've prevented a hell of a lot more. That was smart work, you folks escaping like that and bringing us the word."

"Thank you." She relaxed a little.

"Any sign of our car?" asked Eric. "It's a brown '68 Ford Galaxie."

"We found it. You know your rear bumper was off?" She and Eric exchanged glances. "It's here in Zicksburg. Normally they'd tow it to the Payne County impoundment yard at Lewis Springs, but Ken said they should bring it over here. You can pick it up tomorrow. We'll waive the fee."

"Thank you," they both murmured.

"Don't mention it. Your suitcases'll be here in a couple of hours."

"Thank God for that!" said Eric. "These clothes make us look like a couple of suspects!"

Thinking alike! She sat up straighter and praised God for the man at her side.

"We've also recovered your wallets from the men who stole them," Sturgis went on. "Officially, they're court exhibits, but under the circumstances . . . " He reached in his satchel and pulled them out.

"Money's still here," Eric said, examining his. "I was dead certain it'd gone up in that blast."

"No," the sheriff responded, "though there was a lot that did. Wouldn't be surprised if Cole had it all set to blow if he ever had to get out of there fast, with his bags packed and ready. He took more than weapons, though. The back of that Jeep was piled with records and papers."

Eric's hand went leaden in hers. "How . . . interesting," he said.

"Yeah. There was even some kind of album; at least, we found the remains of a leather cover with a melted blob of silver on it. Nothing much left of the pages. You folks happen to see anything like that there?"

"There was a photo album like that in his room," she volunteered. "He didn't let us look in it, though."

His hand gave hers a grateful squeeze and relaxed.

"Funny he should carry something like that around. A memento of his grandma, maybe."

"May be," she said.

Sturgis snapped the cover of his clipboard closed and stood up. "You folks go get you some sleep. Ken and I'll be talking to the both of you again, say tomorrow around 4:30."

"You want us to come back up here?" Sandy asked. She would rather not, tired as she was. But if they had to, they had to.

"No, we'll meet you down in Osceomenie Falls. At the Falls End Hotel, near the bridge."

"We'll be there," Eric said.

They returned to their rooms and slept until their luggage arrived around 7:30. At eight o'clock the Watkinses collected them and took them home. Thank heaven, they were fed a simple meal, shown to their rooms, and left in peace.

CHAPTER D.26

SANDY'S DOOR WAS STILL CLOSED next morning when Eric got a lift from Allen to the impoundment yard at Zicksburg.

They'd thrown the filthy rear bumper on top of the fishing tackle in the back seat. "Better do something about that," the yard man said.

"Sure. But right now, can you recommend a good antique store?"

"Hah, hah, hah! Planning on selling that heap? It's an antique for sure!"

The mechanic who reattached the bumper was more helpful. "There's one my wife likes in Rains Overlook. Talley's Emporium. She buys and sells jewelry there."

"Sounds like just the place I'm looking for. Thanks."

SITTING IN the wood-panelled living room of Jen and Allen's summer home, Eric had just put down the phone when he heard a rattle at the latch of the french doors that led outside. He got up to let Sandy in.

"Have a good walk?"

"I guess so," she said.

"Well, I was thinking. Want to head into town before time to meet with the sheriffs? The falls are definitely worth seeing."

"Oh, okay." She gave a half-hearted shrug.

"If you don't want to go . . ."

"No, that's fine," she said listlessly. "It's supposed to be a vacation, after all."

She had little to say to him in the car. Was he hurrying things? Maybe she needed more time to recover.

As they entered Osceomenie Falls, he thought she made a noise.

No, not a noise. She was singing under her breath:

D'amour l'ardente flamme . . .

He thought his grin would split his head.

THEY HAD a late lunch and did a little sightseeing.

"Eric," she said as they explored a side lane. "I want to apologize for being bad company earlier. I was having it out with myself."

"No, you weren't bad com—" he began to protest.

"I was. Remember how I said it can be easy to die for Christ, the hard part is living for Him? Since yesterday I've been comparing how grand and exalted I felt when Jeff came for me in the cave with the mess I made of things at the roadblock. I didn't like what I saw."

"Sheriff Sturgis said it actually worked out—"

"Yes. God really did work everything together for good. But I was thinking it was up to me to make it work. 'Stand back, everyone, here comes Alexandra Beichten to save the day!' Like, 'Don't worry, God, I'll take care of it for You'!"

"I'm sure Ken would thank you for not making him shoot his brother. And everyone should thank you for ending that standoff so soon."

"Maybe." She smiled. "Funny, that's what had me in such a knot this morning. If I could tell myself what I did was wrong from start to finish, I could say I'm sorry and not do anything like that again. But good things came out of it along with the bad, and nothing's settled and nothing's clear."

"It'll be all right, I promise."

"I know. God has everything under control and I don't. I think I've finally gotten it through my head that that's just fine."

He put his arm around her, and the closeness of him was life and health and peace.

"I've been thinking too," he said. "I borrowed your Bible when you were out for your walk. I hope you don't mind."

"Of course not," she said decorously, trying not to laugh for joy.

"And I read something about 'bringing forth fruit worthy of repentance.' So, I've called Jacob and Sol and the rest of our Jewish clients— and Neil, of course— and apologized for not facing what was going on months ago. There was no way Hardt could have been dead."

"I wondered, last spring when Jacob and Sam had those close calls. But I didn't want to nag you about it."

He winced. "I doubt I would have listened. I just didn't want to know." He shook his head. "It's different now. They were really decent about it . . . I said maybe they still should be on their guard, in case Hardt's still got some followers up there who'll want to avenge his death."

For a bare instant the fear again seized her— then it quickly passed away. *We can face anything now, in life or in death.* "What did Neil say?"

Eric laughed. "He said he was down for the struggle. Honestly, I think this is all over. But we'll need help in the office, now that Ruth is gone. What do you say I write North Dakota State and ask if they have any qualified Sioux Indian graduates who'd be interested in a job in Wapatomekie?"

She nearly danced in her happiness. "That's a wonderful idea!"

"I thought so. We'll do it as soon as we get back."

"I can hear the falls," she said as they walked along. The sound of rushing water grew louder as they turned onto the main street.

When they drew abreast of a plain jane structure dating from the 1930s, Eric stopped. "The Falls End Hotel."

"Oh, do we have to go in now? It's only a little after 4:00."

"I wasn't planning to, yet," he replied. "In fact, I've saved the best for last. There's the bridge. Come on."

They wandered across the street and onto the wooden bridge over the river. To her delight it was pure Victorian— or at least, a pure Victorian reproduction— and was given over to pedestrian and bicycle traffic only. Others beside themselves were passing over it, enjoying the last of the beautiful late summer afternoon.

At the center of the arched span they stopped. Below them the White River poured in easy stair-step rapids over rocks, past boulders. On the opposite bank lay a sandy beach, and even now, after Labor Day, sand and rocks were populated with mothers, fathers, children, grandparents, sisters, brothers, and lovers, basking in the gentle heat and dabbling in the clean foamy water.

"It's beautiful!" she cried.

"I'm glad you like it."

For some time they leaned over the rail without speaking. Rapids, eddies, backwaters, pools . . . and still the river remained focussed on its goal, running to its God-appointed end.

She lifted up her eyes to the hills that defined and gave meaning to its flow. "I can see everything from here . . ."

"Sandy," he began, "I need your advice."

Such ordinary words. Why did they make her catch her breath? She didn't dare look his way.

"It's about the office . . . I was thinking . . ."

"Eric, wait. Is that Ken coming with Sheriff Sturgis? They're just crossing the street from the hotel."

As she watched, two more men, one carrying a TV news camera, the other a tape recorder and microphone, joined the sheriffs.

He turned her to face him. "Ignore them. This is about our work."

"Our work," she repeated. Despite his wounds— or because of them— he'd never been more beautiful.

From the other end of the bridge Jen and Allen Watkins approached. They'd be having dinner with them later.

His gray eyes captured and held hers. "I was thinking it's time I took on a partner."

"A partner?" A sensation strange and wonderful bubbled up inside her, out of all proportion to the professional meaning of the word. Controlling it— revelling in it as she controlled it— she said, "I think that's an excellent idea . . . as long as the name on the cards says 'Baumann & Beichten.'"

She waited, heart beating, hardly daring to breathe.

From his pocket he drew an object that flashed with pearlescent luster. "I was thinking," he said solemnly, "something more like 'Baumann & Baumann.'"

"Before God and all the neighbors?" As of its own volition her left hand rose to fit itself in his.

"Before God and all the neighbors," he replied, slipping the ring on her finger. "Forever and ever, amen."

And before just those witnesses, in just that way, he gathered her into his arms.

THE END

"God, give me a deep humility, a well-guided zeal,
a burning love and a single eye,
and then let men or devils do their worst!"

–George Whitefield, evangelist, 1737

THE SONGS

<u>Be Thou My Vision</u>

A Hymn
Be Thou my Vision, O Lord of my heart!
Naught be all else to me, save that Thou art
Thou, my best thought by day or by night,
Waking or sleeping, Thy presence my light.

Be Thou my Wisdom, and Thou my true Word,
Thou ever with me, and I with Thee, Lord,
Thou my great Father, and I Thy true son,
Thou in me dwelling, and I with Thee one.

Be Thou my breastplate, my sword for the fight,
Be Thou my whole armor and Thou my true might,
Be Thou my soul's shelter and Thou my high tower,
Raise Thou me heavenward, great Power of my power.

Riches I heed not, nor man's empty praise,
Thou mine inheritance, now and always,
Thou, and Thou only, first in my heart,
High King of heaven, my treasure Thou art.

High King of heaven, my victory won,
May I reach heaven's joys, O bright heaven's Son!
Heart of my own heart, whatever befall,
Still be my vision, O Ruler of all.

Ancient Irish, ca. 6th century, attributed to St. Dallán Forgaill;
translated into English and versified by Eleanor Hull, 1912

D'amour l'ardente flamme

D'amour l'ardente flamme
consume mes beaux jours.
Ah! la paix de mon âme
a donc fui pour toujours!

Son départ, son absence
sont pour moi le cercueil;
et loin de sa présence,
tout me paraît en deuil.

Alors, ma pauvre tête
se dérange bientôt;
mon faible cœur s'arrête
puis se glace aussitôt.

Sa marche que j'admire,
son port si gracieux,
sa bouche au doux sourire,
le charme de ses yeux,
sa voix enchanteresse
(dont il sait m'embrâser),
de sa main la caresse,
hélas! et son baiser
d'une amoureuse flamme
consument mes beaux jours!
Ah! le paix de mon âme
A donc fui pour toujours!

Je suis à ma fenêtre,
ou dehors, tout le jour.
C'est pour le voir paraître,
ou hâter son retour.
Mon cœur bat et se presse
dès qu'il le sent venir.
Au gré de ma tendresse,
puis-je le retenir!

O caresses de flamme!
Que je voudrais un jour
voir s'exhaler mon âme
dans ses baisers d'amour!

The burning flame of love
Consumes my life's best days.
Ah! the peace of my soul
Has wholly fled for evermore!

His going away, his absence,
Are a coffin for me;
And far from his presence,
All things round me seem to mourn.

And so, my poor head
Soon will run stark mad!
My feeble heart will stop
And freeze itself at once to ice.

His walk I so admire,
His bearing, full of grace,
His mouth with smiles of sweetness,
The spell cast by his eyes,
His voice in its enchantment
(He knows it sets me ablaze),
The caress of his hand,
Alas! and his kiss
Of amorous, burning fire
Consume my life's best days!
Ah! the peace of my soul
Has wholly fled for evermore.

I stand at my window
Or outside, all the day
To glimpse his appearing
Or haste his return.
My heart pounds within me
To sense him come near;
O'er-ruled by my yearning,
How can I keep it still?

O caresses of flame!
That I might see the day
When I breathe out my soul
In the kisses of his love!

French lyrics (after Johann Wolfgang von Goethe) and music by
Hector Berlioz, from his dramatic legend, *La damnation de Faust*
English translation from the French by Catrin Lewis, ©2018

<u>Lone Woman Blues</u>

Since my baby left me,
Hear me cryin' all alone.
Since my baby left me,
Hear me cryin' all alone.
I don't get no lovin',
I just hang my head and moan.

Hopped that midnight freight train,
Said he'd ride it down the line,
Hopped that midnight freight train,
Said he'd ride it down the line.
Just hear that lonesome whistle,
Sounds like some poor woman cryin'.

Come on home and love me,
Rock your baby all night long.
Come on home and love me,
Rock your baby all night long.
Ain't never been so lonesome,
Boy, you know you done me wrong.

Take me to the river,
Gonna lay my burden down;
Take me to the river,
Gonna lay my burden down.
Just a poor, lone, lonely woman,
Think I'll jump right in and drown.

Catrin Lewis, © 2018

ABOUT THE AUTHOR

CATRIN LEWIS is the pen name of a woman residing in southwestern Pennsylvania. Besides writing fiction, she enjoys classical, medieval, and Celtic music; history, travel, and foreign languages; art, architecture, and gardening; and herding two ex-feral cats. She is interested in Biblical studies and Reformed Theology and was granted the degree of Bachelor of Theology by the University of Oxford in England. Though trained and licensed as an architect, she has not worked full time in that field for several years, and makes up for it by writing about architects and contending with a house in a perpetual state of do-it-herself renovation.

In her younger days, Catrin spent far too many years thinking up story ideas but never having the courage to write them down. *The Single Eye* is her debut novel, and she is firmly convinced that, now it is out into the world, it will take far less than three-plus decades to publish the next.

CONTACTS & SOCIAL MEDIA

To receive your own copy of Catrin's newsletter
with announcements on her latest releases and future projects,
and for access to great free and discounted offers,
go to HendrickHillBooks.com and click on any Sign Up link,
or email contact@hendrickhillbooks.com
with Sign Me Up in the subject line.

Catrin Lewis blogs at *The Writer Sits Down,*
www.thewritersitsdown.blogspot.com,
You can follow her on Facebook at Catrin Lewis, Writer,
on Instagram at catrin_lewis_writer,
and on Twitter @CatrinLewisAuth

At Hendrick Hill Books we strive to put out
a high quality product that is error-free. If
you the reader should spot any mangled
edits, misplaced or missing punctuation,
erratic spelling, or "creative" grammar not
connected to the story, please notify us at
contact@hendrickhillbooks.com so we can
correct it at the first opportunity. Thank you.

TYPOGRAPHY

The body of this work is printed in
9.5-point ROSARIVO by UGR Design, copyright
©2012 Pablo Ugerman.

Originating from work presented in 2011 to the
post-graduate course in Typeface Design at the
University of Buenos Aires, this font software is
made available under the
SIL Open Font License, Version 1.1.

The SHOPLIFTER typeface by Vic Fieger (page
128) is used under the *1001Fonts*
Free for Commercial Use License (FFC).

The FFF TUSJ typeface (opening title, etc.) is by
Magnus Cederholm, www.formfett.net

The architectural hand-lettering fonts (division
subtitles, chapter heads, etc.) are variants of the
typeface ANOTHER ALL-NIGHTER, and are the
creation and property of the author.

The scene break fleurons are by artists
Ayxan Alizada (weapons),
dreamstate (forest; hiking),
Milta (drafting tools),
Noch (musical instruments),
PiconsMe (architectural drawings),
and Serhiy Smirnov (Bibles),
and are used by license from
Shutterstock.com.

AUTHOR'S NOTE:

Croton oil, the compound Chrissie discusses using as retaliation on one of the pharmacy students is real. It is a potent purgative which can have severe, even fatal effects if used inappropriately. Do not use it.

My novels are written for the purpose of entertainment. However, all written work should, on some level, possess an underlying message. With *The Extern* my hope is that the reader will come away with a better understanding of the ever-expanding pressures, growing complexities, and sometime overt hostilities pharmacists and pharmacy technicians face daily.

Retail pharmacy has been under a relentless siege for more than three decades. This onslaught is the result of a multitude of factors. When insurance companies began paying for prescription services, the industry began to see a steady decline in reimbursements which have trimmed margins and squeezed the bottom line. This has resulted in the need to pump more prescriptions through the pharmacies in addition to providing a wider array of services in order to sure up the bottom line.

Thirty years ago, chain pharmacies began installing drive-thru services in their locations. For the patient this is a wonderful convenience. However, this service has added to the pharmacy staff's workload and level of interruption in an already devastatingly busy and distracted environment.

Changes in pharmacy laws over time have also added to a pharmacist's burden. The addiction and opioid crisis have seen stricter scheduling of narcotic drugs like hydrocodone requiring closer scrutiny of these compounds such as reviewing the Prescription Monitoring Program and tighter accounting by the pharmacy staff. The placement of pseudoephedrine products behind the pharmacy counter and restrictions on their purchases to combat the growing use of methamphetamine and its production requires additional interruptions and monitoring by the pharmacy staff whereas none existed previously.

The addition of immunization services now provided by pharmacists is a vitally important and relatively new aspect of pharmacy services. But this, too, has added stresses. More services and programs will be implemented in the years to come.

Coupled with stagnant labor budgets and the thousands of baby boomers reaching retirement age every day, the demand for prescriptions and pharmacy services has never been greater. This is straining an already fragile balance. Pharmacists and technicians are bombarded by phone calls, faxes, electronic prescriptions, a multitude of interruptions, drive-thru visitors, prior authorization requests, unruly and demanding patients addicted to prescription medications and who take their frustration out on the persons behind the counter. This list does not begin to cover the all the duties a pharmacy team is expected to complete every day.

Along with this plethora of expectations, your pharmacist and their technicians are expected to fill and check your prescriptions quickly—and not make *any* mistakes. Along with the continued and on-going pandemic; with pharmacies now providing COVID testing and vaccinations; these expectations and pressures have only increased the burden and the chances for medication errors.

Having toiled in the retail setting for more than twenty-five years, I speak from experience when I write that these dedicated frontline pharmacy personnel work long hours and, in many cases, under diffi-cult working conditions. Burnout and fatigue are common especially during the fall and winter months.

Chances are good that anyone who is reading this has used a pharmacy. If you haven't already, thank your pharmacy team for their dedication and hard work. And please be patient. Do not rush them! Give them plenty of time to fill your prescriptions and administer your vaccines.

Respectfully,
David